THE MADHATTER'S
GUIDE TO CHOCOLATE

a novel by

RHETT DEVANE

RABID PRESS AUSTIN, TX 2003

Rabid Press
P.O. Box 4227
Cedar Park, TX 78630

Cover art and layout design by Rebecca Greulich

Library of Congress Control Number: 2003094674
ISBN 0-9743039-0-9

Printed in the United States of America
First Edition, 2003

ACKNOWLEDGEMENTS

A heartfelt thank you to all of the fine folks who made this work possible:

My family, friends, and patients—for their constant support and encourage-ment. Leigh Ansley—for yarns about her Big Ma-mer. Michele Burkhead—for sharing tales of her Granny. Talley Morgan—for sharing her story.

Law enforcement experts—Cathy Kennedy, Chris Garrison, Kelly Walker, Dick Barnes, John Walker, Wayne Gellner, and David Turnage. Nursing experts—Jaye Andreasen–RN, Mimi Burkholder–RN, Dianne Sutherland–RN, Mary Menard–RN, and Tonya A. Harris–RN, MN, Associate Professor of Nursing (retired). Legal experts—Trial lawyer Deeno Kitchen, and the Honorable George S. Reynolds, III.

Adoptive mothers—Patsy Eccles and Carol Buckland. My dedicated proof-readers—Ann Macmillan, Thom Saudargas, Talley Morgan, and Joy Hevey. Chattahoochee historian and retired newspaper editor—Grady Turnage. All-time favorite teacher and mentor—Sharon Lasseter. Susan Malone—for her wonderful professional editorial service. Rabid Press Editor in Chief, David Baker, and Marketing Director, Rebecca Greulich—for believing in me.

And, especially to God, for allowing magic, muses, and angels to exist in this tired old world.

For my mother, Theresa
And in memory of my father, J.D.

THE MADHATTER'S

GUIDE TO CHOCOLATE

PROLOGUE

October 3rd, 1960
West Washington Street
Chattahoochee, Florida

MAX THE MADHATTER shuffled slowly down the main street of Chattahoochee, peeking in the store windows, clutching his treasure—a weathered gray notebook. He was going to Mr. D.'s store today. Mr. D always had a chocolate bar for Max, and his little girl Hattie talked to Max like he was just about anybody.

Max touched the brim of his new hat. It was purple and tall, with a wide round top. Nurse Marion gave it to him. Maybe, this hat would keep the voices away.

Suddenly, as if summoned by the thought, the voices came, painting in his mind the bright colors of another place. Max crumpled to the pavement. He clutched his head and moaned. Sometimes, the pictures hurt his head.

When the pictures finally faded, Max found himself staring at the cracks in the sidewalk between his knees. The notebook was open. The voices had made him draw again. He looked at the scratchy sketch on the very last page—a little girl sitting by a spring.

"Mr. Max?"

Max looked up to find lil' Hattie standing a few feet away. In her hands she held a yellow daisy. She offered him the flower with a smile.

"It's for your hat."

Max scrambled to his feet, and carefully took the flower. He fit the stem into the worn hatband, and then tried it on. No voices came. Perhaps this would keep them quiet a little longer. If they talked too much, he would have to go to the room with the bright lights. They would tie him down, and the zap thing would make him not remember.

Hattie was still smiling at him, and Max smiled back tentatively. He picked up his notebook hastily. As he followed Hattie into her father's shop Max decided he would work extra hard for Mr. D today, even if there wasn't any chocolate in return. . .

THE VISITATION

Excerpt from Max the Madhatter's notebook:

November 2, 1960: Little Hattie Davis has a kind soul, and she's easy to bruise. If her daddy speaks harshly to her—not often, she's a good girl, that one—the hurt sparkles in her eyes. She doesn't cry. The tears seem to suck back up inside of her. She'll get solemn for a bit, then dance around or cut the fool—anything to get a laugh. Folks handle pain in different ways.

CHAPTER ONE

"**M**OM'S GONE, HATTIE."
My brother's words echoed in my memory.

"How? When?"

"Last night," Bobby's voice cracked slightly. "In her sleep. Miss Margie found her this morning. She checked on her when she didn't show up for her usual cup of coffee."

"I'll call the airlines and be home as soon as I can."

The emergency return trip from a massage-therapist retreat in Sedona, Arizona—a much-needed vacation to heal the wounds of my latest doomed love affair—combined with the insomnia accompanying sudden grief, numbed my senses. The forty-mile stretch of state highway between Tallahassee and my hometown was so familiar, my mind drifted into automatic mode as soon as the cruise control engaged and the engine eased into a gentle hum. Fresh tears stung my eyes. The edges of the windshield blurred like an Impressionist painting.

"C'mon, Hattie. Hold it together! The last thing everyone needs is for you to wrap your truck around a pine tree."

I dabbed the corners of my eyes with a tissue. "Oh, Mama. I'm just not ready for you to go. There are so many things I needed to talk to you about."

I passed an open field dotted with black and white dappled dairy cattle. The pungent scent of manure penetrated the humid air.

"And, what about Bobby? How can we ever get past our differences without you to run interference?"

The Mount Pleasant Cemetery sign loomed in the distance, and I slowed slightly, intending to visit my father's gravesite as I often did on my way to Chattahoochee.

A flash of my mother's freshly prepared burial site caused me to accelerate sharply. "Better not, this time."

I gestured toward the sky. "Did I spend enough time with you, Mom? Not that I hated Chattahoochee, exactly. It wasn't easy growing up in a small Southern town with a mental institution on the main drag. There was a stigma attached to it. As if crazy could somehow rub off on me. As if the raving-lunatic virus floated through the air. One day, the latent loonies would surface in heavy 5 o'clock traffic, and I'd grab a finger nail file and try to take the inept driver in front of me out of the gene pool. *Understandable,* they would say, *you know she was originally from Chattahoochee.*"

In the formative years before I understood mental illness, the horror of being affiliated with my hometown was profound. I told most folks I was from three miles out of town on the Greensboro Highway. In my estimation, even a small distance from the 'Hooch made one sane.

Once old enough to develop a clear sense of myself, I felt as if I'd been plopped down in the heart of Dixie by accident. After graduating from Chattahoochee High School, I was rabid for release. In the twenty-two years since, I had visited my parents at the farmhouse on Bonnie Hill three miles outside of the city limits and escaped the prying eyes of the town yahoos.

I flipped the radio off and continued the one-sided conversation.

"The questions your friends ask are always the same, over and over, Mother: *Why aren't you married yet, Hattie? You serious with anyone? I'll bet your mama and daddy wish you'd give 'em some grandchildren!* I've always been just

Hattie Davis, Mr. D and Mrs. Tillie's errant daughter. You know, the one who never married and hasn't amounted to much."

In the past few months, as my relationship with Garrett Douglas hacked its final death rattles, I felt a gnawing need to renew family ties. My mother was an only child, and my father had one sister—far from the large extended family of Southern farmhand days. Now, with the death of my mother, the sum total of my kin consisted of my older brother Bobby, my elderly Aunt Piddie, cousin Evelyn and her husband Joe, and Evelyn's two children, Karen and Byron.

As I drove, dazed from grief and lack of sleep, I felt keenly isolated. My parents were gone. In the selfish quest for independence, I had ignored the remainder of the family. Other than an occasional update gleaned during one of the infrequent visits to the Hill, I knew little of the minutiae of their daily lives. Though the townhouse in Tallahassee was less than an hour drive from my hometown, it might as well have been across the country.

Passing the Chattahoochee City Limit sign, I snapped to attention. Noting the first in a series of stark white institutional buildings at the entrance to the Florida State Hospital, I crept below the speed limit. Was it the nineties or the fifties? Hard to distinguish. Other than a row of freshly-planted crepe myrtle trees, the landscape had changed little.

Chattahoochee had been an interesting place to grow up. Where else would one see a guy dressed in a Wild West sheriff's outfit patrolling the sidewalks? Or that little guy who used to come into Daddy's shop all the time, the one with the weird hats?

The truck slowed to a crawl in front of a number of empty storefronts where thriving businesses had once been, their taped, dirt-pocked windows a yawning memorial to a dying town. A chiropractor's office occupied the space formerly housing the Davis Electronics Shop. I flipped a quick U-turn at the second of two signal lights and turned onto a narrow side street.

Avoiding the bustling front entrance, I entered the aged funeral home from a side door. Hidden from the milling crowd in the Memorial Memories viewing room, I cowered behind a towering spray of maidenhair fern and white carnations. 'Jesus Waits' was spelled out in glittering gold calligraphy on a broad white silk ribbon.

Waits for what, exactly? I wondered.

The ingrained Southern guilt immediately clawed at my brain. *Jeez, Hattie. Here you are making jokes at your own mother's wake! Get a grip!*

I stared blankly across the dimly-lit room. A pale pink casket rested on a red velvet draped table surrounded by a moat of flowers.

My mother. She'd been the straight-man half of my parents' slapstick comedy team. For fifty-four years of marriage to Mr. D., she'd patiently tolerated pranks and practical jokes, providing a showcase for his satirical wit. In the seven years since his death, she exhibited an acute sense of humor, as if she, alone, had to carry on the vaudeville show as a one-woman act.

I couldn't bring myself to look at her. I wanted to remember her smiling, bustling around the house on the Hill, intent on some purpose—not cold and still, skin painted like a wax effigy. I watched the surreal scene with the detachment of a movie patron.

Finally, I sighed deeply and allowed myself to be sucked into the swarm of mourners. Dressed in Sunday go-to-meeting regalia, people I'd known from birth murmured comforting words. The women dabbed sodden eyes with embroidered hankies tucked discreetly into the underside of lace cuffs. The suited men looked stiff and uncomfortable, occasionally tugging at collars and waistbands too tight to allow a decent amount of breath.

In one corner, my Aunt Piddie Longman perched on a maroon velvet Queen Anne chair. A tall beehive of lavender-tinged hair swirled in stiff curls atop her head. Miniature blue lace butterflies and silk flowers were stuffed randomly between the ringlets to disguise bare spots.

Actually, she looked pretty darn good for ninety-plus years. Did she still carry my uncle Carlton's driver's license and voter's ID around with her? How long had he been dead now? Had to be close to forty years.

"Hattie!" Aunt Piddie waved a dainty hankie. I took the chair next to my elderly aunt.

She leaned over and planted a kiss on my cheek. "Hi gal, I'm surely glad to see you. I been up most the night worrying you wouldn't be home in time." Piddie shook her head. The rigid mass of curls quivered slightly. "I worried myself sick 'bout your brother plannin' the visitation so fast, what with you half way across the country in Cee-doner, and all.

I didn't think that was right a'tall. I told Evelyn, we could've helt up the funeral for a couple of days to let you get home to help with the arrangements."

Piddie reached over and rested her hand gently on my shoulder. "You holdin' up okay, gal?"

"Yes'm. It's hard, you know...doesn't seem real to me."

We sat in silence for a moment.

"Don't be mad at Bobby, Aunt Pid. He's gone out of his way to annoy me many times, but this wasn't one of 'em. When he finally got through to me at the resort, I told him to go ahead and make the arrangements. I gave him my flight plans, and there was a little time for me to stop by the townhouse to grab some clothes. Besides, Mom had already picked out the casket and paid for the funeral. She took care of it all, right after Daddy died. She wanted to spare us from that part of it." I glanced toward the flower-rimmed casket. "I just talked to her three days ago, right before I left. It's just -"

"Hard to fathom," she finished. "It near 'bout kilt me when your daddy passed. You know, I pretty much raised him after our mama died. I thought on him more as a son than a brother. And your mama, well, she was just precious in my eyes. I couldn't have picked a better wife for Dan than Tillie."

Piddie dabbed a tear from her heavily-powdered cheek. "The sad fact of livin' as long as I have—you lose so many folks to the other side, and it doesn't get any easier with practice. Always hits you square between the eyes. I just keep tellin' myself what my Aunt Ruby used to say, 'The more sorrow carves out your soul, the more joy you can hold later on.'"

I smiled slightly and nodded. My aunt had a wise-ism for every occasion, good or bad.

"You want me to go over with you to see her, sugar?" Piddie asked, her soft voice gentle with concern.

"Um...no."

"You're just like your daddy, Hattie. He couldn't abide lookin' on a person after death, neither. He said he wanted to remember them like they was in life. Well, it's up to you on the way you need to settle things— long as you're easy with it in your own mind."

7

I searched for a subject to lighten the moment. "You still make those great biscuits of yours?"

She reached over and stroked my face. "You and those biscuits. When you was a little bitty thing, you could near'bout eat your weight in my catheads, Hattie."

Years had passed since I'd heard that term. Cathead biscuits— made with lard and big as a cat's head! Tormenting my friends from up North with the expression provided hours of entertainment. Just us God-forsaken Southern folks. No accounting for the stuff we'd eat! I had to work to convince them we didn't actually consume domestic-animal parts. How did all of my aunt's generation live to be so bloomin' old? I was lucky to eat even a gram of fat without feeling guilty.

I held her wrinkled hand. "I only eat your cooking that way, Piddie. You can run circles around any of the upper-crust chefs I know!"

"Oh, you do go on so," Piddie blushed slightly with the compliment. "I don't cook so much anymore, honey. I'm just not able. I've taken to fallin' out every now and then. One minute I'm standin' up and the next I'm flat as flitter on the floor. Fell down the back steps last time, like to have broke my dang neck! Evelyn put her foot down after that one, so I'm livin' with her and Joe now. You know they built a little mama apartment off the big house for me." Piddie's cornflower blue eyes watered.

"Mom told me you were having balance problems, but I didn't realize the addition had been completed. I bet you must miss your little house. You didn't sell it, did you?"

My mind flashed back to the spacious yard surrounding the tiny white frame house at 766 Morgan Avenue. I had once played in the springtime between islands of blooming seven-foot azaleas that divided the yard into magical pink-flowered pathways swarming with bumblebees. In the front yard, the bushes hid the porch so well, I could sit in a rocking chair, shelling peas in the cool shade, watching the occasional car swoosh by, and no one from the road would know I was there.

Piddie smoothed a lacquered curl. "Lord, no! I couldn't bear the thought of letting it go. It's been in the family too many years. We closed it up for a while till Joe decided it would be good to have someone livin' in it. House'll run down without someone livin' in it, you know. We just now rented it out to a nice young fella and his wife. He moved over to work at the Hospital. Believe he's from over around Grand Ridge."

I spotted my cousin across the room. "'Scuse me, Aunt Piddie. Let me go speak to Evelyn. I'll see you in a bit."

Piddie grabbed my hand and patted it softly. "You go ahead, honey. I know you have to talk around to everyone. Make sure to come by for a long visit before you leave town, now. Your mama and daddy would be so proud of you, Hattie. You're always so nice to us old folks." She paused and looked toward the flowered casket. "I'll be there right beside you tomorrow at the service. Don't you worry."

The tears I had been holding threatened to wash over me. "I'll be staying around for a while, Piddie. Bobby and I will have to take care of things out on the Hill. I won't be a stranger, especially not to you. Maybe you can coach Evelyn into making some biscuits one morning. I'll surely come for that!"

Piddie's glossy red lips pinched into a thin line. "The fruit fell far from the tree as far as Evelyn makin' any kind of a cook. She can take a ten-dollar pot roast and turn it into somethin' not fittin' for a stray dog! She don't hold a candle to the slop Carlton's mama used to make, though. That woman cooked ever'thing down to mush—till it was pure gray." She lowered her voice. "I'll see if I can manage long enough to make you breakfast, honey."

I kissed my aunt's heavily rouged cheek and picked a path across the room. A petite pasty-complexioned woman, so drab she could blend into the background, stood next to a mass of floral arrangements studying the card on a tall spray of white carnations. My dear cousin—Evelyn Longman Fletcher.

"Hattie!" Evelyn said when she glanced up. A cloying cloud of flowery scent enveloped me. "I'm so glad you made it home all right. I prayed the whole livelong night for your plane to land on time." Her red-rimmed eyes watered. "I'm so sorry about your mama. I stayed at y'all's house as much as mine after Joe and I were married. It was my second home! I thought she'd just live on forever. She just never seemed like she was any older than the rest of us."

Evelyn dabbed her eyes with a tissue. "Why, just a few days back, she stopped by for a cup of mornin' coffee. She was on her way up to the Cut'n'Curl for her weekly hairdo appointment. Not a day went by that we didn't talk on the phone. It just don't seem real that she's gone."

We studied the line of mourners passing by the pale pink coffin with the rose-trimmed embroidered silk lining.

"I'm so sorry my kids couldn't be here for you, honey. The grand-youngins are still in school right now, so Bryon and Linda couldn't come down with them on such short notice. Ohio's such a long way off. They only get home every other year or so around the holidays. And, Karen…well…"

A flicker of pain washed over Evelyn's features, her hazel eyes downcast. "She's just so busy with her work with the television station up there in Atlanta. But, enough about us, let's have a look at you! You're just pure skin and bones! I told Joe I thought you were livin' way too fast over there in Tallahassee. Lordy, I just don't know how you can stand all that traffic!"

My reply was drowned in a barrage of Evelyn's breathless chatter. Besides being locally famous as a terrible cook, Evelyn was known for frequently redecorating her house, and herself, around a chosen theme. Often, clues to the new décor were echoed in her attire. Small touches to the drab charcoal gray ensemble gave clues to Evelyn's latest animal passion.

The earrings, the necklace…and yes, a ring! Dolphins! Her latest foray into home embellishment was surely "Shades of Sea World." Had she replaced the rooster toilet seat cover in the guest bathroom—a huge red and orange rooster with the words "cock-a-doodle" on the outside and "doo" on the underside? That was during her chicken and barnyard phase. The new lid cover was probably a dolphin sailing high over a wave carrying the Tidy-bowl man in a small dingy.

Acute sorrow and the lack of sleep in the last twenty-four hours had left me punch-drunk. I coughed to cover a giggle.

"Honey, you're not coming down with something, are you? You know your I-mune system takes a beating when you are overcome with grief. You probably aren't eating right, either."

Joe stepped up behind his wife. "Eat a steak every now and then. A little red meat'd do you good!" He leaned over and kissed my cheek.

"She's way too thin, don't you think, Joe? Now, Hattie, you'll have to come and see us after things settle down. I know you're gonna be busy with settling all your mama's affairs, but you can still stop by. It'd do you good to stay over here in the country for a while and breathe some fresh air."

I nodded dumbly.

A murmur rippled through the small room as my older brother entered. He stopped to study our mother's lifeless face. How much he now resembled our father, especially his hands. Like Mr. D., Bobby accentuated his words with expansive gestures, his large strong hands carving arcs in the air. The way he walked, shoulders squared military straight, the uneven smile and receding hairline—all mimicked the giant man I had cherished.

Recently, Bobby and I had drifted apart. The more I prospered and traveled, the more strained our relationship became. After a bitter divorce from his wife of twenty years, Bobby grew more rude and sarcastic when we chanced to visit the Hill at the same time.

The handful of friends who met my big brother experienced the same disdain. Chris, my police-officer friend from Tallahassee, dubbed him Mr. Personality. It was a kind label considering the treatment she received the first time she accompanied me home for a Sunday visit. Chris and Bobby came close to a fistfight over some point of law enforcement. With twenty-eight years' experience as a game warden, Bobby assured her he knew more than she. The picture in my mind's eye was still clear: Chris's Italian temper in full bloom, nostrils flaring slightly, as she tried to control the urge to stuff a dinner napkin into Bobby's smart mouth.

My mother, always the peacemaker, tried to talk with him and me, goading the core of Bobby's anger and pain. "You're not the reason he's so unhappy, Hattie," she told me, "you're just a focus for it to come out."

Bobby's broad shoulders drooped. Though not outwardly handsome, my brother possessed a rugged cowboy demeanor women found irresistible. Unfortunately, his gruff attitude proved an unapproachable barrier. Without Mrs. Tillie's gentle balance to buoy our relationship, how could we manage to mend the rift?

The room was cloaked with a profound stillness. People we had known for years surrounded my family like a protective cocoon. For a

11

fleeting moment, I had the eerie feeling that we were all the same with different coverings hiding identical forms.

Though just the beginning of May, the day of the funeral was unseasonably hot. The near one hundred percent humidity ironed out the heavily sprayed curling-iron waves from my naturally straight hair. The control top pantyhose were stuck permanently to my skin, and several trickles of sweat made a sticky pool on the underside of my bra. To make matters worse, the service was graveside. Only a few immediate family members could sit or huddle in the shade of the narrow crimson Memorial Memories tent. Factoring in the heat and humidity, the press of sweaty bodies swathed in black, and the total lack of even a breath of a breeze, it was a wonder that half the mostly over-fifty crowd didn't pass out.

A cluster of close friends and coworkers from Tallahassee stood to my right side. Among them were Chris and Kathy, two of Tallahassee's Police Department's finest, dressed in formal navy long-sleeved uniforms to show their respect for the family. Visible from several feet away, rivulets of sweat glistened on their faces.

My eyes were sore, swollen, and red-rimmed from bouts of crying. With purple smudges painted from two nights with little rest, I resembled a raccoon with a bad case of mascara runoff. Thank God for dark sunglasses.

Preacher Ghent droned on for over an hour. My head pounded in time with the cadence of his speech.

When was this guy ever going to stop talking? On and on about sin, and ashes to ashes. If we all didn't feel rotten enough, they seated the family practically on top of the coffin! The heat and lack of sleep added to my irritation.

Preacher Ghent heaved a heavy sigh, breathed deeply, and launched into another long tirade. "And, Gawd-AH…"

My lower lip burned where I had bitten down to suppress a giggle. Everything he said ended with 'AH'! Gawd-AH. Heaven-AH. Death-AH.

His deep-voiced litany droned on and on, rolling in waves; quiet and still one moment, enough to shake the rafters, had there been any, the next. To avoid laughing, I focused on counting the AH's.

The preacher heaved a gulp of air before continuing. "And-AH! Our sister-AH in Christ-AH will find her reward-AH in the great-AH by and by-AH!"

I leaned over and shook slightly with the effort not to guffaw. How could anything possibly be funny about a funeral! Aunt Piddie, thinking I was just overcome, handed over a monogrammed hankie and patted me on the back. I held my breath for a full three minutes, just long enough for Preacher Ghent to finish his sermon and ask the crowd to bow in prayer.

Immediately after the congregation responded, I passed out cold— right at the base of the coffin. In the fall forward, two of the standing white carnation and lily sprays tipped over on top of me. I don't recall what happened afterwards. When I could focus, Bobby was holding my head in his lap and everyone was huddled around clucking sympathy for Tillie Davis' poor, pitiful daughter.

Then, oh my God, I saw him. Garrett Douglas. He swaggered toward the crowd with his easy long-legged athletic smoothness.

Damn it! What was he doing here?

"Well, hi there, Garrett!" my brother said as he extended a hand. The two men greeted each other as old friends. Amazing, since they'd met only once.

Bobby tipped his head in my direction. "Seems poor Hattie got a little overheated."

Note to myself: Kill Bobby later.

"She always has been a bit of a delicate flower," Garrett replied in a conspiratorial 'aren't-women-so-weak-unlike-us-good-ole-boys' voice.

If not for the fact that I had just successfully halted the final prayer at my mother's funeral with a half gainer into the flower exhibit, I would have planted a black patent-leather pump in his crotch. It was right at eye level. I could have done it easily.

Garrett crouched and softly stroked my face. "I'm so sorry about Mama Tillie."

I ducked back from his warm hand. "Nice of you to take the time off from work to come."

He flinched. "I hope we can talk soon," he said as he rose.

Bobby helped me to my feet. I brushed a few stray fern leaves from the front of my black dress. "I'm exhausted, Garrett. It's not a really good time for me at the moment, as you can imagine."

Garrett flashed his orthodontist's dream smile. He was the only human I knew who could rival former president Jimmy Carter in the sheer number of teeth he could expose at once.

"Of course. It's a trying time for you. I'll call you later in the week. Good to see you again, Bobby."

As he walked away, I was struck, as always, with his sense of presence. All the women in the crowd, regardless of age or marital status, watched him move toward the sleek black Mercedes convertible. I could've sworn I even caught Aunt Piddie running her tongue over her thin painted lips.

THE DAVIS HOMESTEAD

Excerpt from Max the Madhatter's notebook:

August 17, 1958: I asked Dr. Bruner how it is that I can feel on top of the world and so miserable I can barely look up, sometimes within minutes of each other. He said it was like when it rains and the sun is shining at the same time. Strong feelings can hold hands.

CHAPTER TWO

THE LOCAL PAPER, the *Twin City News*, and its big city counterpart, the *Tallahassee Democrat*, were crammed into the green plastic newspaper box on the opposite side of State Highway 269. That my mother had to cross the busy highway to pick up the paper and mail always concerned me. She had finally contacted the postal carrier the past summer to have the mailbox moved up the sand lane and closer to the house, but the newspaper had to be fetched by either walking or riding an old golf cart.

When Mr. D. was alive, he would pile into the cart, flanked on either side by one or more dogs, and make the mail and paper run. After he died, my mother used the daily paper as a reason to get out, get some exercise, and stop by the neighbors' house for a cup of coffee. This worked out pretty well for everyone except the last of the aging canines who begrudgingly trudged along behind her.

"Howdy, Mrs. Margie!" I called from the road.

The petite woman wearing a red bandana waved from the edge of a patch of tomato plants. "Mornin'! Stop on in after you get the paper. John has the coffee on!"

"Thanks. Some of my friends from Tallahassee are still here. I have to go back up and help with breakfast before they leave."

Spam, my parents' elderly golden retriever/lab/shepherd mix woofed at me to hurry on up the road. I had dubbed the blended mutt a "Florida Cracker Retriever," a hardy breed not yet recognized by the American Kennel Club.

At the turn of the white sandy lane, I paused and studied the sprawling white farmhouse on the Hill. A warm feeling of home washed over me. I had literally been born in that house—on a couch beside the fireplace in the kitchen. My mother had gone into labor in the wee hours of an October morning. I came way too fast for a quick trip to the little hospital in Quincy twenty miles away and had emerged into the world kicking and screaming with my mother, father, Mrs. Margie, and my scared stiff-older brother in attendance.

The house loomed at the top of a small hill as if it had been placed there by an other-worldly Monopoly God who bought the property and dropped a house to improve its value. The grassy lawn sprawled for five acres surrounding the farmhouse, with three large past-their-prime pecan trees framing the edges of the cleared property. My father's workshop was tucked out of view, and an old smokehouse listed dangerously behind the covered carport. A wooden privy once stood at the edge of the woods, but a severe case of wood rot had claimed it several years back. My friends' automobiles were pulled up on the thick lawn next to my truck, and indistinct figures passed behind a rectangular picture window that formed a good portion of the front wall of the kitchen.

I sighed. Except for my graceful dive into the plants, the graveside service was a blur. The numbness prevailed as I heard all the platitudes: She lived a wonderful, full life. She went just the way she would've wanted, Hattie. Your mama wasn't one to stay down for long. Mrs. Tillie's with Mr. D. now. All the well-intended phrases confirmed the wisdom I had gleaned from my father's death ten years prior: It's best to simply say, "I'm sorry for your loss."

The pain lurks, hidden in the wings, waiting for the loyal friends to pack up and go back to their lives. The processions of well-meaning visitors bearing casseroles, heaping plates of cold cuts, cakes, and pies, stop coming up the lane. Contact with familiar things left behind would snare my breath and leave me gasping for air. They were the leavings of a life fully lived: a soil-stained plaid work shirt on a peg by the back door, my mother's frazzled sun hat from the Straw Bazaar in the Bahamas, and a fingerprint-smudged pair of reading glasses propped crossways on an unread copy of *Life on the Nile*.

Chris pushed away from the breakfast table and belched loudly. "Good one!" she boasted.

"You can be so gross," I kidded.

"You're just jealous since you're such the Southern Lady who can't make any good bodily function noises." Her deep-set dark eyes flashed in an expression I had seen many times in the twenty years we had been close.

"I can't help it. My mother taught me that a female neither belches nor farts out loud," I said. We'd had the same conversation countless times.

She toasted me with a coffee cup. "I'll come visit you in the hospital when you finally blow frickin' up."

A sun-faded dark blue Ford pick-up slid into the yard.

Chris smirked. "Time for us to pack up and head back to the city. Especially now that Mr. Personality is here."

Bobby hopped from the truck's cab and shuffled toward the door. "Y'all don't leave on my account, now," he called as he stepped inside.

Chris worked up her best saccharine smile. "Wouldn't give you the satisfaction, sweetie." She pecked me on the cheek. "I'll call you later on in the week. As to that pompous asshole, Garrett, don't worry about him. I have his tag number."

"Don't harass him, Officer Friendly. I'll never hear the end of it."

Her finely plucked dark eyebrows rose slightly. "Would I do that?" Chris grabbed a suitcase and motioned for the rest of the Tallahassee gang to join her.

I ushered my friends outside. They pulled out of the drive in a dust-raising procession.

"What brings you out here so early, big brother? My coffee?" My stomach churned in anticipation of the inevitable confrontation.

"I just came out to let you know that we're supposed to meet with the attorney tomorrow at ten."

"Okay. Fine."

Bobby poured a cup of black coffee. "So, how long you planning on staying in town?"

"I took a month of family leave from the state. All of my massage-therapy clients know I'll call when I'm back, so both jobs are covered. Why? You have a problem with me being around?"

He took a long noisy swill of coffee. His eyes were cold blue. "It was good of Garrett to come to the funeral."

I clenched my teeth and studied my brother. What the hell was he up to?

"Such as it was. I'm sure he had his motives."

Bobby slammed his cup on the table, sloshing coffee onto my mother's hand-loomed tablerunner. "Damn it, Hattie! The man's trying for heaven's sake. Give him a break!"

"You have no earthly idea what you're talking about, and since when do you give a damn about my love life?"

He ran a hand through his thinning light brown hair. "All I know is that half this town thinks you're some kinda dyke. Hell, here you are at forty, and never married!"

Familiar anger knotted my stomach. "Like you're the expert! At least none of my past partners left and took me for everything!"

Bobby's sun-wizened face caved in on itself.

"Oh, jeez…Bobby, I'm sorry. I didn't mean to say that…"

He stood quickly and headed for the front door. "Just be there tomorrow," he muttered.

The silence was eerie and haunting after Bobby left, and I needed to exorcise the anger brewing away at my stomach lining. After phoning Margie and John to tell them I would take care of the daily fish-pond duties, I donned a pair of snake boots and headed to an area my family called the 'back forty.' This was also the direction of what my father referred to as Pete's Mudhole, the mystical place where all of the tremendous summer thunder and lightening storms originated. "It's gonna be a frog-strangler," he would say, pointing to the purple-black clouds above the tree line. "It's comin' from Pete's Mudhole."

The cultivated soil of the field was mushy soft, still rising and falling in the furrows of the last corn crop. The two-lane dirt road gave way to a weedy overgrown path when it entered the hardwood forest at the edge of the ten-acre cleared track. Stepping into the woods, I noticed the reverent hush reminiscent of the foyer of a cathedral. The towering pine, red oak, sweet gum, and hickory trees formed a dappled canopy overhead.

A few feet into the woods, I paused to breathe deeply of the leaf mold and pine-scented air and caught a stealthy movement to my left side. A petite white-tailed doe, frozen in place, watched me briefly before flipping her tail at a ninety-degree angle and bounding out of sight. Unlike a number of locals, I didn't lust for a shotgun as I watched her graceful exit. Mr. D had felt the same. Bright orange *POSTED! NO HUNTING!* signs hung at even intervals along the fence line surrounding the 150 acres. As a child, I often imagined the deer, dove, and turkeys scurrying like the dickens to the safety of our property line.

The catfish pond nestled in a depression at the base of two forested hills, fed by three natural springs that were seldom dry except in severe drought. Although it covered a little over an acre, the pond was deep and cool. I navigated the steep steps leading to an earthen dam. A tin-covered shed and two rusted lawn chairs complete with fishing-pole holders furnished the wide grassy embankment.

I walked over to a rusted twenty-gallon drum and smacked the side several times with a piece of heavy lead pipe. "Dinner!" I yelled, laughing at the absurd notion that the fish were actually hovering near the water's edge listening. It had to be done this way. It was a Davis ritual.

After removing the weighted cover, I scooped a large coffee can full of commercial floating catfish food, reared back like a pro baseball pitcher—*Jeez, Hattie. You throw like a girl!*—and sent the food spraying skyward so that it landed in an arc across the surface of the smooth green water.

I settled onto the sun-warmed grass and watched the greedy catfish wallow and flip, sometimes hemming several pieces into their whiskered mouths before slapping the surface and whipping underwater. The frenzy lasted for several minutes until every piece of food had been eaten, then peace returned to the water.

After my father died, the upkeep of the pond fell to John and Margie. My mother could no longer negotiate the steep steps and had little desire to visit one of my dad's favorite spots. I'm sure it made her too sad. At night, the sound of the peepers and bullfrogs started in slow, steadily rising to a fever pitch—a sound my father loved so much he installed a remote microphone with a receiving speaker next to their bed. Mom didn't appreciate the call of the wild and wore earplugs on the occasions he insisted on falling asleep listening to nature's music.

The faint glimmer of early morning sun on the surface of the water calmed my turmoil. Reflections of my family appeared in my mind's eye like a demented slide show: Fishing with my father and brother. Trying to bait a hook with a wiggling earthworm. Learning to remove a catfish without being finned. Blazing orange sunsets over the pond. My five-year-old cousin Byron falling into the water battling a large fish he was determined to land. My dad's easy laughter. My mom shaking her head at us tracking pond mud onto her clean linoleum floor.

A grief bubble popped to the surface of my mind like a dayglow cork. Loneliness settled into my belly with the weight of a cold stone. An orphan at forty. No parents. One older brother who disliked me for no apparent reason. My two biggest fans were gone, along with their unconditional love. All of my independence sucked right out of me, and I began to sob with heaving gulps of air fueling the next round. My stomach reeled.

Just as I began to feel overwhelmed, a poster that once hung in my Tallahassee office came to mind: A raccoon with two claws on the rail of a floating dingy and the other two clinging precariously to the edge of a dock. It could go either way. As easily as the tears had come, the hysterical laughter ensued. Any minute now, the little guys in the white suits would come to lock me into my own padded room at the hospital uptown.

BREAKFAST AT EVELYN'S

Excerpt from Max the Madhatter's notebook:

February 12, 1959: Piddie Longman made me a cathead biscuit as big around as my double fist! She brought a plate full of them to Mr. Dan's shop. Fresh butter and tupelo honey to go on top. Next to her chocolate cake, it is the best thing I have ever tasted.

CHAPTER THREE

EARLY THE NEXT morning, I rapped hard on Joe's and Evelyn's unlocked side door before entering. The knock was merely an announcement so I wouldn't startle them. As with most folks in Chattahoochee, they had started securing doors primarily at night a few years back following a series of robberies that scared the locals into admitting bad things could happen, even here.

"Come on back!" Evelyn's voice echoed from deep within the house. "We're out here in the kitchen!"

Aunt Piddie rounded the corner, flinging her walker ahead for balance.

"Morning, Aunt Pid." I reached out to steady her. "You're moving awfully fast for first thing."

"Whew!" She blew, holding a liver-spotted hand to her chest. "It's a damn shame, gettin' old!" Piddie lowered her voice. "I had to beat you in there. She's makin' pancakes. Don't you dare touch them. You'll have the stomach scours for a week! I got up early and made you some catheads."

"You didn't have to do that!"

Piddie's nostrils flared, and she pursed her lips. "Yeah, I did. I love you enough to spare you Evelyn's cookin'. Joe's built up a tolerance to it over the years. It's liable to set you back."

"But you eat it!"

"Better than a laxative. Her cookin' keeps me regular."

We laughed like a couple of kids up to no good.

"What y'all doin' out there?" Evelyn called. "The pancakes are almost ready!"

For someone whose cooking was cursed for fifty miles, Evelyn had an impressive kitchen. Copper-bottomed pans were suspended from a wrought iron grate. Every conceivable gadget and appliance stood ready on the long granite countertops. It was a galley to make Martha Stewart wish to do a remote show: Luxury kitchens of the rural South, today on Martha Stewart Weekend. The only thing that impaired the culinary perfection of Evelyn's kitchen was the wild abundance of sea life pictures, figurines, and shells.

Wow. Not just the dolphins, but the entire coast seems to be represented.

"Did you raid Sea World, Ev?" I asked.

Piddie snorted. "Ain't hard to pick up on this year's theme, is it?"

Evelyn sniffed and flipped a pancake that had turned pitch-black on one side. Her starched red gingham apron quivered. Joe glanced at the griddle and swallowed hard.

"I took the opportunity to redecorate the kitchen last year when Joe decided to install central heat and air. Mama'd keep the space heaters in the bathrooms going so hot that you could barely do your business without nearly singeing the hair off your legs! Anyway, we floated a note at Gadsden State Bank for the improvements. Of course, it's the SunTrust Bank now, on account of them bein' bought out, and all."

"I can't help I have low blood," Piddie retorted. "Evelyn would rather freeze her poor old mama out before she'd let loose a red cent to keep the house a degree or two warmer. I'll bet she still has a dime of the first dollar she ever earned."

I grabbed a seashell-embellished mug. The coffee smelled strong. Lucky for me, I liked it that way.

"Sooo..." Piddie said. "Tell us about that good-lookin' feller. Is he your beau? Your mama mentioned you were sweet on some rich business man."

"Garrett? Oh, he's just someone I've been seeing off and on for awhile."

"Lord!" Piddie fanned herself with a manatee print napkin. "What a prime specimen of a male. When I saw him standin' there at your mama's funeral, he near'bout took my breath away! Even at my age!"

Evelyn piled a charred pancake on the growing pile and slipped the plate in front of Joe. He sighed, drowned the stack with butter light syrup, sawed a hunk, and began to eat.

Evelyn gestured with a greasy spatula. "He is a nice looking young man, Hattie."

"Yeah, well. You know what they say. Looks aren't everything." I picked up one of Piddie's cathead biscuits, still warm from the oven. For something made with lard, it was almost weightless.

Piddie's cornflower blue eyes sparkled. "He looks like one of those hunky men on the cover of a romance novel. Face all golden and carved. Sun-bleached blonde hair a'blowin' in the wind. Leanin' over some woman with a cleavage you could drive a truck through."

Evelyn shook her head. "That's stretching it just a bit, Mama."

"Looks like he's one of those smooth men. Is he, Hattie?"

"I'm not sure I know what you mean, Pid." I bit into a buttered biscuit and almost moaned aloud.

She leaned in conspiratorially, her voice barely above a whisper. "Not all ape-hairy like my Carlton was. I can recall as clear as it was yesterday, the first time I saw him without a shirt on…almost dropped the pear pie I was totin'. Hairiest man that ever lived. I had to trim around his neck so his T-shirts wouldn't bind."

"Mama, I don't think this conversation is really appropriate for the breakfast table." She settled into a seat with a slice of buttered toast.

"And balls like a Chia pet!" Piddie stabbed the air with a bony finger.

"Mama!"

"Good Lord, Piddie!" Joe joined in.

"Never in my life would I have ever dreamed I'd have such a prude for a daughter. Me! Liddyanne Davis Longman. Evelyn, do you go to church to repent after you and Joe have sex?"

Joe smiled and ducked his balding head closer to the pancake pile.

"I'm going to choose not to react to that." Evelyn left the table to get a cup of coffee.

"You've been givin' her those thur-apee books of yours again. Haven't you, Joe? She sounds more and more every day like the junk you tell your patients up there in the 'Hooch!"

Joe fell into the trained therapist role, his voice even and calm. "Now, Mama Piddie. Evelyn tries really hard to hold her temper. And, I'd prefer if you would refer to the institution where I am employed by its proper title of Florida State Hospital." Joe sipped the last of his coffee.

Piddie flung her hand in the air. "It'll always be the 'Hooch to me."

"Well," Joe said as he cleared his dirty dishes to the sink, "I think I'll leave it with you ladies. I've got to run up to the post office." He leaned over and pecked Evelyn on the cheek. "Good breakfast, hon."

I bit into a second biscuit. The phrase 'melt in your mouth' had to have come from someone's first taste of a cathead made with lard.

"Good, aren't they?" Piddie glowed. "I didn't scrimp on 'em either, even though I had to borrow some lard from Mrs. Ginny Pridgett two doors down."

Evelyn's hazel eyes widened. "You brought lard into my house?!"

Piddie threw her arms into the air, and the waddles on the under-sides flapped like wet sheets in the breeze. "Watch out! Here come the fat police! Yes, I brought lard into the house. Had to, if I wanted to cook a decent batch of catheads. If not, they would've tasted like hockey pucks—like those dang canned things you beat on the side of the counter to open!"

The two women glared at each other.

I tried to break the tension. "You're lucky to have a guy like Joe who'll at least put his dishes into the sink. I'm so tired of men who expect someone to constantly pick up after them."

Evelyn cast one last smoldering glance toward her mother, then smiled in my direction. "I got him young and trained him right."

"Speaking of men…Bobby said something to me yesterday that I'd really like to know more about. He said everyone in this town thinks I'm gay."

Evelyn shifted uneasily in her seat and cleared her throat. "Well, there were rumors."

"You were partly responsible," Piddie said. She chuckled at my confounded expression. "Close your mouth, Hattie. You'll let flies in."

"I live over forty miles away! And, I'm not even here that much! How could I be responsible?"

"It had everything to do with that busy body Elvina Houston. You remember the first time you came to your mama's driving your new pick-up?"

I nodded dumbly.

"Well, Elvina was there. They'd had a Ladies Circle meetin' at the house, and, as always, Elvina was the last to leave. She can never bear the thought of missing anything. Either that, or she's afraid everyone will talk about her if she goes home early. You came spinnin' up in that shiny red pick-up truck wearin' jeans and boots."

I chuckled. "Yeah, I remember. My mom nearly pitched a fit and fell in it! *Cause*, she said, *ladies don't drive trucks.*"

"Now. Elvina took that football and ran for a touchdown. By the time she made the rounds, folks believed that truck was one hundred percent proof positive why you hadn't married and popped out a load of youngin's...because you swing the other way!"

"Jeez-o-pete! I got the truck because it was easier to carry a massage table. That, plus I wasn't going to pay all the money for a new SUV!" I sat straight up. "I suppose Mom had to listen to the rumors, too?"

"Afraid so." Evelyn nodded." She had her hair done once a week uptown, and most everything that passes for truth comes out of Mandy's Cut'n'Curl. You could learn anything about anybody in there. Your name came up a few times."

"I don't have much control over what people say." I shook my head in disbelief, then smiled with the memory of my mother entering the house with her hair freshly coifed. "Dad used to kid her that she was going up to 'challenge the beauty parlor'."

"It used to make your mama madder than a wet hen when she'd come home with her hair all fluffed up and sprayed stiff, and your daddy would say 'I see they couldn't fit you in today, Tillie,'" Piddie added.

Evelyn nodded "Your daddy was a piece of work, for sure."

Piddie held up her pudgy hand. "Your mama wasn't one to gossip, now. She was…what does Joe call it, Evelyn?"

"A facilitator."

"Yeah, that's it. She'd just sit and nod. Every now and then, she'd own as how 'she didn't know that' or 'is that so?'. Whoever was in the shop could launch off for hours with just that little bit of proddin.'"

"Mama never said anything about hearing any rumors about me."

"She mentioned somethin' to me once awhile back," Piddie said. "She said she'd raised a decent young woman with a good heart and she didn't much care what floated your boat as long as you were happy."

Tears popped into the corners of my eyes.

Piddie offered me a napkin "Here, honey. I didn't mean to make you start up."

I dabbed the corners of my eyes. "You didn't, Pid. I guess it'll be like when Dad died. I'll just have to leak every now and then."

Piddie patted my hand. "You just go right on, whenever you feel burdened. Better outside than in."

Evelyn leaned close. Her floral cologne threatened my sinuses. "You never did tell us about Garrett. You serious about him?"

"I was. It's difficult to be with him."

Evelyn lowered her voice. "He's not married, is he?"

"In a manner of speaking, yes."

My cousin and aunt gasped in unison. The midday soap opera couldn't be as good as the real-life drama of their miscreant relative.

I grinned impishly. "Married to his job. Married to his computer. Married to his car."

"Too bad." Piddie sniffed. "I'll bet you made a fine-lookin' couple."

"Yeah, for about the first six months or so. We traveled together. It was fantastic. He was warm and caring. Then, he just changed. Maybe he was being himself, and I was a brief vacation. There were other things, too. He totally flipped when I broached the subject of adopting a baby. He already has a grown daughter and was dead set against raising another child. I don't know…" I sighed heavily. "I begged for his attention for so long. One day, my flame for him just died."

Piddie jumped like she had been stuck by a cattle prod. "Ohhh! Flame! I almost forgot. Remember your old high school flame, Jake

Witherspoon? He's moved back into town and bought out the Twin City Florist uptown."

"Jake Witherspoon, a florist?"

Piddie nodded. "How can I put this to you easy, Hattie. He was once your flame, now he is a flame."

"Jake Witherspoon is gay!?"

"As a three dollar bill. As the birds in May. As—"

"I think she gets the idea, Mama."

I rolled my eyes and shrugged "It's not that I care if he's homosexual. Actually, it makes a little more sense to me now, thinking back. He was the only boy in town who never tried to coax me into the back seat of his parents' car."

Piddie smiled. Her age-yellowed teeth showed in an uneven line. "You two were an item for a while, weren't you?"

"He was more like my best buddy. I haven't seen him in years. His mama died last year when Garrett and I were in the Tetons. I remember sending a sympathy card to his mom's address when I got home and found out."

One of the silk flowers adorning my aunt's towering mound of curls fell to the floor. She retrieved the fake bloom and pressed it back into service. "You should stop in and see him. He did most of the flowers for your mama's funeral. It's unbelievable what he has done with that old shop. He's also helped redecorate half the houses in town. Not Evelyn's, obviously."

Evelyn smirked at her mother. "Don't start up with me."

I rose and deposited the coffee cup in the sink. "I have to meet Bobby at the attorney's office at ten. Maybe I'll stop by his shop and see if he can have lunch."

DRAGONFLY FLORIST

Excerpt from Max the Madhatter's notebook:

May 2, 1959: Inspiration comes from different places. I see it in the petals of the magnolia blooms beside the Ward A building and in the azaleas flowering in clumps outside the dental infirmary. The smallest thing, once noticed, can lead to the greatest revelation.

CHAPTER FOUR

THE ELABORATE BRICK office of Daniel H. "Hank" Henderson, attorney-at-law, was located on Jefferson Street adjacent to the Chattahoochee Police Station. Bobby's drab green Game and Freshwater Fish Commission truck was parked next to Hank's shiny charcoal gray Mercedes sedan.

Hank's longtime secretary, Janice, looked up from her computer screen. "Hi, Miss Hattie. I'm so sorry about your mama. She taught me business education in high school. Of course, back then the rage was the electric typewriter. I'm not so sure this thing is an improvement, some days. Well...your brother is already back in Hank's office."

Hank looked the same as he had for the last thirty years—overweight, over-stuffed, and over-saccharine. "Well, here she is," he said. "Bobby and I were just catching up on a few things."

I could only imagine what things that would be. "Let's get started, shall we?"

Hank hauled his tailored pants up underneath his distended stomach. "Your mother and father were quite interested in making sure you both were taken care of, as well as being equally treated. There is a sizeable estate for you two to split."

Bobby and I exchanged puzzled glances.

"The hundred and fifty acres of property is to be shared. The only stipulation is that Hattie will own the parcel of property containing the house. Bobby, you will be compensated in kind for the estimated value of the home from the investment accounts."

The leather upholstered chair squeaked in protest when Hank shifted his considerable weight. "I have a breakdown of the cash value of the investments. These funds will be available as soon as I have cleared all outstanding debts, of which there are a few. I will contact you as soon as possible with information regarding the transfer of all funds."

I didn't have to look at my brother to know he was as shocked as I was at the final figure at the end of the column.

"Where'd all this come from?" Bobby asked.

Hank smiled, showing a straight line of perfectly capped Chiclet teeth.

"Your father and mother did two things in favor of their children: They lived simply and invested wisely. Now, if you don't have any questions for me at this time, I have a Board of Directors meeting at the bank that pulls me away."

Bobby stood and walked toward the lobby.

"Oh, I almost forgot, Hattie." Hank handed me a weathered gray wire-bound notebook. "This notebook was with your parents' papers."

On the front, in handwritten oversized block lettering, it read: *"TO MY FRIEND, MR. DAN DAVIS AND HIS SWEET CHILD HATTIE."*

Hank held up one well-manicured hand. "I have no idea, Hattie. Please excuse me now, I must leave." He grabbed an oxblood-red leather briefcase and trundled from the office.

I waved goodbye to Janice on the way out. Bobby's pick-up was gone. As I unlocked the truck door, a City of Chattahoochee police cruiser pulled up alongside me.

A sultry deep male voice said from behind me. "You got a license to look like that, lady?"

I studied the mustached face of the officer. "Why, you going to arrest me?"

"Only if you give me trouble." Officer Rich Burns grinned. "How ya' doin', Hattie? Carol and I been meaning to call you up for dinner. Your mama was a fine lady, even if she didn't turn out to be my mother-in-law like I had all planned out in tenth grade. Lot of folks will miss her."

"Thanks, Rich. You haven't changed a bit. Still have a smile that could stop a five-day clock."

The dispatcher's voice on Rich's radio rattled unintelligibly in his ear. He spoke back in code, then turned to me. "I gotta run, Hattie. There's some drunk causing a scene down at the river-landing bait shop."

He rustled in his uniform pocket. "Here's my card. You call me if you need anything out there on the Hill. Heck, I'll even write down my cell phone number on the back."

"Thanks, Rich. It's good to know I have one of the 'Hooch's finest at my beck and call." I noticed the fine dusting of silver hair between the dark waves.

"As always." He gunned the cruiser to Washington Street and turned west toward the river.

Except for different businesses, Chattahoochee's Washington Street looked pretty much the same as I remembered from childhood. The two lane thoroughfare ran east toward Quincy and west toward the junction of Lake Seminole and the Apalachicola River. The recently renovated Victory Bridge spanning the river near Jim Woodruff Dam was used by locals and a few tourists who desired an easier pace over the high volume of Interstate 10. Only two traffic lights still graced the main drag, not counting the flashing caution/stop light at the top of Thrill Hill.

Thrill Hill wasn't nearly as much fun as it had been in my teenage years. I would turn at the light at Washington and Boliver Avenue, slam the accelerator to the floor, feel the rush as all four wheels left the ground at the crest of the hill, and bottom out the shocks when I landed. I remembered the woozy roller-coaster stomach I used to get as my parents' Ford LTD dropped toward the pavement. Now, a three-way stop bordered the top of the hill.

The larger of the two main intersections had recently been widened to accommodate the rush hour traffic at the entrance to the Florida State Hospital. At one time, the hospital's mental-patient inhabitants made up the vast majority of the local population, as well as providing employment to a large number of townspeople. Over the years, changes in legislation and funding had reduced the number of patients and staff. Recently, several unoccupied buildings had been renovated, and two Department of Corrections institutions were located there now.

I spied the plate-glass window of the Dragonfly Florist halfway down the first block on the north side of Washington Street and pulled into a parallel parking place. Inside, Jake Witherspoon danced behind a large flower-strewn table to an old Temptations tune as he stuck daisies into a basket of ferns and snapdragons.

"Oh, my Gawd! Sister-girl!" Jake whooped when he looked up. He dropped the clump of daisies and rushed to sweep me into his arms.

"I was hoping you'd come by! Sorry I haven't had a break since your mama's funeral to come out to see you on the Hill." Jake held me at arms' length. "You look as sweet and sassy as the last time I saw you!" He reached up and plucked playfully at a stray sprig of my hair. "Well, maybe your 'do could stand a little trim, but otherwise, you're flawless!"

Jake had chided me about my limp do-nothing-famously hair since we were old enough to sprout self-awareness.

"Yeah, I'll have to stop by and see if Mandy can fit me in while I'm home. But you...you look handsome...and movie-starish."

Jake had aged little since high school; still the same boyish facial features, sprinkled with a light dusting of freckles. His sandy brown hair was clipped stylishly short, the tips highlighted light blonde. The calm blue eyes I had loved as a teenager reflected humor and gentleness.

Jake glowed with the praise. "You're too kind, please. I have more than an inch-pinch around my middle and just oodles of smile lines. But thanks for fostering the delusion that I've aged well. I've thought of you often since I moved back. It's been a wild ride getting the business built up again. The shop had gone down a little before I took over."

He frowned slightly. "I'm sorry it took your mama's funeral to bring us together. I'd always hoped to catch sight of you on one of your fly-by trips to the Hill, but I seemed to find out about you being here after the fact. I'm surprised your mom didn't tell you I was back in town."

"I haven't spent much time over here in the past year, I'm afraid. I guess you just never came up in conversation, or I would've come in to see you before this. Aunt Piddie told me you were back in town, just this morning...and, you were at the graveside? I didn't see you."

He tilted his head and smirked. "Of course I was there! I did practically all the flowers. You took out two of my finest carnation and lily sprays with your amazing nosedive! And, I had to deal with that enchanting brother of yours to plan the casket drape." He wrinkled his nose in distaste. "Besides, I know how crazy it gets after a funeral. I was giving you a few days before I made an appearance, armed with an appropriate casserole, naturally."

"Jake, you're so-"

"Flashy? Marvelous? Queer?" Jake supplied, flinging his delicate hands out like a Broadway dancer taking a bow.

"Actually, I was going to say slim. You look incredible. But then, you always were a sharp dresser."

He hugged me again. "Oh, I have missed you, sister-girl!" Jake propped his hands on his slender hips. "Well, let me fill in the awkward spots. Since you've located me, I can assume you've talked to that delightful auntie of yours. You know I am back home to stay, and gay...and you're not, I understand."

"How'd you know that?"

He rolled his eyes. "Oh, let's see. Hmmm... handsome, chiseled man at the graveside service..." he said in singsong. "Obvious! Besides, Elvina Houston told me. She stops by periodically to see if there are any funerals she can attend. That woman operates on the rule of six degrees of separation. If she can even remotely trace her way to any of the folks I'm doing funeral sprays for, she breaks out the mourning clothes and calls it a social function."

"I'm glad Elvina cleared things up. Although I didn't even know I was gay until I came home for Mom's funeral! Imagine my shock!"

"Isn't this town wonderful?" Jake laughed. "Come on back here and sit while I finish this arrangement for the Morningside AME Sunday service. Lucille Jackson will be by shortly to fetch it."

I watched Jake's masterful hands as he turned the arrangement around, plugging flowers into vacant spots. He handed me a cold drink from a small refrigerator.

"How'd you end up back here?" I asked.

"Kismet. Fate. The Gods smiled on me. Actually, my mother, the Countess of the Twin Cities, left everything to me when she died. Got your card, by the way. I tried to live in the Witherspoon castle, but it was just too much. I sold it to a couple from south Florida who've never so much as set foot in town, and bought the store and a rat-trap delivery van that runs most of the time. And...here I am!"

"You like it here? I couldn't wait to get out!"

He crinkled his nose when he smiled, a gesture I remembered fondly. "I love this little burg. I didn't want to leave in the first place. When Cruella de Witherspoon-Ville found out her beloved son walked with a swish, she flipped out. Told me she loved me, but it would just ruin her standing in the community if anyone knew. So, I left with mother's blessings. Went as far away as I could fathom at the time—New York. Mother wrote me, sent money sometimes. I went to school, worked at a little flower shop close to my mangy little apartment to earn extra cash, and got a business degree that I hang in the bathroom. I helped Mrs. Lucy Gray with this shop off and on when I first moved back. She wanted to retire, and it just all worked out. For once."

"If you sold the mansion, where are you living now?"

"I threw a cot in the back." Jake motioned toward a small room in the rear of the shop. "Eventually, I'll find some little hovel to call home. I wish Piddie would sell me her little frame house on the corner of Morgan Avenue and Cedar Road. What I could do with that place! And those azaleas!" Jake paused and considered the flower arrangement from all sides before plugging a wired white carnation into a blank spot. "So...you never married or had kids?"

"No, to both questions. Relationships haven't exactly been my strong suite. The men I've picked so far have either been too scared to commit for the long term, or they've balked at the thought of children. Some day, I may just say to hell with them all and raise a child all by myself. For now, I like my independence. I like to be able to pick up and travel. Besides, I'd have to carry a baby in a suitcase if I had one now...I've had, as Piddie calls it, a 'hysterectum' a couple of years back."

"Oh, sister-girl. I'm sorry!" Jake hugged me.

"Don't be. I'm certainly not. I still get bitchy once a month, but I don't have to go through all that other female stuff. It's kind of nice."

He added an extra fern to the arrangement. "Your aunt is a card. I provide some of the adornments for her hair, by the way. Piddie helped me a lot when I first moved back home. Some folks were a little put out with my somewhat…flamboyant—though charming—personality. Piddie and her bosom friend Elvina Houston pretty much turned things around in my favor. Thanks to them, the business has flourished, and it seems most folks kinda choose to overlook the gay issue."

Jake smiled. "She and Evelyn were in here ordering flowers for Mama Jean Thurgood's funeral several months ago, and she told me she thought the reason she was having her fallin' out spells was because her karate arteries were clogged. Evelyn says 'no, Mama, that's carotid arteries!' Piddie fires back, 'That's what I said, karate!' Turns out, Evelyn's all steamed at her for ruining one of her ace bandages. Mrs. Ginny Pridgett told Piddie she'd read somewhere that you could put a poultice of mustard on your neck and it would unclog your arteries! Well, Piddie didn't want to go to the trouble of going out for dry mustard powder, so she squirted regular old hotdog yellow mustard on an ace bandage and wrapped it around her neck!"

When I caught my breath from laughing, I said, "I would've loved to have seen the look on Ev's face. I'm positive her kitchen was a royal mess! That is classic Piddie!"

A tiny bell tied to the glass door rang, announcing the arrival of a small black woman. "Just in time!" Jake said, glancing toward the front of the shop.

Mrs. Lucille Jackson called, "Mornin', Mr. Jake! Whew! It's heatin' up, out there!"

"Perfect timing, Miz Lucille! I was just finishing your arrangement!"

"Heww! I suwanee, Mr. Jake, you are an artist! It makes me feel cooler just to look at that basket of flowers! I can't tell you how much Reverend Jackson and I appreciate you doin' this at the last minute. Dessa White was supposed to be in charge of the flowers for the altar this week, but she's over in Tallahassee in the hospital. Her sugar went way up and she's havin' problems with her blood pressure. If it wasn't for you, the sanctuary would be awfully plain tomorrow."

"I'm always glad to help you out, Miz Lucille. Y'all send a load of business my way. Oh, 'scuse my bad manners, do you remember Hattie Davis?"

Lucille brushed a strand of gray hair from her glistening forehead and dabbed the beads of perspiration with an embroidered handkerchief. "Why sure! I thought you looked familiar. You're Mama Tillie's little girl! Lord, I don't reckon I've laid eyes on you in a good while. My prayers are with you and your family. Miz Tillie did a lot for this town. She taught my son, Thurston II, to type, and just a couple of years ago, she helped my grandson, Thurston III, in that special readin' program at the elementary school."

I nodded. "I remember her talking about that! Before she started having so much trouble with her arthritis, she joined the mentor program in the county. She said it helped her have a reason to go on after my dad died."

"Yeah. I reckon we all need somethin' to make us feel like we still count for somethin' in this world. I see your Aunt Piddie regular. She's been a friend of mine and the Reverend's for goin' on forty years or so. She comes to services with us 'bout twice a month. Be sure to tell her for me, if you will…some of the church ladies will be bringin' supper by to you all tomorrow. I made a couple of sweet tater pies. Miz Piddie just loves my tater pies, now. One of us'll call before we head over with the food."

She gathered the arrangement and tucked it in the crook of one arm. "Well, I best be gettin' on. Brother Parker is waitin' for me in the car. I'll be by to pay up on the church's bill first of next week."

I asked after she left, "What happened to the other flower shop in town?"

"Silver Moon Flowers?" He shrugged. "Oh, Minnie Blue is gettin' on in years, so I get more and more of her business. We often work together for big events, weddings and funerals."

"How does that stand with the rest of the town?"

"Seems to be okay, for the most part. There're a few folks around that would just as soon keep black and white folks separate forever. I tell them The War is over, every chance I get! Change comes slow, you know. Anyway, I stay pretty busy, although I would like to add on to the shop. I own the other side of this building, as well. I'm just waiting for the inspiration to hit. I want to do something different. Maybe gift baskets. I don't know…that's so overdone nowadays."

"Don't you worry about being so…gay…in this town?"

Jake's boyish face clouded over for a moment. "No, not really." A fleeting expression of anxiety betrayed the brave façade.

"You've had trouble. I can only imagine."

"No one's gonna bother me. I know a lot about the happenin's in this quiet little burg. I see who gets the red roses, and it's not always the person who ought to be getting them, if you catch my meaning. I watch and keep my mouth shut. Besides, it's been nothing serious. Just a few silly pranks, usually after I've helped with a large event for the black community. That seems to get whoever it is going. I suppose they feel the people of color of this town are just supposed to pick field flowers and put 'em in a bucket!"

I shook my head sadly. "That's one of the few things that can't change fast enough about the South."

The door opened and two teenaged boys stepped inside. They poked around for a few minutes before Jake acknowledged their presence.

"Can I help you…gentlemen…with anything today?" Jake fake-smiled in their direction.

The older and more sinister of the two boys smirked. "Nope. Ain't nothin' in this store I need."

The two of them laughed, and then shuffled through the door. They loitered on the sidewalk briefly before continuing down Washington Street.

"What was that all about?"

Jake shrugged. "Oh, those were the Thurgood cousins, in the flesh. They stop in every now and then just to visit the town queer. Must be some kind of testosterone-induced rite-of-passage."

"I bet that bugs the hell outta you."

"They don't concern me one teeny tiny hair. My business comes from the upstanding adults in town, not the likes of those two."

Jake opened the upright cooler and a rush of flower-scented air brushed past my cheeks. He selected a handful of delicate pastel blooms, sprays of white baby's breath, and maidenhair fern. "The ladies of this town have been especially good to me, sister-girl. I had the flu in December right after I first opened. For over a week, your mama, cousin, and aunt brought me chicken'n' dumplin's, stew, soup, and enough Gatorade to turn me into a University of Florida fan."

No Florida State University fan would be caught dead drinking a beverage that carried the stigma of the University of Florida's gator mascot. Being avid FSU Seminole fans practically from birth, we groaned in unison.

Jake laughed hard. "I remember waking up to see Piddie's face looking at me, just painted with terrible concern. 'Son, you don't have the AID, do you?' she asks. Then, Evelyn says, 'Mama, it's AIDS, not the AID! Besides, that's none of your business!' Your aunt fires back, 'That's what I said, the AID! And I don't much care if he has it! But, if he does we need to run him on to Tallahassee, and get him some help!' I told her, 'no, Piddie, I don't have the AID, just the flu.' Lordy, I was so paranoid up in New York after watching so many of my friends die, that I had gotten tested at least once every three months before I came home."

"You don't worry about that now?"

"Sister-girl, there's so much bad stuff goin' around out there, I practically want a validated health card and a blood test before I so much as kiss somebody on the cheek. I'm more of a no-mo'-sexual than a homo-sexual! Oh, I have a closeted friend from the capital that I see for dinner every now and then when I desire company. I really don't need anything. I have it all right here."

"No-mo'-sexual? I like that! That's what I feel like being since dating Garrett Douglas. Maybe I'll get that rumor going around town. Wouldn't that confuse Miz Elvina!" I chuckled. "Why do you like this little half-dead town, anyway?"

Jake finished the pink and white Welcome Baby arrangement, misted the foliage, and returned it to the flower cooler.

"I love Chattahoochee. Always have. I didn't want to leave it to start with! This will always be home to me." He frowned. "It's trying to die, sister-girl. Young folks leave as soon as they graduate, if they wait that long. Don't you remember how it used to be so full of life?"

I nodded. Washington Street reminded me of a dog bone with the marrow sucked out. "I can't say much. I left, too. Funny, I used to think this was the most boring place in the entire world. Now, I can sit by my dad's fishpond for hours and listen to the silence."

He rested a hand on my shoulder affectionately. "Why don't you move home? Is there anything so special about Tallahassee that you can't leave it?"

"I don't know if I could be happy over here. I'd miss my friends, and I do have all my massage-therapy clients to think about. I would not miss the traffic, though, that's one thing for sure."

Jake snorted. "You've never driven in real traffic. It amazes me when I hear folks talk about Tallahassee and all the traffic jams. They need to go to a big city like New York to appreciate what real traffic is!"

"I could move back here, I suppose." I shrugged. "It's weird. I never thought I'd ever not have to think about money. Just between us, my folks left enough that I could retire right now if I wanted to."

He perched on a wooden stool and smoothed the wrinkles from his neatly-pressed khaki trousers. "They always say not to make any major decisions right after losing someone close. You're a bright girl. I'm sure you'll figure it out. At least with the money behind you, you can focus on what you really want to do." Jake pointed to my hands. "What's that notebook you been carrying around?"

"Oh, I don't know why I brought this in with me. I have no idea what it is. It was with my parents' papers. Hank Henderson just gave it to me."

"Lemme see." Jake flipped through the yellowed pages. "Oh, my Lord! Hattie, you know what this is? It's Max the Madhatter's private notebook. Don't you remember him? He was one of those patients that had town privileges back during the sixties. He used to hang out at your daddy's store, along with all the other businesses on Washington."

I vaguely recalled a short impish-looking man.

Jake continued, "He wasn't mental, just kind of slow. You know, they used to lock 'em up when the family didn't want them and they had nowhere else to go. He'd been a patient his whole life, from what I recall. Some of those old Florida State Hospital records had diagnoses like idiot or moron. I remember Max the Madhatter helping out around town doing odd jobs. People would pay him in chocolate. That was his passion! He used to scribble constantly in a notebook he carried all the time. No one had any idea what he was writing, or if he could even write at all."

Jake flipped the pages. "Look at this! Little sketches and...looks like written descriptions of the downtown merchants. It's just full of recipes and comments on all the types of chocolate he'd ever eaten, too. Hey, here's one you will recognize!"

He pointed to a page with a scratchy faded handwritten title.

AUNT PIDDIE LONGMAN'S
BEST DAMN CHOCOLATE ICING

1/2 cup cocoa
5 Tablespoons soft butter
2 cups confectioner's sugar
1 teaspoon vanilla
Scant 1/3 cup milk

Mix your sugar and cocoa together. Mash the butter till it's good'n soft. Add the vanilla and the milk, then start to mix in the dry stuff, a little bit at a time till you got it all in. Blend it till you don't have lumps. You can add nuts, too.

"Imagine that!" I said.

"Can I keep this for a couple of days? I'd like to read it all the way through and make a copy."

"Sure. I'll stop back by to get it. I have to go to Tallahassee tomorrow for a couple of days. I need to call my clients to assure them I haven't disappeared off the face of the earth. And, I want to bring my cat, Shammie, over here. She gets lonely by herself."

"Is that chamois as in 'a soft cloth to dry your wet car' or were you doing your best Carol Channing imitation of the diva herself saying 'Sammy?'"

"It was originally Chamois, but I got tired of having to spell it out at the vet's office, so now it's Shammie."

Jake clasped his hands together. A slight twitch danced at the side of his left eye. "That's a first step—bringing your feline over. We'll have you moved home before you know it! By the way, you do know that your daddy paid for the Madhatter's funeral when he died? From what I heard, they buried Max with a Hershey's Chocolate Bar in his hands."

Shaking my head, I asked, "How do you know so much about this town?"

We looked at each other and grinned.

"Elvina Houston," we said in unison.

Jake rumpled through a stack of papers and florist magazines and handed me a slim bound book. "Study this. It's your assignment until the next time we meet."

"*From Mount Vernon to Chattahoochee*, by Grady Turnage," I read.

"You'll be amazed at the history here."

I tucked the book into my purse. "You want to have lunch with me, today?"

"Only if you go down and get Stephanie or Julie at the Homeplace Restaurant to make us a couple of sandwiches to-go. They both make a mean hot roast beef au jus! I have to make two more baby arrangements and a dish garden for Sweetbay Jones's sister, home from her knee replacement." He pulled a worn leather wallet from his pocket and handed over a twenty dollar bill

"Be back in a flash!" I called over my shoulder.

THE INSPIRATION

Aunt Piddie's Chocolaty Cookies Good for What Ails You

Ingredients: 2 tbsp instant coffee, 2 tbsp boiling water, ½ cup margarine or butter, ½ cup white sugar, ½ cup brown sugar, 1 egg, 2 cups chocolate chips, 1½ cups bleached flour, ¾ teaspoon baking soda, ½ teaspoon salt.

Dissolve instant coffee in boiling water. Add butter, granulated sugar, and brown sugar and mix well. Add one egg, already beaten. Melt ½ cup of chocolate chips and add to mixture. Blend in flour, baking soda, and salt. Add remaining chocolate chips. Bake at 350°F in oven on an ungreased cookie sheet for about nine minutes.

These cookies are good for sour moods, chocolate hankerin's, and fussy youngin's.

CHAPTER FIVE

THE OFFICE OF Garrett Douglas, Inc. filled the first floor of a beautifully restored antebellum house on east Call Street near downtown Tallahassee. Thick garnet carpet muffled my footfall when I entered the richly appointed receiving room.

Jessica, Garrett's petite blonde executive assistant, glanced up from a computer screen and smiled. "Hattie! I didn't know you were back in town!" Her fine-featured porcelain face clouded with concern. "How're you feeling?"

"Pretty good. Day by day, you know. Is himself in?"

"Believe it or not, you're catching him at a good time. He just finished a conference call with the Tampa and Orlando affiliates, and he doesn't have any other commitments until...let's see." She clicked to the computerized schedule screen. "He's free for another hour. Shall I announce you?"

"No, let me surprise him."

I pushed open the heavy mahogany door to his suite. Garrett sat at his massive inlaid cherry desk, studying his Palm Pilot.

"Hattie!" he said as he arose. He circled the desk and gathered me into his arms.

Damn it! Why did he have to smell so good?

His lean body felt familiar, and mine, in direct betrayal of my current state of mind, melted into him like the last missing piece of a 5000 piece puzzle of the scenic Maine coastline.

"I tried to call you a couple of times last week," he said as he ushered me to a buttery-soft leather couch.

"I figured the two hang-ups were you. For someone who eats, sleeps, and breathes technology, you surely hate to leave a message on a machine!"

Garrett ran a finger along the side of my face and touched my hair. "I've missed you, Hattie."

"Amazing. You miss me more now than you did when we were actually dating."

An actual brief flinch of pain crossed his suntanned features.

"Hattie, now-"

I held up one hand. "I'm sorry, Garrett. I didn't come here to pick a fight. I came to offer a truce."

"Really?" He eased back into the sofa and crossed his arms, a smug smile on his full lips. "So, you've come to your senses and given up on that whole parenthood issue. I knew you'd come running back to kiss and make up."

I scowled deeply and gave him my best imitation of Chris's Italian stare of death.

He raised an eyebrow. "But, since that obviously isn't the case, I'll do you the courtesy of hearing you out. I'm very good at negotiations."

I walked into the back door of the farmhouse and deposited Shammie on the floor with her food bowl. Unlike most of the felines who had previously owned me, Shammie could adapt to any change as long as two important criteria were met: I was there and food was within a few inches.

From across the kitchen, I saw the insistent blinking of the answering-machine light.

"Sister-girl!" Jake's voice was high-pitched with urgency. "You must call me right away as soon as you get in. I need to see you, Evelyn, and Piddie as soon as possible!"

Since the line at the Dragonfly was busy, I phoned Evelyn's house.

"Meet me uptown at Jake's shop in fifteen minutes. Something's up!"

"Wha, wha?" Evelyn stuttered.

"I have no idea. He sounded frantic on the message he left here. I'll leave as soon as I can put some groceries in the refrigerator."

Evelyn and Piddie screeched to a halt in her Lincoln Towncar behind my pick-up in front of Dragonfly Florist. Aunt Piddie almost knocked me over with her walker in her rush toward the door.

Jake was calmly misting the ferns in the display window.

"Jake!" Piddie called out.

Evelyn and I were right behind her.

Jake smiled. "Oh! Good! All three of you at once. I'll find some chairs."

"What the devil is wrong?" Piddie clutched her chest. "You're not hurt are you? You've not had any more trouble, have you?"

"No, no. Relax." Jake dropped a couple of old wooden stools and one folding chair onto the floor in the center of the shop. "I needed all of you here to share my divine inspiration!" He spread his thin arms wide and twirled in a circle.

Piddie lowered herself onto the folding chair. "You been nippin' the liquid fertilizer again?"

He scowled "No. I am stone cold sober. Please, Evelyn, Sister-girl, sit."

Jake grabbed the old gray notebook. "This—" he pointed, "is my Godsend. It has provided me with the most marvelous idea for the shop!"

He held his hands in the air, forming a frame. "Picture this. Three small bistro tables draped with red-checkered linen cloths. Matching café curtains gracing the picture window. Sparkling glass display cases filled with every conceivable kind of baked sweetbreads and chocolate confections. Freshly brewed coffee, regular and decaf. Maybe cappuccino and espresso, eventually. This notebook copied, published, and for sale. The book's title: *The Madhatter's Guide to Chocolate*. And…" He spread his hands wide to outline the imaginary writing on the entrance glass. "The name of the shop: The Madhatter's Sweet Shop And Massage Parlor."

All three of us stared at him.

Finally, Evelyn spoke. "Okay, so what do we have to do with all of this?" A thought struck her. "Oh, I get it! My famous chocolate macaroons!" She clapped her hands together. "My recipe makes about three dozen or so. I could easily turn out more with my new double oven."

Piddie snorted. "The boy wants to draw customers, Evelyn. Not flies!"

Evelyn glared at her mother.

"Actually, Miz Evelyn," Jake said, "your part is much more important than cooking. I need you to design the curtains and table covers." He patted her on the shoulder.

"Well, heaven knows, I can sew! You know that for a fact, Jake Witherspoon!"

"Yesssss, ma'am!"

Piddie leaned forward. "What do I get to do?"

"You, Miz Piddie, will be in charge of advance advertising. I need you to talk it up, get folks all excited."

Evelyn smirked. "You can put that old lady hotline to some good use for a change."

Piddie tilted her chin upward and fluffed her towering bouffant with one hand. "We provide an important and much needed service for this community. You'd have to wait all the way to the local news outta one of the Tallahassee stations to hear stuff if it wasn't for our help. Even then, most of what goes on over here doesn't make it past the city limit sign unless someone is kilt!"

Piddie frowned. "It would be a lot easier if we still had party lines. I could tell several folks at once, then let them spread the word." She rested her finger against her lower lip and her brow furrowed. "I got it! I'll call Elvina Houston and let it slip like it's a not-to-be-told. She'll save me a whole lotta callin'."

I nodded. "Great idea, Pid."

Piddie chuckled. "Did I ever tell you all about the time Elvina caused Sissy Pridgeon to near'bout kill herself?"

Evelyn sighed. "Only about a hundred times."

"I haven't heard it," Jake said. He inched closer, his eyes gleaming.

"Well…" Piddie settled herself into the telling. "Long many years back in the 50's, D. J. Cawthon was cleanin' his gun and shot hisself in the foot. Well, Elvina was on the Cawthons' party line. She was, as I recall, two rings to the Cawthons' one short and one long. Anyway, she had a bad habit of picking up and listenin' in. She was a busybody even then! She eavesdropped just long enough to overhear Madie Cawthon say that her husband had shot hisself, before Madie called out 'is someone listenin' in!?'. Elvina hung up and hotfooted it over to Sissy Pridgeon's— she's dead now—to tell her the news. By the time Sissy and Elvina finished callin' the whole town with the news, they had the man shot dead! Course, it was always a race in those days to see who could get the first casserole to the bereaved family. Sissy and Elvina, as I heard it, near'bout kilt each other racin' up the Cawthons' steps. When D.J. answered the door with his foot all bandaged up, Elvina dropped the chicken soup pot she was carryin' on the porch, and Sissy Pridgeon fainted dead out on the front steps. She gashed her head and bled all over the place! She had to have seven stitches to close the hole in her head, not to mention she broke one of her best glass casserole dishes!"

Jake and I hooted. Evelyn laughed in spite of herself.

Evelyn waved her bony hands through the air. "You know, I can just visualize it. I can make the curtains so it looks like a series of smaller windows instead of one big one. It'll be much cozier that way. You have a tape measure?"

"Just a yard stick. Sorry."

Evelyn jumped up and started for the door. "C'mon, Mama. Let's get to the house. I'll get my tape measure and calculator. We'll be back up after we've had some lunch so I can figure how much material I'll need." She held the door for her mother.

I watched Evelyn gun the Towncar onto Washington Street. "So, other than the obvious part, how have you worked me into your little scenario?"

Jake pulled up a stool. "Here's the hard part for me to ask, Hattie. I need a business partner."

"I thought your mama left you fixed for money."

A twitch flickered beside his left eye. "No one around here knows this, and I trust you not to spread it. My mama was rich in her self-imposed title only. When she died, all that was left of the family money was that drafty rundown monstrosity of a house, and a pile of bills. It wasn't only that I didn't want to live there—I couldn't afford to." He paused and inhaled deeply. "I had barely enough to pay off her extravagant debts and buy this business and that half-dead van out back."

"Betsy Witherspoon? Poor? I would never have believed it!"

Jake shrugged. "I've spent my entire life protecting her good name. Moved away to save it. On some level, I suppose I loved her. I've never told anyone how broke she was when she died...until now."

"Weird, isn't it? My parents lived simply and died rich. Your mother lived richly and died a poor woman."

"That's the sum of it, yep. So, I need a business partner. It'll be all legal and binding. I'll have a power of attorney drawn up for you to use in case I get hit by a bus or something." He lurched toward me and enveloped me in a bear hug. "We'll practically be family! I can book your massage-therapy clients when you want them, and run the shop!"

"Don't you think it'll be a bit odd to have a massage-therapy room in the back of a chocolate shop?"

His hands undulated in a wave-like motion through the air. "Just think of it as constant aromatherapy. What better smell to relax by than the scent of sweets and freshly-brewed coffee?"

"There're so many details, Jake. I'll have to get city and Gadsden County business licenses, as well as a massage-therapy establishment license from Tallahassee. We'll have to have a handicapped-accessible bathroom, too. The doors are wide enough to accommodate a wheelchair..." I paused. "Why are you grinning like a goat eating briars?"

A wide smile spread across his smooth face. "You have it in your mind's eye, just like I do."

"I don't know, Jake. I don't really want to live over here full time."

"Don't have to. I'll book your therapy room when you want me to. You can come and go as you please. I can always hire someone to help with the sweet shop."

I imagined that my life was like an old Jason and the Argonauts movies. The Gods floated on high, moving me into position like some kind of chess piece, shifting the surrounding pawns to fit things in as they planned.

"I have one condition, Jake."

"Name it."

"You have to move in with me out on the Hill."

Jake stared at me. "Oh, that'll get tongues wagging!"

"I'm serious. We'll need the space where your cot is now, for storage. If I'm not over here all the time, I'd feel much better with you out on the Hill to watch over things. It's a huge old house. I take up one end. You can have the other. Plus, you can even redecorate."

Jake's eyes twinkled. "Really?" He hesitated. "What about Bobby?"

"It is my house."

I had the money. That certainly wasn't an issue. Dodging the cell phone-distracted drivers on Apalachee Parkway the previous day, I had decided to resign from the paper-pushing state job I loathed. I still wanted to maintain my massage-therapy practice, but I could do that with no trouble.

Oddly, Garrett had provided the final push. Though our discussion had formally ended our floundering love affair, the meeting had laid the groundwork for a tentative friendship. Garrett knew me well enough to understand my need for change, and offered a workable solution that would allow me the freedom to split time between Tallahassee and Chattahoochee. Jillie, his daughter from his first marriage attempt, needed a place to live while attending Business College at Florida State. She could take the second bedroom in the townhouse. Like her father, she was a very driven, serious-minded, bookworm type. I could leave the townhouse in her care, staying in the city overnight whenever I wished. With Jillie in the townhouse in Tallahassee, and Jake on the Hill to watch over Shammie and Spam, no obstacles stood in the way. The big God-hand picked me up and moved me into place.

"Well?" Jake asked.

Sometimes you just have to trust what has been provided, hold your nose, and take the plunge.

"Deal!" I said.

Jake flopped down on the end of my king-sized bed, removed his fuzzy blue slippers, and sprawled on top of the comforter.

"Why don't you put a smaller bed in here, sister-girl? Say, a queen. It'd give you more room."

I glanced up from the mystery I was attempting to read. "I'm not ready to redecorate this part of the house yet, Jake. I promise, when I am, I'll let you have your way with it."

I paused to look around the master bedroom. Since my mother's death, it had remained unchanged. Jake had helped pack her clothes and personal items for charity, a task I couldn't have tackled alone. I wasn't ready to remake the one room of the house where I still felt her and my father's presence.

Jake sniffed. "Okay, sister-girl. You're the boss of the Hill. I guess this room does have a certain…umm…50's ambiance."

"Jakey, I don't mean to sound bitchy, but I've had a long week, and I'm not in the mood for one of our little sisterly chats."

Jake boxed me on the head with a fringed throw pillow. "You can be positively evil when you're tired. I came to bare my soul to you— impart some critical information—and you're being heartless!"

I laid the book face down, careful to mark my place. "Okay, what?"

"Well, you know I do so love you dearly—like the sister I never had."

"Yeah."

"I've been thinking. I want to set my legal house in order. You know—will, power of attorney, that sort of thing."

I studied his face. His expression was neutral.

"I'd like to designate you as my medical surrogate and executor of my, somewhat measly as it is, estate. That way, you could make decisions in case I'm not able to."

An inkling of fear stabbed at me. "What's going on, Jake?"

"Nothing, nothing." He waved his hands in dismissal. "I'd just feel better if I had everything all nice and tidy. You know how I am."

Did I really! The food pantry was alphabetized with the canned-food labels facing forward. I'd never had surroundings as clean and organized as the few weeks Jake had lived at the Hill.

"I'll need to get the name of your attorney in Tallahassee," Jake continued.

"Don't you want Hank Henderson to handle this for you?"

Jake shivered. "Gah! No! That guy gives me the heebie-jeebies! He's never even set foot in the shop. He has Janice call in flower orders for him. The few times I've been around the man since I've moved home, I've just gotten the rolling creeps. There's something not right about him."

I nodded. "He's been a little weird all along. I didn't like him much when we were kids, either. As to legal matters, I have a great attorney in Tallahassee. Her name is Claire Dutchman. You know, I need to update my will, now that I have this house and property. Why don't I call her, and we'll ride over together next week?"

Jake flashed a toothy grin. "That's just dandy! Like me!"

I brushed his hand. "I'm touched you want me to be your executor."

"You are my family, sister-girl. And, I'm yours, whether you like it or not!"

"As long as you don't start to borrow my clothes."

"Pu-lease! Not to be mean, but your wardrobe is way too conservative for my tastes." Jake rolled off the bed and grabbed his slippers. "I'm making some chocolate chip cookies. Want some?"

I glanced at the antique wall clock. "At 10 o'clock at night?"

"Haven't you ever heard of the calmative powers of cookies and milk?"

"I'll be right there."

THE GRAND OPENING

Excerpt from Max the Madhatter's notebook:

October 30, 1961: Heaven puts a person where he needs to be. No use fighting it. I've been here at the mental hospital for as long as I can recall—since I was real little, I suppose. Seen some folks leave. Most stay right on. Especially ones like me who need help battling demons all the time.

I don't hold ill will against my family. Not at all. Don't even remember them much any more. I reckon I was a handful, falling down, flailing about on the floor talking about visions and such.

My chosen family is right here—Nurse Marion, Dr. Bruner, Dan Davis, his wife Tillie and little Hattie, and a few of the other patients who live long enough on this side of reality to have small talks with.

I'm right where I belong. If I wasn't, God would see to it I was moved along. Just like He does for every single one of us.

CHAPTER SIX

OFFICER RICH BURNS poked his head through the back door of the Dragonfly. "Jake? Hattie?" he called as he stepped inside. "Y'all burnin' the midnight oil?"

"Just making sure we're ready for tomorrow!" I called from the Sweet Shop. "Come on in and we'll give you a preview."

Jake admired Rich's pressed uniform. "You on duty?"

"Just comin' on. I have night shift now through the end of July."

"Bet Carol loves that," Jake said.

"Probably does. She gets the whole bed to herself. She swears on a stack of Bibles that I snore. I don't. I just breathe hard."

"Soooo…" Jake said, motioning to the room. "What'd'ya think?"

"You've really fixed this place up nice." Rich said, glancing around. "It's better'n any of those fancy shops over in Tallahassee!"

The Madhatter's Sweet Shop and Massage Parlor was scripted in Old English lettering across the glass entrance door. Evelyn's ceiling-to-floor red gingham curtains hung in four vertical drapes, creating the illusion of separate windows dividing the sheet of plate glass. The drab concrete floor had been tiled with alternating black and white linoleum squares.

Three white enameled bistro tables covered with red and white tablecloths stood in the far corner next to a spring water cooler. Small clumps of daisies, ferns, and baby's breath sprigs in cut crystal vases adorned the tables. The sparkling glass-and-chrome sweets display case spanned the entire length of the room. On one corner of the counter, a white wicker basket was filled with bound copies of *The Madhatter's Guide to Chocolate*. A separate table held a double self-service Bunn coffeemaker, two tall aluminum iced-tea urns, and an assortment of cups, utensils, sweeteners, lemon wedges, creamers, and freshly cut mint.

Rich studied the rows of chocolates and sweet rolls. "Could I possibly sneak a sample?"

"Sure!" Jake placed a chocolate-iced cake brownie on a waxed paper square. "Sorry we don't have any coffee made."

Rich shrugged. "I'll get some of that mud Denise Whiddon has at the station. Won't be as good as what you'll have in here, but I'm used to it."

"Come see the massage therapy room." I slid the pocket door open to reveal my clinic space. "I can't officially open until I get my site license in the mail, but it's ready for people to see."

The massage table stood in the center of the room, draped with pastel sheets and a white dust ruffle I had paid Evelyn to create. The plush carpet was forest green, and an open counter running the length of the room held a small sink, professional lotions and oils, herbal creams, and a display of white candles. Armed with a few sponges and several cans of acrylic paint, Jake had created the illusion of a stand of tall trees on the surrounding walls.

"It'll feel like you're getting a massage in the middle of the woods!" Rich chuckled. "Good thing you didn't paint a big buck's head stickin' out from behind one of those trees. It'd be hard for some folks around here to relax if they saw that!"

Jake and I laughed.

I tilted my head. "You really think the men in this town will come in?"

"I know I will. This gun belt rides low and just kills my lower back. It may take some time for the fellas to warm up to the idea, but it'll come. It's the womenfolk that'll make the difference. Once they see how professional this all is, they'll make their men come in just to stop them from complaining about their aches and pains!"

Rich's radio scrabbled to life. He cocked his head to listen to the receiver on his shoulder. "I better get goin'. By the way, Jake, you need to keep that delivery entrance door locked when you're up here working at night."

Jake swatted his hand. "This is Chattahoochee, Rich."

"I don't care. There's meanness everywhere. Well, goodnight! Good luck tomorrow!" The leather gun belt squeaked as he walked to the back door.

Jake's long face clouded over. "Hattie, there's something I need to show you." He ducked behind the flower shop counter and pulled out a plain white envelope. "I got this in the mail yesterday."

A sheet of copy paper held the typed message:

"ENJOY YOUR DAY, YOU FAGOT. IT WON'T LAST LONG."

A cold chill ran the length of my spine. "Oh my God, Jake! You think somebody's planning something for the opening tomorrow?"

Jake shook his head. "It'd be pretty stupid with all the people in and out."

"I think we need to alert the police just to be safe. It won't hurt to have an officer seen here. Chris and Kathy may ride over from Tallahassee. They won't be in uniform, but they can keep an eye out for trouble."

Jake waved an imaginary magic wand "I'm not worried. I live a charmed life!"

"What did this weirdo, or weirdoes, do to you before?"

Jake motioned to the counter. "In my usual sphinctered fashion, I have kept records and photo evidence." He pulled out an 11x13 manila envelope and spread out a series of glossy magazine centerfolds and Polaroid pictures.

"These vulgar things were scotch-taped to the back door the morning after I worked a large wedding for the black community a couple of months back. Even if I was straight, this wouldn't appeal to me! I never could understand why a view of a woman spread-eagled with the camera lens practically crammed up her wazoo could appeal to anyone!"

He pulled two Polaroid snapshots from the pile. "And, this was a little artwork for my already tacky delivery van."

NIGGER LOVER and *FLOWER FAGOT* were sprayed in crude block letters across the Dragonfly Florist logo.

"You'd think they'd at least learn to spell," he said. "Faggot has two g's."

"You told me you had informed the police."

"Right."

"You shouldn't be up here anymore by yourself at night, Jake."

Jake stamped his foot. "I will not be run off from my rightful place of business by an ignorant redneck bigot!"

"I just think—"

"No, Hattie. This town's too good and kind to allow this kind of trash!" He held my chin in his hands. "Sister-girl, I promise I'll be careful. But, I can't just run off and hide. I've done that before."

The late-June summer morning dawned with a flawless pink and rose-painted sky. Jake and I stood sipping hot black coffee on the cement sidewalk in front of the shop.

"Hard to believe that dust and ashes from some distant volcano could cause such incredible colors," Jake said. He took a loud slurp of his cream-laced coffee. "If I was God, I'd take my best pleasure in giving folks a mornin' like this one!"

"Uh-huh."

We stood side by side in the shared silence.

"Jakey, can I ask you something personal?"

Jake smiled crookedly. "Oh, Jeez-o-Pete! Here it comes, some weirdo sex question. I knew you'd come out with one, sooner or later."

"No, it's not that. Give me a little credit, will you? I'm not naïve, and I have a pretty fair imagination. Besides, I wouldn't ask you to give details about what goes on in the privacy of your own bedroom, for God's sake."

Jake's left eyebrow shot up. "Well, Excuse-mm-wah!"

"I was just wondering—when did you know you were gay? I mean, did you know when we were sort of dating, back in high school?"

"First of all, I'd hardly justify what we did as dating. We just kinda hung out together, really. Heck, I wore your sweaters more than you did!" A faint smile played across his lips. "We did get in some pretty good kissing practice, from what I recall. Thanks for that. Second, I've always felt like I was, shall we say, cut from a different bolt of material, from conception practically."

"So, you've never—"

"Slept with a woman? Yes, for your information, I have. Tried it once. A dismal mistake." Jake sipped his coffee and stared into space for a moment. "Ruined a perfectly good friendship."

"This was after you moved to New York?"

"Um-hmm. I went through this whole gay-boy crisis for a while. Thought I could will myself straight. Didn't take—I felt like I was trying to wear somebody else's old worn jeans—might've fit them like a second skin, but they hung on me like socks on a rooster."

I smiled at the familiar Southernism. "You miss the city at all?"

He shrugged. "Sometimes. The plays, oh heavens, the plays! And the restaurants! There's a lot to recommend living there. But, my heart has always belonged to the 'Hooch."

"I'm kinda shocked how people, in general, don't seem to mind your, um—"

"Keen sense of fashion? Other-worldly boyish charm?" Jake's blue eyes sparkled. "Funny about little towns like this. Folks will be bigoted in the most strict sense of the word, swear up and down they just can't tolerate someone, or something—well, like me bein' gay, for example. But, if they like a particular person, know him pretty well, respect him as a stand-up kinda guy, then they'll fight, tooth and nail, anyone who says a bad word against him. It's the darndest thing I've ever witnessed!"

I laughed. "He might be queer, but he's our queer, huh?"

Jake whipped one hand into the air as if to testify. "Honey, you done broke the code!"

The shop opened promptly at 7 AM, in time for the first influx of state weekend workers trudging in for coffee and sweet rolls. Soon, the little shop overflowed with customers.

Jake smiled as he studied the room. His white linen sports coat provided a perfect overlay for the blue-striped Polo dress shirt. "Looks like Piddie did a great job of advertising. Oh, remind me to send a 'thank you' note to Mary over at the *Twin City News* for putting the announcement in last weekend's paper."

Since it was a Saturday, most of the townfolks put in an appearance later in the morning. Evelyn, Joe, and Piddie stayed for a couple of hours. Piddie held court from one of the bistro tables while Evelyn described the curtains' design and construction to anyone who would listen. A group of my Tallahassee friends drove over as well.

Kathy boxed me playfully in the arm. "You sure you're not turning back into a small town gal?"

"I think I'll try timesharing the two places. I'd miss all of you guys too much to leave Tallahassee for good. At the same time, I really enjoy the peace and quiet on the Hill."

Jake stepped up and joined the conversation. "Hey, ladies! You can always come over and stay at the resort on the Hill. There's an extra bedroom all decorated for you!" He flitted off to greet another customer.

Chris slurped her coffee. "I saw Garrett the other day. He was out at Chez Pierre all over some skinny little blonde."

"It's okay, Chrissy. He and I have had a long talk. No expectations. I may call him sometime to meet for dinner when I'm over there. Besides, his daughter, Jillie, is going to be living in my townhouse."

Chris rolled her eyes. "He still makes me want to puke. Maybe you'll meet someone decent over here."

"I'm not really looking."

Chris grinned. "Right."

"Jake had any trouble today?" Kathy asked.

"No."

Kathy looked around the crowded shop. "I really don't think anyone would be stupid enough to try anything with a crowd of people around. Nonetheless, you and Jake better keep up your guard."

"My thoughts exactly. Now, convince him!"

The booming roar of a rusted-out muffler sounded. I glanced toward the street. A beaten-up faded green pick-up crept by. Through the sunlight glare on the front window, I could barely make out the shadowed silhouettes of two people. The passenger hung a hairy arm from the window, yelled obscenities, and fired several vulgar gestures toward the shop. The truck accelerated and sped from view.

I muttered. "So much for the local color."

Chris frowned. "Want I should go after them?"

I shook my head. "Don't bother. They're only out for attention. I'd hate to accommodate them."

By the time we closed at five, the display counter looked like a war zone. I'd seen just about the entire population of Chattahoochee and a few folks I recognized from Sneads, Greensboro, Mt. Pleasant, and the communities over the Georgia line near the lake. Jimmy T. Johnson, the venerable mayor of Chattahoochee, came in for a brownie and a cup of coffee, and most of the police and fire personnel had stopped by as well. Stephanie and Julie from the Homeplace Restaurant came down during their break, and Carol Burns, Rich's wife, visited with their twin girls. The biggest surprise was seeing Bobby at the counter with an attractive raven-haired woman he introduced as Leigh Andrews from over near Grand Ridge. Could it possibly mean he was starting to forgive me for allowing Jake to move into the farmhouse? Any step toward defrosting our relationship would be welcome.

"Whew!" Jake blew out a long breath. "I'm glad tomorrow is Sunday. It'll give me a chance to come up in the afternoon after church and restock! If today was any indication of things to come, I'll need to bump up the dessert orders and hire some help pretty soon! It's not like I don't already have enough to do with the flower shop. What was I thinking?"

"A little late to pull out now, Jakey. Looks like the sweet shop will definitely pay for itself," I said. "I can't believe we sold over thirty copies of *The Madhatter's Guide to Chocolate!* Word's out that it has a lot of town history in it, and people are buying it to see if any of their relatives made the pages. Of course, I know more than a few folks who dove at the chance to get hold of Piddie's icing recipe."

Jake swept chocolate chip cookie crumbs from the top of a bistro table. "It was great to finally meet your friends from Tallahassee. One can never know too many law enforcement officers."

Jake cocked his head. "Hey, was that your charming brother I glanced on his way out with a take-out bag?"

"Yeah. Imagine that?"

"That's the first time I've ever seen him with a woman. And, now that I think about it, the first time I've seen the man smile since forever. He actually looked like he might be having a good time! It's certainly no stretch to see how he'd flip over her—that dark hair and blue eyes—and those cheekbones! To die for! She must have Native American blood mixed in somewhere."

"Miracles happen. Maybe she had something to do with him putting in an appearance." I sighed. "I wish I could talk to him without starting a fight. He doesn't seem to like me much the last few years."

Jake grabbed a broom. "You ever considered that he might be a little jealous? I mean, there you were with your college education, livin' a good life with plenty of money, traveling, not tied down—"

"Hey, he chose to live here and raise a family!" I snapped.

"Ewww…we're a little sensitive, aren't we?"

"I'm sorry, Jake. It's just that I get a little tired of being blamed for not staying here and being the good little hometown wife and mother."

"And that's all I really wanted to be! 'Boo-hoo…always a bridesmaid and never a bride,'" he quoted from an old Bugs Bunny cartoon. He grabbed a folded napkin and dabbed dramatically beneath both eyes. "Sister-girl, don't you worry your pretty little head, blood is thicker than water. Bobby'll come around."

I hesitated. "Did you catch the action on the street?"

Jake flipped his hand. "Not everyone loves success."

"I'm serious, Jake. I'm worried."

Jake shook the dustpan into the garbage container. "Don't be."

THE FOURTH OF JULY

Excerpt from Max the Madhatter's notebook:

November 4, 1958: Why is there meanness in the world? I see it reflected in the eyes of some of the folks I share the ward with. Hard places in their hearts where love doesn't live. Wonder what carved out the holes they fill with darkness?

CHAPTER SEVEN

THE CITY OF CHATTAHOOCHEE, for as long as I could remember, had sponsored an impressive fireworks display over the waters of Lake Seminole. From the intersection of Boliver and West Washington Streets, the curving, hilly road led north for a half-mile before crossing the Georgia border and continuing its route as the Booster Club Road. At the base of a skateboarders' dream hill, the land spread out, revealing tennis courts, public bathrooms, and a wide-angle view of the expansive tree-studded lake. The tall stands of pines and rolling hills reminded me of the mountains. Any local could explain that this part of Florida was actually part of the foothills of the Appalachian Mountain chain further north.

During the fireworks, the south boat landing was closed to traffic, providing a secure launching area. Across a small canal once used for boat slips, the main parking lot held concession stands and a large portion of the population of several surrounding counties. Five small covered picnic tables dotted the grassy periphery, and a massive concrete covered group-shelter stood to the left side atop a wooded hill. Every patch of ground was covered with the blankets, coolers, and chairs of the community waiting anxiously for dusk to turn to darkness.

"I can't believe you're still there working!" I raged into the phone. "I'm almost finished packing our picnic for the fireworks, and you aren't here yet!"

"Get your panties out of a wad, sister-girl. I told you it would be a little bit more before I could come home. Miz Lucille is counting on me for these flower baskets for the Jackson family reunion tomorrow."

"But we'll miss the start of the fireworks," I whined.

Jake sighed. "If you'll stop calling me, I can finish. I have one more arrangement to do. As soon as I do that, and load some stuff in the van, I'll be on my way. I'll fly. Give me thirty minutes, tops."

"Okay. I'll wait on you for a little bit. But when the sun starts to set, I'm leaving whether you're here or not!"

I filled Shammie's water and food bowl, then went out back to the carport to feed Spam. He sauntered up slowly, and I patted his golden-red fur.

"Those old hips are hurting you today, aren't they boy?"

He woofed and wagged his tail. After I served his food, I sang his favorite song, The Florida Cracker Dog Song—sung to the tune of the theme song of the Beverly Hillbillies:

> *"I wanna tell you all a story 'bout a dog named Spam,*
> *Florida Cracker Retriever, he said 'that's what I am!'*
> *Late one day, he came walkin' up our road,*
> *So, we fed him 'till he stayed*
> *Best dog we ever knowed!*
> *Hell-of-a-dog. Full-blooded. Pedigreed."*

Spam slopped in appreciation as I played air banjo to complete the set. I packed vegetable sticks, dip, and stuffed mushrooms into a covered wooden and wicker basket along with a bottle of Merlot and two wine glasses. After forty-five minutes, I called the shop again to no answer.

How did I end up with a workaholic partner? Wasn't it enough that I had to go through this whole thing with Garrett Douglas for the past two years?

After fifteen more minutes, I packed the truck and left the Hill in a huff to drag his butt away from the shop.

Washington Street was deserted. Only the Dollar Store remained open. Everyone for miles around had already secured a perfect spot on the banks surrounding Lake Seminole to watch the light show. I clenched my teeth at the prospect of fumbling around in the dusky dark, tripping over people, in order to find a decent spot to spread the blanket.

As I approached the front of the shop, I noticed the lights were off. I didn't pass him coming into town. If he had gone to the lake without me, I would strangle him!

I swung the truck into the delivery alley. The Dragonfly Florist delivery van stood idle with the side door ajar. The hair stood erect on the nape of my neck.

I parked and approached the rear door. It was unlocked and slightly ajar. When I pushed the door open and stepped inside, I almost lost my footing on a slick place on the concrete floor. I grappled with the light switch.

My heart almost stopped dead still. Flowers were strewn in every direction. I stepped cautiously into the room. Total destruction met my shocked gaze: broken glass, earthen potted plants upended and broken, and the words *FAGOT. FAGOT. DAMN FAGOT* were scrawled over every wall and surface in black spray paint. Barely breathing, I backed up slowly toward the door, almost slipping again. I looked at my feet. The sticky moisture was dark red.

Blindly, I raced to the truck, fumbled with the keys, and almost dumped the transmission, taking off in a roar of screeching tire rubber. Fortunately, the streets were deserted, because I didn't stop at a single intersection between the alley and Jefferson Street. *Damn it! Why had I never gotten a cell phone?*

I slammed the truck into park and raced into the Chattahoochee Police Station, leaving the truck door open.

Denise Whiddon looked up from her book.

"Hattie Davis! Girl, what's wrong? You're pale as a sheet!"

I gasped for breath. "Jake! Something's happened to Jake! The shop! Blood on the floor. Oh, God!" I sobbed.

Denise rushed to the radio. "Chattahoochee 220, Chattahoochee 227?"

Rich's deep voice replied,"220."

"Be 10-51 to Dragonfly Florist, 304 West Washington Street. Possible signal 17, possible signal 55."

The sound of a siren filtered through the radio with Rich's reply. "Copy. 220 in route."

A second male voice responded. "227 in route."

"Hattie, come on here and sit down. You look like you're gonna faint!"

I was already heading for the double doors.

"Don't go back over there, Hattie! Rich and Don are only a minute or two away! The suspects could still be there! Hey!"

Denise chased me out the door, but I beat her to the truck, flipped a quick U-turn, and headed back uptown. Rich's cruiser screeched to a halt in the alley. From the opposite end of the alley, Don Hall, the second officer on duty, slipped his cruiser into place in front of the delivery van.

Rich pulled his service revolver and motioned for Don to follow. When he saw my truck, he shook his head hard, and I sat back in my seat. The two officers entered the building cautiously.

After a couple of minutes, they appeared at the door. Rich came to my window. "Sit tight, Hattie. I've got to put in a call out to Lieutenant Harrison and establish a crime-scene periphery. Please go on back to the station. No one else can enter that shop until I can get our crime-scene investigator here."

"But, Jake!"

"Don is calling right now to put out a BOLO on Jake. I need you where we can talk as soon as I get back to the station!"

Back at police headquarters, Denise fixed a cup of the worst coffee I'd ever tasted. I drank it and made a face.

"The boys like it strong," she said with a shrug. "You want me to call anyone to be with you while you wait?"

I thought of Evelyn and Joe. "No, everyone's out at the lake. I'll be okay, Denise. I just feel so helpless."

Denise took the seat next to mine. "We've got a BOLO—that's a be-on-the-lookout—to Gadsden County, city of Sneads and Chattahoochee, Florida Highway Patrol, and the Georgia boys. We'll find him, honey."

"How, Denise? We don't even have any idea who has him or what they're driving!"

Denise patted my hand. "You gotta have faith, honey."

The radio erupted in a barrage of sound. I caught the code for an ambulance call-out. Denise dashed back to her dispatcher post.

"Denise! What?"

"I don't know, honey. It could be Jake, but we got a load of people out there at the landing. It could just be someone out there needing assistance. I know Rich will come by with information as soon as he knows anything."

An hour dragged by. The radio chattered on in code. Something was going on somewhere. Even though I'd been around my law-enforcement friends enough to pick up on a little bit of the jargon, I couldn't understand most of it. Denise was busy chattering back in the same secret language. Finally, I could stand it no longer.

"Anything?"

Denise looked up. Her kind brown eyes were rimmed with red. "Rich is on his way back to the station. They've found Jake."

I began to pace, my mouth sour with the aftertaste of bad coffee.

The double doors flew open behind me, and Rich rushed inside. "Sit down, Hattie," he said.

I perched on the edge of an orange molded plastic chair.

"A couple of kids found Jake. He's in route to Tallahassee Memorial Hospital by ambulance. He's alive."

Tears clouded my vision. "Where was he?"

"A couple of teenagers slipping away from the Fourth festivities found him tied to a tree at Turkey Point lookout, by the lake. He's been beaten up pretty badly, Hattie. He was unconscious when they found him. The kids ran back and informed the Chattahoochee officer who was at the celebration. Luckily, the ambulance was already up there on stand-by, so they got to him pretty quick."

"Why would someone take him to Turkey Point? Isn't that place crawling with people watching the fireworks?"

"Usually. A sinkhole took out part of the road a week or two back. The road leading up from the lake was barricaded."

"That doesn't make any sense, Rich. How'd someone get him in there?"

He ran his hand through his thick unruly salt-and-pepper hair. "Same way we took the ambulance in—from the back entrance. Two of the barricade barrels had been run over to one side. Those kids walked up there on foot, probably to sit on one of the benches near the water to have their own private show."

My stomach lurched. "I gotta get to Tallahassee."

Rich's hands held me down. "You're in no shape to drive alone right now. Is there anyone I can call to go with you?"

I couldn't think. "No one except Evelyn and Joe, but I can't call them. I wouldn't want to get Piddie upset. She'll find out soon enough."

"Let me phone Carol. If she can get Jan next door to watch the twins till I get off my shift, I'm sure she'll go with you."

My mind raced. "Jake's insurance information and papers. I'll need to stop by the house."

Rich left, then returned shortly. "Carol's on her way. You can stop by the Hill on the way, then hit the Interstate. And Hattie, don't you two get in an accident trying to get there fast. Jake's in good hands now, and he'll need you later. It will do no one a bit of good if my two girls get themselves cracked up on the highway."

"Oh, Rich!" I sobbed onto his shoulder. "I'm so lucky to have you and Carol for friends!"

Carol pulled up in the family Jeep Cherokee.

Rich grabbed my elbows and pushed me gently away. "Leave your truck keys here, Hattie. I'll pull it around back and make arrangements to get it to you. Now, go! You're taking the creases outta my uniform!"

I smiled weakly and wiped my nose with the tissue he offered. Rich blew a kiss to his wife and returned to his cruiser.

THE HOSPITAL

Excerpt from Max the Madhatter's notebook:

November 13, 1557: What does it mean, really, that it is darkest before the dawn? I stayed awake for three nights to see. Far as I could tell, it was true. The fourth night, Dr. Bruner ordered a sleeping pill.

CHAPTER EIGHT

THE TRIP FROM the Chattahoochee I-10 interchange to the emergency entrance of Tallahassee Memorial Hospital took less than forty minutes. Carol ignored the posted speed limit and floored the accelerator. We both decided it was worth the risk of a ticket to push the envelope under the circumstances. We alternated between my hysteria over Jake and Carol's calm voice coaxing me to have faith and breathe deep.

"Carol, I'm so glad you who could come with me. Rich was right. It wouldn't have been a good idea for me to drive right now. How do you manage to stay so calm in a crisis?"

Carol's smile was lit by the soft glow of the dashboard lights. "I learned this deep-breathing trick in Lamaze class. As for the calm part, the twins have helped me to develop that ability. When you have kids, there's nearly a crisis a day."

We pulled into the parking lot behind the emergency room at 1:00 AM. Even with the late hour, the emergency room was crowded with people. From the times I had ridden a shift with Chris—as part of the Tallahassee Police Department's citizens' ride-along program—I knew this was the place for interesting folks to congregate from all parts of

Leon and surrounding counties. On any given night, there could be a combination of simple ailments like cold or flu, domestic violence victims, automobile accidents, and the aftermath of brawls brought on by too much alcohol and too little sense. Tonight was no exception. The harried personnel at the check-in desk barked names in succession.

"I'll go to the side door of the unit and see if my friend Mary's on tonight."

Carol followed me through one set of double doors, then down the hallway to the threshold of a second set.

"I need to see Mary Mathues! Is she on tonight?" I asked the first scrub-suited person I spotted.

"Yeah, I just passed her. She expecting you?"

"No, but it's vitally important that I speak to her as soon as possible!"

He nodded and headed down the main corridor. The interior of the emergency room looked to be as hectic as the waiting room. At several points, less critical patients reclined on sheet-draped gurneys lining the hall. Triage nurses dashed in and out of the rooms carrying charts and equipment.

Mary appeared from a doorway, and waved. "Hey, what's up?" she asked. "Kind of late for you to be out wandering around town."

"They just brought my friend, Jake Witherspoon, in by ambulance from Chattahoochee. Do you know anything about it? I was going to stop at the desk, but they looked swamped."

Mary tucked a chewed pencil behind one ear. "I did see someone bringing a guy in with police escort about a half hour ago. That's probably him. Let me see what I can find out."

"Thanks! I have all of his insurance papers. I also have all the legal papers he drew up a couple of months back. I'm his medical surrogate."

"Well, that will certainly make it easier for you to be included in on everything if you're not related." She scuttled off in the direction of the main desk deep within the unit.

Carol smiled. "You know everyone, Hattie. Police. Nurses. It sure helps to have friends like that."

"Mary used to be my next-door neighbor way back when I first moved to Tallahassee. We don't see each other very often, but we know we can count on each other. I don't know what I would've done without her over the years. She was incredible when Dad was in here with heart problems. I met a lot of the other nurses here, too."

Mary appeared at the double doors. "He's still up in x-ray having a CAT scan. He was unconscious when they bought him in. He has a head injury, along with at least one broken bone, and several knife wounds to the legs and arms." Mary's petite features held genuine concern. "The head injury is the most life-threatening. They'll check for intracranial bleeding. That's about all I can tell you. Since you're his medical surrogate, I'm sure the ER doctor will want to speak with you as soon as he has a report. It may be awhile before they know anything."

She rested a warm hand on my shoulder. "Why don't you go back to receiving and give Bonnie his insurance information? She's in the office next to the front desk. The hospital will want a copy of the medical-surrogate form for his file, too. I'll have the Doc come find you."

I hugged Mary. "Thanks tons. I don't know where I'd be tonight without my buddies."

She scurried back to work, and Carol and I returned to the bedlam of the waiting room.

"I guess it's true what Aunt Piddie says about this place," I said as we picked a path through the clumps of ailing people. "If you have to come here, you should fall out on the floor. You get more attention that way."

I found Bonnie tucked in a small office, clicking madly away on a computer keyboard, introduced myself, and completed the paperwork for Jake's file.

Then we waited. And waited. And waited. The crowd ebbed and flowed around us in an ever-changing kaleidoscope of human pain and folly. By the time the ER physician called my name, Carol and I had both consumed so much coffee we had to pace to maintain a semblance of sanity.

"Hattie Davis?" the young baby-faced doctor called from the entrance door.

"I'll wait for you out here, Hattie. I need to call Rich, "Carol said.

The doctor held the door open for us to pass. "Are you his next of kin?"

67

I hesitated. "Yes, well—I'm the only family he has. He's...he's my best friend, and I'm his legal medical surrogate."

"Here, let's sit down away from all the commotion." He motioned to a small file room off the main corridor. "I thought you might prefer more privacy than what's available out there."

He cleared his throat and referred to the chart. "Your friend has taken a heck of a beating. He has suffered a head injury. He has a compound fracture of the right femur—the long bone of the thigh—that will require extensive reconstructive surgery. He received multiple cuts, possibly from a knife, across the legs and torso. There was evidence of rectal hemorrhaging upon initial examination. There is a possibility that he was sodomized, probably with the same sharp object."

"Good Lord." I closed my eyes to hold back the impending barrage of tears. "Be upfront with me. Is Jake going to die?"

"The outcome of a severe blow to the head is hard to predict. The neurologist will be able to answer your questions once he has completed an evaluation. If there is no evidence of bleeding inside the brain, he will have a reasonable chance of full recovery. As soon as the surgical team has clearance, they will take him in for repairs to the rectal lining and initial correction for the compound fracture of the femur."

His smiled slightly and reached over to hold my hand. "Would you like for me to find Mary Mathues for you?"

"Yes," I said shakily. "I'll be in the waiting room."

It was almost 5 AM when Rich Burns walked into the surgical waiting room on the first floor. "Lordy, Hattie. You look 'bout like the southbound part of a northbound mule!"

I stood and gave him a warm hug. "I could say the same about you, but you're the best thing I've seen since your wife left here. 'Cept she's prettier than you."

He flopped onto an upholstered chair. "Whew! What a night! I don't think I've had one to compare in the twenty years I've been in law enforcement! What's the word on Jake?"

"He's still in surgery. They're setting a compound fracture of his right leg and repairing some cuts."

He reached down and loosened the bulky gun belt. "You talked to his doc yet?"

I shrugged. "Only the ER physician. Jake has a head injury and the neurologist is supposed to talk to me at some point, but you know a hospital operates on its own time schedule. I guess they'll fill me in after he's in recovery. I figure they probably wouldn't be doing the other work if his CAT scan came back showing a problem. I really wanted to tag Mary again to answer some questions, but I haven't seen her in a couple of hours since I first talked to the ER doctor."

He settled back into the chair. The leather holster squeaked in protest. "I bought your truck over with me. I got one of the Gadsden County boys to follow me over. They're going to be trading out with Leon County and Tallahassee Police Department to keep a watch over Jake. Until they find the perpetrator, he could conceivably still be at risk. They'll also need to be here when he comes around, so they can contact the investigators to hear what, if anything, he can recall about the attack." He leaned over to gain access to a pocket and handed over my keys. "I'll hitch a ride back home with the Decatur County, Georgia officer who spent the night over here last night. I'll buy him breakfast. That'll pay him back for the side trip through the country."

"I really appreciate all you and Carol have done for Jake and me." I kissed him on the cheek.

"Hope you kissed her like that too, Hattie. She's a jealous woman." His dimples flared at the corners of his mouth. Two teenagers with angry dark eyes plopped down in the row opposite ours. When they noticed Rich's uniform, they stood and relocated to the far side of the room.

"I know you probably can't talk a lot about it, Rich, but do you have any leads yet?"

"Florida Department of Law Enforcement, FDLE, and the Georgia Bureau of Investigation, GBI, are crawling all over the two crime scenes. Since this involves a kidnapping and hate-crime, the FBI is also sending some people in. It's complicated because the perpetrator took Jake over the state line." He paused and used a cloth handkerchief to wipe the sweat from his brow. "I'm glad we'll have all the resources of the combined agencies. This is a lot more than a small local police department could, or should, handle alone. Gadsden County Sheriff's

Office and Decatur County, Georgia, Sheriff's office are also helping with the case." His eyes were droopy and bloodshot.

"You just get off?"

"I had one of the other officers cover the last couple of hours of my shift. I wanted to come on over and get your truck to you. I figured you'd need it to get around once you left the hospital. Carol's gonna call Margie and John to look after your animals. They've always had a key to the farmhouse from when your mama lived up there on the Hill by herself after your daddy died. Carol will go tell Joe, Evelyn, and Piddie the news, too. It wouldn't do for them to hear it on television."

He stretched and yawned. "I spent some time up by the lake at the crime scene before I left to come over here. Last night, with the road closed, Turkey Point overlook was deserted. Otherwise, most nights, Decatur County Sheriff's officers have to run kids off from the area where Jake was found. It was damn lucky that Ashley Wood and her boyfriend decided to walk up there for some privacy. She told our officer that Jake did the flowers for her sister's wedding in December of last year. That's why she recognized him right off."

I smiled. "Maybe not so lucky for little Ashley when her mama and daddy get through grounding her for slipping off to smooch at Turkey Point."

"We've all done it, haven't we?" Rich winked. "After the scene they witnessed, I reckon it'll be a good long while before those kids want to slip off anywhere!"

"How long would it have taken to identify him if the kids didn't know who he was?"

"One of our boys was on duty with the ambulance team at the fireworks and heard the alert on Jake over his radio. Without him, or the kids knowing Jake, it would've taken a bit longer. The Georgia officer who was one of the first on scene found a Dragonfly Florist billing invoice in the pocket of a shirt he found hanging on a shrub. Even without the invoice address, the alert was out with Jake's description, and it wouldn't have been much longer before his identity was confirmed. It just expedited things having the kids there to identify him so quickly."

"I suppose it's also a good thing, too, that it was a warm July night," I said.

"Yep, it would have been worse for him if the weather'd been damp and cold."

I sighed. "I'm stretching for things to feel thankful for, but all I can feel right now is anger mixed with a good serving of helplessness." I combed my fingers wearily through my knotted hair.

"There'll be a lot of that to go around before this is all over with, I suppose," he said, nodding. "Well, let me go con myself a ride to the country." He stood and pinched me playfully on the cheek. "That little truck drives pretty smooth. Engine cuts out a little around ninety, though."

"I don't know how Carol puts up with you," I said.

"It's the boyish charm." He flashed an impish grin. "One of us'll be in contact with you. As soon as the media gets a'hold of this, our little town is gonna be a crazy place to be." He shook his head. "I have a funny feeling it's only just begun."

THE FIRST DAY

Nurse Marion's Old Fashioned Fudge

Ingredients: 2 cups white sugar, ½ cup corn syrup, ½ cup milk or cream, 1 tspn butter, 1 tspn vanilla, 2 tbsp cocoa.

Mix the first four ingredients, stirring occasionally. Simmer until soft. Remove from heat and beat in vanilla and cocoa with a wooden spoon until stiff. Add nuts and cherries if desired. Spread on waxed paper and let cool.

Cut into squares, wrap up in pretty napkins and give away as party favors or treats to guests.

CHAPTER NINE

AT THE INSISTENCE of the neurologist, I went to the townhouse for a few hours of rest. Jake was out of surgery, stable, and settled into a bed in the neurological intensive care unit. I didn't think I could sleep, but I was out as soon as my head hit the pillow.

I jerked awake at noon, quickly showered, changed into a clean pair of jeans and a shirt, grabbed a crossword puzzle book, and headed back to the hospital.

Jake looked worse than when I'd seen him fresh out of recovery in the wee hours of the morning. His bruises had darkened to shades of angry deep red and purple, and his eyes appeared sunken into his swollen, pale face.

"He's breathing on his own," Mimi Sullivan, the neurological intensive care unit nurse commented. "If he remains stable, he may get to move out onto the floor by tomorrow."

"Even if he's still unconscious?"

"Yes." She checked his monitor. It amazed me how technology had improved patient care. Jake's heart rate, blood pressure, respiration rate, and blood oxygenation were displayed on the screen.

I touched Jake's hand. "I feel so helpless."

"Talk to him. About anything—everything. We don't know how much he can hear, but often people who come out from a coma report hearing the voice of a loved one while they were unconscious." She made a few notes in Jake's chart. "Keep your visits short—ten minutes once an hour. And, only two visitors at a time while he's here in the unit."

"Mimi, how long do you think he'll be this way?"

She flipped the chart closed and rested it on her hip. "Depends. As the swelling in his brain decreases, he'll be more likely to wake up. With severe trauma to the body, it's partly the shock as well. I've always felt like the patient will wake up when the body's healed enough to deal with outside input." She nodded toward the bed. "You talk to him, Hattie. You're the best medicine." Mimi possessed the calm demeanor of a seasoned caregiver. Her neatly pressed uniform, clean white shoes, efficient movements, and even-toned voice garnered trust.

"Thanks, Mimi. I've always said if you want to understand something, don't ask the doctor, ask the nurse."

"It's cause we speak plain English!" she called over her shoulder as she turned to complete the rest of her rounds.

For a moment, I studied his bruised face. The turmoil of conflicting emotions threatened to choke any words. The soft whir of the machinery, interrupted by the occasional whoosh of a respirator, broke the stillness of the ten-bed unit. I pulled a small bedside chair to Jake's side, held his hand, cleared my throat, and began to speak quietly.

"Jake, do you remember what Chattahoochee was like when we were kids? I can see it just like it was yesterday. Picken's Drugstore on the corner. It had a long white glitter-sparkly counter with thick padded seats on polished chrome bases. Black and white tile on the floor. And, the trim on the walls was bright red. There was a long mirror that ran the length of the bar with lines of clean glasses." I sighed. "Those incredible fountain floats, made with whole milk and real ice cream. They were heaven on earth for twenty-five cents. Bobby used to take us with him while Mom was grocery shopping. When we were older, we'd go by ourselves, just you and me. Do you remember?

"And, the theatre? We went every Saturday afternoon for the matinee." I giggled. "You hated the horror flicks. I loved them. *Beware of the Blob*-that was a doozy, for sure. Scared you half to death!"

"Oh, and the Western Auto store! You wanted the red wagon in the display window, only your mother refused to buy it. God, she was stingy. No offense, Jake. Remember when we used to take the bikes and ride down Thrill Hill when we weren't supposed to? And, the time when what's-her-name fell off half way down and was picking gravel out of her knees for weeks?"

With the intermittent beep of a monitor, I traipsed down memory lane in ten-minute increments until my voice grew hoarse.

I concentrated on the crossword puzzle on my lap.
Sixteen down…three-letter word for law officer. 'Cop!'

Weird stuff happens. Kathy walked into the neuro waiting room right at that moment, still wearing her navy Tallahassee Police Department uniform. "Hey, I just got off and thought I'd swing by and check on things. How's Jake?"

I filled her in on his status. "I can't stop thinking about the Fourth. What if he'd been lying there in the shop bleeding to death, and I just left him? I don't know what came over me! When I saw all the broken glass, the word *faggot* painted on the wall, and the smeared blood where I'd stepped, I turned and ran out as fast as I could!"

Kathy rested a hand on my shoulder. "You did the right thing, Hattie. When you come to a door that's open when it should be locked, and you at all suspect that security has been violated, you need to get the police as soon as possible. Yeah, Jake could've been in there hurt. By the same token, you could've walked in on the suspect and it would have been your blood on the floor."

"It's good to have your input, officer." I mock saluted her. She's fond of that.

Kathy explained the intricacies of working a crime scene and the semantics involved with coordinating different levels of law enforcement. We turned toward the door when the metallic click of a walker sounded in the hall.

Dressed in a mid-calf length floral moo-moo, my aunt leaned into the room. "Is this a private waitin' room, or can just any ol' body off the street come in?"

Evelyn walked in behind her. "Joe's hunting for a parking space. That garage is nearly full. It's a marvel there's so many sick people in the world!"

"Look at you, Miss Kathy!" Piddie said. "You always look so imposin' in your po-leese uniform!"

Kathy hugged my elderly aunt. "Yeah, old woman. You give me any lip and I'll run you in."

Piddie's blue eyes twinkled. "That'd mean I'd get to ride in the back of a squad car like a common criminal!"

Evelyn sat down. "There's nothing common about you, Mama."

Piddie's hair reached new heights. To match her bright floral shift, she had stuck small, fuzzy, black and yellow pipe cleaner bumblebees between the lavender curls.

I smiled. "Your hair is a work of art today, Pid,"

Evelyn snorted. "Don't encourage her, Hattie. If Jake were to wake up and see that hair, he'd think he was being attacked by killer bees!"

"You leave my bees alone, Evelyn." Piddie patted her hair. "Jake ordered these bees, 'specially for me, outta one of his florist magazines! He has supplied me with tiny tree frogs, butterflies in every color of the rainbow, and these adorable bumblebees. It's becomin' quite the thing in town, you know. Mandy over at the Cut'n'Curl has asked Jake to order a few for her to have at the shop." Piddie smoothed her dress. "When can we see our boy? Are they allowin' us family members in?"

I checked my watch. "I was getting ready to go back in shortly. Two of us can go in at a time for only ten minutes."

Evelyn glanced up as Joe entered the waiting room. "We'll just sit and catch up, then, while we're waiting."

Piddie studied me closely. "You don't look as wore out as I thought you would."

I pushed a limp hank of hair behind one ear. "I went to the town-house and took a quick nap and showered."

Piddie's eyes watered. "How is our boy?"

"Stable. Pretty bruised up. He's still unconscious."

Piddie shifted and arranged her dress. "You should have heard Elvina Houston carrying on. She swears on a stack of Bibles she had some kinda spell about dark-thirty. Said it was like the claws of death gripping at her heart. Now, she's calling everyone in the Big Bend, telling them she had a premonition of the evil that got a'holt of Jake Witherspoon the night he was taken. She just can't stand it when she's not the absolute first to know something! That old woman wears me out."

Evelyn shook her head. "Everything wears you out, Mama. I think we need to focus on one thing, don't you?"

I glanced at my watch. "It's been long enough. I think we can go in, now."

Evelyn nodded. "Why don't you take Mama on back? Joe and I will sit and pass the time with Kathy."

We checked in with the Gadsden County Sheriff's deputy at the door to the unit. Piddie shuffled slowly toward Jake's glass-walled cubicle. Several of the nurses looked up from their monitors, and she nodded hello as she passed the main desk.

Piddie circled the bed and stood by Jake's left side. Her blue eyes watered.

"Talk to him if you want, Piddie. The doctor and nurses all said it was a good thing."

Piddie touched Jake's hand tentatively. "What have they done to my boy? Huh?" Her voice shook. "Now you listen to me, Jake Witherspoon. You're gonna wake up soon, when you're good'n ready. We'll be waitin' right here for you. Don't you worry about a thing! I got it all figured out. I'll make you some cathead biscuits, chicken'n dumplin's, and one of my best damn chocolate iced layer cakes!"

She paused. Her eyes strayed to Jake's tightly encased leg. "Your leg's gonna take a little time healin', honey. I've got a pearl-handled cane I'll give you, and I'll teach you how to use it right. I don't use it since my balance's gotten so bad. If I can get up and go after all the fallin' out I've done, so can you. Hattie told me I can't stay so very long, or I'd think of a story to tell you. Next time I see you, you'll be good'n awake. I'm gonna send up some prayers for you. I'm asking my Carlton to put in a good word from the other side. He didn't know you, but he'd like you if he was able to be here."

Piddie leaned over and pecked Jake softly on the cheek. Her lower lip started to quiver. She nodded, and we left the bedside.

"It just near'bout tears me to pieces to see him all beat up and hurt. How could anyone do that to him—such a sweet lovin' man never did nothin' unkind to nobody!" she said as we entered the hall. "I'd take it all on myself if I could."

"Kathy had to go," Evelyn explained when we came into the waiting area. "She said she'd stop back by later on."

I settled Piddie onto a chair. "What's going on at home?"

Joe pulled his reading glasses off and folded the daily copy of the *Tallahassee Democrat*. "It's just getting cranked up over there. We passed three TV vans getting off the Interstate when we started over here."

Evelyn inched forward until she balanced on the edge of the vinyl chair. "And you wouldn't believe Jake's shop! They won't let anyone within ten feet of it. All kinds of law officers coming and going!"

Piddie began, "Stephanie at the Homeplace said she served up breakfast for a couple of G-men this mornin'. Said they had black suits and sunglasses on just like in the movies, and she nearly passed out when one of 'em looked her right in the eye. Said it was almost like they could stare right through her and see she hadn't reported all her tips for the last few years."

"Joe keeps telling us that it's only just begun," Evelyn said. She stood and smoothed the wrinkles from her pale blue dress. "Hattie, Joe and I have decided to wait to see Jake when he's a little better. He needs his rest."

"We're gonna take Mama to eat at the Golden Corral on Monroe Street before we head home," Joe said. "Can we bring you anything?"

I shook my head. "No, I'll be going back to the townhouse later on tonight. I want to get a good night's sleep so I can be up here first thing in the morning. They may move Jake into a regular room tomorrow. Piddie, could you tell everyone to hold off on sending flowers and cards until after he's in a room? There's no place to put them right now."

"I'll call Elvina Houston when we get home. Saves me a lot of breath."

THE REVELATION

Excerpt from Max the Madhatter's notebook:

July 4, 1959: I see the map of a person's life written on him like a see-through film. Not always, but often, for just a brief blink of time. Hidden secrets glow like the light from a dim candle—buried deep. Secrets ready to rise up and cause hurt. Or heal it.

CHAPTER TEN

SHORTLY AFTER JAKE was settled into private room 4411 around 10:30 AM, Mary Mathues knocked softly on the door. "I'm glad it's the same officer as yesterday," she said. "She didn't give me the third degree for trying to visit you guys today."

"I know a few more police people now, that's for sure. I'm glad they're here, though. Actually, I know Kelly from the days I used to work with the state. My building wasn't in the city limits—that was before Tallahassee decided to annex everything within forty miles—and she worked our part of Leon County. She came on duty about the time I left the building after working late, so she'd drive by and keep an eye out for me getting to my car. She's great!"

Mary leaned in close to Jake, her calm green eyes echoing concern. "Any signs that he's coming around yet?"

"He's moaned a couple of times this morning," I replied as I straightened his sheet.

Officer Kelly Powers stuck her head in the door. "Hattie, there's a Mr. Thomas Thurgood here from Chattahoochee." She wore the dark green uniform of the Leon County Police Department.

I shot a puzzled look toward the door. "That's odd. He's not particularly someone I would think of as one of Jake's friends. I'll come out there, Kelly."

"I'll stay here with Jake," Mary said.

The tall fifty-ish man in the hall stood with his Atlanta Braves hat in his hands, "Miss Hattie," He dipped his head in greeting. "I'm sorry to disturb you, but I need to speak to you in private…if I may."

After making sure Mary could stay with Jake for a while, I returned to the hallway. "Why don't we go down to the cafeteria on the first floor and get a cup of coffee."

We rode the elevator in awkward silence. Thomas Thurgood didn't speak until we were seated with our mugs at a corner table away from the milling nurses, staff, and visitors.

"I just did the hardest thing I've ever had to do in my entire life." He stared absently into space. The loose skin bagged around his rheumy brown eyes. "I turned my son over to the police in Chattahoochee. I thought you'd want to know. I'd tell Mr. Jake if he were awake. I understand he hasn't come around yet."

I frowned. "Are you telling me that your son did this to Jake?"

Thomas sighed deeply and his thin shoulders drooped. Deep creases formed around his mouth. He ran a hand through his unkempt thinning dirt-brown hair. "No, Matt didn't do the beatin', Miss Hattie. It's a long story."

I sat back and crossed my arms. "Seems I have the time to hear it, and if you can tell me anything that can make this nightmare make sense to me, I'm certainly willing to listen."

He fortified himself with a long swill of black coffee before speaking. "I'm a twin. So's my wife Lottie. She and her sister, Louise, are from over near Bonifay. My brother and I married them in '80 in a double wedding. Tim and I were almost thirty by that time. It was a mistake for my brother from the start. You see, the whole family knew he was a homosexual. You just didn't admit that, 'specially if you're from a small town. We railroaded my brother Tim into getting married."

I quickly did the math. It was difficult to fathom that the sad-faced man in front of me was only six or seven years my senior.

"Louise and Tim had their son, Marshall, first. Matthew, our son, came almost a year later. Couple of years after Marshall was born, Tim ran off. Louise said my brother told her it was to go 'find himself.' I hadn't seen him for years until Mama Thurgood, our mother, passed, end of last year. He called me at work, and I met him at a little truck stop outside of Tallahassee to talk." He paused to take a sip from the mug.

"He didn't sit with the family at the funeral. They didn't even know he was in town. He said he was afraid of what Louise and Marshall would do if they knew he was around. Someone told me later that they saw him slip into a pew after the service started. But, I knew he was there. I could just feel his presence. Then, just like he appeared, he was gone. He's livin' somewhere on the west coast. Says he's happy." His thin bottom lip quivered slightly. "I miss my brother."

Thomas swallowed hard. Tears formed at the corners of his eyes.

"Louise went to drinkin' heavy after Tim left her. She was a mean drunk—always carryin' on about Tim in front of Marshall. There were a couple of times when it got real bad, and we'd take Marshall to live with us. Louise would make a big play like she was dryin' out, and she'd come and take him home with her. We heard that there was a parade of no-account men in and out.

"Marshall grew up hating his daddy. Louise always threw it in Marshall's face that he was a son of a fag, when she was dead drunk. Marshall was bad seed from early on—mean as a cut snake, a bully, and vicious to anything smaller and weaker than him—animals and people. Hated black folks, too.

"I prodded Matt to spend time with him. Thought he could be a good influence. I can see that was my mistake, now. Marshall stayed in trouble with the law, drinkin' and fightin', but always shy of ending up in jail. I even heard rumors that he was involved in runnin' drugs up in south Georgia."

He sighed deeply and dissolved into a fit of phlegmy coughs. "Louise cleaned up when the boy was around fifteen, but, by that time, it was too late for Marshall. His hatred had ruined him. I always feared he would come to no good one day."

Thomas stared blankly across the room before continuing. "I'd heard the boys talking before about that flower faggot uptown. I told them to hush. So, when I heard about Jake, I had a sick feeling deep inside my stomach. Matt wouldn't admit to having anything to do with it at first, but I could tell something was eatin' at him. Finally, last night I cornered him. *Son,* I said, *these federal fellas are gonna find out who did this terrible thing. They're talking kidnapping and murder now, 'specially if Jake dies. You know anything, you best come clean to me now. 'Cause, you'll be knee-deep in it when it comes out if you don't.*"

Thomas took a noisy drag from his coffee cup. "He told me everything about how he and Marshall jumped Jake going into the back of the flower shop, bound and gagged him, then rubbed cow manure all over the walls. Marshall was the one who wrote the bad words all over the place. They were both dead drunk."

"Matt wanted to untie Jake and leave him be. Marshall said it would teach him a lesson if he woke up and was tied up and couldn't talk—he would be so embarrassed when someone found him the next mornin', he would surely tuck his tail 'twix his legs and hightail it outta Chattahoochee."

I couldn't believe what I was hearing. God help us.

"Marshall drove Matt home and dropped him off. We figured Marshall doubled back, picked up Jake, and took him off over the Florida border to the lake." He fidgeted in his pocket for a worn pack of cigarettes and grimaced when he noticed the no smoking sign. "We called Louise from the police station. Marshall's not been home since the night of the fourth. He goes off for days at a time. She's lost all control over him, so she didn't think a thing of him not being around. There's a manhunt on now for Marshall. Your brother's helpin' the law to try to find him."

I cocked my head. "Bobby?"

"He volunteered—knows every pig trail and huntin' camp for miles. From what Matt told us, Marshall was dead drunk. He had no money on him to amount to much, so they figure he's probably hidin' out somewhere close by."

I felt faint. "I don't know what to say to you, Mr. Thurgood."

Thomas shrugged. "I don't expect understanding. I feel the weight of a lot of this. My whole family does. We tried to make Tim into somethin' he wasn't, and forced him into a marriage he couldn't live in. Oh dear God—now, look what's come of it."

He started to cry, then stopped and blew his bulbous nose loudly. "I can't say as how I understand Mr. Jake or Tim. I wasn't raised that-a-way. Then again, neither was my twin brother. I reckon a person can't much help what they are. Can't judge either of them anymore. Nobody deserves what was done to Mr. Jake. When Mama Jean Thurgood had her knee replacement right before the stroke took her Home to her rest, Jake was good to her. He brought her fresh flowers every couple of days and called to see how she was getting on just about every day."

Thomas stood to leave. "I just wanted you to hear it from one of us. My family will be prayin' for Mr. Jake's recovery."

He walked away, his wrinkled clothes hanging on him as if they belonged to a taller, heavier man.

I sat in stunned silence, oblivious to the clanging of utensils and conversations around me. I checked my watch and rose to find the elevators. A wave of nausea hit me in the hall. Fortunately, I found a vacant women's room. The coffee went first. When nothing else remained for my stomach to repel, I endured the dreaded dry heaves for a couple of minutes. I eased down to sit on the commode and hugged my midsection. The events of the past few months came crashing down: my mother's death, the loss of my damaged relationship with Garrett, Jake's abduction and assault, and Thomas Thurgood's revelation. Although I fancied myself as a resilient steadfast forty-year-old woman, I wished desperately for the comfort of someone's arms—just to hear, it's going to be okay.

THE AWAKENING

Excerpt from Max the Madhatter's notebook:

September 9, 1956: Nurse Marion sat by me in the common room today. I had one of my spells, and I was feeling like the world was closing in on me. She said some folks go through life never feeling a thing. They are like ghosts moving in time, taking up space.

No matter how bad I feel, at least I feel.

CHAPTER ELEVEN

AS IF SOMEONE had launched a flare over Tallahassee, flowers and cards started to arrive with a steady stream of pink lady volunteers in attendance. The first massive arrangement came from the owner of Blossom's Flowers, a florist whom Jake knew well and frequently called for phone orders. Soon, every corner and shelf was filled with cut flowers in vases, ferns, towering prayer plants, and silk arrangements. Visitors came and went during the day: Reverend Ghent and his wife, Clarice, Mrs. Lucille Jackson and her son, and several nurses from the neuro ICU.

I settled into the vinyl upholstered chair beside the bed. "Remember how your mama and Aunt Piddie used to get together to do their art? Who else? Oh, yeah, Sissy Pridgeon and Elvina Houston. The four of them. Mama still has one of the god-awful paint-by-numbers pictures Piddie did during that time. It's hanging front and center in one of the back bedrooms. Your mama would always shoo us away when the girls were coming over. I think they took a little nip in their tea, the way those paintings turned out!" I laughed, then clasped my hand over my mouth. "They're going to throw me out of here if I don't pipe down.

Anyway, you had the good taste to make Betty Lou hang her beloved landscapes upstairs where nobody could see them."

The monologue continued until I grew hoarse and couldn't dredge up even one more silly Chattahoochee anecdote.

By 4:00 PM, the room was quiet except for the low drone of the overhead mounted television. Jake slept peacefully, though he twitched and moaned a few times. To pass the time, I imagined the community of my hometown as a living organism—perhaps, one big cell. Elvina was the cell wall. Everything coming in or leaving had to pass by her. The nucleus consisted of the older generation, such as Piddie, who protected the history of the community. The younger people were in charge of the future: cell division and the movement of the group forward. All the workers supplied the organism with energy, protected it, helped it communicate, repaired the tears, and removed waste: firefighters, police, city utility workers, sanitation, phone service, health workers, food service, and government.

I drifted off to sleep.

"Am I in heaven?" Jake mumbled.

I jerked awake and lunged toward the bed. "Jake?"

He opened his eyes and struggled to focus. "I must be in heaven, 'cause Oprah's on, and I love me some Oprah!"

Relief washed over me, and I laughed.

Jake reached for my hand. "Dorothy, we're not in Oz anymore, are we?" He looked around the room. "If we are, then I must be the Wicked Witch and someone just dropped a farmhouse on my head." He tried to reach up to touch his face.

"Easy, Jake. You've got all these IV's and monitor wires attached."

"How long...?"

"Two days, close to three. Jake, do you recall what happened to you?"

He closed his eyes and breathed deeply. "Last thing I remember, I was going into the back of the shop. Something hit me from behind." His brow furrowed.

"Jake, I've got to go let someone know you're awake." I stepped outside long enough to tell Kelly to call the nurse and contact the FDLE investigator.

The shift-charge nurse bustled into the room, checked Jake's vital signs, chirped as if she had just won the lottery, and hustled away to inform the doctor. In a matter of minutes, Investigator Tom Watkins bustled into the room with an assistant carrying a video camera bag. We waited for half an hour for Lt. Harrison from Chattahoochee PD to arrive.

The local investigator's temple pulsed as he alternately clenched and relaxed his jaw. A nondescript black suit, white shirt, and dark gray tie, along with his stern demeanor added to the air of authority he wore like a tight-fitting second skin. "Mr. Witherspoon. I must apologize for having to question you so soon after your return to consciousness. However, it is important for us to get a statement from you as soon as possible."

"I'm starting to remember a little bit. It's kind of fuzzy."

When the video camera and microphones were in place, the investigator began. "I am Lt. Bill Harrison of Chattahoochee Police Department, along with Florida Department of Law Enforcement Investigator Tom Watkins. It is 5:45 PM , July 7th. I am speaking with Jake Witherspoon from Tallahassee Memorial Hospital Room 4411. Mr. Witherspoon, please tell in your own words what you recall of the events of the evening of July 4th."

"I was taking some flower stands out to the delivery van behind the shop. I came back in through the alley door and something hit me over the head." Jake's brow furrowed. He closed his eyes. "The smell of water…I remember the smell of water…" He was silent for a minute. "Some kind of gun blast or, like, cannon fire close-by."

Jake opened his eyes. "I couldn't focus." He squinted as if trying to see into the darkness of his memory. "My hands were tied. It was hard to breathe…they were fastened to something above my head."

He shook his head and wrinkled his nose in disgust. "Some kind of fishy, foul rag was stuffed in my mouth." He took a deep breath and swallowed. "There was a figure in front of me." He pointed toward the wall. "There, just a few feet ahead of me. Pacing back and forth…stumbling."

He looked down. "The person was muttering…a word I could catch every now and then."

Jake shook his head.

"Daddy…he kept saying daddy over and over."

He pursed his swollen lips. "He was talking as if someone else was there…I strained to see another person."

Jake breathed faster. I held his hand. "He had a stick…or bat…something in his hand." Jake's hand squeezed mine hard. "He's walking toward me…I can see his eyes."

He stopped and hung his head. "Oh, sweet Jesus, his eyes! All glassed over and…evil!"

Jake's speech quickened. "My heart—hammering. He saw me looking at him. And he screamed!" He squeezed his eyes shut. "It was the most awful sound I've ever heard…Oh my God, I'm going to die!" He dissolved into deep, racking sobs.

I climbed onto the side of the bed and held him as he shook. Finally, he stopped and looked at the investigators.

"Can you continue?" Lt. Harrison asked.

Jake nodded. "He reared back and hit my leg with the object in his hand—maybe a bat? Excruciating pain and the bile rose in my throat…trying not to choke, trying to breath through it. I must've blacked out. Then, I heard Oprah's voice." He looked over at me.

"And I saw Hattie's face."

"Can you identify your attacker?" Tom Watkins asked.

"It was one of the boys who came in the shop a few times. Just loitered around a bit, then left. I used to call them—oh, what was it!"

Lt. Harrison leaned closer. "Take your time, Mr. Witherspoon."

"One of them was a little older, and he lorded over the younger one. They looked like brothers. I called them Matt Dillion and Festus, like on Gunsmoke." Jake nodded. "His name—Marshall. Marshall Thurgood."

I sat with Jake, relishing the silence in the aftermath of the harrowing interview. He pinched his eyes shut and winced.

"Let me call the nurse and see about getting you something for pain."

"Sister-girl." He grunted. "I've been back in the world less than three hours and you want to put me out again!"

"No, Jake, I…"

Jake held up his hand. "I know what you're trying to do. It's kinda good in a bizarre sort of way to feel every part of my body—even if it's pain. It reminds me that I am alive." He moaned. "I sure could go for one of your lovely full body deep tissue massages."

I looked him over. Very little area was not covered in bruises, snaked with wires and tubing, or wrapped in bandages. "Your left foot! It's the only thing not covered. I can do some reflexology! That would make your whole body feel better, and it wouldn't hurt anything!"

Jake moaned. "Lordy, yes! Ask Nurse Nancy for some lotion. I'm sure they'll add $30.00 to my bill, but I really don't care at this point."

I rummaged in my purse. "I have a sample of massage cream in here somewhere…Ah-hah!" I held the small plastic container up like a trophy.

"Sister-girl, we need to get you onto Let's Make a Deal! I'm sure there's nothing Monte Hall could ask for that you don't have somewhere in that bottomless pit you call a purse. You hidin' a couple of hard-boiled eggs in there, too?"

"No, but…I do have half of an energy bar."

He rolled his eyes. "Like I said!"

I sat at the end of his bed and gently started to work the pressure points on the bottom of his left foot.

He flinched.

I stopped. "Am I hurting you?"

"No, no. It's not you, my right leg's doing a cha-cha under the splint."

He closed his eyes and fell silent for a few moments, releasing himself into the pleasure of the foot rub.

"Sister-girl, tell me what happened…"

"Jake, haven't you been through enough for today?"

"There's no way I could feel any worse. I have to understand. You are my eyes and ears." His boyish face was marred by purple-black bruises and slashes of tape. My soul felt as if it was crumbling under a weight of tremendous sadness. "Why would Marshall Thurgood do this to me? I've never tried to hurt anyone, at least consciously, in my whole life! Why me?"

"Jake, I…"

"Please, Hattie." He closed his eyes again. Tears glistened on the tips of his eyelashes.

As I continued to massage his foot, I unfolded the story of what I knew of the attack—my arrival at the shop, the trip to the ER, his surgery, the hours of worried vigil by his bed, and the extent of his wounds. Then, I recounted Thomas Thurgood's visit.

The slight whir of the electric wall clock accompanied the silence.

"Could you get the nurse, now?" He asked in a soft voice. "I think I will take you up on the pain medicine."

HORNET'J NEJT

Excerpt from Max the Madhatter's notebook:

July 23, 1958: I stepped on a fire ant hill. The ants boiled out of the top, raging mad. I got bitten so many times, my feet swelled up twice their size. Can't blame them. They were just being ants.

CHAPTER TWELVE

NEWS OF ANY KIND, especially bad news, travels through a close-knit community like telepathy. When a few folks saw a Gadsden County Sheriff's Office cruiser pull away with Matt Thurgood riding in the seat reserved for criminals, it struck like a bolt of lightening. Where Matt was involved, that bully cousin of his was often leading or some-where close behind with a cattle prod. Even before word of the wide scale manhunt was officially released, Chattahoochee residents suspected the worst—one of their own had committed the unspeakable crime.

I washed my bowl in the sink, and helped myself to a coffee refill. "Thanks for the cereal, Evelyn. I was just going to get something later on. God knows, the milk at the house is probably sour by now."

Evelyn smiled. "Glad to help out, Hattie. You heading back on over to the hospital now?"

I rolled my eyes. "As frivolous as it sounds, I'm actually going up to see if Mandy can squeeze me in for a trim."

Piddie, Evelyn, and Joe stared at me.

I cocked my head and shrugged. "Jake insisted. He said that if I didn't get this mop of stringy hair cut, I shouldn't bother coming back!"

Piddie chuckled. "That boy's going to be okay."

"So, after I take care of that, I'll stop by the Hill on the way out and gather some fresh pajamas. He's mortified someone will pass judgment on his delightful hospital gown."

The phone jangled and Piddie picked it up before the second ring. Piddie clapped the phone headset on the table. "That was Elvina Houston. She says the Thurgood boy, Matt, just turned hisself in at the police station."

Evelyn looked up from the cookbook she was studying, *You Can Cook Thai!* "Matt Thurgood!? Thomas's and Lottie's son? He's such a nice young man! I can't fathom him doing such a thing!"

"Elvina didn't have all the details yet. Seems they're lookin' for Matt's double first cousin, Marshall," Piddie said.

Joe shook his head. "Now, there's one troubled young man."

"I told Elvina to snoop and call me as soon as she finds out anything new."

Evelyn squinted at Piddie over the rim of her reading glasses. "Mama, just yesterday you were saying she wears you out!"

Piddie huffed. "She does wear me out! But, I'm not able anymore to go sniffin' around on my own. I gotta turn that over to the younger generation, and Elvina seems to be naturally inclined toward surveillance."

Piddie checked the clock on the counter. "Evelyn, you better get a move on if you expect us to make our appointment at the Cut'n'Curl!"

"We got time! It's only a minute away from here! Besides, I gotta wash my hair before we go."

"You beat all I've ever seen. Washin' your head before you go pay someone to do it for you is the silliest thing I've ever heard! That'd be like cleaning the house before the maid comes!"

Evelyn walked out of the kitchen. "I'll not be seen out of this house with dirty hair!" she called over her shoulder.

"Well, you better hurry up! Mandy's got a new shade of nail polish for me." Piddie held out her hands. "It's called Kiss of the Harlot red!"

Evelyn snorted back into the kitchen. "Mama, why on earth do you have to wear such whorish colors! When are you going to start actin' your age?"

Piddie stared a hole in her prudish daughter. "Red, for your information, little Miss Smarty Pants, is a royal color of queens and kings! And, I'll wear it painted on my bare behind and sashay down Washington Street if you don't hush!"

I ducked my head and stifled a snicker.

"Is it safe for me to leave you two to go to the bank?" Joe asked.

Neither woman said a word.

I patted him on the shoulder. "Don't worry, Joe. I'll be here for a bit."

Joe shook his head. "Actually, Evelyn, it's pretty wild out there with the media in town, and all the traffic. Y'all may want to allow yourself some extra time so you don't miss your slot."

The standoff ended, and Evelyn disappeared into her bathroom. Joe gathered his billfold and checkbook and left for town. A few minutes passed before we heard a loud argument on the front lawn. Piddie picked her way to the front picture window and looked outside. A group of strange men stood facing a nice-looking young fellow dressed in a suit. The group's leader was scarlet red in the face, yelling at the top of his lungs.

Piddie swung the front door open. "Hear, hear!" she called. "What's the fuss?"

The group turned to see an elderly, lavender-haired woman in a bright red housedress clumping down the concrete walkway with a walker.

"What do y'all mean, standin' out here on our property shoutin' loud enough to raise the dead?!" Piddie's blue eyes flared like crystals.

The handsome young gentleman in the tailored sport coat spoke first. "My apologies, Mrs…"

"Longman. Piddie Longman," she said.

I watched from the porch as the tall, handsome man with swarthy features approached my aunt. "Mrs. Longman, I was just coming to see if your family would grant me the pleasure of an interview, when I seem to have somehow offended these men by refusing to back down to their insults. They were hurtling words not suitable for a lady—at your house. Seems as if the local hate group militia have stumbled upon your home as the residence of friends of Jake Witherspoon." He pointed toward a stack of hand-lettered poster boards affixed to wooden stakes. "They were attempting to plant these anti-gay signs in your front yard when I interrupted them."

The pimply red-faced leader of the small group spewed obscenities.

Piddie picked up her walker and swung it through the air. "Lissen here!" she shouted. "You can pack your filthy potty mouth and mutt-ugly buddies back in that rat-trap truck and head on back up town. There ain't any cameras here to help you end up on the national evenin' news. And, that's what you're after, am I right?"

The greasy-haired leader started to speak.

"Git!" Piddie punched the air with the walker turned battle-ax.

The five men grumbled under their breaths as they piled back into the truck and peeled off toward town.

She aimed a diamond encrusted finger toward the astonished man standing beside the driveway. "Now, as for you—come with me." She turned and made her way toward the house.

Clad in a lavender chenille housecoat and matching fuzzy house slippers, Evelyn rushed into the kitchen, leaning over to towel her wet hair. "Five minutes, Mama. Give me five minutes and I can be ready to leave." She looked up to see me, her mother, and an attractive stranger being obviously chummy over coffee.

Piddie gestured. "This is my daughter, Evelyn. She looks better when she dresses right."

The color drained from Evelyn's face. She modestly grabbed the front of her robe where it had gaped open. "Mama? Who…who's this man?"

Piddie smiled. "This happens to be Mr. Holston Lewis, a writer all the way from New York City, here to do a background interview about our lovely Hattie and the shop." Piddie smiled adoringly in Holston's direction. "The three of us have just been sittin' here gettin' acquainted."

Holston stood to leave. "Mrs. Longman, Hattie, you've been most enchanting. And, Mrs. Evelyn, pleasure to meet you. Hattie, may I come by in a few days after Mr. Witherspoon is released from the hospital?"

I shrugged. Words had stuck to the roof of my mouth.

The skin around his blue eyes crinkled when he smiled. "I'll leave you now so that you can make your appointments on time. I will look forward to seeing you, Mrs. Piddie, and you, Mrs. Evelyn in the future. Please forgive me if I have interrupted your morning."

Evelyn blushed. "Of course you didn't bother us, not one little bit. If I'd have known you were out here, I would've offered you a piece of homemade sour cream cake to go along with your coffee."

"You better get out while you can, Holston. Evelyn's killed stronger men than you with her pound cake."

Evelyn glared at her mother, and then smiled in Holston's direction. "Please, do stop by again. I'm sure Hattie will grant you an interview as soon as things settle down, and anything we can add, we'll be happy to help you out."

The two women stood side-by-side at the front door and watched Holston leave. I hung back slightly, peeking from one corner of the window sheers.

Evelyn stomped to the kitchen. "I don't believe you, Mama! A complete stranger comes up to our house, and you just roll out the red carpet!"

"Actually, I invited him in." Piddie turned to go back to the kitchen. "Go get dressed, Evelyn. I'll not abide you if I don't get to see my new nail color!"

In the years I had lived in Florida, I came to understand that disaster and times of trouble brought out all types of people. Residents of the hurricane-ravaged coastline were familiar with the fact. In contrast to the tireless relief workers, countless weasels loaded up the backs of rental trucks with electric generators and bottled water and hotfooted it to the areas hardest hit to peddle their wares at triple the original purchase price.

As soon as the words 'gay-bashing' and 'hate crime' appeared in print, Chattahoochee and the surrounding areas experienced an influx of media: legitimate newspaper and magazine writers, freelance authors, major TV news affiliate teams, and bottom-feeder trash rag magazine scribes. In addition, Chattahoochee floated in a quagmire of hate group representatives, rubbernecking onlookers, and a small pod of white supremacy thugs with nothing better to do.

One swing through town told the story. Both small hotels were simultaneously booked to capacity for the first time in the town's history. Vans and RVs filled the sites at the East Bank campground on Lake Seminole across the Georgia border. The local IGA food store strained to keep the shelves stocked, and the restaurants hired extra help to cook and serve the heavy load of customers.

Even though the individual members of the visiting crowd were disparate, the group seemed to move as one giant amoebae-like being. We watched as it oozed between the heavily guarded crime scenes at Turkey Point and the Dragonfly Florist/Madhatter's Sweet Shop and Massage Parlor. An ever-changing crowd hovered at the Chattahoochee Police headquarters on Jefferson Street, hungrily lunging at each law enforcement official who passed within range. Stephanie from the Homeplace was mobbed with questions when she delivered a bulging sack of sandwiches and a tower of soft drinks to the team of investigators inside the conference room.

Inside the safe womb of the Cut'n'Curl, news was updated hourly with the arrival of appointed patrons.

Mandy sectioned off a wet strand of my hair and snipped. "You know what Margie from out on the Hill told me?"

Piddie and Melody, the nail specialist, stopped their conversation and looked toward the hair care side of the shop. Mrs. Tamara Johnson and Evelyn leaned completely forward to free their ears from the whistle of the hair dryer.

Mandy paused to relish the attention of her audience. "A couple of reporters came barreling up the lane out at your farmhouse, got out, and started toward the door. Margie watched them walk around the yard for a few minutes before she decided to come up the hill. She told them, *the owner of this house is not home, and I'd advise you to get off her property before I phone the law!*"

"We've had some of them hanging around our house, too," Evelyn said. "Mama even invited one in!"

The women shifted attention to Piddie. She held up a half-manicured hand. "He was a nice gentleman from New York City, now. He ran some roughnecks off the front lawn. Besides…" She winked at me. "He's handsome and I didn't notice a wedding band."

Mandy giggled. "You match-makin' again, Miz Piddie?"

Piddie raised an eyebrow. "Cupid needs a little shot in the butt every now and again."

Melody spoke up. "All I know is that this town's gone crazy. It took me almost five minutes to get down to the bank yesterday!"

Mandy ran her fingers upward through my hair to dislodge the loose trimmings. "Chattahoochee looks like Tallahassee before Florida State plays the University of Florida in football! It's been good for business, though. Julie from the Homeplace came in for a touch-up on her roots, and she's just dead on her feet, but rollin' in tips!"

She rolled a hank of damp hair onto round brush and set the handheld dyer on the lowest setting. "You know what else? I had one of those trash magazine folks in here this morning tryin' to dig up some dirt on Jake and Hattie. I sent her packin', let me tell you!"

Melody glanced up from Piddie's extended hand. "When you reckon they'll let Jake come home, Hattie?"

"Maybe a few more days. He's beginning to eat more solid food now. He may have to have more surgery on his leg later on, though. The Thurgood boy really smacked the bone in Jake's thigh. He'll have to have therapy to walk again."

Piddie shook her head. "I shore hope they find Marshall soon. I 'spect everyone'll rest easier when they do. You know they've kept a police officer right at Jake's door the whole time?"

Melody gasped. "Is that right?"

"Yeah, you have to check in before you get to visit. 'Course, most of 'em recognize all of us now, we've been over there so much." Piddie admired her wet nails. "Melody, this is surely a purty shade, even if Evelyn insists that red makes me look like a two-bit tramp."

Mandy threw her head back and let out a deep-throated laugh.

"Lordy! You two!"

Evelyn ducked her head from beneath the dryer and shot Piddie eye-daggers across the shop.

MANHUNT

Melt-In-Your-Mouth Dark Chocolate Brownies

Ingredients: ¾ cup unsalted butter, 2 ounce unsweetened chocolate, 2 ounce semisweet chocolate, 1 cup white sugar, ¾ cup light brown sugar, 3 eggs, 1½ cups bleached flour, ½ tspn salt, 2 tspn vanilla, 1½ cups coarsely chopped walnuts or pecans.

Preheat the oven to 375°F. Melt the butter and chocolate in a large saucepan over low heat, stirring often. Remove the pan from heat and mix in the white and brown sugar, eggs, flour, salt, vanilla and nuts. Spread the batter into a well-buttered 9x9x2 inch baking pan. Bake the brownies uncovered for 35 to 40 minutes, or until the brownies begin to pull away from the sides of the pan.

Serve with plenty of milk and napkins.

CHAPTER THIRTEEN

FOLLOWING MATTHEW THURGOOD'S confession and the confirmation of Jake's statement, the manhunt for Marshall Thurgood swung into a well-organized fever pitch. Clusters of law enforcement personnel from Decatur, Georgia, Gadsden, Jackson, and Leon counties, FDLE, GBI, and the FBI converged on Chattahoochee police headquarters. After Matt Thurgood was grilled for his take on possible locations where his cousin might hide out, the team put all available personnel into action. A bulletin was released with Marshall's physical description and the make, model, and year of his truck.

Marshall's '77 faded green Dodge 4x4 pickup resembled a number of hunting trucks roaming the backcountry roads. Once the word spread through the surrounding counties, Chattahoochee PD was bombarded with calls from all across the tri-state area. Vehicles similar to Marshall's had been seen simultaneously at a fish camp on Lake Talquin near Quincy, Florida, parked beside the road two miles north of Pelham, Georgia, and outside a roughneck bar near Youngstown, Florida, halfway to Panama City Beach. Denise Whiddon's cousin, Jennifer, was enlisted to help her field the calls. After a couple of intense hours, she and Denise resorted to drinking the spoon-dissolving coffee to stay alert.

Inside the conference room, the officers shuffled, waiting anxiously for assignments.

"You know this area probably better than most of us, Bobby. What about any old abandoned houses or hunting camps?" Rich Burns asked. The room full of officers listened intently.

"Well, as I see it, Marshall was drunk and half-crazed by the time he left Turkey Point. His mama said there was no way he could've had a lot of cash on him, and all of her credit cards are accounted for. So…I reckon he's still around here close-by, probably waiting to slip back into town for money and food. There're a slew of old hunting and fishing camps up in the edge of Georgia. I'd bet he didn't come back down toward town, but ducked up there to lie low."

"Still, I think we ought to make a list of the hunting areas in Gadsden and Jackson counties and not rule them out," Chattahoochee Police Chief, David Turnbill said. "I know a lot of them, but, Bobby, you can help the officers with any they might not be aware of."

Denise appeared with the updated list of truck sightings. Within a few minutes, cruisers pulled away from CPD heading in all directions, leaving a trail of puzzled, frustrated media in their wake. Chief Turnbill came out long enough to make an official statement, then returned to the command post.

Bobby drove his blue Ford pick-up over the Florida-Georgia border into Chattahoochee City limits. It had been a frustrating day of dead ends. He had remained in cell phone contact with Officer Rich Burns, giving him new sites that came to mind as he rode the heavily wooded back roads.

Though he'd never given much thought to his stand on homosexuality, the senseless brutality of Jake's assault had made Bobby white-hot mad. Jake wasn't a bad fellow. From all accounts, he was a decent, stand-up guy. Hattie certainly held him in high regard. That had to account for something.

Bobby's growing affection for Leigh Andrews nudged the deep-seated knot of anger in the center of his gut. She was all about family, loved every Sunday dinner, birthday and anniversary. She kept up with special dates, favorite songs, and cherished memories. Leigh couldn't fathom his lack of regard for his sister and the remaining few members of his extended family, and took every opportunity to nudge him in their direction.

He'd been giving it some serious consideration. How many times had Hattie reached out to him, only to be cut to the quick? Bobby shook his head. It was a small wonder his sister would still give him the time of day.

The need for reconciliation had driven him for the past long hours—up and down every pig trail hunting camp road, past deserted fishing shanties, and over back dirt country lanes so rutted and over-grown, the tree branches carved deep gouges into the shanks of his pick-up.

Bobby talked aloud to himself. "Maybe I oughta rethink this thing. Marshall could've come back toward town and turned west toward Sneads, but who in his right mind would head across that narrow Victory Bridge...drunk...at night? Then again, we aren't dealing with a boy in his right mind."

He turned west and headed for Jackson County. As he drove, he allowed his mind to wander, mulling over any place he knew where a kid might run. Rich Burns' words floated briefly through his mind: *Don't be a hero, Bobby. You have any leads, you call me and I'll get someone on it right away! That boy's scared, half-crazy, and possibly armed with at least a deer gun."*

Following a gut hunch, Bobby turned south on Florida Power Road, closely paralleling the winding route of the Apalachicola River. As he approached the site of the Florida Power Plant on the banks of the river, he slowed. During the winter months, the abandoned factory buildings were a hangout for local teens looking for a place to smoke pot and drink.

Hidden from the main road, he spotted Marshall's 4x4 in a thatch of oak and pine saplings. He pulled his truck nearby and cut the engine. For a moment, Bobby toyed with the notion of contacting Rich. Slowly, he left the truck and approached the 4x4, listening for any unusual noises.

Marshall's truck had rolled half-throttle into the patch of woods. Deep gashes ran the length of the sideboards and the front hood was crimped in three places where small trees had stopped his forward momentum. Spider web-like veins spooled outward from a crack on the driver's side windshield. Bobby peered though the open window. The lingering sour smell of spilled whiskey permeated the cab, and he noted dried blood and a few strands of dark hair hanging from the center of the fracture in the windshield. A long piece of rounded cypress wood lie on the seat, one end dark with what he supposed was Jake's blood.

Bobby followed a set of uneven shoeprints toward a listing tin outbuilding with broken windows and a ruined roof. The musky smell of decaying freshwater mussels floated on the wind. As he cautiously moved closer to the shack, an even stronger odor accosted his nose. He knew this scent from discovering the aftermath of illegally poached animals in the woods he patrolled. It was the smell of death.

When he opened the rickety shed door, the rancid odor hit him full in the face. He grabbed a bandana from his back pocket and cupped it over his mouth and nose.

The remains of Marshall Thurgood lay splayed on the concrete floor beside an old wooden chair. An empty bottle of Jack Daniel's whiskey sat on one side, and Marshall's 30 caliber Marlin lever action deer gun lay on the other, his right index finger still caught in the trigger. A blood encrusted hunting knife was close to the body. Pieces of Marshall's 17-year-old face, and the majority of the gray matter that had been his brain were sprayed in a fan-shaped arc across the walls and floor. A mass of flies, nature's vultures first on death's scene, maintained a constant stream through the broken windows.

Bobby staggered outside into the fresher air and vomited violently.

Bobby stared blankly into the deep thicket of trees on the periphery of the power plant parking lot. There were times when he thanked God for his eyesight. When he looked out over the salt marshes at St. Marks Wildlife Preserve on the Gulf coast—the rippling marsh grasses dotted with islands of palm and palmetto bushes and fingers of brackish water teaming with bird life and alligators. Or, when he studied the dips and valleys of the Appalachian Mountains, blue green and cloud-dappled for miles in the distance. His mind would take a snapshot and store it for the future...to recall and enjoy again.

Unlike the pleasant visual memories he'd stored over his lifetime, Bobby knew that the freeze frame of Marshall's final suicide drama would be permanently burned into his mind's eye. Even if he tried to push it out, it would never leave him. He squeezed his eyes shut.

Within minutes of his call into headquarters, the abandoned power plant grounds swarmed with law enforcement officers.

"Damn it, Bobby! I can't believe you went in there alone!" Rich Burns swore as he paced beside his squad car. "That was really stupid! If he'd been alive, that could've been your brains on the floor!"

Bobby wiped the beads of cold sweat from his face. "I know...I know...I don't know why I did it. I'm sorry I did it!" He rubbed his eyes as if trying to cancel the image in his head. "I'll never get that picture out of my head." He held his pounding temples.

They watched as the swarm of investigators and Jackson County law enforcement ebbed and flowed around the shed.

I watched the local news as I packed a small duffle with fresh underwear and clothes. The hunt for Marshall Thurgood was the lead story. On the video footage, the police headquarters in Chattahoochee teamed with law enforcement and mobs of reporters. Chief Turnbill looked as if he hadn't slept since the abduction.

The doorbell sounded and I bounded down the townhouse stairs. My brother stepped in. "I've been looking all over for you! I thought you'd be up at the hospital." His eyes were red-rimmed.

"I needed some fresh clothes."

He pushed by and loped into the living room.

"Bobby, I really don't have time for a confrontation. I need to hurry on back to the hospital so I'll be there when Jake's doctor makes rounds."

He spun around. His thinning hair stuck out at odd angles, and his shirt looked as if he had worn it for several days. "I need to talk to you, Hattie. Please." His voice sounded ragged.

"So, talk."

"I found Marshall Thurgood."

I watched as my brother, a thorn in my side for over a decade, fell apart in front of my eyes. He sat on the couch and hung his head in his shaking hands, a sigh passing out of his body in a great shudder.

"I can't get that got-damned smell out of my nose. It's like it's burned in there forever. Damn, I could use a drink."

A cold shiver brushed the fine hairs at the base of my neck.

He buried his face in his hands. "The flies! The god-damned flies covered everything!" Beads of acrid sweat clung to his skin. "I puked my guts out. I couldn't stop."

Racking sobs shook his body. I sat next to him and held him, rocking back and forth.

When Bobby finally quieted, he said softly. "I did it for you, Hattie. I know I ain't been much of a brother to you."

I wiped the tears from my cheeks, and for the next four hours, we had the first real conversation with one another since childhood.

THE WAKE

Excerpt from Max the Madhatter's notebook:

January 6, 1956: Sometimes, I have to do things I don't like. Like eat liver. Nurse Marion says that's what dessert is for—to take the taste of something bad from my mouth. I think friends are what takes the bad taste away, too, when the bad comes from somewhere besides the cafeteria.

CHAPTER FOURTEEN

ON THE ELEVATOR, I flipped to the obituary section of the *Tallahassee Democrat* and read:

> **Marshall James Thurgood** of Chattahoochee, Florida, 17, died on July 4th. Graveside services are planned for Wednesday at 2 PM at Mt. Pleasant cemetery on Highway 90. Family will receive friends from 1 to 4 PM Tuesday at the residence of Thomas and Lottie Thurgood.
>
> A native of Chattahoochee, he was a junior at Chattahoochee High School. He is survived by his mother, Louise Thurgood of Chattahoochee and his father, Timothy Thurgood of California, his uncle and aunt, Thomas and Lottie Thurgood, and cousin, Matthew Thurgood. (Memorial Memories Funeral Home: 663-5010)

As I started to enter Jake's hospital room, a young man in a finely tailored charcoal-gray suit stepped out and held the door open for me to pass.

"Who was that?" I asked.

"Pull in your hormones, Josephine, he sings in my choir, not yours."

"Is that your—"

"Dinner partner? Yes. Let's just call him…Mike." Jake smirked. "Not his real name, of course. That man is so far back in his own custom-made closet, I'm surprised he doesn't have a shoehorn crammed permanently up his wazoo!"

I picked up a teetering stack of magazines and plopped down. "I'm surprised you haven't read him the riot act!"

He shrugged. "I used to be all up in your face—queer and here, when I was in New York—all full of righteous indignation and anger. I would've blown the closet doors clean off the hinges of someone like him."

"This is certainly a side of you I haven't seen. You don't try to hide anything yourself, but you put up with it out of your…dinner partner?"

He winced. "I still believe in not hiding—for myself. But, I just feel like each person has a right to decide what floats his, or her, boat. And it's up to that person whether or not to call a press conference about it. It's Mike's own business. Not mine. Not anyone else's."

"It was nice of him to come by and visit you."

Jake motioned to a crystal vase filled with a dozen yellow roses, fern, and baby's breath. "See the flowers he brought the queen?"

I curtsied. "Your highness, how are you going to deal with it when you leave here and don't have everyone waiting on you hand and foot?"

"Piddie and Evelyn have it all planned. I'll stay with them until I get my walking cast. Piddie is going to cook for me, though. She and Evelyn had it out over that one!"

"Speaking of spoiled royalty—you've single-handedly ruined my cat. Margie went up to feed the animals yesterday, and Shammie was piled up in the middle of your comforter with an open bag of kitty treats!"

Jake rolled his eyes boyishly. "Uh-Oh…Miss Fluffinella found my stash by the nightstand."

I propped my hands on my hips. "So! That's how you've bought her affection."

He grinned. "Tuna is a girl's best friend."

I pushed a stack of home design magazines onto the floor and sat down. "Where are the back-up troops from the 'Hooch?"

"Down getting Joe some breakfast. They dragged the poor man over here today without a dab of food! From what Piddie was telling me, he has actually enjoyed eating in the hospital cafeteria. Evelyn's cooking must be pretty dismal."

"She means well. Did you see the news this morning?"

He shook his head. "The nightly drug lord gave me something to help me sleep. I missed the early report. Why?"

"They found Marshall, Jake. He committed suicide. Bobby came and told me the whole story a little before it made the news."

"Sweet Jesus." Jake looked down. A slight tremor shook his hands. "You going to the funeral?" he asked softly.

"No, I don't think I can handle that. It just wouldn't feel right to me. But, I am going to stop by the wake later on today after I catch up a few loose ends over here."

"Please, just…give his family my regards," he said.

Joe and Piddie appeared at the door, and I waved them in. "Good timing. I'm just leaving to head on over to Chattahoochee in a bit."

"We'll keep Jake company today." Piddie said as she studied the flower-infested room. "Lordy! Looks like your shop in here. You're sproutin' more flowers by the minute!"

"Not to mention, the cards," Evelyn said. "Look at the postmarks. I'll bet there's one here from nearly every state!"

"Bet those pink-lady volunteers just love you, what with havin' to drag your loot up here!" Piddie said.

Jake grinned. "Actually, they do!"

In the early afternoon, I pulled my truck into place in front of Lottie and Thomas Thurgood's house.

"Miss Davis! Miss Davis!" a chorus of reporters called as I left my vehicle.

I held up one hand. "No questions, please! Not today!"

A police periphery had been established to corral the media. Rich Burns nodded to a Gadsden County police officer to allow me to pass.

The living room of the Thurgood's house was packed with people milling around and talking in low tones. Thomas conversed with an elderly gentleman. He looked up, caught my eye, and excused himself, nodding his appreciation for the man's condolences.

"Miss Hattie." He shook my hand warmly. "It's so nice of you to stop by."

"Jake wanted me to come." I paused. "I wanted to come."

He motioned toward a study off the main room, and we settled on a small leather couch.

Thomas was clean-shaven and neatly dressed in a coat and tie. Fatigue showed in the downward droop of his thin shoulders. "How is Jake?"

"Better, every day. He's eating well...and we talk a lot about what happened. It's going to take time." I smiled slightly. "I left him with Evelyn, Joe, and Piddie. They're going to watch the Atlanta Braves game together this afternoon."

A smile twitched at the corners of his mouth. "Mama Jean Thurgood and your Aunt Piddie used to wager on those games when Mama was alive."

"Piddie was trying to get Jake to, as well. He told her he wasn't a gambling man."

Thomas studied his massive nicotine-stained hands for a few moments. "My brother Tim called yesterday."

"Is he coming home for the funeral?"

Thomas's eyes watered. "No. He said he couldn't face the press. With the whole story out about Marshall and the family troubles, he just couldn't handle being portrayed as the gay father who deserted his young son. He's carryin' a heavy load of guilt, he told me, always will."

"You think he might come back after this dies down?" The cloying scent of flowers permeated the small room. I breathed through my mouth to avoid gagging.

"I don't know. I left the door open. I don't think even Louise would rail against him. She's not the same woman she was years ago. She's taken on some of the blame, too."

"Is she here? I'd like to speak to her...give her Jake and my condolences."

Thomas reached over and held my hand in his. For a moment, I felt like a little girl with her daddy. His large bony hand dwarfed my smaller one.

"I'll be sure to tell her for you, Miss Hattie. It will mean a lot. Dr. Kennedy had to give her a mild sedative. She's had such a bad time of it. She's so scared she'll start hittin' the bottle again. Lottie and I have moved her in here with us—at least for a while. Her friends in AA have been so kind. They've been here from the beginnin'. 'Course, I don't pry as to which folks are in her group—some of 'em have told me. I don't know who her sponsor is."

"Is your son going to be allowed to attend the funeral?" I asked.

He dropped his gaze. "They're still debating that. He may get to come under guard."

"Mr. Thurgood, I'm not going to Marshall's funeral. I just can't do it right now...so close after Mama's."

Thomas patted my hand. "Of course, Hattie. I know how I felt after losing my mama. Are you heading back to the hospital then?"

"Probably not until late tomorrow. I want to clean up the shop a little. Jake'll be exposed to the pictures in the magazines and papers, but I don't want him to have to actually see the shop that way. I don't want to wait for the insurance company to send someone in. That could take awhile. Evelyn and I are going to start on it tomorrow. Piddie and Joe will go back over and stay another day with Jake."

We stood. Thomas guided me into the living room. "Miss Hattie, let me show you something." He led me toward a towering arrangement of flowers: bird of paradise, palms, and exotic topical blooms. "This came a little while ago—delivered by a nice florist from Tallahassee." He removed the small white card that read: *With heartfelt sympathy for your family, Jake Witherspoon.*

I looked up to Thomas Thurgood's weary brown eyes, speechless.

Early the following morning, I met Evelyn at the shop. Once the police had cleared the crime scene, I was allowed, as a shop owner, to reenter the building. I stepped carefully over the broken pot shards and display case glass and sighed heavily. What the vandalism hadn't destroyed, painted, or shattered, the investigators had. Fingerprint dust smudged every surface, and bits of flowers, dead plants, and food from the sweet shop had been crushed underfoot. Since the door to my massage room had been closed at the time of the attack, Jake's forest mural had been spared.

Evelyn stood, indignant, with her hands propped on her hips. "Just look at my draperies! Those boys painted all across the windows! They'll have to be remade!"

I plopped a bucket of supplies on the floor. "It'll take us hours to clean up all of this mess, but I can't have Jake coming home to face this." I sighed. "Guess we better get started."

Before too long, a rap sounded on the front glass door. "We're closed!" I called.

The insistent knocking continued. A crowd of people stood at the door.

"What the...?" I picked my way across the floor and flipped the latch.

"Miss Hattie," Lucille Jackson said, "we're here to help."

One by one, five women and four men from the black community filed through the door carrying buckets, rags, cleaning supplies, brooms, and mops.

"I...don't..." I began.

Thurston Jackson II put up his hand. "We want to help out, now, Miss Hattie. Mr. Jake's been awful good to all of us. He's come through many times for our community. Plus, your mama tutored my son. He was failing down at the elementary school a couple of years back. I don't know how she did it, but she lit a fire under my boy. He reads up a storm, now. All of us want to help you and Mr. Jake. He surely doesn't need to come home to see this right off!"

The group scattered into the shop and began to load debris into heavy-duty trash bags. After a half-hour, a second group appeared outside the shop. Six members of my mother's ladies circle waltzed in carrying wicker baskets filled with sandwiches, brownies, and drinks, as well as buckets of cleaning supplies.

"Well," Elvina Houston commented eyeing the roomful of people.

"Looks like we're gonna have ourselves a party!"

Evelyn whispered in my ear, "Mama's going to be fit to be tied when she and Joe come back from Tallahassee and find out Elvina's been up here cleaning,"

"Maybe, but she can always take shelter in the fact that she was keeping an important bedside vigil at the hospital," I said.

Evelyn's eyes lit up. "Looka here! It's that writer friend of Mama's from New York!" She dropped the cleaning rag and smoothed the wrinkles in her peach-colored linen dress.

For the first time in my life, I wished I was someone else. Anyone else. I've never really been known for my incredibly good looks—more the nice personality, good sense of humor type of girl. Even at its coifed and sprayed best, my medium-length sandy brown hair was average. My eyes were just green, not the startling crystal blue of my mother's or aunt's. I was neither willowy tall, nor stumpy and short. I wasn't thin, or heavy. Just average, average, average.

"Mr. Lewis!" Evelyn gushed. "How nice to see you again!"

Holston Lewis walked behind the florist counter and extended his hand. "My pleasure, Mrs. Evelyn."

Evelyn's hand fluttered bird-like at the base of her throat. I wanted to thump her back into reality. "My!" she finally said. "Where are my manners? You've met Hattie, of course."

His dark eyes rested on me. A slow burn started in the pit of my stomach and moved lower.

Evelyn's eyes glistened. "And, the rest of these fine folks are our dear friends and neighbors. Are you here to do an interview for your book?"

He glanced around the room filled with busy people. "Actually, I'm here to help."

"Well!" Evelyn said. "Come on, and we'll find you a bucket and sponge!" She led Holston around the room, introducing him as she went.

I stood, speechless and stunned—unfamiliar feelings for me. Holston flashed a warm smile over his shoulder in my direction. A heat rush gushed all the way to my big toes. Though I smelled a lavender-haired matchmaking rat, I loved my Aunt Piddie intensely at that moment.

Before the end of the day, we had cleaned, scrubbed, and touched up the damaged paint. After most of the helpers had left, I painted over the bleached remainder of the dark red dried bloodstain at the back entrance. Even though Jake would have to reorder flowers and restock the sweet shop, the store was sparkling clean and renewed. Before he and Mrs. Lucille left, Thurston Jackson II said a blessing prayer for the "protection and healing of the wounds to the spirit" inside of the shop. The biggest surprise of the day came when Bobby and Leigh stopped by to measure the display cases for replacement glass.

THE HOMECOMING

Sweet Chocolate Treats for the Youngin's

Ingredients: 1 cup brown sugar, 1 cup white sugar, ½ cup milk, 1 tspn vanilla, ½ cup cocoa powder, 3 cups oats, 1 cup shredded coconut, ½ cup chopped walnuts.

In a saucepan over medium heat, combine brown sugar, white sugar, cocoa powder and milk. Stir until sugar is dissolved. Pour into bowl. Stir in vanilla, oatmeal, coconut, and walnuts. Cool to room temperature. Shape into 1½ inch balls, and roll in sugar. Store in airtight container in single layers between waxed paper.

Make certain that these treats are kept in a cookie jar far above any child's reach or you won't have any left for yourself!

CHAPTER FIFTEEN

BY THE TIME the paperwork for Jake's release from the fourth floor was completed, the steadily building heat of a mid-July north Florida day was sending waves of radiance through the humidity-thick air. Ushered by a throng of his new medical friends, Jake's wheelchair-led procession of well wishers, bobbing helium balloons, and pink lady volunteers pushing flower-laden carts extended for several feet.

"I'm so glad you brought the Lincoln, sister-girl. I can't imagine riding home in your little pick-up with all these plants and flowers."

"The queen in a commoner's cart? Never!" I helped him maneuver his splinted leg into the passenger seat of Evelyn's car. "I talked Evelyn and Piddie into letting me come to bring you home. Thought you'd rather have a few minutes of peace and quiet before you're barraged with people. You can thank me later."

"You betcha. No matter what, the ride home will certainly be an improvement over the ride here." Jake glanced out into the vehicles ebbing and flowing on Centerville Road.

"I saw that incredible arrangement at Marshall's wake," I said as I butted the Lincoln into the flow of lunch hour traffic. "How the heck did you get them delivered so fast? I'd just left you a few hours before."

"Piddie," Jake answered.

"Piddie?"

"She called my friend, Jesica, from Blossom's, and told her the story. By the time she was finished, poor dear Jesica not only agreed to create the arrangement to Piddie's specifications, but to personally deliver it to the wake herself! That woman could talk the fuzz off a peach."

"She never ceases to amaze me."

We chatted absently while I navigated the sea of cars, SUVs and delivery trucks. After I merged onto the westbound lane of Interstate 10, I noticed I had been talking to myself. Lulled by the smooth hum of the powerful engine, Jake was sound asleep.

"We home yet?" Jake asked when I slowed forty minutes later to make the sharp turn off State 269. He smiled when he saw the rambling old white house atop the hill. "What a welcome sight."

A small crowd of press cameramen and reporters stepped aside to allow the Lincoln to pass. I parked as close as possible to the concrete walkway leading to the front door.

"Just wave and tell them you are doing well," I instructed. "No comment seems to work pretty well, too."

Jake balanced carefully on the crutches and beamed at the gathering. "Thank you all for coming to welcome me home!" A jumble of questions erupted from the crowd.

Jake held up his hand. "There's a pot of chicken'n dumplin's calling my name right behind that door." He pointed dramatically to the kitchen entrance. "As much as I'd really love to stay and make my Hollywood debut, that's more important to me right now!"

Evelyn opened the door. "He's home!"

"I got eyes, Evelyn. I can see he's home." Piddie said. "Come on in! You must be starvin'.'"

In the true Southern tradition of weddings, funerals, and home-comings, members of the surrounding communities had brought enough food to feed a small army. The table was laden with an array of dishes: Stephanie's sweet-potato soufflé topped with rainbow-colored marsh-mallows, Elvina Houston's Shepard's pie, Mandy's famous tuna with English pea casserole, homegrown tomatoes and bread'n'butter pickles from Julie, an oversized pot of freshly picked turnip and mustard greens and creamed sweet corn from the Jacksons, Piddie's chicken'n dumplin's and cathead biscuits, and Evelyn's Heal Your Heart Chakra Frittata.

Jake clasped his hands. "It's like Christmas!"

Joe nodded. "There's more in the refrigerator. You won't believe all the food folks have been bringing out."

Piddie added. "The Reverend Ghent and his wife, Sara, brought a congealed ambrosia salad. They'll come out later on—once you've had a chance to settle in."

Townspeople continued to visit in a constant stream bringing food, drinks, ice, and supplies of paper plates, cups, and napkins. Finally, Evelyn and Joe corralled Piddie into the Lincoln and headed for town. Sensing that all events worthy of news had transpired, the media packed and left as well.

Bobby, Leigh, Jake, and I surveyed the kitchen. The local women had cleaned the dishes, removed the leftover food to the refrigerator, and made a freshly brewed carafe of decaffeinated coffee.

Jake raised his hand like a second grader with the right answer. "You know what I want most right now?"

All three of us jumped up at one time.

Jake laughed. "Wow! This is great! It's like having a remote con-trol!" He paused. "I want to go sit by the pond and watch the sun melt into the horizon."

Bobby helped Jake onto the bench seat of John and Margie's ATV, leaving Leigh and me to follow on foot. When we reached the pond, Bobby carried Jake in his arms and negotiated the steep, grassy steps.

"Ewwww…" Jake pinched Bobby's biceps. "You're such a strong man!"

Bobby nearly lost his balance. "Careful, Princess, I'll chunk you right down this hill into the water!"

"Don't worry, Bobby-boy. You're not my type," Jake said with a wicked grin.

Leigh and I chuckled as we hopped down the steps behind them.

The oppressive heat of the summer day began to break, and a cool stillness descended on the woods. Occasionally, the snap of a twig in the underbrush behind the dam broke the serenity. Soon, the deep bass croaks of the bullfrogs and the higher chirps of the peepers would reverberate around the water's edge.

"Miz Evelyn's frittata looked…interesting," Leigh said.

Jake laughed. "I'm pretty sure that color doesn't exist in nature."

I nodded. "Piddie pulled me aside and warned me not to dare touch it. Evelyn got the recipe from her new cookbook, *Channeled Recipes for Cosmic Healing*. Piddie said it had one of those triangular-headed, bug-eyed green guys on the front cover."

We shared a chuckle.

"I sniffed it," Leigh said. Her tanned nose crinkled. "I picked up the scent of curry—and, maybe mint? And, something else I couldn't identify."

I held up both hands. "Being a child of the '70's, and somewhat familiar with this—not that I ever partook, mind you—but, I could swear the crumpled brown herb under the top layer of cheese was marijuana!"

Jake, Leigh, and Bobby regarded me with wide eyes.

I added. "That is…if I didn't know Evelyn the way I do. She'd die before she broke the law. She's such a rule-abiding sphincter queen; she wouldn't sleep nights if she didn't return a shopping cart to its corral in the parking lot at Wal-Mart!"

Jake nodded. "Say what you will about Evelyn, but she and Piddie have been so good to me. Piddie was my savior while I was laid up in the hospital. She smuggled food in to me every time they came over. Evelyn always checked with the nurses to make sure I could have it, of course."

Jake rested his gaze on the still water of the one-acre fishpond. "I wish I could recuperate out here instead of uptown."

"I know you do, Jake, but I'm going to be staying some in Tallahassee starting next week. My massage clients over there think I've deserted them. It wouldn't be good for you to be out here on the Hill alone. Sure, Margie and John are fairly close by, but it still wouldn't be a good idea."

"What about the kids?" he asked.

"Margie has volunteered to feed Spam and Shammie for the few days I'll be gone," I said. "I'll pick you up as soon as I get home on Wednesday evening."

Leigh smiled and patted Jake on the back. Her dark blue eyes twinkled. "I can come by and drag you out of house after I get off from work. We'll find something to get into."

"And, it'll be only for a few weeks until you have a walking splint on your leg," I added.

Jake sighed. "All right. I'm going to start ordering for the shop next week. Mrs. Tamara Johnson's son, Harrison, wants a job as the delivery person until school starts back. I'll have to hire someone to help with the sweet shop customers. I want to go back to work as soon as I can; I can still hobble around and do my flowers!"

Bobby chewed on a sprig of grass. "I could run you to work in the morning on my way out until you can drive again."

"See! It'll all work out," I said. "You know Evelyn and Joe will pitch in, too."

Leigh grinned. "Piddie told me she's going to be overseeing the cooking so you don't end up back in intensive care."

"Poor Miss Hapless Gourmet Evelyn. Am I the only one who understands her? She's just trying to find a way to shine for her mama. I spent years trying to do the same." Jake shifted his weight and winced.

"You need to go on back up to the house, bud?" Bobby asked.

"Bud? Imagine that! Bobby Davis calling me his bud! A few minutes ago you were threatening to chunk me in the pond!"

Bobby smirked.

Jake laughed. "No, I'm fine. I just have to change positions every now and then when my hip starts to rumba. Oh, I forgot to tell you guys—they want to turn this whole ordeal of mine into a made-for-TV drama! Can you believe that?"

"Wow, doesn't take the circling vultures long to zero-in on a potential profit," I snapped. "You going to sell the story?"

Jake shrugged and skipped a flat pebble over the water's surface.

"It's already been plastered all over the newspapers and magazines. This little town has been through a lot. On the other hand, it might help to raise awareness. Maybe keep something like it from happening to someone else."

"One thing I wondered about. That twin thing. One gay and one straight. I've never even heard of such," Bobby said.

"Why would you, Bobby-boy? Not exactly your frame of reference." Jake winked. "I don't have any statistics to quote, but I personally know four sets of identical twins where one is salt and the other, pepper."

"Did anyone hear what's going on with Matt Thurgood?" I asked.

Bobby nodded. "Only bits and pieces from Rich Burns. I'm sure we'll all hear more later on. Since he wasn't involved in the abduction and final assault and hasn't had any prior trouble with the law, his attorney will try to keep the case in the juvenile justice system. Rich says that, given the high profile of the crime and the national outcry, he may be tried and sentenced as an adult."

Leigh shook her head sadly. "That would mean prison time, no doubt."

Jake toyed with a sprig of dry grass. "I don't know how I feel about all of that. I know he can't get off with just a slap on the wrist, but it seems so awful to have his life ruined by sending him off to be around thugs."

Bobby's face turned red with emotion. "Lord have mercy, Jake! The boy was in on wrecking your shop—and your life, for that matter! How can you be so damn forgiving?"

"I just think there should be a way for it to come out, somehow, I don't know…less tragic. Matt never struck me as being a mean kid—just one that was pushed around. He made the mistake of following the wrong person. Besides, everyone around here has sure been busy making me look like Mother Teresa!" Jake retorted. "I'm not perfect. There were times when I lived in New York when I didn't give a flying shit about anyone but myself. I could've easily been like Matt, given a different set of circumstances. I'm not a saint!" He grinned. "Although, I would look fetching in a flowing white robe."

The awkward silence was broken when Spam slapped at the edge of the water, chasing a frog.

"He can move like a puppy when he wants to," Bobby said.

I jumped up and burst into song. *"I wanna tell you all a story 'bout a dog named Spam—"*

"You ain't never been right," Bobby said after I completed the Florida Cracker Dog Song and took a bow.

Spam dashed back and forth, sending sprays of water into the air. For a few moments, we were silent, enjoying the balmy evening.

"You know," Jake began. "I dream about it. Joe says it's Posttraumatic Stress Syndrome. I see Marshall's demented face...so close I can see every pore of his skin and the line of spittle on the corners of his mouth." Jake shuddered, and I put my arm around his shoulders. "In the dream, I'm not gagged. I'm talking and talking to him, trying to talk him down—telling him my name is Jake. I'm not who you want to hurt! Please, hear me!"

Bobby ran a hand through his thin hair. "I don't know if he would've listened, Jake. Drunk and mean is a bad combination."

"I just felt so helpless. He was beating the life out of me, and there wasn't a damn thing I could do to stop it!" Jake wiped the tears forming at the corners of his eyes. "Joe insists that I see a counselor, and I will. I just look forward to a time when I can close my eyes at night and not see his face."

Bobby nodded. "There're some things your mind just burns into your memory."

Leigh reached over and grasped Bobby's hand.

Jake breathed deeply. "Anyway, Piddie has hooked up with a book author she has fallen in love with, I think. Some guy named Holster or something—"

"Holston Lewis," I said, my voice a tad too dreamy.

Jake raised one eyebrow. "Well, do I sniff the Virgin Queen perhaps coming out of her early forced retirement?"

"I just met him, Jake."

Jake snuffled. "Then, I suppose you won't be interested in the fact that I am considering granting him exclusive book rights to the story."

I shook my head. "I thought you didn't want to have anything to do with all of that."

"If Piddie is right about him, he's the only one I'd want to write it. You know someone will, and, if I can depend on him not to portray Chattahoochee as some hick Southern town full of half-breeds bent on hate, I want him to handle it."

Jake studied the orange reflection of the sunset mirrored on the pond's surface. "And, sister-girl, as far as your obvious attraction to Mr. Lewis goes—one thing I decided through this ordeal—I will not close myself off to love anymore. When I came back to Chattahoochee after the Countess Witherspoon passed away, I was searching for a place to hide away from the world. I do love this place. But, I will not allow myself to bury my heart anymore...and neither should you."

A bullfrog thumped a deep bass note and was quickly joined by several more. Soon, the air was filled with the evening frog opera.

I pointed to a rusted pole on the far end of the dam. "You know, my dad used to have an intercom receiver over there so he could lie in bed at night and listen to this."

Bobby chuckled. "Used to drive Mama nuts."

Leigh traced her fingers across Bobby's chin. "It's good sometimes to remember the past."

Jake slapped a hand on his left knee. "Speaking of remembering the past—the other reoccurring dream I've had since the attack is one where I am walking down Washington Street repeating the names of the shops, over and over, and sometimes stopping to tell some inane little story about the owner. I wonder what that all means?"

It took a moment to connect. All the hours I'd spent recounting the town's history to Jake as he lay unconscious. I started to laugh– hard. I snorted and tried to catch my breath. The puzzled expressions on their faces only made me laugh harder. Pretty soon, they joined me, caught up in my craziness, not sure what the heck was so funny.

THE MADHATTER'S FESTIVAL

Everyone's Favorite Chocolate Cake by Piddie Longman

Ingredients: ½ cup margarine (I love to use real butter), ½ cup oil, 2¼ cup white sugar, 2 eggs, 2/3 cup cocoa, 2 ½ cups flour, self-rising, 2 cups buttermilk, 1 tsp vanilla.

Mix your margarine, oil and eggs until just soft. Add the sugar and vanilla. Dab some vanilla behind your ears to make you smell good like baking day. Sift your cocoa and flour together. Then, alternate mixing in the buttermilk and dry ingredients into the margarine/egg/oil blend. Beat until the lumps are smoothed out.

Bake in a 350°F oven for 35 minutes. I use a greased bundt pan. After it has cooled, top with my Best Damned Icing.

CHAPTER SIXTEEN

October 21st, Two Years Later

I STOOD ON the west bank of the Apalachicola River watching the coffee-brown water churn in muddy swirls over the submerged concrete boat ramp a few feet from the base of the old Victory Bridge. Though the river was broad at this point, the swift current often made launching a light boat an interesting proposition.

Indian Summer heat and humidity had recently given way to the pleasant, clear blue-sky days of late October. A cool breeze kissed my cheeks. The predictably cooperative weather had been the main factor in the city manager's decision to officially slot the third weekend in the month for the annual Madhatter's Festival.

A broad grassy meadow near the landing was surrounded by sprawling ancient live oak trees festooned with hanks of Spanish moss, a stringy, gray parasitic plant we called witch's hair when we were young and trying to scare the bejeezus out of each other at Halloween. A black and white-checked welcome banner hung across the entrance to the grounds with the festival's title, year, and an enlargement of a line drawing of Max the Madhatter gleaned from an old black and white print from the *Twin City News* archives. Jake's standing sprays of red and white carnations adorned the covered performance stage, and all of the food and craft booths were decorated in a red and white picnic theme. Huge black wire and papier-mâché ants, Jake's and Stephanie's creation, were scattered randomly between the stage and seating area.

Since Jake's abduction and assault, a change had washed slowly over Chattahoochee. Driven by the national media frenzy, people from across the country had visited the town. The release of Holston Lewis's book, *Twin Tragedy of the Twin Cities: the Jake Witherspoon Story*, focused the spotlight on our area.

Sensing the small-town appeal and potential for profit, an investor from south Florida had purchased a section of vacant buildings on Washington Street and created the Madhatter's Antique Mall. Small specialty shops had recently opened, selling antique glassware, silver jewelry, and hand-thrown pottery. The shop owners had created a committee to beautify Washington Street. The proceeds from the festival, after expenses, were added to the renewal fund. The first Madhatter's festival had provided money for new sidewalks, faux antique pole lanterns, and wrought iron park benches. A brick paved courtyard with a center fountain, benches, and a flower garden were planned for a vacant lot a block down from our shop. Similar to the town of Havana, Florida, north of Tallahassee, Chattahoochee was evolving into an arts and antique center.

As a result of the influx of business, housing sales had increased. Several antebellum homes had been renovated. Surrounded by rose gardens and neatly trimmed hedges, the newly opened Madhatter's B&B welcomed guests to a cheerful house that had once been a dilapidated eyesore a block from downtown.

I turned from my vigil of the river to watch the frenzied activity. A total of sixty-five arts and craft booths were scattered under the overhanging arms of the giant trees, twice last year's number. As the day progressed, the crowd would grow in size, sending a mixture of bluegrass music from the covered stage and laughter filtering through the air.

Jake wove his way through the throng, moving as quickly as his cane and the uneven ground would permit. At last count, he owned thirty canes: an eclectic assortment of intricately carved oak and cherry, chrome, and fantastically painted wooden walking aides. Once Elvina Houston spread the word of Jake's passion for variety, he'd received canes every month. Sometimes, he would find them propped against the alley entrance to the shop with a hand scrawled 'get well' note. For special occasions such as today, he used his favorite—a black, pearl-handled cane—Piddie's homecoming gift.

Rich Burns waved from across the meadow. The local deputies were on duty, parking cars and milling through the crowd for security. Rich pointed to his shoulder and pantomimed extreme pain. Must have been out target practicing for too long—always his shoulder and forearm. I'd have to call him and get him in soon.

A sense of deep connection flowed over me. For the majority of my life, I'd known many of the vendors and locals who had come out to enjoy the food, music, and pleasant weather. Because today was to be special for Jake, I had invited the nurses, doctors, law-enforcement officers, and emergency personnel who had been involved with his case. My friends from Tallahassee were in attendance, along with many of my massage-therapy clients from both Tallahassee and Chattahoochee.

Rich Burns had been on target with his prediction concerning my massage-therapy practice in town. A trickle at first, it had developed into a steady stream. Elvina Houston, Piddie, Evelyn, Bobby, Joe, and Leigh blazed the trail initially. Shop owners, city officials, and hospital employees followed. Although many of my male clients waited until a strained muscle or sore back drove their wives or girlfriends to make an appointment, the females came regularly.

Bit by bit, I gleaned the details of their families and daily struggles, shared in confidence during the sessions. Though I strived to maintain a level of professional distance, the act of providing safe, relaxing touch to another human created a bond. Stephanie, formerly of the Homeplace Restaurant, was now a licensed massage therapist. Using her hard-earned tips, she had attended night school in Tallahassee. After passing her national board examination and receiving a Florida license, she added her practice to our shop, using the treatment room on the days when I was out of town.

I waded into the crowd toward Jake.

"Sister-girl!" Jake called, "Isn't it great this year? Our booth is swarming with people buying *The Madhatter's Guide to Chocolate*. I'm goin' to have to put in a print order, again." He wiped a chocolate crumb from the corner of his mouth. "Michele Newman from Quincy sold two of her queen-sized quilts to the new family who moved into the old Jones house. And, have you seen the redneck wind chimes? They're just flattened beer cans hanging from a piece of driftwood, and they're selling like mad!"

"I'll have to buy some for the shop," I joked.

Jake's blue eyes twinkled with mischief. "I'll be sure to hang them smack dab in the middle of your treatment room, if you do." He scanned the crowd. "Where's that love-struck brother of yours?"

"Flat on his back with a terrible head cold. My future sister-in-law—God willing—is nursing him back to health." I crossed my fingers.

Jake shook his head. "Too bad. I actually look forward to being around Bobby. Amazing how sobering up and finding the love of your life can change a guy." His eyebrows shot up. "Guess who I spotted in the parking lot?" He paused dramatically. "Just a certain beautiful male author from New York…"

I scanned the crowd. "Holston? Holston's here?" I turned back to Jake. "Don't give me that look. I barely know the man. He only emailed me when he couldn't get information out of you."

"Who do you think you're foolin'? I may have had a head injury, but I could be deeply affected mentally and still see the look on your face every time his name comes up."

I snorted.

Jake swung his cane in a circle. "I know something you don't!"

I grabbed the end of the cane, stopping it in midair. "Give it up, Jake."

"Easy, easy! You'll tip your hormonal balance." Jake wrestled the cane from my hand. "You know I told you that Mama's mansion was up for sale again? Well, you'll never guess who picked it up for a song!" His eyes glittered.

"Okay. Who?"

"You are just a tidbit irritable today, sister-girl. That peevish look really doesn't work well for you." He patted my shoulder. "The buyer is just your future husband from New York City! And, this is going to bite your butt. He has hired me to decorate after the repairs are completed. Is that not so circular?"

Holston Lewis living in Chattahoochee?

Jake motioned toward the stage. "C'mon, go with. I was heading over to get Piddie."

Aunt Piddie rested on an upholstered, red taffeta-covered, high back chair, the queen of all chocolate cake judges. Numbered plates of sliced layer cake were scattered half-eaten on the table in front of her.

Elvina Houston stood beside the booth, officiously recording Piddie's comments. "I think we have a winner," she said. "Wouldn't have been who I would've chosen, but…"

Piddie snatched the tally from Elvina's thin hand. "Just give it over, Elvina, for God's sake! It's not like I asked you to help pick the next president."

Jake leaned over the table. "C'mon Piddie! Let's start over toward the stage. They'll need you to announce the winner of the Best Damn Cake and Icing Contest." He helped Piddie with her walker, and we started slowly toward the performance stage.

At the podium, our squat, pompous mayor, Jimmy T. Johnson, cleared his throat into the microphone.

"Oh, Lord help," Piddie remarked. "We'll be here all afternoon if that windbag gets started up."

Evelyn and Joe walked up, carrying folding chairs. "Shhh…Mama! Someone'll hear you!" Evelyn said in a loud whisper. They walked ahead to the ground in front of the stage, and set the chairs in place.

Jimmy T. cleared his throat and tapped on the microphone before he spoke. "This working? Well, suppose it is, now. As Mayor of Chattahoochee, I'd like to thank all of you for attending the second annual Madhatter's Festival. As best as we can tell, we have over 2,000 people here this year!"

A smattering of applause sounded from the audience.

"Before I call Mrs. Piddie Longman to the stage to announce this years' chocolate cake and icing winner—"

"That's *best damn* chocolate cake and icing, Jimmy T.!" Piddie yelled. The crowd laughed.

The mayor paused. "Yes…well. I stand corrected. I'd like to thank all the sponsors who have been instrumental in making this festival a success: City of Chattahoochee, The Madhatter's Antique Mini Mall, the Downtown Merchant's Committee, and the Dragonfly Florist and Madhatter's Sweet Shop and Massage Parlor."

Mayor Johnson paused to allow the applause to subside.

"At this time, I ask Hattie Davis, co-owner of the Madhatter's Sweet Shop and Massage Parlor to join me at the podium."

Jake's eyes were round with suspicion. "What are you up to, sister-girl?"

"You'll see." I patted him on the back and wove through the crowd to the stage. From the higher vantage point, I spotted Holston Lewis smiling up at me. A lump the size of China formed in my throat. Good thing I didn't have to speak.

"In the past two years," the mayor continued, "our city has seen an amazing revival. We've profited from a boom in local business openings, and have welcomed many fine folks into our community. The City of Chattahoochee would like to honor one of its native sons, a man who has been an ambassador and promoter for our town…Mr. Jake Witherspoon!"

The crowd exploded with applause and whistles.

Piddie punched Jake playfully in the arm. "Get on up there!"

Jake inched slowly to the stage. "Remind me to slap you silly, later, sister-girl," he mumbled as he stepped to the podium.

"Hattie Davis and I now join in presenting Jake Witherspoon with the key to the city!" We handed the three foot gold key ceremoniously to Jake.

"Speech! Speech!" Piddie called. The crowd echoed her demand.

I gave Jake a gentle nudge toward the microphone.

For a moment, he studied the audience, purposely looking in every direction. "I feel a little emotional right now." He mimed dabbing the corners of his eyes with an imaginary hankie. "There are so many people in my life to whom I would like to extend my deepest appreciation and love. Thanks to Hattie Davis, they all seem to be here today. Hmmm..." He rubbed his square chin as if in thought. Laughter trickled through the gathering.

"I love this town, always have. Everyone knows each other. It was that fact that I credit with saving my life." He searched out Ashley Wood, who stood next to her fiancée, and nodded in her direction. "Hattie and I have talked a lot about the history of Chattahoochee. This town has always opened its arms and hearts to different types of people."

"Now we're stuck with the likes of you!" A voice called out from the edge of the crowd.

Jake identified the heckler. "You best watch out, Officer Burns, or I'll tell your wife, Carol, just how many iced cake brownies you eat in a week!"

Laughter rippled through the audience. Carol Burns playfully punched her husband in the shoulder, making him wince.

Jake continued, "Chattahoochee deserves to grow and prosper...just not so much that we ever lose contact with our neighbors. I do believe, if Max the Madhatter could be here right now, he'd love what's happened to Washington Street, especially our sweet shop! Thank you all deeply, from the bottom of my heart!"

The crowd cheered as Jake held up the key, then awkwardly executed his best curtsy.

"Now," the mayor said, "let's have Mrs. Piddie Longman up on stage!"

Joe and Evelyn helped Piddie to maneuver the steps onto the platform.

"Good afternoon!" she called out to the crowd.

Several people in the audience good-afternooned back.

"Before I announce the winner of the Best Damn Chocolate Cake and Icing Contest, I've thought of a little story to tell y'all. It's about the time my daughter, Evelyn, tried to make Joe, her husband, a five-layered chocolate cake for his birthday. Now, I know some of the firefighters in the crowd will remember this one..."

"Have mercy," Evelyn muttered.

124

RENOVATION

Excerpt from Max the Madhatter's notebook:

April 23, 1956: I like to play dominoes. We don't play them in the ward like the game is supposed to be—lining up the dots so the numbers match. Nurse Marion taught us to put them in a straight line on the floor like little soldiers marching. Then, you tap the first one and they all click down, one by one! I just set them up again and again to watch how one tipping over makes all the rest fall.

CHAPTER SEVENTEEN

GARRETT DOUGLAS STEPPED into Cabo's Tacos on Lafayette Street in Tallahassee, sweeping the crowded dining area with the baby-kissing smile of a Leon County politician running for a heavily disputed election. His gaze finally settled on the corner booth where I sprawled, nursing a bottle of light beer and a scowl.

"Sorry, Hattie." Garrett removed his custom-tailored suit jacket and flung it loosely across the end of his side of the booth. "I had a last-minute call I had to take."

I shook my head. "You know, this used to be the one thing that just ate me alive about you, Garrett. Everyone else's time was always less important than yours."

He held up his hands in surrender. "Guilty as charged. I'll buy you dinner to make up for my one unfortunate character flaw." All fifty of his mega-watt incisors beamed at me at once.

"Damn, Garrett. Did you have your teeth bleached again?"

He rolled his eyes, then motioned to our waitress. "I'll have a Dos

Equus with a twist of lime, and, let's see…an order of chicken nachos with guac' and sour cream, please." He studied my face in the dim light. "You look tired."

"I've been doing massage therapy all day. Tends to wear me out. My shoulders were killing me by the end of the day. Luckily, Anna fit me in for a quick shoulder fix. Best perk of the job. I can usually get one of my coworkers to help me out when I get stressed. Of course, I return the favor in kind."

"You have one of your football players in today?"

"No, just an array of stressed-out computer-tortured state employ-ees."

I sipped my beer and dipped one of Cabo's tortilla chips into the homemade hot salsa. The flavors of onion, tomato, jalapeno pepper, and cilantro filtered over my tongue. Though I had never been well known at any of the capital city's pubs, the personnel at a few of Tallahassee's eateries knew me by name and favorite food. It warmed my heart to have a server smile when I entered the room, knowing that a tall glass of unsweetened iced tea with lemon would be in front of me when I sat down. Here, we went through the same dance each time. I would be handed a menu to peruse, my tea would appear, and they would wait for my order as if they didn't know I always had the bean burrito wet supreme, hold the onions, with hot salsa. I had stressed them this after-noon by ordering a beer.

Garrett took a long swig of the imported beer the waitress had delivered. "You heading back to the country in the morning?"

"Thought I'd go on back tonight. I couldn't catch up with any of my friends to play on a Friday night, so I'll beat it back to the Hill."

He pointed to the bottle in my hand. "Better not drink too many of those, then."

"You know me better than that, Garrett. Piddie says she's pretty sure someone rings a victory bell in hell every time I drink, I do it so sel-dom. Besides, after two of these, I would probably be underneath some-one's chair with my shirt half off, singing a sappy love song at the top of my lungs."

Garrett's movie-star laugh emanated deep within his chest and res-onated like shock waves from a pebble skipped over smooth water.

Several of Cabo's patrons turned to enjoy the sound, smiling in his direction. The man should have been either an evangelical preacher or a Southern political icon. No wonder I had once been swept up in his charismatic web.

"So, Mr. Douglas. Don't keep me in suspense. Why did you call me for dinner? Need advice for the lovelorn today? Or, are you just feeling lonely?"

Garrett scowled. "You can be so sarcastic sometimes, Hattie. It really is quite unbecoming. Maybe I just wanted to see you. We are friends, after all."

I ran my hands wearily through my hair, then let them fall heavily onto the countertop. "I'm sorry. I'm tired and ready to head home. I shouldn't take it out on you."

Garrett reached over and covered my hands with his. "Maybe you should stay at the townhouse tonight instead of driving to Chattahoochee."

"No, I told Jillie I wouldn't be staying. I think one of her study groups is meeting there tonight. I have to hand it to you as far as she goes, Garrett. I don't worry even a second about leaving my property here under her watch. She's repainted her room and bathroom, cleans like a fiend when she's not crouched over the books, and has even fixed the leaky flush valve in the downstairs half-bath."

"Her mother did a great job of raising her. I can't claim too much credit, unfortunately. We've been able to spend some decent time together since she's been up here attending FSU. I'm just pleased that she's not living over close to campus. I don't worry about her too much in your neighborhood."

Garrett cleared his throat. Something urged me to lean forward and listen carefully. The sound was Garrett's this-is-really-what-I'm-setting-you-up-for signal.

"Actually, I did want to speak to you about something."

Here we go! Lock up the little old ladies. Hide your women. Get those wagons in a circle!

"Hattie? You with me?" Garrett asked.

"All ears."

"I would like to buy your townhouse for Jillie. As a gift. She'll be graduating next fall, and plans to stay on for her master's studies, maybe even law school. She hasn't decided on that part yet. I'd like to provide her with her first home."

I stared at him in disbelief. "Gee, I don't know. I hadn't thought that far ahead. Right now, I kinda like having a place over here."

Garrett flashed a smile. "C'mon, Hattie. I've noticed you spending more and more time in Gadsden County. Admit it. You really want to move over there full time."

Amazing how someone outside of your skin can nail a situation. The Hill had slowly wormed its way into my concept of home. It was the place where I kept my electric toothbrush. My best underwear. My rattiest jeans. My cat!

"I really hadn't given any thought to selling it, Garrett."

The waitress arrived with our food. Because the noisy surroundings didn't call for his best manners, Garrett dug into the mountain of nachos with his fingers and crammed a mouthful of the Mexican goo into his mouth. "You don't have to give me an answer now. Just let me have first dibs when you sell." He said around a mouthful.

"If I sell."

Garrett stopped chewing long enough to give me a conspiratorial wink. "Right."

Without conscious realization, I often sent blazing signals into the universe. The impulsive on-the-way-home purchase of a brand-new, parchment gold metallic Ford Escape XLT Sport Utility Vehicle (with power accessory package and in-dash CD radio audio system with seven premium speakers and a subwoofer) sent a blaring announcement to the powers on high. I was ripe for change.

I merged onto the entrance ramp of Interstate 10 West at the Highway 90 interchange and accelerated smoothly into the evening flow of traffic. The tight, powerful straight-off-the-assembly-line engine roared. After driving a four-cylinder pick-up truck powered by three hamsters and an anemic gerbil for the last seven years, the rush of the large V-6 tipped my hormonal balance heavily in favor of testosterone.

The first few licks of *Respect Yourself* by the Staple Singers played on

106.1, the oldie FM radio station. At times like this, I imagined having at least a smattering of Motown soul buried deep inside. I smiled, remembering lazy childhood afternoons at Piddie's white-frame house on Morgan Avenue. Piddie would spin one of her Motown records on a suitcase-style vintage turntable, and we'd sing and dance as if we'd lost what little sense we had. Aunt Piddie told me once that if she had one wish, it would be to change into a black woman, even if only for one Saturday night. *They just have more passion!* she claimed, *Not all washed-out and fake-proper like most of us white folks!*

I turned the volume up full-tilt and sang and gyrated as much as I could and still keep the SUV on the road. The driver of a passing semi tractor-trailer truck tooted his air horn.

The pungent scent of new upholstery and vinyl tickled my nose. If they could find a way to bottle the aroma, it would be a lot easier to heal new-car fever. I imagined a plastic-faced department-store salesperson spritzing unsuspecting customers, breathlessly saying, "I'm Mercedes 2000!"

Relishing a new vehicle alone is not acceptable. I had a burning need to share the spoils of my insanity. On a straight monotonous stretch of the Interstate, I used my cell phone to contact Jake. No one answered on the Hill, so I breezed past our driveway off Highway 269 and cruised the three miles into town. The interior lights were off at the Dragonfly. Jake's van wasn't parked in either the delivery alley or the front parking lot of the Homeplace, his usual Friday evening French Dip and fries after-work retreat.

I turned left at the signal light on to Boliver Street and approached the empty intersection at the crest of Thrill Hill. On a blind let's-see-what-this-baby-will-do impulse, I gunned past the three-way stop sign and lifted off as the Ford Escape cleared the pavement. The new shocks cushioned the return to Earth. I let out an ear-piercing redneck whooeee! Quickly, I checked the rear view mirror for signs of police pursuit. Okay! I won't do it again…ever!

Generally, I'm not a reckless driver. Ask anyone who knows me. I will drive five blocks out of my way to avoid making a left hand turn against traffic without the safety of a signal light and rarely exceed the posted speed limit. I'd have to watch myself in this new monster so that my decadent twin, an entity Jake fondly called 'Evil Rita', would not become the predominant operator.

The only place I hadn't checked for Jake was the Witherspoon mansion. Lately, he'd spent a great deal of his spare time with the construction team working on the renovations for Holston Lewis. Still flushed with the adrenaline rush of my Thrill Hill coup, I negotiated the winding azalea and dogwood-lined drive leading to Jake's mother's house. Even though Holston Lewis now owned the property, the locals would continue to refer to it as 'The Witherspoon Mansion' until the end of time immortal.

The sun-bleached white antebellum house loomed over a vast expanse of green lawn gone to seed. Islands of pine and Spanish-moss-draped live oak trees surrounded with overgrown flower beds gave way to a circular cement drive at the once-grand entrance. From afar, the structure looked like a *Gone with the Wind* movie set. A closer view revealed crumbling woodwork and ragged curls of peeling paint. Six Doric columns supported the porch, and two cement lions stood at fierce guard on either side of the steps leading to the double doors.

I pulled alongside the Dragonfly Florist's delivery van and killed the engine. Since the front door was open, I bounded in without knocking.

"Yoo-hoo! Jakey!" I called in singsong. "I've got something to show you!"

At the doorway to the parlor, I stopped dead like a rookie starlet stunned by twenty floodlights. The scene would be permanently etched in my mind's eye: Holston Lewis—sweaty, paint-flecked, no shirt, jeans sitting low on his slim hips. He turned toward the sound of my noisy intrusion, the paint roller poised in his right hand—one of those slow-motion movements, as if I was on some kind of drug, or in a music video. The flesh at the corners of his dark eyes crinkled as he smiled in recognition. "Hattie! How nice of you to drop by! Are you home for the weekend?"

"Umm...ummm...ummm," I stuttered. I felt like Ralph Cramden in an old Honeymooner's episode where his wife, Alice, nails him for some infraction, and he just stands there stupidly repeating 'ah-ba...ah-ba...ah-ba,' over and over.

Jake came up behind me. "Hattie!" he yelled as he tapped me on the butt with the end of his 'everyday' sweetgum cane, "snap out of it!" Then, to Holston, "she gets stuck sometimes—kinda like a broken record with a skip. Isn't it a relief that we're all old enough to actually remember what a record is?"

We laughed, and I finally released the breath I'd been holding.

"You come by to help paint?" Holston asked.

A heat rush prickled the skin on my face. "No, that is… I could help. I didn't know you were working… I mean, I don't want to interrupt you…" God, I sounded like a lovesick teenage queen!

Holston dropped the roller in the paint pan, and wiped his hands on a rag hanging from his front pocket. "We can always take a break to welcome a visitor."

Jake peered out of the doorway toward the front door. The front fender of the Escape barely showed through the opening.

"Sister-girl! What have you done?" He shrieked.

"Oh, Yeah," I said, as if the real reason I had searched for Jake for a half-hour had just been announced to my brain. "I wanted to show you my new truck."

Jake hobbled quickly from the room, and we followed. "She is beautiful! You didn't tell me you wanted a new truck! What bank did you rob!?"

I handed Jake the keys and he crawled into the driver's seat. He closed his eyes as he relished the new car aroma. "She is su-weet! And you got an automatic 'cause you love me."

After two follow-up corrective surgeries on his damaged right leg, Jake still walked with a slight limp. Luckily, the delivery van's automatic transmission saved him from the discomfort of shifting gears. He refused to undergo further treatment, emphatically stating that he couldn't let go of his impressive collection of walking canes!

Holston walked around the SUV. "V-6. Smart move. More powerful than a four cylinder, but not too much harder on the gas mileage."

I nodded. "The salesperson said the average was around 23 mpg in town, with up to 28 mpg on the open road."

Jake hopped out of the driver's seat and surveyed the outside of the SUV. "When did you get her?"

I smiled sheepishly. "I bought it on the way home today."

Holston and Jake looked at me for a long moment.

"Well…I had noticed them when they first came out. Saw a few in traffic. I don't know what came over me. I was driving by the dealership on the way home, and I pulled in to just look. I ended up putting the down payment on my Visa and driving it off the lot."

Jake blinked and studied me like I was an alien life form. "The Queen of No Debt put a down payment for a vehicle on her always-paid-off credit card?" He held his hand to his forehead. "I'm having a spell. I think I need to sit down."

"Actually, I have a certificate of deposit maturing at the end of the month. I figured I could pay off the credit card and most of the remainder of the debt. It's not like I'm destitute, Jake."

Jake snorted. "Well, I certainly feel better." He narrowed his eyes. "Am I recalling this right? Didn't you buy your last truck the same way?" Jake threw his hands into the air. "You wanton hussy! You've left Pearl in some used-car lot in Tallahassee at the mercy of God-knows-who! How could you?"

Holston's brow wrinkled. "Who's Pearl?"

Jake propped his hands on his hips. "Just the precious little gray pick-up truck who has faithfully shuffled this ungrateful wench around for the past seven years."

Holston shook his head.

"Hattie always gives her automobiles names, you see," Jake explained.

"Wait a minute! Get your panties out of the wad they're in," I said. "For your information, I didn't trade Pearl. The salesperson helped me drop her by the townhouse. I'll pick her up later. She can retire to her home in the country for her golden years."

Jake sighed. "Well, I'm glad you didn't lose your mind completely. That little girl will be running long after all the rest of our vehicles have gone to the big metal heap in the sky. She deserves to stay in the family. We'll have to get her back over here to the Hill as soon as we can."

"Would you like to come in for a while?" Holston asked. "We don't have anything special, except fresh coffee and some iced tea. I could use a break. How 'bout you, Jake?"

The three of us settled onto a canvas drop cloth in the entrance parlor. Jake winced as he stretched his right leg. "I haven't been able to do as much as Holston. My leg won't bend enough to allow me to do the trim work."

Holston sipped his coffee. "You've picked the color scheme and shuffled paint and supplies. That's been a huge help."

I glanced around the cavernous room. "What are you planning to do with this big place? I can't imagine one person rambling around in all this space."

Holston shrugged. "I may keep the back bedroom and sitting room as my private quarters. As for the rest, I don't know yet. I thought about paying someone to move in and open a Bed and Breakfast, but the Madhatter's B&B uptown is doing so well, I wouldn't want to cause a problem. I don't know if this area would support both. For now, I'll just complete the renovations and hope some notion strikes me."

Jake took a sip of iced tea. "There are rumors afloat that an out-of-town investor may be looking to buy the state golf course by the hospital."

"I hadn't heard that," I said.

"Piddie told me." He stuck his tongue out like a bratty first-grader. "If you hung out at Mandy's Cut'n'Curl as much as she and Evelyn, you could get the scoop on upcoming events, too."

I stretched out my legs. "I don't have the leisure of passing the time at the beauty parlor like they do. I guess you'll just have to depend on Piddie."

Jake picked at my hair. "You could use a trim."

I waved him off. "I'll call Mandy for an appointment next week."

Jake's blue eyes lit up. I knew the look—a set-up. "Why don't you help us paint this weekend?"

Holston smiled warmly. Unlike the I-want-something-from-you smirk I had just endured from Garrett Douglas, Holston's expression was genuine. Heat settled deep within my heart, then it crept lower.

"Umm, sure! I don't think I have any massage clients at the shop until Tuesday afternoon."

"Great! This'll be fun!" Jake clapped his hands like a two-year-old at a birthday party.

MASSAGE THERAPY

Southern Chocolate Pecan Pie

Ingredients: 4 whole eggs, 2 cups sugar, 4 tbsp melted butter, 8 oz semi-sweet chocolate, a pinch of salt, ½ tspn lemon juice, 1 cup pecans

Prepare my Chocolate Pie Crust and set aside. Beat the eggs well, add the sugar, and continue to beat until light and creamy. Add the melted butter and the chocolate. Stir in the salt and lemon juice. Add the pecans and pour the filling into the unbaked pie shell. Bake in a 375°F oven for 30 minutes, or until set.

Enjoy on a long summer day with a scoop of ice-cream, homemade iced tea, and close friends.

CHAPTER EIGHTEEN

UNDER JAKE'S CAREFUL WATCH, the new color scheme for the mansion unfolded as we worked through the house. The rooms off the front entryway we painted with gentle, calming shades of cream and muted green, the colors becoming warmer and more inviting as the traffic flow entered the rooms in the back of the house. Having chosen the shades for the downstairs public portion of the house, Jake was currently busy fussing around with paint samples, choosing the hues for the upstairs bedrooms, baths, and sitting rooms. He stopped by at different times during the day to check the colors as they changed character with the quality of light.

Although I spent Wednesday through Friday in Tallahassee, I had begun to look forward to the trip home at week's end. I stopped on the

Hill long enough to slather Shammie with love and adoration before changing into an old T-shirt and a ratty pair of shorts in preparation for an evening of mindless trim painting. Spam, our ancient retriever, had died peacefully in his sleep the previous winter, so Shammie now ruled the farmhouse. Small caches of her prized possessions, gleaned from upended trashcans or the tops of bureaus and nightstands, graced hidden nooks in every room. When I moved the living room couch during a spring-cleaning frenzy, I located one of her hidey-holes. The neat mound contained a wad of used mint dental floss, a Heineken beer bottle cap, two pieces of aluminum foil, and a gold ball earring I'd been missing for several months.

If ever a drug needed to be developed, it was one that mimicked the euphoria of a budding affection. I wasn't willing, or even cognizant enough, to call it love. Love is reserved for star struck-teenagers, and the way I feel about rich, dark chocolate. At forty-plus, I found myself floating in a dreamy, pastel-dipped fog, appreciating the blooming azaleas, dogwoods, and bridal veil spirea as if I hadn't seen them each spring of my entire life. A sappy, misty-eyed love song made me choke up. I couldn't eat or sleep. Piddie had a cliché that fit perfectly: a woman headin' for a fall.

My past romantic entanglements felt more like an extended hormonal imbalance. After the heated physical component waned, the inevitable bland aftermath settled into sad discontent when I realized I really didn't like the person with whom I was sharing my life.

Why had I felt the need to remain friends with ex-lovers? Most folks turned their backs on past relationships, severing contact completely. Loose ends annoyed me. With the exception of one past love who later married an obsessively jealous woman, my relationships had come full circle. We often met for lunch or dinner, Dutch treat, and kept up with the events of each other's lives. With the expectations of a love relationship removed, I once again found reasons to locate common ground with a partner I had once lusted for, loved passionately, then wanted to choke. I hadn't been promiscuous in the twenty-plus years my eggs had been viable. Four serious relationships dotted my past, one coming dangerously close to matrimony with a person I later found totally undesirable.

Holston Lewis was, as Piddie phrased it, an azalea of a different color. Since I spent time each week in Tallahassee, I was spared the daily humiliation of following him like a homeless puppy. Visitors to the mansion came in a constant stream: construction workers, neighbors, bored city police officers on patrol, and Elvina Houston. She stopped by on a biweekly basis to get an update on the renovations. Her information hotline fed the surrounding counties, preventing their entire populations from traipsing through the double doors.

In the few moments we had alone, I gleaned snippets of Holston's life before he moved south. He had been married once to Claire Beaumont Lewis, an upwardly mobile socialite with aspirations of glory. When he left the pressured world of day-trading on Wall Street to pursue his dream of writing, she dumped him after twelve years of marriage. Claire immediately hooked a rich oral surgeon from Manhattan. Fortunately, Holston and Claire's union had produced no children to reap his ex-wife's cruel version of his retreat into obscurity. And, Holston's former occupation and careful investments had left him financially solvent.

Other than occasional contact with his previous mother-in-law, a sweet woman he adored, Holston had cut all emotional ties to the city. According to his account, fate had led him to Chattahoochee following the lead story of Jake's assault, and he had fallen hopelessly in love with the area and its people. Like me, he was a mid-life orphan. His father had died when he was young, leaving him to be raised by his doting mother until her death three years prior at the age of seventy-eight.

I pushed a damp hank of unruly hair away from my face, and studied the wall in Holston's private study. "You know, I didn't like this color initially. It looked a little muddy on Jake's sample. Now that I see it on the walls, it reminds me of a rich mocha latte with whipped cream."

Holston wiped a trickle of sweat from his temple. "Hattie Davis, you do have a way with words! Now, I'll crave designer coffee every time I come into this room."

Jake waltzed into the room holding a ragged, half-starved puppy in one arm. "Look what followed me home!"

He put the ugly patchwork brown and tan puppy on the floor. It sniffed around for a few minutes, then peed on a corner of a drop cloth.

"Jake!" I scolded.

"Hey, a man's gotta do what a man's gotta do! Don't worry, I'll clean it up. Can we keep him, Ma? Can we?" Jake bounced from side to side.

Holston bent down to ruffle the wiry hair on the pup's back. The dog wagged his tail and licked him on the hand. "He's so ugly, he's almost cute."

When the orphaned puppy's sad brown eyes looked directly into mine, I was a goner. "Only if you take him to the vet first thing tomorrow, Jake. He's probably loaded with fleas and worms. I want him to have all his shots and to be on heartworm prevention. If we're going to adopt him, he has to be taken care of properly."

"Well, of course. I'll take him by Doc Swanson's in the morning before I start work."

"You given him a name yet?" Holston asked.

Jake spread his arms wide as if to present the dog to the world "In keeping with the Hattie Davis tradition of pet names starting with an 's', I have named him 'Spackle.'"

I ruffled the puppy's dirty fur. "Great name! How'd you come up with that one?"

"Two things. First, notice the white smudge on the tip of his nose, here. Second, he comes to us during the marvelous renovation of the Witherspoon mansion—a time of much spackle action."

Jake gathered Spackle in one arm and headed for the door. He called over his shoulder, "Dinner at Evelyn's tomorrow night! You're both invited! No refusals allowed! Aunt Piddie's supervising the cooking. Special event of some sort. Don't know the details. Be there at seven!"

I stared after Jake. "Wonder what that's all about?"

"No telling with your family." Holston immediately did the backstroke. "Didn't mean anything bad by that, now. They just tend to be a bit on the eccentric side. But, some of my most favorite people are eccentric."

Holston rubbed his right shoulder and winced. "Maybe doing some of the work myself wasn't such a bright idea. My shoulders feel like they are about to seize up completely."

"Why don't we stop for the day? Mine are a little sore, too. I hear a hot bath calling my name."

He rubbed the back of his neck. "You're lucky to have your own place. The tub at the hotel is barely big enough to turn around in. I'll be glad when I finally have all this finished and I can move."

He could come home with me… "Yeah, I'm sure you will be. Why don't you come to my clinic tomorrow at 1:00? I have an opening for an hour massage. I'll work on your neck and shoulders for you."

He closed his eyes and moaned. "That'll work."

Though the ceiling fan in the master bedroom was set on high, I spent the night feverishly churning the sheets with images of Holston's back muscles rippling surrealistically in my jumbled dreams. Around 6 o'clock, I gave in to frustration and Shammie's impatient yowls for food.

I sipped coffee and rocked gently in my father's old porch rocking chair. The hummingbirds danced in zippy circles around two red nectar-filled feeders hanging from overhead beams. I inhaled deeply. The mixed scent of rich damp soil and tea olive blooms filled my nose. Molded by years of supporting my father's weight, the woven wicker seat of the rocker dipped four inches lower than the white oak frame, and a few strips of reed had broken around the edges. By far, it was the most comfortable rocker on the Hill, and I'd fight anyone for the privilege of sinking into its creaky cocoon.

After jotting a quick note to Jake on the notepad next to the coffeemaker, I donned a worn pair of hiking boots and grabbed my mother's walking stick. Growing up in the rural south had taught me the importance of always taking a stick on a walk through the woods to double as a weapon in the event I startled a rattlesnake. In years not too far past, most country folks held with the adage: *the only good snake is a dead snake*. Unfortunately, as did many of the early beliefs, this one had led to the endangerment of some species. I would use the stick to keep the snake at bay so that I could get away, if I didn't fall out from fear first.

Exercise for its own sake bored me immensely. I'd probably spent close to three thousand dollars in my lifetime on various Tallahassee gym memberships. I had never lost a single pound at one of them. Apparently, I'd missed the small print in the contracts: *You have to show up.*

The way I viewed it, the extra minutes I added to my life span with each half hour of brisk workout might be added to the end of my lifetime—four to five months more at the extended care facility of my choice at $4,000.00 a clip.

Margie waved from a flowerbed at the rear of their property as I reached the end of the lane. I turned right, walked a few feet through the tall Bahia grass on the shoulder of the highway, then turned right onto Dolan Road. The packed clay and sand roadway had been recently grated by the county road crew, and I walked close to the churned soft edges. Creek Indian tribes had once roamed these hills bordering the Apalachicola River, and a newly plowed field or dirt road often provided a prize find of a flint arrowhead or spear points.

Dolan Road spanned three miles through hardwood and evergreen forest in the direction of the river, coming to an abrupt dead end before intersecting with the water's edge. A few families owned land along the road. Whenever I walked this route, I pulled a quick U-turn at the edge of their properties. A couple of mixed-breed dogs guarded the ramshackle farmhouses with snarling glee. One particular steel-jawed pit-bull mix named Precious would rather chew off a leg than breathe. I judiciously avoided contact with her. She could quickly take the joy out of a stroll on a country lane.

As the early morning mist cleared, the sun winked through the tips of the evergreens. The budding hardwoods were adorned in shades of lime green and glowed in the soft light of sunrise. Occasionally, the startled scrabbles of small rodents and lizards rustled the underbrush near the road. Dew-dipped spider webs glistened like garland between the weeds. I breathed deeply the mixed aroma of fertile wet earth and vegetation.

In the middle of the summer, this walk would not be tolerable. The heat would roll in visible waves from the dry, packed earth, and the humidity would slow all life to a sluggish crawl. July through September in North Florida could be enough to send a person packing in search of a cooler climate, but the remainder of the year was delightful. Winters were seldom harsh. I could only recall seeing snow once during childhood. Even then, the accumulation was less than an inch, and I had to gather the entire side yard to get enough snow to build a snowman a foot tall. January and February were the coldest months, affording the cozy luxury of a roaring fire built from hardwoods cut from the property, with creamy marshmallows cooked slowly on a straightened wire coat hanger over the glowing coals.

Jake was bustling around the kitchen when I returned. "I'm making Western omelets. Want one?" He broke an egg into a stainless mixing bowl.

"I'm not really hungry."

Jake grinned. "You got it bad, sister-girl." He grabbed a wire whisk and whipped the eggs and milk mixture to a bubbly froth.

"I don't know what you mean," I replied as I removed my boots.

"Oh, pu-leaze! You've got it so bad for Holston Lewis you can barely see straight!"

I stood with my hands on my hips. "For your information, I barely even know the man."

"You've emailed him on a regular basis since my incident by the lake, and you practically killed yourself dashing for the phone whenever he called to ask me something for the book! Of course you know him! Your trouble is that you want to know him in the, as Piddie puts it, biblical sense."

"I admit I'm attracted to him, Jake. That doesn't mean he feels the same way. He only wrote to me for tidbits of information. I don't have any reason to believe he feels anything toward me except friendship."

Jake expertly flipped the omelet. As many times as I had tried the same trick, my omelets always turned into scrambled eggs instead of a perfect half-moon.

"Oh...he's interested," Jake said. "Trust me, I know an interested man when I see one."

"Whatever happened to your big resolve to allow love to come into your life?"

Jake smirked. "One just can't will Cupid to flit by, sister-girl. It's not my turn yet. But, it is yours and Holston's. This isn't about me this time. Quit trying to distract me!"

I headed in the direction of my bedroom. "Love to stay and dissect my love life with you, but I need to shower. I have a client at nine."

Jake swung his spatula in an arc. "Fine. Leave me to my solitude.

Shammie and I will enjoy your part of breakfast."

Shammie, curling in circles at his feet, yowled in agreement.

I parked Betty in my reserved space in the alley behind the Madhatter's Sweet Shop and Massage Parlor. Though I had washed her the day before, Betty was covered with a thick greenish-yellow sheen of pollen. The new SUV owed her name to a long-time friend and client who had unfortunately lost an extended battle with pulmonary fibrosis the previous year. Betty had packed an amazing blend of fight and zeal for life in her petite frame. My new truck was honored to be her name-sake.

Sally had been my first car, followed by Jenny, Miz Scarlet, Rosie, and Pearl. All of my vehicles, with the exception of a brief stay by Bonnie Blue, a subcompact traded after seeing a car like her nearly destroyed in a low-speed collision, had been longtime companions. Since I couldn't bear the thought of leaving a beloved auto at the mercy of uncaring strangers, I traded quickly before I had a chance to get all fussed up over its fate. Pearl remained in the family. She was handy around the Hill for carrying supplies and firewood. Thanks to my parents' estate, I was finally able to afford the insurance for two vehicles.

"Mornin' Glory!" Stephanie called from behind the Sweetshop display case. "Your 9 o'clock just cancelled. I tried to reach you, but you'd left the Hill, and your cell phone wasn't on."

I helped myself to a cup of freshly brewed decaf. "That's okay. I'm tired this morning, anyway. I'll just clean the room and piddle around here. Holston's coming at 1 o'clock, and I'm slammed with clients all the way till after five."

Stephanie cocked her head. "You've been tired a lot here lately. Look a little pale, too. Maybe you should take a few days off and rest."

"I think it's all the manual labor catching up with me. I feel okay, for the most part. I actually went for a long walk this morning!"

"Now, I am worried about you!" Stephanie squirted the glass enclosure with cleaner and polished the display case until it sparkled. "Hey, it's past the busy part of the morning. Why don't you let me practice my foot reflexology on you? I'm sure Jake can hold down the fort for an hour."

Jake came through the delivery entrance of the Dragonfly Florist and called out, "Mornin' Glory!" We immediately drafted him to watch the Sweetshop.

From the viewpoint of a massage-therapy client, I studied the room. Jake's abstract forest mural continued upward to meet a painted ceiling filled with fluffy white clouds and a crystal blue sky. A few V-shaped slashes of color provided the illusion of high-flying birds of prey circling lazily above.

The acrylic sheepskin table cover under the sheets was gently warmed from below by an electric mattress pad. I allowed myself to sink into the soft sheets as the tension melted from my sore muscles. Stephanie tapped gently on the door, then entered after I responded. For the next hour, she rubbed and worked the pressure points on both feet. Other than a couple of times when she hit a sore spot, I drifted off, waking myself with an embarrassing snort.

"Boy, a couple of those pressure points were awfully tender," I said.

She consulted the brightly colored foot-and-hand chart hanging behind the door. "Those are the points for the colon...see?" She pointed to an area near the heel on both feet.

I shrugged. "Can't imagine why."

The reflexology session left me calm and mildly euphoric. I drifted aimlessly around the shop, plucking dead leaves from the potted plants.

Jake handed me a freshly brewed cup of coffee. "Here, sister-girl. You'd better caffeine up before your handsome client arrives. At this rate, you'll fall asleep on the poor man."

Holston appeared at 12:45, cleanly shaven and freshly laundered.

"Is he a hunk, or what?" Stephanie mumbled to me as he stepped through the door.

Holston completed a brief medical-history intake form, and I led him into the therapy room.

"You can go to your level of comfort as far as clothing, Holston. Some people prefer to keep their underclothes on. Except for the part I am working on at the time, you'll be completely covered by the sheet. I'd like for you to be face up, tucked between the covers. I'll give you a bit to get settled in."

After a few minutes, I knocked for permission, then entered the room. "What type of music would you like? Classical? Piano? Guitar?"

"Your choice," he replied.

"In that case, I'll play my favorite acoustic finger style guitar artist, Bill Mize." I slipped a CD into the player. "Have you had a massage before?" I asked as I warmed the lotion in my hands.

"Only once. I felt totally beaten up afterwards. I never tried it again."

"I'll try to make this more relaxing for you. Feel free to speak up if you want me to modify my pressure. Otherwise, I will honor the silence of the massage treatment and allow you to tune in to your body."

When I touched Holston's face, a spark of heat traveled through my hands. The hair on my forearms stood up as I felt a warm flush radiate through my body.

Get a grip, Hattie! Time to turn on the professional mind. Let the feelings go.

The session followed my favorite sequence. I began with a facial and scalp massage, followed by neck, hands, forearms, upper arms, and shoulders. I then moved down to work the anterior portion of both legs. I spent ten minutes on the feet, working in a brief foot-reflexology session.

After positioning the U-shaped face cradle at the head of the table, I held the sheets for Holston to flip over onto his stomach. I proceeded to massage the posterior of both legs, the entire back, posterior neck, and buttocks.

The full-hour massage session was a combination of Swedish strokes with exotic sounding names such as effleurage (long fluid strokes) and petrissage (kneading), percussion, and deeper neuromuscular friction techniques designed to manipulate the muscles at their attachment sites. The session ended with a gentle rocking motion of the entire body.

"Did you kill him?" Jake asked when I came out. "I think you killed him, Hattie!"

"Hush, Jake. He'll be out in a minute. As hard as he's worked on that house lately, he may have fallen asleep. It sometimes takes a few minutes to get yourself together after a massage session. You know that."

"I know if he's not madly in love with you after one of your fabulous massages, he's Mississippi mud inside!"

I shushed him when the pocket door to the therapy room creaked open.

Holston had the dreamy bemused expression of a person high on endorphins, nature's own pleasure-pain relief chemicals released during massage.

"How do you feel?" I asked.

"Uh...good. You know..." He studied his reflection in the wicker-trimmed mirror by the door. "I look like the victim of a night at a bad drive-in movie."

"I know what you mean, honey," Jake said as he waltzed back to the florist side of the shop.

After he paid for the session, Holston started toward the door.

"See you at Evelyn and Joe's tonight!" Jake called to him.

Holston waved. "Yeah...right..."

Jake cocked his head. "That must have been one hell of a massage!"

I pulled a pair of imaginary six shooters from a gun belt, spun them in the air, fired, then blew the end of the barrels before twirling them back into the holster. "I'm good at my job."

PARTY AT EVELYN'S

Excerpt from Max the Madhatter's notebook:

February 14, 1958: The Chief sings all the time. When he's not busy giving Nurse Marion a hard time. Today, special for Valentine's, he sang all the love songs he knew. For hours. I don't know much about it. I haven't been in love.

CHAPTER NINETEEN

"OWW! ARETHA! Time to crank her up!" Jake reached over and bumped the volume. Betty's sound system blared. "This girl Betty sure has one sweet stereo system!" He gyrated in the passenger seat.

I courteously waited until the DJ chattered at the end of the song before reaching over to lower the volume. "You have any idea what this dinner party's for?"

Jake smoothed the sides of his heavily-gelled hair in the illuminated mirror behind the sun visor on his side of the SUV. "No clue. I have a sneaking suspicion Evelyn's redecorated, though. She ordered a special arrangement of exotic tropical flowers for a centerpiece."

"The marine theme's history?"

Jake shrugged his shoulders. "I do believe. She always went for the subdued natural flora during that phase. I hardly think yellow, scarlet, and hot pink would blend."

"She's incredible."

Jake shifted to face me. "Did you know that the last time her son and daughter-in-law visited from Cleveland with the kids, she redid the entire house in art deco just for their visit?"

"I can't believe how much fun I've missed the past few years by limiting my trips into town whenever I visited Mama and Daddy on the Hill."

"Your cousin's gone through at least five decorating themes since I've been back home! Heaven knows how many before that! She keeps me artistically challenged to find compatible floral accompaniment."

"And she seems to do it all on a shoestring budget."

"I'm tellin' ya, sister-girl, the woman is channeling Martha Stewart…without the back-up staff, of course."

The entrance to Evelyn's and Joe's house was lined with flaming wicker tiki torches. A distinctive Caribbean beat flowed from the open windows.

"Of course! It's Carmen Miranda and the whole tropical thing!" Jake exclaimed. "That explains the tiny paper umbrellas Piddie had me order."

Since we were attending a special dinner party, we shunned the side door in favor of the brightly lit front entrance. Aunt Piddie answered the door in her motorized wheel chair.

She said in a sultry voice, "Welcome to the islands."

Aunt Piddie's hair was a volcanic monument to the wonders of hair spray. Mandy's recent semi-permanent color had imparted a vibrant light blue sheen to her curled mountain of locks. Each level supported minia-ture paper umbrellas in bright tropical fruit-drink hues. A Batik print moo-moo flowed around her in delicate folds. For the crowning touch, she wore a series of silk flower leis around her neck.

"Aloha! Or whatever they say in the islands…" She motioned for us to bend low enough to slip a silk lei around our necks. "Okay, I've done my part! Everyone's in the kitchen." She backed the electric wheel chair expertly and wheeled off toward the rear of the house.

Evelyn's living room had morphed into an island retreat complete with wicker accessories, colored accent lights, and tall silk palm trees and birds of paradise. A multi-hued room-sized rug splashed color over the hardwood floor. Two of the walls were painted a bright purple shade to match the rug.

"I can't wait to see the dinnerware!" Jake said.

Bobby, Leigh, Joe, Evelyn, and Piddie were grouped around the island counter in the center of the kitchen sipping pina coladas from plastic pineapple mugs with green straws.

"Good!" Evelyn hugged Jake and me. "Now, we're just missing Holston."

Jake grinned. "If he comes. Hattie gave him a massage today and he looked like he was ready to hibernate until this time next year when he left the shop."

The group laughed and nodded. I'd worked numerous times on each of them in the past couple of years.

"Maybe you should've waited until after my dinner party to give him a massage," Evelyn said.

Jake threw his arm around Evelyn's shoulder. "So, sugar, what's this party all about? Hmmm? We know one reason is to exhibit your fabulous new island décor, but what's the other one?"

"Actually, she's throwing this party at my request," Bobby answered, "and...you'll find out soon enough."

Evelyn held out her arms. "Let's all go to the living room and visit until Holston arrives."

I followed closely behind Aunt Piddie. "You know anything?" I whispered in her ear.

She whispered back. "I think Bobby and Leigh are going to announce their engagement."

Several minutes passed before the doorbell chimed. Piddie swept forward to go through her island-airport-greeting routine for Holston. He chuckled as Piddie slipped the yellow lei over his head, then he bent to kiss her on one heavily rouged cheek.

"Lordy, boy! If I wasn't so damn old, you'd be in a heap of trouble!"

Holston held her chin delicately in his cupped hands. "You're not old, Miz Piddie Longman. You just got here before I did, that's all."

It was the only time I'd ever seen Piddie blush.

Holston glanced in my direction as he stepped into the room. He held my gaze long enough to make the sip of coconut-pineapple punch I'd just swallowed burn in my throat. He quickly looked away and greeted the remainder of the group.

Evelyn admired Holston's attire. "Why, if I didn't know better, I'd

147

think you had ESPN! You're dressed just perfectly for our party theme."
She twirled a piece of her light brown hair like a flirtatious teenager.

ESP…N? I shot an amused glance toward Jake.

Holston wore a tropical-weight tan sports coat with khaki pants, and a tasteful Hawaiian print shirt open at the neck. He could've stepped straight out of the old 80's television series, Miami Vice, except that Holston, unlike the show's star, Don Johnson, was clean-shaven.

Joe clapped Holston on the shoulder. "C'mon back, Holston. I'll buy you a drink at the Tiki bar. We got whatever you want: beer…something sweet and tropical…or something with more of a kick."

Holston followed Joe into the kitchen.

"God Almighty," Piddie said. "Did you see the way he looked at you, Hattie?"

"He's just being nice, Pid. I really don't think he's interested in me. Look at him. He could have any woman he wanted!"

Piddie frowned. "Don't underestimate yourself! He'll come around. I chased your uncle Carlton for nearly a year before he caught me!"

Evelyn served dinner promptly at eight. Fresh fruit salad with vanilla yogurt dressing on ceramic pineapple plates was followed by cold butternut squash soup in coconut cups. The main course, Hawaiian baked chicken with wild rice, was presented with green beans almandine and Aunt Piddie's cathead biscuits.

"We went round-and-round about the biscuits," Piddie said. "Evelyn insisted they didn't eat cathead biscuits on the islands! I told her they probably just ate the cats instead!"

Evelyn snorted. "Mama! I think that's a horrible thing to say! They don't eat cats in the Caribbean!'

Piddie flipped one hand in the air. "Whatever…anyway, I got to make the biscuits."

"And we're glad you did," Holston said. "These are as wonderful as the first time I tasted them a couple of years ago!"

Piddie giggled. "Oh, you do go on so!"

Evelyn's crowning glory was a ten-layered buttery tropical cake.

Aunt Piddie complimented her in a round-about way. "I've told Evelyn all along. If you're not a natural-born cook, stick to the recipes like white on rice! You can't go wrong that'away. Looks like she finally took my advice to heart."

"Thank you, Mama. I think."

Bobby tapped the edge of his water glass with a fork. "Okay. Time for the big moment." He turned to Leigh and took her by the hand. "Leigh and I were married last weekend."

Everyone at the table stared in shock.

"M-m-married?" Piddie said. "What happened to the engagement announcement? And the weddin' plans?"

Bobby smiled down at his new wife. "Leigh and I agreed we didn't want a big fuss made over us."

Tears formed at the corners of Leigh's blue eyes. "I'm so sorry if we've hurt your feelings."

Jake leaped up and hugged the newlyweds. "Nonsense! We're all thrilled! This means we can plan a reception party!"

Evelyn clapped her hands. "Of course. Bobby, Joe and I can stand in for your folks since your mama and daddy have to attend in spirit! I can just see the decorations in my mind!"

"Don't you worry, honey." Piddie patted Bobby's new wife on the hand. "This gives us all somethin' wonderful to look forward to."

After dinner, we retired to the living room where Evelyn served decaffeinated coffee with cream and sugar. The party guests each received a miniature piñata filled with candy.

"Well…" Holston stood to leave. "I've got to call it a night. It was most enjoyable."

Evelyn jumped up. "Oh, I wish you didn't have to go. We're going to play a game of spoons! It's a fast and furious card game. You might not have heard of it, you being from the North, and all. We'll teach you."

"Maybe next time," Holston said as he walked toward the door. "Thank you so much for a wonderful evening."

Evelyn held the door. "Please, don't be a stranger, now."

Piddie punched me in the side. "Walk him out!"

Holston and I stood between the tiki torches on the front walkway.

"I'm booked with massage clients during the day, but I can come by after work on Monday and Tuesday to help you finish the trim in your private quarters."

He looked into the distance. His strong jaw was outlined in the torch's glow. "You can if you'd like. Jake has a key. I'm leaving for a couple of weeks. Got to fly to New York to tie up some loose ends with my publisher."

"Oh. Okay. Well, I'll guess I'll see you when you return, then. Have a safe trip."

Holston gave a small wave over his shoulder as he walked toward his car. I watched him drive away. A slight haze of dust from his hasty departure hung in the air—a statement or question mark. I was unsure which.

Piddie met me at the door. "Well?"

"He's leaving town for a couple of weeks," I said. My voice sounded as flat and washed out as I felt.

"If that don't beat all." Piddie sighed. "You remember when your daddy used to take you fishin'?"

"Yeah. Why?"

"When you snagged a big ole' fish that was a keeper, it would take off to the bottom like a shot. You'd give it some line to play with. Pretty soon, it just gave out, and you got it in the boat!"

"It's not my intention to trick anyone into being with me," I said. "If he wants me, he'll have to make the moves."

"All I'm sayin' is…be patient."

Jake stood. "I'm all pooped out, sister-girl. Let's take it to the Hill, shall we?"

FUTURE SIGHT

Excerpt from Max the Madhatter's notebook:

March 28, 1959: Life is not only here on this earth. I see the ghosts of the past mingling in the park outside my window. Most of the time, they carry on their existence with barely a notice of our own. One old gentleman in a top hat sometimes follows Nurse Marion around, but I won't tell her.

CHAPTER TWENTY

THE WEEK FOLLOWING Holston's departure, my clients benefited from my need for distraction as I threw myself into work with a mad-scientist passion. By Thursday afternoon, I walked around the Tallahassee clinic in a weary, sleep-deprived fog.

Anna rested her hand on my shoulder. "You look just awful, Hattie. Is there anything I can do?"

"No, I'm just working through some stuff." I ran my fingers through my hair. "I wish I could just wave a magic wand and get all the answers!"

Anna's long purple skirt swished with her slightest movement. "Why don't you make an appointment for a reading with Phil Waters? He helped me a lot last year when I hit the wall during the custody battle for my daughter. He may not give you all the answers, but I certainly felt comforted by the session he did for me."

Friday morning, I did what any sane woman would do when confronting a personal crisis. I consulted a psychic.

"You're in luck," he said over the phone. "Although, we know there is no such thing as luck. My two o'clock consultation just cancelled.

Otherwise, it'll be around three weeks before I have an opening."

Phil Waters' townhouse was nestled midway in a row of older brick structures off Beard Street. A thin, thirty-ish man with sandy blonde hair and kind brown eyes answered the door and welcomed me into a light-filled sitting room scattered with plants and books. Sunlight refracting through crystals suspended in the windows sent rainbows dancing on the parquet floors.

Phil served tall glasses of ice water, and we settled into the over-stuffed cushions of his couch. We talked casually for a few minutes before he began the session.

"I usually open myself to the spirit family surrounding you at the beginning. I am not a trance channel. I close my eyes to focus inward, but my consciousness stays here with us as I communicate with the guardians around you."

He moved to a high-backed cushioned chair, closed his eyes, and took a series of deep breaths.

In a few moments, he began to speak in a pleasant, soothing voice. "As I enter your energy field, I am aware of the friends and family around you. They are very excited to be here. You have been asking for help in lifting a burden, and to find answers to help you find a peace you have been working toward. There's a lot to be said and much healing that can take place today."

After a brief pause, he continued, "Your spirit family is ready, willing, and able to come to your aid…to bring you the strength to carry on…to help you find the faith you need when you doubt…to let you know their presence is real. Their involvement is based on a deep commitment to who you are as an individual.

"They want to tell you that the reason your life has been touched with pain is to open your heart…to prepare you for a life of compassion, for yourself and others. The pain has made you realize that you don't want to create the same experience for others. Compassion and service to others is a central theme for this life."

Phil tilted his head slightly to the right and paused. "You have some old ghosts hanging around you regarding your self worth. Spirit is adamant that you let these go…let go…that you never doubt yourself, not even for a second, for the contribution you make to the world simply by your being here.

"The word they give me is courage. They are very pleased with the amount of courage you have displayed in this life and they say job well done…job well done."

The silence was punctuated with the rhythmic ticking of an oak wall clock. "There's a part of you that blocks off the experience of your value…a part of you that wants to turn some of your best qualities of compassion—gentle, caring, loving—into negative qualities. Spirit is adamant that this wound be healed. This critical voice in your head that doubts your life's purpose must be silenced." His eyes opened slowly.

Phil drew a large imaginary circle in the air with his index fingers. "The physical world where we live offers us doubt, fear, limitation. We lose sight of the fact that the universe only has our best interest at heart. The source of our pain comes from living in the physical world. The spiritual world holds no such judgment."

His voice became very soft as he closed his eyes. "Yes, you have suffered loss and pain. There have been times when it felt as if everything has been taken from you. But, you're still here. You are growing and evolving every day. You are still here.

"Spirit says you don't need to work so hard at yourself. All you really need to do is acknowledge the self you already are. Who I am as a spiritual being is just fine. There's no reason you can't make the choice today to not listen to the voice of doubt that lives within you. Turn off that voice. It pulls you down into heaviness. All you have to do is call off the search and say, *this is me*. This is who I am, and I'm fine.

"It doesn't mean that all the problems will go away…or the challenges will stop. You are not a problem. You are a gift."

Phil's face eased into a warm smile. "Life doesn't need for you to exhort effort at it. You are doing the best you can do given the circumstances. Spirit wants you to know that life doesn't have to be about suffering. Choose to see what you can learn and grow out of this to become a richer, fuller being."

Phil paused and took a deep breath. After a brief moment, he continued, "Your father and mother are both in spirit. They are showing me a baby girl with them."

"Baby?" I thought for a minute. "Sarah?"

"Your sister."

Sarah hadn't crossed my mind in a long time. She had been born between my older brother and me. She lived for two days before succumbing to a systemic infection contracted during the lengthy birth. My parents seldom spoke her name, preferring to hold their grief inside. As an adult, I had learned the story of my sister's short life from Aunt Piddie, but my parents shielded my brother and me from the loss.

"Sarah is with your mother and father. It is okay to remember and honor her brief time with your family."

Phil opened his eyes. "Are there any questions you wish to ask?"

"Just a couple. First, are there any health concerns I need to address?"

Phil's eyes rested on me briefly. "There is an imbalance here. Part of it relates to, and is involved with, blood. Some type of internal problem...possibly with the assimilation system—digestion, utilization of food and nutrients. You should be aware of this imbalance."

I leaned closer. "How about relationships, particularly romantic..."

"There is someone who may have already entered your energy field. There was contact...written correspondence. This person may not be aware of the potential for the union. I get the sense that there are old burdens left over from childhood...an oppressive parent, perhaps. This person is working through old scars."

"There is an aura of family surrounding you—extended family. I am getting a picture of a bubbling brook...spring-fed...and a field of small wildflowers, perhaps daisies."

Phil studied me for a moment. "There are two children in your energy field. Although there is a connection to both, I don't sense a biological commonality in one of the children."

After the session, I walked around Lake Ella, grabbed a chicken tetrazzini salad at Hopkin's Eatery, took myself shopping at the Tallahassee Mall, then went to the townhouse.

I planned to go to the Hill first thing Saturday morning.

Since Jillie was at the university library buried in research for a project, I had the townhouse to myself for the evening. I wandered around the rooms in search of something to lift my growing sense of melancholy.

I entertained the idea of ordering out a pizza, a luxury Chattahoochee didn't provide, but food didn't appeal to me. Even though the townhouse glowed under Jillie's careful household maintenance, I cleaned the bathrooms. The smell of bleach soothed me with the notion I was doing something fruitful by destroying hordes of helpless microscopic organisms.

Friday evening in a city big enough to actually support a night life, and here I was schlepping around in a terry cloth robe riddled with holes and pulled threads, with a spray bottle of bleach in hand. I thought of phoning Garrett, then wiped that notion away. No need to spend an evening providing a mirror for his blonde, overblown ego. Besides, he was way too popular to be free on a weekend night.

I rummaged through what was left in Tallahassee of my CD collection, and selected one of my favorite jazz standards, Love Season by Alex Bugnon. The rich tones flowed from the Bose speakers surrounding the room.

"I need to move my system to the Hill when I take Pearl home," I said aloud.

Shocked, I looked around the townhouse, realizing how little I felt connected to the place. Bit by bit, I had loaded books, mementos, pictures, and small pieces of furniture into the truck for my weekly sojourn to the country. Where traces of my life once graced the walls, floors, and drawers, evidence of Jillie's young personality exerted itself like a patient opportunistic virus waiting for the host to weaken so that it could flourish in its own right.

I bolted up the stairs and threw on my jeans, tank top, and shoes. I scribbled a quick note to Jillie explaining my sudden departure, killed the stereo, and dashed out to the parking lot.

Driven was a good description of my mood and intent. My evil twin Rita came out as I cussed, dodged, and accelerated my way out of the city to the Interstate. The drivers in front of me operated their vehicles as if the pavement was made of molasses. I wouldn't have been surprised if a misguided plane landed in front of me. Thanks to the help of several harried guardian angels, I reached the Chattahoochee exit intact. No need to look at the speedometer to know I was exceeding the posted 70 mph speed limit. The fact that I'd passed cars, buses, and semi-trucks as though they were stapled to the asphalt was proof enough.

The farmhouse was lit with welcoming light at the top of Bonnie Hill. I expelled a huge sigh as I reached the head of the driveway. Spackle lifted his dopey puppy head and woofed at Betty's arrival. I parked, hopped from the truck, and almost ran to the front door. I scooped him up, and he splashed my face with wet puppy kisses. Jake stood behind the screen door watching us.

"I'm so glad you decided to come home, sister-girl." His voice cracked with emotion.

I flung open the screened door and hugged him. "I just had to get here as soon as I could! It was weird…" I stopped. The tears glistened at the corners of his eyes.

"Jake! What's wrong? Come sit down." I guided him to the loveseat in the kitchen's seating area.

"It's been a one hell of a day, sister-girl." His shoulders drooped. "Thomas Thurgood dropped dead of a heart attack last night around midnight. His wife called me today to tell me of the arrangements and plan the flowers for his memorial. Then, this afternoon, she received word from San Diego. Timothy Thurgood, her husband's twin brother, had died from coronary failure…within minutes of Thomas's time of death."

The room was silent except for the monotonous ticking of the antique mantle clock. Jake wiped his eyes with his sleeve. "They're flying Timothy's ashes home to be interred with his brother."

A visual memory of Thomas Thurgood's massive, strong hands holding mine at his nephew's wake flashed in memory.

"They'll finally be reunited," I said softly.

I held Jake as he sobbed. The scars of family hatred and violence cut too deep to have healed over completely. Jake and I cried together for the futility of lives spent in shame, fear, and regret. Because of Marshall Thurgood's vicious attack on Jake, the lives and lies of their family were permanently intertwined with his. Because he was my best and truest heart-friend, Jake's pain was mine.

"I didn't expect you till the morning," Jake said shakily as the wave of grief ebbed.

"I just felt like I needed to be home."

We looked at each other and said at the same time, "ESP-N!"

I began to giggle. Then, he did. Spackle started to yip and howl. Shammie sauntered into the kitchen and meowed loudly. Jake and I laughed harder, spurring Spackle to new heights of coyote-pitched yowling. Shammie sat down and studied all three of us with the absolute disgust only a cat can project.

"Aren't we one freaked-out family," Jake said when he caught his breath.

"Best kind in my book."

RECONCILIATION

For Anything Everything Chocolate Pie Crust

Ingredients: ½ cup sifted flour, ¼ cup sugar, ¼ cup cocoa, ½ tspn salt, ½ cup shortening, ½ tspn vanilla, 3 tbsp ice cold water.

Sift flour, sugar, cocoa, and salt into a large bowl. Cut in shortening until pieces are the size of small peas. Add vanilla and water and mix lightly to form a dough that holds together. Roll out to 11" in diameter and fit into a 9" pie pan. Bake at 400°F for 8 minutes. Crust will be soft when it comes out, but it sets as it cools.

For an extra-flaky crust, must sure all ingredients are chilled beforehand. This is the perfect pie crust for my Southern Chocolate Pecan Pie!

CHAPTER TWENTY-ONE

UNLIKE MARSHALL'S media-saturated funeral three years past, Thomas and Timothy Thurgood's memorial service was small and sparsely attended. Jake and myself, Louise and Lottie Thurgood, their extended family, a smattering of Thomas's coworkers, and naturally, Elvina Houston, were in attendance at the dual burial. Reverend Samuel Morrison of the First Presbyterian Church of Chattahoochee performed the brief service. A last-minute judge's order had permitted Matthew Thurgood the privilege of attending his uncle's and father's service under police guard, before returning him to the state prison where he was serving a ten-year sentence for his part in the initial assault and desecration of Jake's shop.

Since I'd cancelled my massage clients for the day, I followed Jake home to the Hill, and we rode Margie's and John's ATV to the fish pond. A warm spring breeze chased swirls of pollen across the glassy surface of the water. An hour later, we negotiated the steep grassy steps to the parked ATV and returned to the farmhouse.

Though Tuesday's clinic schedule was full, I remarkably had spare energy to burn at the end of the day. After changing into a pair of old shorts from the back of the SUV, I procured Jake's keys to the Witherspoon mansion. A couple of hours' labor completed the trim work in the back bedroom in Holston's private quarters.

A twig snapped behind me in the dusk dark as I crouched by an outside faucet washing the paint tray and brushes. Startled, I spun around.

"Holston? Lordy! You scared me half to death! You're home early!"

"What're you doing back here?" he asked.

"Washing out some brushes. I painted the trim in your bedroom. Jake's anxious to get the wood floors refinished so you can move your furniture in. I had some spare time, and I was bored. I got the key from Jake. Hope you don't mind me being here…"

"No." He stood still, watching me with his hands propped on his hips like the King of Siam.

"Well. Um…I guess I'll get on home now." I brushed past him and headed for Betty.

He appeared by the driver's side of the SUV and motioned for me to roll down the window.

"Hattie, I'm not very good at this…"

"At what?" Being a jerk?

"I'd like to apologize for the way I left you last week. I had some soul-searching to do. I'm afraid my dealings with women, thanks to Claire, have left me a bit gun-shy."

"Holston, you show me one man or woman our age who hasn't been shot in the foot several times in relationships, and I'll show you a person who's been in a monastery! Besides, I thought we were doing pretty well being friends."

"Yeah. My fault for the confusion." His full lips curled into a slight smile. "Actually, I was hoping to reserve some of your time this Friday evening."

Was he asking me out? "I'm all ears."

"Have you found anyone to help you bring your truck back yet?"

"No. Jake's been so busy, and I hate to bother anybody. I need to do it soon, though. Pearl's battery is going to be dead as a doornail from just sitting around the townhouse parking lot."

"Good! That is…I have a proposal to make. I met with my agent while I was in New York, and we talked over an idea for my next book. Last year, I met a wonderful couple, Patricia and Rainey Hornsby, while I was in Tallahassee doing a piece during the legislative session. They'd adopted a little orphaned Chinese girl. Given the somewhat strained relations between the U.S. and China, I thought it might be a good time to write a book documenting the experiences of the adoptive parents." Holston smiled at me as if I had a clue as to my role in this whole thing.

"And…?" I prompted.

"Oh, okay. Here's the deal. Patricia and Rainey have invited me to a social function Friday night where I can be introduced to several of the families, set up interviews for the book, that sort of thing. Jake is going over to have dinner with his legislator friend that evening, as well. If you'd like, I could hitch a ride with him, come by and take you to an early dinner, attend my meeting, then help you drive Pearl back to Chattahoochee."

He hesitated. "Of course, you can attend the social with me, if you'd like. Patricia and Rainey are incredible people. I think you'd hit it off with them immediately."

"Sounds like an interesting proposition. Why not? What time, and what do I wear?"

He patted Betty's door. "Great! Patricia said it was very casual — jeans and T-shirts. I'll have Jake drop me off at the townhouse about 6:00 pm. Will that give you enough time to get home from work?"

"Sure. I schedule my last client on Fridays at 3:00. I like to be clear of Apalachee Parkway before the 5:00 Demolition Derby begins."

Holston flashed a smile. "I'll see you then, Friday night around 6:00 p.m.!"

I didn't feel Betty's tires hit the pavement all the way to the Hill.

❧ ❧ ❧

Since I had been craving barbecue all week, Holston and I had dinner at Sonny's Real Pit Bar-B-Q. I immediately splattered a dime-sized blob of red sauce on my clean white FSU T-shirt.

"I don't know why I don't just smear something on me when I first sit down and save the suspense!" I grumbled as I pulled a spot removal wipe from my purse.

Holston smiled. "Looks like you're prepared."

"I try to be. Growing up in the country, one learns to be resourceful. Besides, I come by this trait genetically. My mother used to say, if it's not worth wearing, it's not worth eating!"

Laughter eased the tension between us.

Patricia and Rainey Hornsby's five-bedroom home graced six wooded acres in the Chemonie Crossing development several miles out Centerville Road. The grassy side yard was filled with tables, chairs, and people of mixed ages milling around with soft drinks and plates of food. Smoke billowed from a brick grill on the side patio. Throughout the crowd, small girls of Chinese descent dashed and played like honeybees tipping between spring blossoms. A few American-born children, the biological offspring of some of the couples, also mixed with the group.

A petite forty-ish strawberry blonde woman broke away from the crowd when she spotted us walking across the front yard. Her impish green eyes and ruddy cheeks made me want to call out—*well, if it's not Mary McShane*—in a thick brogue.

Holston bent to give her a warm hug. He introduced us.

"I'm so glad you could come," she said.

Holston searched the crowd. "Where's Rainey?"

Patricia waved her hand in dismissal. "Last time I saw him, he was tightening one of the seats on the swing set. Have you eaten? There's a ton of food!"

Holston glanced toward the informal buffet. "Actually, we had something earlier."

"I should've told you to eat with us. I'm sorry! Anyway, come on over and I'll introduce you to the families here this evening. This isn't all of us. The Bronsons left last week to pick up another orphan. This'll be daughter number two for them."

Since Holston was busy speaking with the adoptive parents, I wandered over to the playground to watch the children play. One little girl of about four ran up and grabbed my hand.

"Come on Mama chuntian, come play with us!"

I didn't bother trying to explain to her that I wasn't anyone's mama, unless Shammie and Spackle counted.

She led me over to the play area and introduced me, one by one, to the other little girls, referring to me as Mama chuntian each time.

Patricia appeared from the edge of the crowd. "I see you've met our daughter, Ruth. She's not shy, that one."

"She's made sure I got to meet her friends. She's been calling me Mama chuntian. Do you know what that means?"

Patricia shrugged. "The mama part is obvious, as to the other word...I haven't a clue. Ruth likes to give her friends nicknames." She called her daughter.

Ruth ran to her mother and tipped her head in a slight bow.

"Honey, Miss Hattie would like to know what Mama chuntian means. Can you tell her in English?"

Ruth smiled at me. "Sure! It means mother spring."

Patricia rested her hand on her daughter's shiny black hair. "Why'd you name her mother spring?"

Ruth shrugged. "May I go now?"

"Yes, honey." Then, to me. "Who knows? Maybe you remind her of springtime."

"Holston told me he met you two last year during the legislative session."

"Isn't he an adorable man? I work for the legislature, mostly dealing with domestic violence issues. Rainey and I met Holston at a fundraising dinner for the Refuge House, the Tallahassee shelter for battered spouses and their children. We had just returned from our trip to China to adopt Ruth. It was a pretty hectic time."

I was surprised. "She's only been here for a year?"

She glanced toward the children and smiled. "Ruth's an amazing kid. I had expected to adopt an infant, but, my psychic set me straight on that one!"

"Your psychic?"

"Phil Waters. He's incredible. Let go of your expectations, he told me. Your daughter will be who she is meant to be. Age means nothing to spirit."

"He did a reading for me a couple of weeks ago, too."

"Small world, isn't it?" Patricia smiled slightly as she watched her daughter from across the lawn. "Ruth was nearly three when we got her. Within a year, she'd totally grasped the English language. Her first word was McDonald's. She can spot the Golden Arches from miles away!"

We laughed.

"I noticed most of the children are female. Why?"

"Politics. Chinese families are allowed one child per family. Anymore than one, and they are fined. Boys are desirable. Girls are not. Lately, a few older boys have been orphaned. They are usually left behind because of poor health. The Cooper family adopted their son last year. He was nearly five years of age when they got him. He can remember his parents. Still, most are little girls who were orphaned as infants."

"That's incredibly sad. It just makes me furious to think they'd just throw a child away!"

Patricia sighed. "I felt that way too, initially. Still do, for the most part. Their culture is so much different than ours. After meeting the gentle women who were caretakers at the orphanage, I still believe it would be heart wrenching for a mother, any mother, to desert her infant daughter. I'm just glad we can help some of them have a better life."

"What was involved in the adoption?"

"Months of waiting, reams of paperwork, testing, and money—lots of it. We had to travel to China with a group of prospective parents from all over the States. We used every mode of transportation known to man—short of camel procession—to reach the orphanage where she lived. Then, we spent three weeks meeting with their counselors, and our counselors."

Patricia smiled in Ruth's direction. "It's all been worth the effort. She possesses such an insuppressible spirit. She also has compassion and a knack for healing. I've actually had the beginning of one of my migraine headaches, and she's held her hands on my head until the pain completely vanished. I've seen her cradling one of the animals when it's

163

hurting. Sometimes, she tells me things before they happen. I tried to squelch that talent initially. Now, I see it's one of her gifts."

Patricia turned to me. Her green eyes glistened with moisture. "Gosh, I just met you, and here I am hogging the conversation. You're as easy to talk with as Holston. Please, make yourself at home. I've got to mingle a little." She left to attend to her hostess duties.

Across the yard, I watched Holston as he spoke with the adoptive families. It wasn't difficult to see why people found him attractive. His manner was open and attentive, a reflection of genuine interest. He seemed unaware of his effect on women, young and old—a trait that increased his allure.

By the end of the evening, Holston had made appointments with twenty families for research interviews. Patricia and I had become fast friends.

She hugged me warmly. "Please call us. Rainey and I would love to spend some time with you two. You're such a cute couple!"

"Actually," I said, "we've only just begun to get to know each other."

Patricia's eyebrows shot up. "Wow. I thought you'd been together for a while! You seem to fit each other."

Rainey and Holston joined us, and we promised to meet again soon.

At ten o'clock, we pulled into the parking lot at the townhouse. The inside lights were off, as Jillie had traveled to south Florida to visit her mother for the weekend.

"Want to come in?" I asked. "I'll grab Pearl's keys."

I bounded up the stairs to the second floor, and gathered the truck keys from the top of my bureau. When I returned downstairs, Holston was standing in the center of the living room.

"This townhouse doesn't feel like you," he said.

"Funny. I came to that exact conclusion myself the other night. I'm seriously considering selling it."

"Sounds like Chattahoochee has captured your heart as much as mine."

For a long moment, we stood staring at each other in the low illumination from the entrance hall light. He stepped forward and gathered me into his arms, brought his face close, and hesitated briefly before touching his lips to mine.

I'd always poked fun at the smarmy, lust-filled romance novels Aunt Piddie loved to read. At that instant, any of those authors' descriptions of the way I felt inside would've fit...and then some.

He drew back slowly, and held me gently, safe and cradled next to his heart.

"Do you really feel like driving all the way back to Chattahoochee tonight?" he asked softly.

"No," I managed to squeak.

"Neither do I." He held my hand as he led me up the stairs.

I stopped midway. "You know what this means, don't you?"

He looked at me over his shoulder.

"I can't be your paid massage therapist anymore."

He raised his eyebrows.

"Ethics...I can't be intimately involved with you and be your massage therapist."

Holston laughed. "That's okay, Hattie. This time when you touch me, I want to touch you back."

DINNER AT THE MANSION

Excerpt from Max the Madhatter's notebook:

April 4, 1962: Next time I come back to this earth for a visit, and I believe we all take turns returning here, I would like to have the love of a good woman—or man, depending on which I was and how I was persuaded. I have seen the evidence of that special kind of love, and it's a true gift.

CHAPTER TWENTY-TWO

SEX, FOR THE most part, is overrated. That's how I'd felt before my physical union with Holston. In past relationships, sex had been a biological urge—just a messy part of the package. Previous relationships seemed to start out hot and heavy—long weekends spent in bed, emerging only to pay the pizza-delivery person. Then, they gradually cooled into a mutual apathy devoid of touch. With Holston, my initial shyness about the ridges and bumps of my over-forty body gave way to a wanton erotic playfulness. I morphed into Xena, Warrior Princess, to complement Holston's Caveman Jack. Holston was the most affectionate man I had ever encountered. He had no qualms about holding hands in public or giving me warm hugs at regular intervals.

We agreed to confine the over-night erotic forays to the Tallahassee townhouse. Jillie was wrapped up in final studies, and seemed oblivious to meeting us over coffee in the mornings. Our lives settled into a comfortable routine. Sunday through Tuesday, we spent in Chattahoochee at our respective abodes. Wednesday through Friday, we stayed in Tallahassee. Holston spent his days, and some evenings, meeting with the adoptive families as work progressed on the book he'd tentatively entitled *Daughters of the Rising Moon: China's Lost Children.*

I attended a few of the social gatherings the group regularly planned, and began to see them as one large, supportive family. The parents agreed the children needed to retain contact with their cultural heritage. Frequent meetings allowed them to play together and speak in their native tongue, as well as perfecting the English language. Because the problems the families faced were similar, the adoptive parents drew strength from understanding each other's struggles to raise their children in the best way possible.

The fact that Holston and I spent so much time together didn't escape the rumor mill in Chattahoochee. According to Evelyn, Piddie and Elvina Houston had a major fallin' out over Holston and my weekly cohabitation.

Apparently, I had gone from dismissing the male species entirely to being crowned the town hussy. Amazing! Piddie had reportedly called Elvina a bug-eyed busybody. Elvina countered with a drawn-out lecture on Baptist morality and Piddie's part in the downfall of modern society. Piddie allowed that although she and Carlton had not actually consummated their union before marriage, they had come pretty close. *I didn't sample the fruit first, I just wanted to make sure it was ripe!* She and Elvina didn't speak for a couple of weeks. Like most news tidbits, updates on our sordid liaison lasted a short span before the crew at the Cut'n'Curl moved on to more interesting topics.

The delight of a new relationship lies in ferreting out the minor faults and idiosyncrasies of one's partner. Early on, Holston busted me for my tendency to put the pickle and olive jars back in the refrigerator with just juice. I noted his habit of passing gas three times each morning as he shaved. He couldn't fathom why I felt the burning need to coin a song for the daily occasion.

Toot Three Times by Hattie Davis:
(Sung to the tune of *Knock Three Times*
   by Tony Orlando and Dawn)
Toot three times in the bathroom if you lo—ooove me!
   Twice on the porch (clap, clap) if the answer is no—oooo-oo!
Pfftt, Pfftt, Pfftt means you'll meet me in the bedroom!
   Twice on the porch (clap, clap) means you ain't gonna show—ooow!

At least once a week after I'd heard him in the bathroom, I'd dance around the bedroom singing *Toot Three Times*, doing my best Tony Orlando imitation with a hank of hair held under my nose to approximate a mustache. He'd listen patiently behind the door before answering, "You need therapy." No matter how many times I heard his reply, the phrase always sent me into hiccupping fits of laugher. Who wrote the rule that you can't have fun with bodily functions?

Holston jokingly chided me about the attractive half-lens reading glasses I kept in the bathroom to assure I was putting the makeup on my face. The cruelest trick of the natural aging process lies in the fact that, at a time in my life where I sprouted at least one new chin hair a month, my close-up vision had waned. Presbyopia seemed to occur overnight. I could recall exactly when I first noticed it. Garrett and I were seated in a fancy-pants restaurant in the Florida Keys, and I couldn't read the scripted menu in the low light. Too embarrassed to ask Garrett to recite the entries, I just asked the waiter to bring me the chicken.

As far as daily facial maintenance, I tried my mother's trick with a 3x-magnifying mirror. Good for the overall view, but mascara application was impossible. I appeared to have one giant eye in the middle of my forehead. I'd long given up the idea of eyebrow plucking. Now, I subjected myself to the grueling waxing torture where an esthetician yelled *cowabunga!* before she ripped the flesh and hair-imbedded wax strips from my face.

Around the same time, hormonal imbalance reared its ugly head. For a couple of years following my hysterectomy, I gloated over the fact that my ovaries were still producing the necessary chemical cocktail. Then, I began to have the hot flashes I'd kidded my mother about, and Evil Rita came out on a regular basis. One day, I honestly wanted to get out and rip the lady's head off in the car in front of mine at a stoplight. She was chatting on her cell phone and caused both of us to miss the brief left turn signal. I knew at that point I needed professional help. Within days of starting naturally derived compounded hormone replacement therapy, I was my old loveable self. Most of the time.

A book I'd like to see on the shelf: *From Babe to Bitch (or Gonna Take a Peremenopausal Journey).*

Fortunately for both of us, Holston and I had crossed paths at a time I felt relatively balanced. Though life's events were tumultuous the first time I met him at Joe's and Evelyn's, I was a rock inside. Crisis brought out the best in me.

Holston melded into my family as if he'd always been an integral part. Other than the fact he was a Damn Yankee—a trespass that Aunt Piddie graciously forgave him—his easy charm and sense of the absurd helped him hold his head above my family's constantly churning waters. Eventually, Evelyn found a way to speak to him without tripping all over herself. My only grief was the knowledge that neither of my parents had the pleasure of knowing the man I treasured more than double chocolate cake…with almonds.

A heavenly blend of aromas wafted though the door as the family entered Holston's newly remodeled kitchen.

"Come on in!" he called as he ushered Evelyn, Jake, Leigh, and me into the room. "Where're the rest of the crew?"

Evelyn gestured over her shoulder. "Joe and Bobby are helping Mama negotiate the front steps. She can make it without the wheelchair, but she's a little slow."

"Guess I need to put in a ramp if I use this house for any commercial purposes," Holston said. He wiped his hands on the dishtowel hanging over his shoulder. "Dinner's ready as soon as the garlic rolls are warm. Please seat yourselves at the table. I'm sorry I don't have any sitting room furniture yet."

Jake pulled out a chair. "As soon as the painters finish the upstairs, I can bring the floor refinishing team in here. I'd hate to have workers traipsing in and out with their dirty shoes on my…umm…our newly varnished wood floor!"

Holston nodded. "Soon enough, soon enough. I'm just glad to finally be out of the hotel room. I'm also glad we decided to pay someone to complete the painting. My shoulders are still reminding me that I had no business doing the walls down here. This is a huge house!"

Jake clapped his hands together. "I can't wait to start on the grounds! You should see the water garden Sheila at Native Nurseries has planned for the back yard."

"You're sure good at spendin' Holston's money, aren't you?" Piddie called from the kitchen door. Flanked by Joe and Bobby, she inched her way to the large round oak table and plopped down. "Whew! I feel like I've run a mary-thon!"

Holston opened a bottle of Piesporter Michelsberg and poured a glass of the sweet white wine for everyone at the table. I helped him bring the platters and bowls from the stove. Other than an occasional Sunday morning brunch, this was the first time I'd tasted his cooking. Tonight, he had prepared turkey cutlets in a creamy picatta sauce with capers over linguine, glazed carrots, a mixed spring-greens salad with raspberry walnut vinaigrette dressing, and homemade Italian garlic knot rolls.

When we were all seated, Evelyn volunteered to say the blessing. Following family tradition, we held hands and bowed our heads. "Lord…we thank you for this gathering of family and friends…"

After a couple of minutes, Piddie grumbled. "Someone stop her, or the food'll be stone cold."

Evelyn gathered religious steam and droned on with another long litany of prayerful insights. Finally, she said "Amen."

"Amen," we echoed.

"Lordy-be, Evelyn! You sure can go on with a food blessin'! I bet the Good Lord sits Himself down when He hears you start up a'prayin'! 'Well…it's that woman again! I better take a load off cause it's gonna be awhile!'"

Evelyn shot eye daggers across the table at her mama. "Well, at least my blessing makes it past the ceiling."

"Now, ladies," Joe said in a soothing tone, "let's just settle down now, and enjoy Holston's hospitality."

As soon as we got busy passing the plates, Evelyn and Piddie forgot to be mad at each other.

Piddie wiped a thick haze of sauce from her lips. "This turkey is so moist. Not like the Thanksgiving turkey Evelyn made a couple of years back."

Evelyn shot her mother a warning glare. "Mama…."

Piddie laughed. "She decided to fry the turkey like she'd heard about from someone at the Cut'n'Curl. She went out and bought this contraption special for it. Well, when she was done, the white meat was so dry you could've used it for a hockey puck! Seems she heard the turkey was 'sposed to float to the top when it was done!" Piddie stopped to chuckle again. "I don't know much about fryin' a turkey myself, but I can honestly swear that nothin' weighin' in at twenty pounds is gonna float to the top of anything, 'less you throw it in the pool with a life preserver wrapped around it!"

Piddie howled with laughter until tears formed at the corners of her eyes. Everyone at the table, even Evelyn, got caught up.

"Whew!" Piddie said, wiping her eyes. "It feels good to belly laugh like that! I think it gives your insides exercise." She reached over to Evelyn. "I know you do your best, honey. And, you've been improvin', here lately."

Hearing the rare compliment from her mother, Evelyn smiled in spite of herself.

Over a dessert of chocolate torte with white chocolate sauce and coffee, Aunt Piddie filled us in on the latest news from the Cut'n'Curl.

Holston stood. "I have a proposal to make!"

"I sure hope it's a weddin' proposal," Piddie mumbled.

"I have the opportunity to write a piece on the cruise industry— mainly, how they cater to the entire family. I'd like all of you to accompany me on a seven-day Alaskan cruise to help me with the research."

After a moment of shocked silence, everyone spoke at once.

"Wait! Wait! Let me explain. I have four staterooms available, enough for eight people. The problem is, the dates are from June 3rd through June 10th, less than two months from now."

"I can take time off," Joe said. "I'm retiring next year, anyway. What are they gonna do, fire me?"

Evelyn said, "I don't have anything planned."

"That's enough time for me. I'll just mark off the schedule books in advance," I said.

"Well, shoot!" Jake said. "I'm not going to be left out. Anybody who plans a last minute wedding now...they'll just have to use another florist. I'm in!"

Bobby and Leigh were excited to go, as well.

"It'll be like a honeymoon for us!" Leigh said.

The group turned toward Aunt Piddie. "I hope you all have a good time." Her lower lip quivered slightly.

"You don't want to go?" Holston asked.

Tears gathered in her blue eyes. "I can't go on a boat! I need a wheelchair to get around. I can walk a little ways, but not far. I'd just slow you down."

Holston rounded the table and squatted by her chair. "Ah—but, you're an important part of my plan. I need the viewpoint of family members with all levels of ability and disability."

Piddie's face brightened. "I can go?"

"Most definitely. We can make arrangements with the cruise line for your wheelchair. The airlines are most cooperative, too."

Piddie slapped her palms on the table. "Sign me on as the senior citizen corrie-spondent!"

Holston stood. "Okay then! Here's the main problem I see. We have a short time to finalize the arrangements. I can take care of the airline reservations. The only hitch I see is this: because we will be in Canada for a brief time before boarding the ship, we'll each need a picture ID and either a valid passport or certified official copy of a birth certificate. The latter will probably be the quickest to procure."

"My passport is still valid." Jake said. "I traveled into Canada a few times while I lived up North. It was easier to flip out a passport at the border, so I got one a few years back."

"Good, I have a passport as well. As for the rest of you, the driver's license will suffice for the picture ID, and I can help you apply for a certified birth certificate over the Internet. The fee is small, and it takes a couple of weeks to process. I wouldn't advise taking your original birth certificate on the trip."

"What about Mama?" Evelyn asked.

Piddie's face lit up. "Oh, I have a driver's license."

Evelyn's face mirrored our unified shock. "What?"

"They keep sendin' me renewal notices, and I pay 'em. I could drive if I wanted to."

Evelyn snorted. "I surely wouldn't ride with you."

Piddie pointed a pudgy finger toward her daughter. "Don't start up with me, missy! I'm not the one who's had three fender benders in the last year!"

"Ladies—"Joe said.

"Piddie, the fact that you do have a license certainly makes things simpler," Holston said as he returned to his chair. "I'll have brochures soon, so we can review our options for the extra excursions in the three ports we'll be visiting: Juneau, Skagway, and Sitka. There will be two stops on the way up to Glacier Bay and one stop on the return trip."

Piddie clapped her hands. "We gotta go clothes shoppin', Evelyn!" She stopped and frowned. "Oh, no. What about the party we're goin' to plan for Bobby and Leigh?"

"Let's save that 'till we get back home," Bobby said.

Leigh nodded. "It'd be too much to cram all of that in, and plan a trip, too."

After the family left, I helped Holston clear the dirty dishes.

"So…what's really up with this trip?" I asked as I loaded plates into the dishwasher.

"We're taking a trip to Alaska," Holston answered, all sweetness and innocence.

"Holston, I know as well as you do that nobody would foot the bill on four staterooms for publicity on an article. One, maybe two…but, four?"

Holston closed the dishwasher and toweled dry the countertops. "I'm paying for the majority of the trip, okay? If you tell them that, they won't go. I'm getting a great group rate for us, and, I really want to do this. You and your family have given me so much and never once expected a thing in return." His eyes glistened with moisture. "That means more to me than you can imagine."

I wormed my way into his arms. "You're the sweetest Damn Yankee I've ever met."

WAGON'S HO!

Chocolate Baked Alaska—Cake Recipe

Ingredients: ¾ cup sugar, 1 cup flour, ½ cup cocoa, ¾ tspn baking powder, ¾ tspn baking soda, egg, ½ cup milk, ¼ cup vegetable oil, 1 tspn vanilla extract. ½ cup water.

Combine sugar, flour, cocoa, baking powder, and baking soda. Add and mix for 2 minutes 1 egg, ½ cup milk, ¼ cup vegetable oil, 1 teaspoon vanilla extract. Mix in boiling water. Pour into prepared pan and bake for 30 to 35 minutes. After the cake has cooled, remove it from the pan and cut off the raised center of the cake so that the top is level. Let cool for at least two hours.

Shape one quart of ice cream (your favorite flavor) into a layer the same size as your cake and return to the freezer. Let it harden for at least two hours. 15 minutes before you are ready to serve desert, make the meringue.

CHAPTER TWENTY-THREE

JAKE SWEPT INTO my bedroom on the Hill wearing a form-fitting pair of dress pants and a silky rayon shirt. "Does this make me look fat?" he asked as he pirouetted on his good leg to show me all viewpoints.

"You couldn't look fat if you tried, Jake. Besides, don't you need to look hot so you can catch some unsuspecting tourist?"

Jake snorted indignantly, his hands on his slender hips. "Why does everyone assume that all gay men are horn-dogs just lurking in shady bathrooms looking for action? You know I'm not that type of girl!"

I laughed. "Perhaps it's the air of suppressed sensuality you exude."

His scowl lightened. "Gotta be it!" He surveyed the mounds of clothes stacked on my bed. "Gaaah…I'm glad I don't have to cart your bags around! You look like you're going to Alaska for a month!"

"I want to be prepared," I said. "Holston says the weather can be unpredictable in early June. I have to take clothes to layer in case the weather's cool."

"If you don't have it here, I can't imagine you'd need it. Did you find a dress for formal night?"

"Oh! Yes! Wait!" I grabbed a plastic-wrapped hanging bag. "I'll try it on for you."

"Sister-girl!" Jake cooed when I stepped into the room. "You are a dish of Baked Alaska in that dress! Maybe, Cherries Jubilee. Well, something sweet on fire, anyway."

I sashayed around the room like a runway model in the slinky, formal-length, strapless black dress, then whipped a velvety-soft cashmere pashmina throw around my shoulders.

Jake lurched to pet the wrap. "Cashmere. Honey, you are intent on spending your inheritance."

"You only go to Alaska once, maybe twice, in a lifetime, right?"

"Exactly. That's why I bought a new tux. I'll pick it up tomorrow at the mall." Jake's expression darkened. "You have lost a lot of weight, sister-girl. Maybe you and lover-boy should take a break from breeding and eat some decent food."

"I've been eating, Jake. Besides, I kind of like being able to wear a dress like this without seeing all the bulges and lumps sticking out in obvious places."

"You don't need to lose any more. A woman looks better with a few curves."

"Now you sound like my mother."

Jake rested a hand on my shoulder. "No kidding, you have been looking a little worn out. I think you need to stop all this back and forth nonsense. Travelin' between the two towns is wearing you out! It's so much calmer over here." The loving concern on his face caused tears to form in my eyes. "You sure you're okay?"

"I do need a vacation, I think. I'm not sure I'm ready just yet to give up on Tallahassee all the way...maybe some day soon, though. This place kinda grows on you, after a while." I smiled at him. "Don't worry about me, Jake. It's just...I haven't had my usual amount of energy."

"You may have...how does Piddie put it? Low blood."

I walked to the bathroom to undress. "I could be a bit anemic. I've felt this way before. I'm due for a check-up. I'll call when we get home from the trip and schedule with Dr. McCray."

Jake yelled through the door. "I talked to Evelyn this morning while you were in the shower. The woman is just beside herself with excitement. She's sewing up a storm for herself and Piddie."

"I can't wait to see how she dresses for the cruise! I wonder if she'll carry the Island theme to the cold country."

Jake smoothed an unruly lock of my hair when I stepped from the bathroom. "Actually, I think she's going with more of a L.L. Bean out-doorsy-girl look."

"Good. It'd be hard to see a tropical print transposed on the view of the Inland Passage."

He tilted his head. "I'm proud of Evelyn. She's really a trooper. As amusing as your Aunt Piddie can be, I'm sure it's no picnic living with her 24-7. Then, there's that heart-wrenching daughter thing."

"My weird cousin Karen?" I twirled a finger in a circle by my temple.

Jake curled up on the bed with a throw pillow. "Yeah. I don't remember a lot about her from our growing-up years. I vaguely recall this odd little girl who used to hang out with us sometimes. Since I've been back home, I had not heard anyone mention her at all! I finally got the scoop from—"

"Elvina Houston," we said in unison.

Jake threw his hands into the air. "How'd you ever guess?

Anyway, Karen changed her name to Mary Elizabeth Kensington immediately after she graduated from FSU. She's now living in a huge house north of Atlanta with a couple of cats. She has a great job with Georgia Metro Public Television. But, get this...she speaks with a British accent and no longer acknowledges her connection to the family. It's as if Karen had an out-of-body experience, and some free-loading British woman with an attitude stepped in while she was out!"

I stuffed a wad of underwear into the open suitcase. "I didn't know any of this! I suppose that's why the only pictures of Karen are from before graduation."

"Joe and Evelyn have both been very hurt by all of it. Evelyn has tried to keep in touch by phone. Karen, or Mary Elizabeth, refuses to answer by her real name, and treats her parents like they're some people that she met on a holiday and doesn't remember very well."

I shook my head. "That is so unbelievable!"

"She seems to function okay. I've caught sight of her a couple of times on interview shows on GMPTV. She has a crisp British accent. Certainly, you'd never pick her out as being from the South!"

Jake turned to leave the room "Elvina says that it's as if everyone's decided to leave it alone. It's a taboo subject. No one wants to hurt your family. Listen to me, standing here yakking like I don't have thing to do! I gotta finish packing. I can't believe we actually leave in three days. I have to set up the VCR to tape Oprah while we're gone. Thank the stars for modern technology!"

The procession that screeched to a halt in the departing flights lane at Tallahassee Regional Airport looked more like a parade on the Beverly Hillbillies show than an excited gathering of Alaskan-bound travelers. All we lacked were the shovels and buckets for road-kill collection hanging from the back bumpers. Stephanie had graciously volunteered to chauffeur Holston, Jake, and me over in Betty. The rest of the gang followed in line.

"I still feel bad you're not going with us," I said as we pulled to the curb.

Stephanie shrugged. "Someone has to hold down the fort. Besides, I start skin specialist school in Tallahassee end of next week."

As if we were missionaries heading off to some mosquito-infested third-world country, a large contingency of Chattahoochee citizens, as well as a few close Tallahassee friends, had turned out to see us off. Patricia and Rainey stood near Gate A-3 with Ruth. The Delta personnel at the gate commented that they didn't recall a crowd of this size since the Florida State University Football team had returned victorious from the 1999 National Championship game in New Orleans.

Ruth handed me a small red velvet box after I hugged her mother and father.

I knelt down. "What's this?"

Patricia smiled down at her daughter. "Ruth picked this out herself. She was quite adamant that she be able to give it to you today."

I opened the box to reveal a delicate gold and porcelain daisy on a fine gold chain. I knelt down. "This is beautiful. Ruth! Thank you!"

"It will keep the bad thing away from you until you come home, Mama chuntian."

I opened the minute clasp and slipped the pendent around my neck. "I won't take it off for a second!" I held the small girl to me.

The intercom crackled with the call for first-class passenger boarding. I hugged Patricia and Rainey goodbye.

"First Class?" I asked when Holston approached and ushered the family toward the ramp.

"Better for everyone. Larger seats, more room. It's going to be a long day." The gray morning had dawned with a light drizzle, and Aunt Piddie motioned for Jake to halt her wheelchair to gain assurance from the handsome, gray-haired captain that he could handle the plane in bad weather.

"It's clear in Atlanta, ma'am," he said. "We'll be up and over these few clouds in a very short period of time. I've logged many hours in weather much worse than this."

Since Holston, Jake, Joe, Bobby, and I had previously flown, we settled Aunt Piddie, Evelyn, and Leigh into the window seats. Piddie was immensely interested in the flurry of preflight activity surrounding the plane. The first leg of the trip spanned from Tallahassee to Atlanta. A commonly held notion in this part of the country held that when you died, you'd have to circle Atlanta before moving on. We watched as the procession of coach passengers filed past, lugging bulging carry-on bags. The sound of overhead bins being stuffed to capacity and snapped shut echoed from the rear of the plane.

Piddie wrung her hands. "I sure don't know how they're gonna get this heavy thing off the ground with all these people on it!"

Jake patted her. "Wait until you see the plane we take from Atlanta to Seattle. It will make this one look like it wasn't big enough to be taken away from its mother. By the way, I saw you over there talking with Elvina Houston. Was she crying?"

Piddie swatted the air. "Lordy-be! She's such a drama queen! She wasn't really all caught up in us leaving. She's just upset she's being left out of somethin'. I promised to bring her a souvenir."

The plane pushed back from the ramp and aimed toward the entrance ramp to the runway. The monstrous jet engines started to hum, then roared louder as the Boeing 737 taxied toward the head of the runway. Aunt Piddie held a white-knuckled grasp on the armrest.

Jake reached over and put his hand over hers. "Hold on, Piddie. Here comes the best part!"

As the 737 lifted from the earth, Aunt Piddie let out a loud "Whooeee!" and began to laugh hysterically. "Whew!" she said when we leveled off above the cloud ceiling. "That was faster than Carlton's '54 Chevy at top speed!"

The trip between Tallahassee and Atlanta's Hartsfield International Airport took less than fifty minutes—just long enough for the attendants to serve beverages. Everything about the experience fascinated Piddie: the beverage cart, the complimentary package of nine salted peanuts, and especially, the lavatory.

"Wonder where it goes when you flush it?" she asked. "Hah! Wouldn't it be a hoot if it fell right on Elvina's new hairdo?"

I didn't want to ruin her fun by explaining the holding tank to her, or the fact that we were, at thirty minutes into the flight, miles from home, probably over Macon, Georgia.

After a forty-five minute layover in Atlanta, we boarded the plane for Seattle. As Jake had forecast, the Boeing 767 was the huskier big brother of the smaller plane we'd taken from Tallahassee. By this time, Piddie was an old hand at flying. Taking both her doctor's and Elvina Houston's advice to heart, she stood and walked around at least every thirty minutes to prevent blood clots from forming in her legs.

We circled Seattle, Washington, for a few minutes before gaining clearance to land. The impressive snow-capped peak of Mt. Rainer loomed in the distance. The first thing I noticed when we deplaned was the air quality. The lack of humidity made breathing easier and my entire body felt light. A short commuter flight with Alaskan Airlines connected us to our final destination of Vancouver, British Columbia, Canada. The cruise line personnel had taken our yellow-tagged luggage to the awaiting shuttle buses. On the other side of customs, several smiling, nautically-clad attendants held block-printed signs for the major cruise lines.

A twenty minute bus ride through the clean, colorful streets of downtown Vancouver led us portside to Canada Place, Vancouver's main cruise ship terminal, and the first sighting of our ship, the Regal Queen.

"I gotta find a phone!' Piddie said.

Evelyn dug in her purse for the ticket packets. "Whatever for, Mama?"

"I always call Elvina and let it ring three times, just to let her know I've arrived safely. She won't rest easy till I triple-ring her, and she'll have it all over town that we've been fallen upon by a band of thieves if I don't."

JUST CRUISIN'

Chocolate Baked Alaska—Heavenly Meringue

Ingredients: 8 egg whites, ¼ tspn salt, 2 cups sugar, 2 tspn vanilla extract.

Preheat the oven to 500°F. In a large bowl beat egg whites and salt until foamy: Slowly add sugar and vanilla and beat until whites are stiff but still moist: Put the chocolate cake on a cookie sheet, place the ice cream on top of the cake and cover the cake and ice cream with a thick layer of meringue. Immediately place in the hot oven for about 5 minutes or until the meringue is slightly brown. Serve as soon as possible.

Put any leftovers in the freezer before the ice cream melts. You're sure to eat the rest!

CHAPTER TWENTY-FOUR

HOLSTON HAD BOOKED four outside rooms on the Caribe deck. Jake was assigned to the room with Holston, Aunt Piddie roomed with me, and the two sets of old married farts, Joe & Evelyn, and Bobby & Leigh, had rooms together. The mounds of luggage we hadn't seen since it disappeared on the conveyor belt in the Tallahassee airport had been delivered into our respective staterooms.

"Hey! Hattie! Come in here right now and bring that video camera you brought!" Piddie called from the small bathroom.

"You okay? What's the matter?"

Piddie hooted. "Aim your camera on this sign, first off..."

"Wha...?"

"Just follow my lead, gal! This will be a stitch to watch later on when we get home."

I focused the video recorder on the illustrated sign above the toilet displaying a stern warning about closing the lid before pulling the flush mechanism.

"Okay, now...zoom in on the toilet." She began to gesture like a contest-show model. "You just push this little button—here." Piddie panned for the camera. "And, whoosh!" The vacuum toilet made a loud sucking noise. "It'll suck your dang butt clean out of the boat!" Aunt Piddie cackled. "And, I thought the john on the airplane was fun!"

I shook my head. "C'mon, Pid, we need to get ready for dinner."

"Is this one of them dress-up nights?"

I flipped through the daily flyer provided by the hall steward. "Nope. That's tomorrow night. Just casual tonight."

Following our 6 o'clock seating for dinner, we toured the ship to locate the casino, bars, viewing decks, and grand ballroom. The lighted shores passed slowly by as we headed north into the Strait of Georgia toward the entrance to the Inside Passage. Since we were all tired from the long day of travel, we turned in around eleven.

"Now I see why they have these blackout curtains on the picture windows," Piddie said. "It's still good light outside. It's a wonder these folks up here don't wander around like a bunch of zombies."

The first full day of cruising was spent on the open water. Without the protection of land masses on both sides of the ship, the white-capped five to ten-foot seas as far as you could see tossed the boat in long rolling waves.

Bobby pointed toward the pool in the center of the Lido deck. "Look at that! The boat's rocking so much that it's making an Alaskan wave machine!"

"And there are actually tourists in the water," Leigh added. "Man, we don't go in the water in Florida until it's at least eighty outside. It can't be much over fifty today."

"It's 'cause we got thin blood," Piddie explained. "I bet their blood's thick as pea soup up here."

Bobby hugged Leigh around the shoulders. "Hon, you still look kinda green around the gills. Breakfast didn't help any?"

"I thought it would. I've got these sea-bands on." She pointed to the elastic acupressure bands around her wrists. "I think it's because it's so rough today. I feel like I'm walking around half drunk."

Piddie snorted. "I know what you mean. I forgot to set the brakes on my chair this morning, and I rolled backward into one of the waiters carrying a full load of coffee cups! He was fast on his feet, though. Danced around for a minute, but never dropped one thing."

"It'll be smooth by tomorrow," Holston said. "We'll be on the Inside Passage with land on either side of us again to block the rough seas. If any of you start feeling too bad, the ship has a doctor and a full pharmacy. Leigh, why don't you go on down and see if you can get something for sea sickness?"

The group scattered. Holston and Jake left to sign us up for our in-port excursions, and check out the gym. Bobby and Leigh left for the infirmary, and Evelyn dragged Joe to the shopping decks. Aunt Piddie and I located a couple of lounge chairs blocked from the wind and sat in the bright sun.

"Lordy, I'm havin' a good time! I can tell right now that Joe and I are gonna be in withdrawal when we leave the boat and have to eat Evelyn's cookin' again!" She reached over and patted my hand. "You gotta a good man in Holston. I'm sorry about you havin' to share a room with me. I know you'd a lot rather be with him."

"I wouldn't want to send Evelyn into a moral outrage by shacking up on this vacation. Besides, I'm having a blast rooming with you!"

We rested in shared silence. The singing of the stiff breeze against the Plexiglas windows surrounding the Lido deck muffled the noise from our fellow travelers.

"I'm proud as punch to see your brother so happy, too. Your mama was pretty worried over his drinkin' after the divorce."

"I didn't know until recently."

"He's on the straight and narrow, now. But, he had a time of it for awhile."

"I wish Mama would've let me know."

Piddie reached over and patted my hand. "She didn't mean no harm by it, gal. She barely let on to Evelyn and me about it. I suppose she didn't want it spread around. Bobby came near to losin' his job over it, from what your mama said. He hit rock bottom, and looked up, I reckon. Anyway, he got hisself some help, and started goin' to them Triple A meetings." Aunt Piddie brushed a stray curl from her eyes. "That's where he met Leigh."

"Leigh's a recovering alcoholic, too?"

She shook her head. "I believe she has some family member, maybe her daddy, that is. She goes to a supporter group."

"Guess that's why he hasn't touched even a sip of the wine they've served with the meals."

Piddie nodded.

❦❦❦

"Auntie, I need to ask you something…privately."

Always on the lookout for a secret, Piddie perked up.

"I've been having some…um…bleeding."

Piddie studied my expression. "I thought you'd had all that taken care of with your hysterectum a few years back."

"No, I mean…rectal bleeding."

She jerked upright, her brows knit in concern. "Is it real bad?"

"Sometimes. It's happened a few times in the past couple of months."

Piddie fanned the air with one hand. "Probably just your 'roids raging. That comes with age."

I rolled my eyes. "Hemorrhoids? How enchanting!"

"Then again, you might want to get yourself checked out. Your daddy had some plops removed from his colon when he was…oh…seventy, or so. As I recall, one of them was cancer. They took a piece of his bowel out."

I vaguely remembered him telling me about having his hemorrhoids repaired.

"Why didn't I know about this?"

"Your daddy and mama were bad about not wantin' to worry you kids."

"That's true. They'd call up about two weeks or so after something happened and say, oh…your daddy cut his leg off. We didn't call 'cause we didn't want to bother you. The doctor sewed it back on. "

Piddie chuckled. "Yeah, that was my little brother, all right. He'd have to be near to death before he'd let on anything was wrong. Your mama wasn't much better."

Piddie's blue eyes reflected the perfect Alaskan sky. "You given up on bein' a mama, gal?"

"No…maybe…I don't know. I had given some thought to adopting a baby. Actually, I thought about doing it alone. That was before I met Holston."

"I think you'd make a good mama. Why, look at the fine example your own mama set up for you!" She reached over and patted my hand. "Don't you worry none. If it's meant to be, the good Lord will find a way. There're plenty of youngin's out there with nothin' to call their own."

A waiter appeared beside our chairs. Piddie and I ordered hot chocolate with whipped cream. What the heck, we were on vacation.

Piddie licked the foam mustache from her upper lip. "A person could get spoilt easy. Someone's always there bringin' you something even before you know you want it. And none of them have made me feel like I'm older than dog dirt!"

I sipped the creamy hot chocolate. It was obviously not the lite variety, thank the heavens. "It feels so good to finally relax. It seems like so much has happened."

"We had ourselves a cluster, now, didn't we?"

Aunt Piddie had a theory worked out for almost any situation. I suppose by her age, you'd have studied life's subtleties long enough to see the underlying patterns.

AUNT PIDDIE'S CLUSTER THEORY:
Life is full of bad and good. Things happen in clusters—both bad and good. Like, for example, death comes in three's. When you're in a cluster, you just have to keep your head above the surface and tread water like the dickens till the cluster passes you by. When the bad cluster goes away, you're due a period of smooth sailin'.

Another theory she held as honest-to-goodness truth was the Southern Bootist Theory:

AUNT PIDDIE'S SOUTHERN BOOTIST THEORY:

Whenever you say the words forever, never, ever, and always, and especially in combinations like always and forever and never, ever, this big boot comes right down outta the sky and kicks you into the situation you were never, ever, always, or forever gonna be in…or out of…

Made perfect sense to me. The one time I received a traffic ticket was immediately after I'd bragged that I'd never even gotten a speeding ticket! The God in charge of moving violations almost broke his neck to park a trooper running radar in the median in front of me.

The cruise line planned the formal dinners for the evenings following a day at sea. Most of the nights after we were in port would've been too hectic to spend the extra time dolling up for the occasion. I was reserving my long black gown for the second formal evening. For tonight, I planned to wear a sky blue cocktail length dress.

I tugged at the off-center seam. "Now I remember why I hate panty hose so damn much!"

"That's one of the joys of getting on up there in years." Piddie pulled her caftan up to reveal ankle-length hose under her sparkly gold sneakers. "Everyone's so busy marvelin' at the fact you're still alive, and they don't much care how you look. It's very freein'."

We left to meet the rest of the family on the Promenade level, where a three-deck-high cocktail party with complimentary drinks was underway. My breath left when I saw Holston enter the room in his formal attire. Not one to be outdone, Jake strolled in behind him, pausing briefly to case the room before making a sweeping entrance.

"My, my! You boys are handsome! Both of you clean up real nice!" Piddie said.

Holston held my eyes and smiled seductively. "I'd say the very same about you, ladies."

How many days would it be until we could be alone again?

Joe and Evelyn spotted us from across the crowded room. Evelyn wore a clingy scarlet mid-calf dress. Joe slipped his arm proudly around his wife's waist.

Piddie whistled. "If it's not the Harlot of the 'Hooch."

Evelyn blushed. "It's too much. I knew it! I'll go change."

Joe squeezed her. "Don't you dare!" Evelyn fluttered her eyelashes like a schoolgirl. Was she flirting with her husband?

"Where are Bobby and Leigh?" Holston asked.

Evelyn tore her gaze from her husband. "They'll meet us at the table. The doctor gave Leigh something real mild for nausea."

A three-piece ensemble of piano, drums, and guitar played for a handful of dancers. Holston led me on to the floor, and we slipped easily into the samba beat. We danced together like we made love: teasing, approaching and retreating, then blending together into the rhythm. Cruise photographers circled through the crowd snapping pictures of couples and groups. That evening, we coined the phrase Cheesy Photo Opportunity, or CPO.

Bobby and Leigh appeared a few minutes after we were seated for dinner.

"You feeling better?" Evelyn asked.

Leigh waved the wine steward away from her glass. "Much better, thank you. The doctor gave me some freshly ground ginger root for the nausea."

"Why didn't he give you something stronger than that?" Piddie asked.

Bobby and Leigh exchanged meaningful glances. "You want to tell them—or shall I?" Bobby asked.

"Lord help us all!" Piddie clutched her chest with one hand. "Last time you two made an announcement it damn near gave me a heart attack!"

Leigh smiled. "It seems as if the motion of the boat wasn't entirely responsible for my sickness."

We all stared in silence.

"Umm...the doctor had to test me before I could get any strong medication for sea sickness. As it turns out, I'm pregnant."

The announcement sent ripples of excitement around the table.

"This is outstanding!" Holston said. "And, what a wonderful place to celebrate!"

MENDENHALL GLACIER

Excerpt from Max the Madhatter's notebook:

April 19, 1957: I like surprises. I really do. Well, not the kind like when I have one of my spells in front of folks. It scares them. Scares me, too. Nurse Marion bought a box of fancy chocolates to share after Valentine's Day last year. With one bite, I found a creamy rich filling flavored with something exotic. Each one I tried was different. They looked so innocent on the outside, but the most delicious surprise waited inside.

CHAPTER TWENTY-FIVE

THOUGH THE SUN rose at 3:30 a.m., we didn't reach Juneau, our first port of call, until 1:00 p.m. Cloudless, robin's egg blue skies greeted us as we stood on the viewing deck observing the pilot's careful maneuvers into port. The seafront was awash with a flurry of activity. Floatplanes soared overhead and smaller departing fishing vessels criss-crossed our wake. Towering forested mountains loomed behind the strips of level land where Juneau spread out along the shores on either side of the Inside Passage. The Regal Queen's sister ship was moored at the dock behind the space reserved for our boat.

Bobby leaned over the rail. "I'd sure hate to know I had to park this baby."

We watched in fascination as our boat slowly paralleled Juneau's Steamship Dock. The engines on the sides of the ship kicked on, and the Regal Queen inched sideways until she was aligned perfectly with the space provided. Massive cables were deployed fore and aft. When the ship was secured, the metal gangway was lowered and fixed into position.

"Where's everyone off to today?" Evelyn asked. "Joe and I are going to ride the chair lift to the top of the mountain, then shop till we drop when we come back to town."

Joe smirked and shook his head, then smiled brightly when Evelyn turned his way.

"Piddie and I are going on a nature-boat tour. We're supposed to be on the lookout for seals and whales," Jake said.

Piddie's blue eyes lit up. "I've always wanted to see a whale—other than Elvina Houston in a bathing suit."

Bobby reached over and grabbed his wife's hand. "Leigh's a little tired today, so we're going to the museum and maybe hit a few of the stores."

Holston rested his arm across my shoulders. "I guess that leaves us to be the adventurous fools. We're ice hiking on the Mendenhall glacier!"

"Well, ain't that somethin'! Okay—" Piddie fussed with her purse and wind jacket. "We'll all meet up at the salmon bake this evening. Let's go, Jake. I don't want to miss our boat."

Since our excursion wasn't scheduled to leave until two, Holston and I visited a few shops. Three cruise ships were docked, and the Juneau streets were teaming with credit card toting tourists. Eager to support the local economy, we bought embroidered sweatshirts for ourselves, as well as souvenirs for Stephanie, Jillie, and Margie, and John. We located the Juneau Police Department, where I exchanged Tallahassee and Chattahoochee police departments' arm patch badges for Juneau Police Department patches for Chris, Kelly, Kathy, and Rich.

At two, we met the Alaskan Wilderness Excursions van near the dock. Along with the ship's doctor and cruise entertainment director, Holston and I were the other two brave souls heading for the glacier. The hike was a recent addition to the Queen Lines' long list of excursion choices. 'Dr. Tom' and Jane were going along to rate the trip for time constraints and level of required fitness.

The van deposited us at the outfitter's headquarters, where we were fitted with bright red Gore-Tex wind jackets and pants, grinders for clamping rescue ropes in the advent of a mishap, mid-calf waterproof boots, and nylon girders over the boots.

"Make sure you pee before you get all this on!" I warned Holston as the outfitter cinched the grinder strap around my waist. I looked like the Pillsbury doughboy with an L.L. Bean fixation.

We were each given an ice ax and a set of crampons to clamp on the sole of the boots when we reached the glacier. After posing for a CPO, this time with our disposable water-resistant camera, we boarded the van for Juneau International Airport.

The helicopter rested on an asphalt pad at the far end of the landing strip. Long canals of water stretching the length of the paved runway provided space for the arriving and departing floatplanes. Near the terminal, an Alaskan Airlines jet taxied toward the buildings.

"Don't hit the side of the 'copter with these shoes," the bearded outfitter explained. "These boots are made of space-age material, and they're actually harder than the shell of the 'copter. We don't want any new dents today, okay?" He flashed us a smile that read: maybe this group will be bright enough to follow instructions.

We strapped into the seats, and the pilot handed us headsets with voice-activated microphones to use while in flight. The engine droned, and we lifted straight up and away from the landing pad.

Initially, our course followed a small river as it snaked away from the city. The terrain changed quickly to the blinding white of the Alaskan ice fields, broken only by the surrounding brownish-gray rock peaks.

"There's a mountain goat and her kid." The pilot pointed to a sheer rock facing. "We don't buzz too close this time of year. Most of them have their young with them, and we try not to upset them with the noise."

The 'copter swung around to face our destination, the Mendenhall Glacier. Below, a small camp dotted with waving red flags and two guides awaited our arrival. The pilot guided the helicopter gently to rest on the ice, and waited until we walked away before lifting off for his return to Juneau.

"Okay! Hello! My name is Ray and this is my buddy, Chip. We'll be your guides today!" Ray bobbed his curly head. "Time for a little in-service training before we do the ice!"

Great. We'd pulled Bevis and Butthead for tour guides.

"First thing! Your crampons." Ray slipped the steel shoe-shaped forms on to the sole of his boots. "These spikes on the bottom will keep you from sliding and falling down on the ice."

The crampons reminded me of my first pair of roller skates in the late '50's. I would wear my Red Ball sneakers and strap the skates on around the shoes, and hurtle myself into a skinned knee in no time flat. I still have the scar from the time I got the bright idea to skate down Thrill Hill. Believe me, it's much safer in a car.

Chip demonstrated the correct way to hold an ice ax so that it could double as a walking stick and a brake in case of a fall. We walked around in a circle a few times to learn the proper way to maneuver on solid ice. "Don't roll the foot from heal to toe like you normally do on land. Stomp your foot down flat with each step so that the spikes on the crampon can bite into the ice."

Walking in the awkward footgear, I felt like I was high stepping with the FSU Marching Band at halftime. Chip led the small procession with Ray bringing up the rear. Both guides carried coiled ropes and extra clamps for emergency rescue use. Ray and Chip took turns amusing us with an informative commentary on the history and geology of the glacier.

Holston waved. "Come a little closer, Hattie." The gaping blue slit though the ice was two to three-hundred feet deep with a frigid white-water stream gushing at its base.

"I can see it just fine from here, thanks."

Holston zoomed in on the crevasse with the camcorder for a few frames, then swung the camera to face me. "And…here's Hattie Davis, a good quarter mile back from the edge."

I rolled my eyes and stuck out my tongue. Everyone's a freakin' comedian.

After crossing the crevasse at the narrowest point, we hiked for another quarter of a mile to a fifteen-foot vertical wall of ice.

"Who feels like trying their hand at ice climbing?" Ray called.

Every great expedition needs a camera operator—someone to stay at the base of the hill and record the adventurous ascent.

"I'll take the camcorder," I said.

I'm not a coward. Yellow is not my base color. Since the time in sixth grade when I shot up five inches in height in three months, I have had no internal gyroscope. Thin air can trip me up, if it gets in my way.

I'd learned to forgo any trial involving the need for balance.

Coached by Ray and Chip, Holston borrowed my ice ax, and used the pick ends to grab the ice above him and pull his weight up the wall. Since the crampons had spikes on the toes, he kicked the tips of the boots into the ice as if he were ascending stairs. When he reached the top, the entire group waved to my camera from their vantage point above.

Ray descended first, demonstrating how to balance against the wall using the ice ax and the sides of the boot crampons to aid in winding downward. When we were once again on the same level, Ray offered each of us a nut and granola bar and a bottle of spring water. After a brief break, we hiked back toward the helicopter landing site. Ray and Chip chatted easily as they walked, oblivious to the two Florida lowlanders heaving for breath in their wake. We had hiked for less than two miles by the time we reached the flags surrounding the camp—the equivalent effort of a five-mile land hike. It was all that dang marching.

Holston motioned to my backpack. "Let me have the camera." He handed the camcorder to Chip and showed him how to operate the controls.

"Okay!" He put his arms around my waist. "Smile for the folks back home."

I mustered a weary smile and my best parade wave. "Hi, everybody!"

Holston grappled in the pocket of his wind jacket and pulled out a small velvet box. He knelt in front of me.

I thought the altitude had finally gotten to him. "What're you doing?"

"Hattie Davis," he said, dramatically, "would you do me the extreme honor of becoming my wife?"

There's a tilt mechanism in a person's mind that zorks out at times of stress, even the good, giggly kind. My mind drifted into a *petit mal*, Sound-of-Music dream state. I was Julie Andrews, blue chiffon swirling around my slim body, gazing raptly into Christopher Plummer's eyes. The accompanying tune played in my head—something about how I must've had a wretched childhood and miserable youth. But I must've done something good, because here you are, standing there, loving me. The orchestra music swelled in the background.

I snapped to reality. Holston was still kneeling at my feet, holding a diamond engagement ring like an offering to the revered goddess of the glacier, a rapt expression on his handsome face.

"Yeah…I mean yes!"

I stripped the heavy glove off and Holston slipped the golden ring onto my finger. The icy shimmer of the two-carat diamond rivaled the glacial blue ice at my feet.

"Unbelievable," I mumbled.

"Yes, you are that," Holston said as he rose and scooped me up. In the bulky Gore-Tex wind suits, we were Mr. and Mrs. Doughboy in love.

A faded orange former school bus delivered us to the Native Alaskan salmon bake. Nestled in a small clearing in the woods, the cook-out site resembled a festive traveling circus with blue-striped tents. Two long baking racks over a smoldering alder wood fire pit were tended by several aproned Alaskans keeping watchful eyes over rows of cooking chicken, ribs, and salmon filets. One wooden table contained an assort-ment of salads and freshly baked cornbread and muffins. A second table supported platters heaped with the smoked poultry, meat, and fish, and large tins of baked barbecued beans. A side table held an array of soft drinks, iced tea, and freshly brewed coffee.

After serving our platters, Holston and I settled on to a section of the bench surrounding an octagonal picnic table cloaked in a red and white cloth.

Jake smirked. "About time you two dragged in! We were beginning to think you'd taken a detour by the staterooms."

"I hope your day was as good as ours," Piddie grinned, her face still red from the wind. "We saw a whole herd of humpback whales in Auke Bay! With babies! I almost wet my Depends!"

Evelyn shook her head. "Pod, Mama. A group of whales is called a pod."

"Pods are where peas live. Jake and I saw a herd! We saw harbor seals, too! Even spotted an Alaskan black bear along the shoreline of a cove comin' back in!" Piddie wiped the baked bean sauce from her mouth. "That captain was so nice. He settled me on a cushioned chair on the back of the boat. I got a good view of everything."

Jake chuckled. "He got Piddie's cathead biscuit recipe. He didn't come out so bad."

"Look here what my Joe bought for me." Evelyn swept her hand in a circle for everyone to admire her new inlaid opal ring. "He's the sweetest man!"

"Wow, that's beautiful, Evelyn." I studied the ring up close. "You know, opal's my birthstone, but I've never seen a ring like this before. I wish we had more time here to see all of the shops."

Joe smirked. "We pretty much covered it for everyone, Hattie."

Leigh pointed to my ring finger. "Looks like you found a souvenir somewhere, too."

I blushed slightly. "Oh...this..."

Piddie grabbed my hand and leaned in close. "Diamond as big as the Rock of Gibo-bo and she says, *oh...this!*" Her eyes twinkled. "Well...give it up. We seem to be on a roll with the announcements in this family."

"Hattie has agreed to be my wife," Holston said.

Piddie clapped her hands. "Lordy mercy! I prayed to sweet Jesus this was going to happen! Whooo-eee! I can die a happy woman!"

I smiled at my ancient aunt in her yellow L.L.Bean anorak and polar fleece hat. "Not anytime soon, I hope."

"Especially not 'til I finish my Alaskan cruise. Anyway, I got just a few more years left yet 'til I get my hundred-year official birthday card from the Pres-e-dent. I ain't leavin' the earth without that."

SKAGWAY ADVENTURE

Warm You to Your Toes Hot Chocolate Soufflé

Ingredients: 2 tbsp butter, ½ ounce semi-sweet chocolate, 2 tbsp flour, ¼ cup sugar, ¼ tspn salt, 2 eggs, ¾ cup milk.

Melt butter in a saucepan and gently mix in flour and salt. Stir in the milk until smooth and thick. Add melted chocolate, sugar, and egg yolks, lightly beaten. Last, fold in the egg whites, beaten dry. Bake in individual soufflé cups at 350°F for 30 to 40 minutes. Serve hot with whipped cream flavored with vanilla.

CHAPTER TWENTY-SIX

GIORGIO, THE ITALIAN waiter assigned to our dining room table, peaked around the side of the breakfast buffet. He picked Aunt Piddie from the group and stood behind her chair. "You don't lave me anymore?" He pronounced each word carefully with a thick Italian accent.

Piddie patted him on the hand. "Well! If it isn't my favorite little Eye-talian boy! What'cha doin' up here?"

His creamy Mediterranean skin made his smile appear dazzling white. "Sometimes, I work other places on the Queen, but my favorite is your table."

Piddie rolled her eyes. "Oh, you do go on."

"You weren't at dinner last night," he scolded. "I was lonely."

"Oh, we were all at the salmon bake, honey. Don't take it to heart, now."

"You will be at dinner tonight, okay? I have something special planned for you, yes?"

Piddie grinned. "We'll be there with bells on!"

"You going off the ship today?" Giorgio asked, glancing around the table at the rest of the family.

Piddie pointed to the brochure on the table. "Jake, Evelyn, Joe, and I are taking that train ride up the hill. The other youngin's are takin' a hike in the woods."

Giorgio shook his head. "Okay. You be careful. I see you at dinner tonight."

"Oh-wee!" Piddie said as she drowned a stack of French toast with syrup. "I could take him home with me!"

Evelyn's drew her mouth into a thin line. "Now, Mama! Don't be silly. What would you possibly do with him?"

Piddie tapped a red nail on her chin. "Tell Elvina Houston I'd taken on a lover."

"You beat all, Mama." Evelyn turned toward our end of the table. "When does y'all's hike leave?"

Holston answered, "Around eight, I think…pretty close to the time we pull into port this morning. I think we dock in Skagway about seven."

Jake slurped his coffee with an expression of sheer pleasure. "Our train doesn't leave 'till noon, so we're takin' a shuttle into town to do a short walking tour."

"I'd really like to buy a piece of Alaskan gold—maybe a pendant— while we're here," Leigh said.

Holston checked the brochure. "Our hike lasts about four hours. We can look around when we get back into town. We don't even leave port until eight tonight. That's plenty of time to putt around a little."

Piddie took a sip of her coffee. "There's not a thing wrong with any of the food or drink I've had on this trip. This coffee is good as gold. Holston, I've been keepin' a runnin' account of the trip from my senior citizen point of view for your research. I'll be sure to take good notes on the train ride, too."

I shot a loving look in Holston's direction that did not go unnoticed.

Jake slammed his coffee cup down with a bang. "Gaahhh! You two! I can't wait till I can be around you without worrying about being caught in your sappy lover's-look line of fire! Between you and your brother, it's a wonder I don't catch a case of hetero-love sickness."

What the port at Skagway lacked in size, it made up for in color. The entire tree-studded granite mountain face adjacent to the dock was covered in large blocks of painted signs. The logos for the cruise lines that frequented the port were represented in detailed color, as well as abstract art and initials of the brave artists who had suspended themselves to paint on the billboard nature had generously provided. Small vans and buses shuttled visitors into Skagway. The companies in charge of excursions lined the dock waiting for the passengers who had signed up for the various hikes, tours, and fishing and nature sighting trips.

A giant bearded man wearing a tan T-shirt and khaki hiking shorts unfolded himself from the driver's seat of an old Dodge passenger van and loped toward us. In addition to Holston, Leigh, Bobby, and me, the adventurers included a young married couple from Ohio and a second couple from California's Sacramento Valley.

"You all the overland excursion party?" he bellowed.
We nodded dumbly.

He spread his beefy arms. "Welcome to Skagway, Alaska!" He flashed a smile of large, white teeth. "My name is Buckwheat, and I'll be your guide today! Y'all hop on into the van, and we'll get going! There're choppers waiting."

"We'll ride the chopper up the mountain to the head of the trail in the Tongass National Forest," he explained in a deep booming voice as he teased the van through the clumps of tourists walking the route into town. "We'll hitch a ride back on the train."

By this point, I was an expert, if somewhat uneasy, at the helicopter experience. If the motor stalled, we'd fall to earth like a lead weight thrown from a ten-story window. Danger was now my middle name, so that fact didn't faze me. Two helicopters were enlisted to transport us to the trailhead. Following a twenty-minute flight over the Juneau Icefield and the adjacent forest, we touched down near the top of a steep graded hill next to a set of railroad tracks. Buckwheat and a second guide unloaded the supplies, then the helicopters lifted off to return to Skagway.

Buckwheat pulled a bulky black internal-frame backpack over his shoulders. Two bear repellent canisters the size of hairspray cans dangled from clamps on each shoulder strap. Mark, the younger guide, handed out hiking sticks and belt packs loaded with bottled water.

Buckwheat caught me staring at the repellant cans. "Don't worry 'bout these, now. Chances aren't real good that we'll bump into a bear on this trail. We'll be hiking next to a glacial-runoff river, and it doesn't contain salmon because of the dissolved silt in the water. No salmon—no bears. Besides, there's only enough pepper spray in one of these to annoy a grizzly and, maybe, buy us enough time to get away." He let out a deep throaty chuckle. "Just make sure you can run a little bit faster than the slowest member of the group, and you'll be okay!"

We glanced uneasily at each other. Clearly, it would be a toss-up between me and the lady from Ohio with the knee brace as to who would be bear-bait.

Buckwheat reared back and let out a loud bellow. Although I'd never heard the mating call of a lovesick male moose, the sound had to be close. "It's a bee-utiful day for a walk in the woods in Skagway, Alaska!" He turned to us and grinned. "Shall we?"

Having just recently been stranded on the top of a mountain, miles away from Nowhere, USA, we had little choice but to follow the burly man with the backpack into the forest. The level alpine meadow soon gave way to a well-traveled, packed-dirt footpath that snaked between towering evergreens. Buckwheat stopped at intervals to call attention to a particular type of vegetation or wildflower, identify the spoor left by a passing wild animal, and point to the scarred bark on a tree six feet from the ground where a bull moose had scratched his antlers.

The song of rushing water filtered through the foliage as the trail turned to parallel the Skagway River. Buckwheat stopped and dropped his pack on a large flat boulder on the bank. He handed out Hershey's chocolate candy and granola bars from his pack. We took turns posing for pictures with the ice-capped peaks, evergreens, and the coursing river for a backdrop.

Holston nuzzled my ear as he slipped his arms around my waist. "Miss you," he whispered.

I studied the majestic postcard scenery. "Me, too."

"Jake's a good stateroom mate. But—don't tell his highness I told you—he snores."

I laughed. "No secret to me. I was up late one night on the Hill when I couldn't sleep. I went down to the kitchen to rummage in the refrigerator, and could hear him cutting the Z's from there! It's a good thing our bedrooms are on opposite ends of the house."

Holston brushed a stray sprig of hair from my eyes. "You feeling okay? You look a little tired."

"We ice hiked for four hours, then stayed up until after the midnight buffet—way past my bedtime. I'll catch up on my sleep. I'm fine. Really!" We plopped down on the sun-warmed rock. "I just had a thought. What're we going to do with Jake after we're married? I mean—will he still live with us? He's family, and I can't imagine just asking him to leave with no place to go."

"Actually, I've given that some thought. He'll probably want his privacy, as well, Hattie. I have a business proposition for him, if he'll take it. I'd like to rent the mansion out. I'm not sure exactly for what purpose just yet. That'll come. Do you think Jake would consider trading living quarters there in exchange for overseeing the place? I could let him have free reign."

"You want to live on the Hill?"

Holston smiled. "The Hill means more to me. It's where you are."

A warm rush of affection swelled inside of me, closing my throat. It's a wonder people in love can breathe at all.

"I'll keep my study in the back. I think I'd be more motivated to write with an actual office space to report to regularly," he added.

I pitched a loose pebble into the rushing water. "Jake'll probably like the idea of living in the mansion. Ask him. He may have some ideas on how to use the rest of the house, too."

Buckwheat bellowed in his best bull-moose voice for us to continue toward the top of the trail. After a few minutes of climbing, we reached our destination, a boulder-strewn plateau at the base of a small waterfall.

"Whew!" Leigh plopped down on a smooth sitting rock next to me. "This pregnancy thing takes a lot out of a person."

I sat next to her and rubbed the cramp from my left calf. "You doing okay?"

"Oh, sure. It's a great excuse for just about everything. I'm having a blast watching your brother wait on me hand and foot."

"It's good for him, Leigh."

Bobby and Holston were busy quizzing Buckwheat and Mark on the area's geography. From this vantage point near the falls, we could see Laughton Glacier in the distance. I snapped photos for my scrapbook of Buckwheat, Mark, Bobby, and Holston in earnest manly conversation.

"Okay, gang!" Buckwheat said as he gathered his pack. "We gotta beat it on back to the trailhead so we don't miss our ride home. Otherwise, it's a ten mile hike down the tracks back into town."

"You ever missed it before?" the man from Ohio asked.

"Only twice—the first time and the last time! And, I don't wanna do it again!"

Since the return trip was downhill, we made it to the trailhead in a little over half the time it took going up. At the bottom, Buckwheat opened the weighted lid on a heavy wooden box and retrieved two coolers. One ice chest was filled with spring water, soft drinks, and locally bottled beer. The second held crackers, chopped fruit, and Buckwheat's salmon pate'. In addition to being an accomplished mountain wilderness guide during the warm months, he was a gourmet cook, and wrote poetry for children.

Soon, the mournful blast of an air whistle sounded as the yellow and green White Pass Railroad Train rounded the mountain pulling a line of boxcars with names like Big Salmon and McClintock written in bold block letters on their sides. Buckwheat pantomimed a well-rehearsed display of standing in the middle of the tracks waving down the slowing engine.

We hopped aboard with the gear and coolers as soon as the train came to a complete stop. Buckwheat bellowed once more for the benefit of the puzzled passengers. The train jerked as it continued its steep descent into Skagway station.

The town of Skagway resembled an old mining settlement. Wooden boardwalks spanned the sides of the narrow main street. Many of the buildings were reminiscent of the days of gold rush fever. All four of us bought authentic gold nugget pendants at the Ole Gold Mine Gold Shop. While Bobby and Leigh mulled over a selection of sweatshirts,

Holston and I located the single-story wooden building that housed the Skagway Police Department. As I had in Juneau, I traded Florida police badges for the colorfully embroidered police collectibles.

Piddie held a set of dangling gold earrings above the dining table. "Look what I bought Elvina!"

"They're pretty. Kinda unusual," Leigh said.

"They're gold-plated gen-u-ine moose turd earrings." Piddie broke up with laughter. "Just wait 'till Elvina gets a load of these!"

I studied the small oblong drop earrings. We'd seen the real thing on the trail a few hours earlier. "These are fantastic! Very bizarre. I wish we'd have seen these."

"Don't worry," Piddie said. "I bought all of us a pair. Except, of course, for the boys. For y'all, I bought moose turd tie pins."

Jake's face contorted. "Oh…that'll look fetching with a tux."

"That's an idea! I'll make sure to give them to you all so we can wear them on the last formal night."

Bobby shot eye-daggers at Jake. "Big mouth."

Piddie, Jake, Evelyn, and Joe chatted on, often talking at the same time, about the three-hour train ride through the mountains on the narrow-gauge railroad.

Evelyn clamped a hand to her chest. "I'm tellin' you—one sneeze the wrong way, and we'd've been at the bottom of that Dead Horse Gulch!"

"Oh, now, dear. It wasn't that frightening," Joe said.

"Maybe not for you," Evelyn replied tartly, "but I have an inner ear problem."

Piddie sniffed. "It's cause there's so much air separatin' them. Makes you dizzy."

Giorgio appeared at the table before the two could get worked up any further.

"I told you I would have a surprise for you," he said. He presented a perfectly turned-out chocolate soufflé and positioned it on the table in front of Aunt Piddie. With a practiced flourish, he snapped a linen napkin into a triangle and tied it in a loose bib around Piddie's neck. He smiled down at her. "I feed you."

Piddie was delighted beyond words, a rare occurrence.

Giorgio served heaping warm spoonfuls of the spongy soufflé on to small china plates and topped each with a warm heavy cream sauce from a small silver pitcher. After he passed a dessert-laden plate to all of us at the table, he proceeded to spoon feed Piddie, coaxing and cooing to her in Italian. Between bites, she giggled and blushed at the lavish attention.

"Lordy-be!" she said on the way back to the stateroom to rest before the nightly activities, "I never thought havin' a second childhood would be such a grand experience!"

GLACIER BAY

Double Chocolate Cake with Almonds

Ingredients: ¼ cup vegetable oil, 2 ounces semi-sweet choco-late, 1 egg, 1 cup white sugar, ¾ cup milk, 1¼ cups bleached flour, ½ tspn salt, ½ tspn vanilla extract, ½ tspn baking soda, 1 cup semisweet chocolate chips, ½ cup sliced almonds.

Combine oil, chocolate, egg, sugar, milk, flour, salt, vanilla, and baking soda in a 9 inch round pan. Mix until smooth. Sprinkle with nuts and chocolate chips. Bake at 350°F for 30 minutes. Don't burn your fingers!

Let cool on a wire rack, slice, and serve the largest piece to the birthday girl.

CHAPTER TWENTY-SEVEN

THE FACE STARING back from the small mirror over our lavatory didn't look familiar. Deep purple under-eye smudges made me look like a nocturnal animal shocked by the bright light of day. Although I didn't normally wear make-up, except for special occasions, I grabbed the cosmetic pouch and rummaged for the powder base and blush—any-thing to mask the sallow, blotchy skin tone. The weight loss I had at first heralded as a gift from the thigh gods, had robbed my face of fullness.

Who'd've ever thought that I, Bertha Butt Davis, could look anorexic?

The new pants I'd purchased three weeks prior to the trip hung on my hips like the tattered ruined sails of a ghost ship. A deep, gnawing fear lodged stone cold in the pit of my stomach. The bleeding I'd expe-rienced sporadically was now a daily occurrence as my body sent scream-ing smoke signals—call 911!

Get a grip, Hattie! You can hang in there four more days without keeling over!

I took a shaky breath and squared my shoulders. Today would be spent entirely on a long slow trip around Glacier Bay—a much easier pace from the last two days.

"You okay in there?" Piddie called from the other side of the door.

"Yep…just putting on my face!" I answered.

Piddie eyed me suspiciously when I stepped from the small bathroom.

"Girlie, I'm really startin' to fret over you. I've seen dead folks with more color. Maybe you should go on down and see the ship's doctor."

"I'll be all right, Pid."

"The bleedin'…is it happenin' again?"

I sighed heavily. "Yes. But, I want this to be our secret, Piddie. I don't want to ruin everyone's trip. I'll call my doctor as soon as we get home."

She jabbed a bejeweled finger in the air in front of my face. "If you don't, I will. I mean that!"

At 6:00 a.m., the Regal Queen reduced speed to embark two National Park rangers at Bartlett Cove, then sailed into the entrance of Glacier Bay. By nine, we slowed to view the Lamplugh and Johns Hopkins Glaciers, then came in close to the Grand Pacific and Margerie Glaciers. As we approached the Margerie Glacier, the pilots cut the engines to allow the boat to slowly inch parallel to the blue wall of ice. The National Park rangers narrated with a steady flow of information on the glaciers over the loud speaker system on the viewing decks.

Around us, the two glaciers spoke in snaps and deep echoing growls like thunder. Without warning, massive chunks of ice broke away from the wall and crashed into the frigid water. Afterward, the crowds along the viewing rails clapped, *ooohhhed*, and *ahhhhed* like North Florida locals gasping over a 4th of July fireworks display. Holston, Jake, Evelyn, Leigh, Joe, and Bobby were stationed at different points along the starboard side of the ship with cameras in tow. Piddie and I were positioned toward the rear of the viewing deck in a less crowded area we shared with a nice Chinese gentleman who introduced himself as Dr. Paul Wong from Beijing.

"Dang it!" I growled as I swung the camcorder around a split second too late to capture the ice as it calved from the glacier.

"Go on over there more toward the middle," Piddie instructed. "Maybe you can swing either way faster if you're midway. Go on, now. I'm right here with my wheels locked. I'm not going to fly away. I'll just stay here with Dr. Wang."

"Wong, Paul Wong," he politely corrected.

"All right. If you're sure you'll be okay here without me. I'll be back as soon as I catch one of these babies on film." I dashed to the center of the most crowded spot and jockeyed for position. Capturing the glacier in action obsessed me.

A short time later, a series of sharp cracks and moans set the camera crew on edge. Multiple lenses scanned the length of the glacier, trying to predict the areas most likely to produce a spectacle worthy of filming. An immense chunk of ice calved into the water immediately in front of my viewfinder. Giggling, I caught the entire episode complete with the splash and rippling waves.

The cheers and applause from the jubilant crowd were pierced by a sharp "Ah-Yee! Ah-Yee! Chinaman overboard! Chinaman overboard!"

I caught a frantic motion to my right, and turned in time to film my elderly aunt standing near her wheelchair with a bright orange life ring in her hands. As if we were stuck in syrup, we watched in stunned awe as Piddie swung the life ring in a wide arch high into the air. The lifesaving float landed within a few inches of Dr. Paul Wong, who was frantically treading water. Within minutes, the well-trained cruise staff rushed to rescue the shivering man who clung to the life ring Piddie had so expertly thrown, and hustled him to the infirmary. Dr. Wong's wife, a petite woman standing in our midst, cried out in Chinese. The uniformed attendant took her by the arm and led her below.

Aunt Piddie held her hand dramatically to her chest. "I told him he was leanin' over way too far. Lordy! He just crawled up there on top of the rail—leanin' over with his camera, and *Whoop!* There he went!"

Evelyn threw her arms around Piddie. "Gosh, Mama. You're a hero! I'm truly amazed."

Piddie stuck her chin high into the air. "Well, I guess this ol' girl still has a few moves left in her. If I'd been ten years younger, I'd've gone in after him."

For a good half-hour, Piddie posed for pictures by the rail. I chuckled to myself when I imagined them looking at the snapshots later. My adorable blue-haired aunt in her purple Polarfleece outfit and red tennis shoes, smiling to beat the band. Because of the video cameras, Aunt Piddie's unselfish act had been captured on film from several angles. I felt certain it would be featured on a television show about amazing rescues, as well as making the major news networks.

Piddie and I were back in the stateroom resting before dinner when a sharp rap sounded on the door. "Mrs. Piddie Longman?" The uniformed attendant asked when I opened the door.

"That's me back here!" Piddie called. She shuffled slowly to the door, holding on to one wall for support.

"Mrs. Longman." He smiled. "May I personally express our gratitude for your act of heroism." He handed her a white envelope embossed in gold with the Queen Line logo. "The Captain asked me to deliver this invitation to you and your party."

He waited silently as Piddie tore into the elegant envelope. "It's an invitation to dine at the captain's table tonight!" she called out. "You go tell Mr. Captain that we'd all be downright thrilled to eat with him. I'll round everybody up. You can count on that!"

"Thank you, Mrs. Longman. I will inform him of your acceptance." He clapped his well-manicured hands together. A second young man carrying a bouquet of a dozen long-stemmed yellow roses entered the stateroom. "From the staff of the Regal Queen." He set the bouquet on a small side table.

"If there is anything you require at all during your stay with us, please feel free to call upon me." He handed my aunt a calling card. "I will personally make it so." He left in a flash of starched white.

"Well! Now isn't that a fine how-de-do? Can you call the family? I gotta get started on my hair."

After phoning the other staterooms to announce our date for the evening, I stretched out on the bed and fell into an exhausted sleep listening to Aunt Piddie humming in the bathroom as she coaxed her hair to new heights.

❧ ❧ ❧

"Pid, you've pulled out all the stops for tonight's dinner," I said, studying her festive outfit. As if she'd foreseen her part in Dr. Paul Wong's mishap, Piddie had packed an outfit with Chinese flair for the semiformal dress night. Evelyn's design, the red silk pantsuit sported a mandarin collar and six black-knotted satin buttons. Gold sneakers completed the ensemble. The crowning touch was Piddie's hair. It was a towering monument to hair fixative products. Tonight's 'do stood at least a foot and a half above her head—mounds of three-inch curls layered like cooked pasta. Miniature folding fans with dangling gold tassels were interspersed between the curls. Her new moose-dropping earrings complemented the look. Spots of dark rouge matched her lip and nail color. Compared to Piddie, my emerald green silk jumpsuit looked plain and understated.

"Piddie, you're a feast for sore eyes!" Jake said when we met him and Holston in the hall. "Leigh and Bobby will be along shortly. She's having a bad hair attack, and he's doing his best to help her style."

I snickered. "Bobby? A hairdresser? There's a stretch for you. Amazing what impending fatherhood will do for a man."

"Where're Joe and Evelyn?" Piddie asked.

Holston answered. "Joe wanted to drop by the ship's library before it closed for the day. They'll meet us in the restaurant."

"Wait on me a minute." I ducked back into the stateroom to replace my earrings with the moose-poop gold dangles.

The Court Restaurant was abuzz with activity. The maitre d' led us to a section in a different area from our assigned seating. Captain Raella stood when we arrived at his table. Although we had seen him from a distance on the second night's cocktail party when the crew and staff had been presented, I hadn't noticed how handsome the Captain was. His thick salt-and-pepper hair curled around his face, framing smiling dark brown eyes.

"Ah! Mrs. Piddie Longman." He tipped his head, then leaned to kiss the back of Piddie's extended hand. Holston, Jake, and I introduced ourselves.

"But…where is the remainder of your party?"

"They'll be along soon," Piddie answered. "You'd think it'd be easy keepin' everyone hemmed up together, but we're spread out all over this boat! We spend most of our time ramblin' around lookin' for each other."

Evelyn and Joe approached the table. "I'm sorry we're a bit late," Evelyn said. "Joe got caught up at the library. I just can't keep him away from the spy novels." Evelyn's moose-poop earrings glittered in the light.

Three waiters swarmed the table, filling water glasses and taking drink orders. After a few minutes, Leigh and Bobby appeared.

"My hair has developed a mind of its own," Leigh whispered to me as she took her seat. She, too, was wearing the earrings Piddie had purchased.

"So, how long you been driving these big boats?" Bobby asked the Captain.

"My first appointment as Captain was in 1983, but I have been in the business since 1964."

Leigh smiled. "You must really like it, then."

"I've been around ships since I was old enough to walk. My father and his father before him were captains. I can't imagine any other life." Captain Raella stood. "I have invited Dr. and Mrs. Paul Wong to join us, as well." He welcomed the couple to the table.

"How're you farin' after your spill?" Piddie asked when Dr. Wong took her hand in greeting.

He bowed. "I have had excellent care. I was a little chilled, but otherwise, unharmed. Thanks to you."

"P'shaw!" Piddie waved her hand in dismissal. "Anyone would've done the same." Piddie studied Dr. Wong for a moment. "Somethin' I been wonderin'…how do you come by such an American-soundin' first name?"

Dr. Wong chuckled. "Ah…it is for the convenience of the Americans I deal with in my work. I am one of many government liaisons between my country's orphanages and the hopeful couples who seek to offer our children homes in your country."

Holston and I exchanged glances.

"My Chinese name often proved difficult for Americans to pronounce. I adopted the name 'Paul' to make communications more effective."

Evelyn turned toward Mrs. Wong. "Are you enjoying the cruise?"

Sushan Wong turned to her husband for interpretation, then answered in Chinese with a nod and smile toward Evelyn.

"My wife has a limited grasp on your language," Paul Wong explained. "She relates to me that she has been very warmly received by Regal Queen's crew."

Sushan spoke again to her husband.

"My wife comments on your beautiful golden earrings. Are they from your home?"

Piddie flipped her finger at one of the moose-dropping earrings, making it dance and dangle. "Nope, I bought all of us a pair of these in Skagway. They're gen-u-wine moose poop earrings!"

The surprise registered on Paul Wong's features, then spread to his wife when he related Piddie's disclosure. She nodded with a sheepish smile.

The waiters arrived with the salad course and baskets of freshly baked bread with sweet cream butter.

"I understand you are from Florida," Dr. Wong said to my family.

Piddie swiped her hand in a circle. "Yep. We're all from a little town named Chattahoochee in the north part of the state—except for my niece, Hattie. She lives part-time in Tallahassee, the capital. It's not too far from our home."

Paul Wong leaned forward. "Tallahassee? My! The world is, indeed, very small. One of my favorite adoptive couples is from Tallahassee—Rainey and Patricia Hornsby. Their daughter, Ruth is delightful. A most unusual child."

"Rainey and Patricia are good friends of ours," Holston said. "We adore little Ruth."

Dr. Wong chattered excitedly to his wife. She nodded with a broad smile.

"Ruth predicted Sushan and my meeting each other. I will never forget it—such a small, intelligent little girl. She reached up with her tiny hand to touch my cheek and said, 'Sushan...Sushan'. Two months later, I met my wife. Like me, she had been alone for many years following the death of her spouse. We were married two weeks ago in Beijing. This is

209

our marriage trip."

"Honeymoon!" Piddie clapped her hands. "Well, isn't that something? Looks like this table's just full to runnin' over with good news." She pointed to Bobby and Leigh. "Leigh just found out she's expectin' a baby." She motioned toward Holston and me. "These two just got engaged right here in Alaska, right on top of a glacier. Now, here we find out you two are honeymooners!"

"This calls for something special!" The Captain spoke to the waiter. The wine steward appeared with iced champagne for the group and sparkling alcohol-free wine for Leigh and Bobby.

"Salud!" the captain called out. We raised our champagne flutes into the air.

The conversation flowed easily around the table as the main course was served. Piddie passed the breadbasket to Dr. Wong. "This bread's mighty tasty. If you ever come to Chattahoochee, I'll make you some cathead biscuits. That's my specialty."

Paul Wong translated for his wife. They exchanged puzzled glances, and she replied in Chinese.

"My wife and I are entertained by Americans. You wear gold excrement on your ears and eat your cats baked in bread."

My family broke into hearty laughter. Paul and Sushan Wong and Captain Raella, still looking rather unsettled, joined in.

I finally caught my breath long enough to explain. "Cathead is just an expression. The biscuits are made by hand, and they are as large as a cat's head. No animals lose their lives."

"Ah!" Paul translated to his wife.

After an exquisite desert of Cherries Jubilee cooked tableside with tall rippling flames, we sipped cups of rich freshly brewed coffee with cream.

As we rose to depart, Dr. Wong took Aunt Piddie's hand. "Mrs. Piddie Longman, we will always be in your debt. Because of your bravery, you are now part of our family. If there is anything I can ever do for you or your family, you have but to ask."

Following dinner, we split off in different directions. Evelyn, Joe, Leigh, and Bobby went to the International Showlounge on Deck Seven for the evening's show. Jake and Piddie decided to take in the casino, and talked the Wongs' into accompanying them.

Seizing the opportunity to be alone, Holston and I begged off from the planned activities, and strolled around the ship, huddled together in the evening chill.

"Are you thinking what I'm thinking?" Holston asked when we spied the vacant bubbling hot tub on the stern. Giggling like two kids up to no good, we tore off toward the staterooms. We met in the hall in swimsuits and the thick white terry cloth robes provided by the cruise line.

Piddie had been extremely impressed when she spotted the fluffy white robes hanging in our closet. "Terrier cloth! Isn't this a fine how-de-do!"

Terrier cloth—would that be wire fox terrier or rat terrier? I envisioned scores of hairless dogs shivering with embarrassment, sheared to the skin in order to make robes for the cruise industry.

My sore muscles moaned in relief as I slid into the hot frothy water. Holston slipped in beside me. We watched in shared silence the wide V-shaped wake curling behind the boat as we left Glacier Bay. We would reach Sitka, our next port of call, early the following morning.

"I've been thinking about something." I wiggled my pruned toes in the frigid air before plunging them back into the water.

Holston opened his eyes. "Hmmm?"

"How would you feel—about possibly—adopting a Chinese orphan after we're married?"

Holston sat bolt upright and studied my face. "Hattie, I thought you were opposed to having children."

"Giving birth to a child, yes. Moot point since I no longer have the piece-parts, but...to help a baby who's already here, and who's been deserted? I've just been giving it some thought."

Holston slid over to encircle me in his arms. "I would be proud and thrilled to be a father." He kissed me deeply and we held each other as the water bubbled around us—one of those moments, highlighted in bright yellow day-glow marker that stands alone in memory.

"You want to catch the midnight buffet?" Holston asked as he held my robe.

I felt a wave of dizziness wash over me. I grabbed Holston for support.

"You okay?"

"Bad case of the black twirlies—probably the heat and excitement."

"Perhaps it would be best if I tucked you in. I'll catch up with Jake and Piddie and make sure she gets in okay. We'll be kayaking in Sitka tomorrow morning. You'll need your rest."

JITKA BAY

Excerpt from Max the Madhatter's notebook

May 14, 1957: Why are so many people searching for peace? All you have to do is look inside. I guess if you have your insides right, the rest will follow.

CHAPTER TWENTY-EIGHT

THE REGAL QUEEN picked her way between the forested islands of Sitka Sound, approaching our final port of call. A second cruise ship anchored offshore dwarfed a nearby boat half its size. The Queen nestled among the ships and dropped anchor. The trips ashore would be accomplished with the ship's tenders, small covered boats used to ferry passengers to the docks of Sitka.

Holston, Leigh, Bobby, and I scurried to Deck Six to meet the eight a.m. group boarding for the kayaking adventure. Evelyn and Joe were departing at the same time for the Historic Russian America and Eagle Raptor tour. Since the weather had turned gray with the threat of light rain, Piddie and Jake had opted to sleep in, possibly leaving later for the shopping district.

The bay pitched the tender boat, making the initial step into the small craft an act of bravery and timing. Two attendants stood on either side to help us balance long enough to step aboard and find a seat for the brief ride to the long gangplank leading upward to shore.

Yet another Cheesy Photo Opportunity awaited the six of us at the top of the metal stairway. Two cruise employees, one dressed as a goofy moose and, the other, a polar bear, hammed for pictures with arriving passengers. A third snapped quickly-posed snapshots of the shore visitors hemmed between the two characters.

Evelyn scowled. "I'll hear about this later."

"Why's that?" Leigh asked.

"Mama's bought every single picture they've made of her since we stepped on the boat. I bet she's spent over a hundred dollars so far. She'll be fit to be tied she missed one!"

Joe reached for his wife's hand. "Maybe the weather'll clear up, and she and Jake will come over later on. Those two stayed up pretty late with the Dr. and his wife."

Holston chuckled. "It was after 11:30 when I left them at the Bengal Bar, and they were still going strong. Piddie was charged up about going to the champagne waterfall."

I sighed. "I can't believe I missed that!" The stacked tower of champagne flutes overflowing with bubbly was a spectacle I'd heard about from everyone who'd ever gone on a cruise.

"Don't worry. I'm quite sure Mama'll tell you about it in detail. No doubt, she'll have the pictures, too."

"Here's our group!" Joe pointed to a sign held by the tour leader. "See y'all back on the boat later."

The four of us met the remainder of the kayaking adventure tour gathered by a nearby dock.

"Just want to give you folks a brief safety spiel." Zachary, the tall red-haired tour leader, motioned for us to be seated on a series of benches.

After he explained the safety procedures and provided bright orange life vests, all ten of us loaded onto a twenty-foot rubber boat with twin engines for the ride across the bay. A narrow inlet off the main bay opened into a small mist-dappled cove. The kayaking outfitter's shack floated on pontoons at the far end of the waterway, surrounded by a series of short docks. Bobbing gently, multicolored kayaks of various sizes were corralled between the wooden walkways. The runabout deposited us on a long extension of the main dock.

"I hope we can do this without it ending up looking like a Three Stooges routine," Leigh remarked as we watched the rowing demonstration.

Holston steadied the rocking two-person boat as I crouched low on the dock and transferred my weight slowly into the forward seat. I steadied the front of the kayak by bracing the end of my paddle on the dock, allowing him to slip into the seat behind me. One deck over, Leigh and Bobby almost tipped before settling into place.

Bobby laughed. "It won't be the first time I've fallen out of a boat. But, I sure wouldn't want to ride back in the wind in wet clothes."

"Not to mention, having to hear about it from me the whole way back," Leigh added.

Holston and I soon synchronized our paddling rhythm. The small sliver of a craft sliced through the water with little effort. Holston maneuvered two foot pedals to alter its course to the left or right.

Cool mists curled like tongues licking over the clear smooth cove. Profound peace. I could have died right there—right at that moment. Perhaps, it was because my distant ancestors had once oozed from the sea; many of the times I'd had this feeling involved being in or around water. Stillness. An awareness of my heart beating, holding a predictable, steady rhythm. Breath pulling in, flowing out—all the billion chemical and molecular processes twirling along at their preset paces. For the first time since the loss of my parents, I felt truly content.

When the mist lifted, the tree branches became visible, lush and velvety green.

"Look at that," Holston mouthed in an awed whisper.

Poised like Disney animations, bald eagles were perched on every other branch. The entire cove was surrounded by towering evergreens dotted with the majestic sentinels. As if a choral director had flipped an invisible switch, a ripple of motion jolted the aviary community. Eagles took to wing, dipped, dove, and scooped fish from the water all around our pack of kayaks. In vain, I tried to rough-count their numbers. I gave up at forty, and simply enjoyed the pageant.

Human activity ceased while the eagles performed in the freefall circus. No one twitched. No mechanical whir of a camera film-advance disturbed the magic. As we slowly inched our way around the cove, the curious sentinels tipped their heads to follow our progress with piercing predatory yellow eyes. A few posed with wings outspread, drying their feathers in the cool air. The guide kayak led us single file as we snaked along the shoreline.

"I don't believe I've ever seen so many eagles in this cove at one time," Zachary whispered. "That was the most amazing thing I've seen in all the years I've been leading these trips."

We moored the kayaks, helping each other negotiate the docks without overturning. Inside the rustic cabin, the outfitters had prepared warm, spiced apple cider and hot chocolate. On the return trip, we were still too dumbstruck to talk as the twin engines pushed the boat across the bay to Sitka.

I awakened from a pillow-drooling nap to a series of sharp raps on the stateroom door. My head was blasting a raucous show tune of a headache as I stood and stumbled to answer.

"Eewwww, am I glad I stopped by." Jake pushed his way by me and flopped onto Piddie's bed. "You look like death on a holiday. Put your clean panties on, sister-girl, I've made an appointment for you. The spa just happened to have a last minute cancellation. C'mon…chop, chop!" He clapped his hands.

I ran my fingers through my hair. "Jake, I—"

"C'mon. My treat! It's a full body sea salt scrub and exfoliation and La Massage treatment. After that, Julianne's going to do a fashion upsweep with that nappy hair of yours. And…" He paused dramatically. "You get a complimentary application of California Sun Kiss makeup. You will look fab-uuuu-lllush in that slinky black dress you bought for tonight!"

Jake had never been a person who heard the word no. I had no energy to argue. I slipped on a pair of sweat pants, sweat shirt, and shoes.

Jake stood with his hands on his hips. "Nothing says I don't care quite as much as sweat suit." He shook his close-cropped head. "Well, at least yours doesn't have studs or gobs of cutesy ribbons and playful animals on it. I'll never understand why women think that looks attractive."

"Not everyone is perfect like you."

His long face lit up. "Good for me. It improves the contrast. Now, c'mon!"

"You're going, too?"

"Juan is giving me a half-hour massage. Don't worry, sister-girl. I'm sure it won't be as magical as one of yours."

Three hours later, I emerged from the Regal Health and Beauty Spa with skin as smooth as a baby's behind, a healthy sun-kissed glow on my face and neck, and a fancy upswept hairdo.

Piddie whistled when I stepped into our stateroom. "What I wouldn't give to be your age again! Holston's gonna trip over his tongue when he sees you tonight. By the way, he's stopping by to escort you to dinner at 5:45. I'm going out with Jake. We're joining the Wongs'."

"Two nights in a row?"

"You oughta see Paul doing karaoke. Got a little accent, but he's darn good. His version of Love Me Tender near'bout brought tears to my eyes!"

"All I have to do is slip on my dress. My makeup and hair are done, and I couldn't possibly get any cleaner. The salt scrub was heavenly! I sure hope Stephanie adds that in when she gets her skin care specialist license."

"I better get started. The older you get, the longer it takes to put on your face—it's all the fill-in work you have to do." She cackled and shuffled to the bathroom.

Clad in a black tux, Holston appeared at my door promptly at 5:45. "For you…" He handed me a single long-stemmed red rose.

I was still waiting for him to morph into a foul-mouthed, beer-swilling slob. Not that I had him perched on a pedestal—my past experiences with men had left me somewhat doubtful about the gender in general.

Holston helped me drape the cashmere pashmina around my shoulders. "You look edible in that dress."

He nuzzled my neck. It seemed like months since we'd been intimate. Deep inside of my soul, Xena Warrior Princess screamed a war whoop.

How many more days are we going to be on this cruise?

After posing for formal photographs on the Promenade Deck, we made our way through the milling crowd of evening gowns and tuxedos.

"I'm grateful you have such good, refined taste," Holston whispered in my ear. "That woman over there—I'm pretty sure—is wearing an unwashed poodle."

A lanky jewel-bedecked lady with a Bride of Frankenstein hairdo sashayed toward us. Her lower body was packed like link pork sausage into a tight black dress that trailed behind her in ragged wisps. Something exotic had lost its life to create the black, shaggy-dog wrap barely covering her ample bosom.

"I don't know," I said. "After seeing her, I feel somewhat underdressed."

We spied the family gathered near the entrance to the Court Dining room.

Jake, Joe, and Bobby were resplendent in their black tuxedos. Evelyn and Piddie wore Evelyn's custom-made fashions. Leigh wore a simple spaghetti-strapped emerald green formal with a matching shawl.

"We're all beginning to look like we've always dressed up fit to kill!" Piddie said. "That black frock fits you like a second skin, Hattie."

Jake tapped his black and gold cane on the parquet floor. "You lookin' fine, sister-girl! Unlike that woman in the mastodon jacket who just went past us. It's a shame when folks have all that money and no fashion sense."

"It's like readin' those magazines about the rich and famous. I'm thoroughly convinced that the more money you make, the tackier you dress," Piddie added.

The line for the first seating for dinner started to move ahead of us. We were well-appointed cattle on the way to the trough. Tonight's dinner was the crowning glory of the Regal Queen's accomplished culinary staff. A roving photographer took a group shot of the family with Piddie, Jake, Evelyn, and Joe seated, with Leigh, Bobby, Holston, and me standing behind them.

Following the gourmet meal, a loudspeaker announced the arrival of dessert. To the tune of the Macarena song, lines of tuxedoed waiters, holding platters of flaming baked Alaska aloft, snaked through the room. Our dessert waiter stood beside a small sidebar next to our table, where he carved the dessert into serving portions. The creamy frozen dessert with crisp meringue coating was, as Jake so cleverly put it, a mouth orgasm.

Giorgio pulled Piddie to her feet as the Macarena song started up for the second time. "You will be my partner."

"Oh, Lordy! I don't know how to do this dance," she said.

"I will teach you." Giorgio helped Piddie to balance as he showed her the sequence of motions. "It's easy once you get it down."

Piddie swiveled her hips to the Latin beat. "Whoop-de-do! Look at me!"

Jake grabbed his cane. "Dance with me, sister-girl. We need to practice so we won't be a laughing stock at your wedding."

Bobby and Leigh and Evelyn and Joe joined us in the aisle. All around the room, people were laughing and dancing beside their tables, both passengers and staff.

Piddie threw one of her butterfly hair accessories high into the air as if she were the queen of the Mexican hat dance.

HOMEWARD BOUND

Excerpt from Max the Madhatter's notebook

November 3, 1956: Nobody gives me any credit. When you are invisible, you can see a lot of things, and no one will ever know you are there.

CHAPTER TWENTY-NINE

A S THE LAST straggling partygoers retired to their staterooms around 1:30 a.m., the Regal Queen left Sitka Sound sailing at full cruising speed for Vancouver. The pilot navigated the Dixon Entrance and approached Triple Island about 3:00 a.m., where we set a southerly course.

At seven, our group arrived by two's for the breakfast buffet in the café. On this final day of the trip, I could navigate the ship without consulting the laminated foldout map. I've always been directionally challenged. My friends have often said that the hearse driver at my funeral would make several wrong turns before arriving forty minutes later than the anxiously waiting mourners. Because I stayed hopelessly turned around the first six months I lived in Tallahassee, I had ferreted out every back street shortcut in town.

After breakfast, everyone went in different directions. I found my cousin-in-law, Joe, sitting in the sun on Deck Twelve.

"Hey, gal! Where're you heading?" He put his book beside the coffee cup on a plastic table near his chair. "Stop and sit a spell."

"I'm just wandering around the boat aimlessly." I settled onto a lounge chair next to him. "It's nice today, compared to yesterday."

"Yeah. I'm glad of that. I thought I'd sit up here and finish my mystery. It's due back in the library before five."

I noticed a thin gray booklet. "Is that a copy of the *Madhatter's Guide*?"

"Sure is. I've never taken the time to read it. Evelyn keeps me busy with honey-do projects when we're at home."

"It's pretty interesting, isn't it? I don't remember much about Max. Guess I was too young."

"He wasn't one of my patients, so I don't know a lot about his history. But, after reading some of his journal, I have my doubts the man needed to be incarcerated at a mental institution. His thoughts are too focused…too in depth. But then, many people who suffer mental illnesses have clear thoughts, at times."

"Something else I noticed." Joe flipped the pages to a small sketch of a man. "See this drawing? According to the paragraph above, this is a rendering of Big Sam Blount. He owned the Five and Dime back during the fifties. Notice the way Max drew the little dark bleeding heart on his shirt?"

"So?"

"Big Sam died of a massive heart attack not long after the date listed on this page. I remember, because it was pretty soon after Evelyn and I moved into our house."

"Weird."

"I'm finding more examples of the same sort of thing."

"You saying he was some kind of physic?"

Joe shook his balding head. "I'm too traditionally trained to jump to any conclusions, right off. It's just interesting to me at this point."

"It's fun to think there's magic in the world."

"Suppose it is." Joe smiled. "I guess everyone's scattered out this morning. I saw Holston and Jake heading down to the gym. Evelyn, Piddie, Leigh, and Bobby are doing some last minute shopping."

"Bobby amazes me more every day. I've never seen him quite so…domestic."

"He's gonna be a good daddy, I'll betcha." Joe shook his head. "I hope we can fit all the souvenirs Evelyn's bought in our suitcases. She has Alaska sweatshirts for the kids and grandkids."

His face clouded over. "She bought an expensive golden pendant in Juneau for Karen. She'll mail it off to Atlanta next week. It'll be the same as before—in a couple of weeks, she'll get a formal letter in the mail to Mrs. Evelyn Fletcher. Sometimes, Karen will keep the gift. Others, she mails right back. I'm sure this one will come back. She won't accept an expensive gift from folks she claims not to know."

"I find it hard to believe that she really thinks she's from England."

Joe sighed heavily. "I've been in the mental-health field for over thirty years, and I don't understand, either. She's doing quite well for herself. Big house, fancy clothes, and expensive cars. I suppose, as a parent, I should be glad to see my daughter successful." He stared out of the Sun Deck windows at the forested land masses passing by the boat.

I reached over and rested my hand on his shoulder. "I'm sorry, Joe."

He managed a weak smile. "Well, things'll work out like they ought to, I suppose. This trip's been good for all of us. There's no doubt Piddie's having the time of her life. I bet she sleeps for a solid week when we get home."

"I don't think I'll ever forget the sight of her holding up her dress and swiveling around in the dining hall last night. I didn't know she could still move like that!"

Joe laughed. "Jake told me she sang a duet with Paul Wong in the Bengal Bar."

"Let me guess... *You Are My Sunshine?*" It had been one of Carlton's favorites.

Joe nodded. "Evelyn's really had a ball, too. I haven't seen her this relaxed in years. She's like the girl I married—funny and ready to try anything!" He nodded his head. "I've made some decisions on this trip. Life's too short not to enjoy it! I can put in for my retirement from the state the first of next year. I'm gonna get out as soon as I can, and then I'm taking my wife on a Mediterranean cruise with these Queen Line folks. Jake told me he'd be glad to stay at the house and watch over Piddie. Those two are a little scary together." He chuckled. "Don't breathe a word of this to Piddie or Evelyn, now. I want it to be a surprise."

"I wouldn't dream of it. You know, I've been really impressed with Evelyn's eveningwear designs. Maybe she can parlay that into a money-making thing. She's very talented."

"Once she got it into her mind to use some color and freed herself up a bit, her creative side just seemed to flower. I know you see your cousin as a strange woman who only lives to go to the beauty parlor and redecorate our house, but I know the real Evelyn, and she's the apple of my eye."

"I think this trip's colored all of us in a new light," I said. "Well, I gotta go find Piddie and Evelyn. They wanted to go to the Eye and Neck Care seminar at the Bengal Bar at two. Then, I have to pack. We're supposed to leave our luggage with the white tags attached in the hall before eight, except for the carry-on bags."

"All right, gal. I'll call you if I need someone to help me sit on top of the suitcases to get them closed."

The final day aboard the Regal Queen was the most relaxing of the seven-day trip. No schedules had to be met. All souvenirs had been purchased, and we were beginning to long for the familiar surroundings of home.

Piddie put her hand over Giorgio's at the end of dinner. "There's a little somethin' extra in the tip envelope for you, honey. You've been awfully good to this old lady. Put it with what you've saved toward that restaurant you want to open one day."

Giorgio leaned over and planted a soft kiss on Piddie's forehead. "You will never be an old lady in my eyes."

"You should've said that before. It'd doubled the ante!"

As we slept, the two Canadian pilots who had embarked as we passed Pine Island steered us past Seymour Township, then continued on a southeasterly course in the Strait of George toward Vancouver. At 6:30 a.m., we passed under Lions Gate Bridge and entered Vancouver Harbor. By seven-thirty, the Regal Queen was safely moored alongside Canada Place cruise ship terminal in Vancouver.

After having the breakfast buffet at the café, we vacated our staterooms and watched from the deck as the passengers disembarked in accordance with the color-coded sequence. The deck was buzzing with activity. Crates of fruit, food, and supplies were loaded onto the ship in preparation for the next batch of excited passengers. What had been a seven-day adventure for my family was a repetitive occupation for the crew and staff. Would Glacier Bay appear less grand if you saw it every week for three months of the year? I suppose it was the same thing as the mountain folks from North Carolina heading for Florida's beaches, while we lowlanders headed for the hills. The beauty around you dims when it becomes commonplace.

Giorgio appeared by Piddie's side. "I came to say goodbye." He flashed a wide, white grin. "I have something for you." He handed her a small paper bag embossed with the Queen Cruise Lines logo.

"Ewww!" Piddie squealed with delight.

"What is it, Mama?" Evelyn hunkered down to peer into the bag.

Piddie held a miniature plastic replica of the Regal Queen aloft. Looky here! A whole bag of little boats to go in my hair!"

Evelyn patted her mother on the shoulder. "I'll have to make you a nautical-theme outfit when we get home," she said with a gleam in her eyes. I knew what the new decorating scheme would be at Evelyn and Joe's.

Since our flight to Seattle wasn't scheduled to leave until six, we had several hours to loiter in the airport. With our luggage piled around, we napped in shifts until we were allowed to proceed through customs to the Alaskan Airlines gate.

Following a two-hour layover in Seattle, we boarded the jet for the second, and longest, leg of our return trip. I dearly love to travel by plane, but I've never developed the ability to sleep sitting up. The extra two inches you gain by reclining don't seem to help.

My consistent companion on every airline trip was some flight-related song that played in an endless loop in my mental CD player. Once, on an early flight to Tampa, the song was *Up, Up, and Away* by the Mama's and Papa's. Though I couldn't recall all of the words, the same verse played over and over. Tonight's selection featured the words *Big Ole Jet Airliner* with the accompanying electric guitar licks.

Jake jabbed me and rolled his eyes toward the woman who settled into the window seat behind him and Piddie. Her teased bleached-orange hair hung in thick, stiff hanks over her shoulders. She sported a black sweat suit covered with silver studs and small mirrors in various sizes and shapes. As soon as the unsuspecting seatmate joined her, she began a loud monologue in a gravely voice thick with cigarettes and whiskey.

Jake scribbled a note and handed it to me across the aisle. *Why is it that the one person who's a non-stop motor mouth with an obnoxious voice always sits close to us? And, did you see the outfit? Looks like she got a stud-setter for Christmas!*

Soon, we were aloft, and the steady drone of the jet engines muffled her conversation. I closed my eyes and dosed slightly, only to awaken with a start as she exaggerated the first word of each barrage of chatter. *That!* or *And!* was all I heard, interrupted by an eh-eh-eh-eh cackle of laughter that sounded like a car with a faulty starter.

Jake passed another note. *Mrs. Stud-setter and her husband have been together for nine years. The only channel she lets her brilliant child watch is the Discovery Channel because TV is such trash. Her loving husband brings her coffee in bed every morning.*

After a couple of hours, her chatter blended into the background noise, along with the phlegmy cough of the man immediately behind me. Piddie and Evelyn made frequent trips up and down the aisle to allow Piddie to move her legs during the long flight. Leigh, Bobby, and Joe slept peacefully in their seats. Holston was oblivious to everything around us, having lapsed into an open-mouthed snoring slumber twenty minutes after take-off.

Atlanta's Hartsfield International Airport was nearly deserted when we emerged at 5:30 a.m., bleary-eyed from the cross-country flight.

"That woman behind us was worse than Elvina Houston when she's off her medication," Piddie grumbled.

Jake nodded. "She only shut up the last twenty minutes of the flight, right before the pilot announced our clearance to land in Atlanta."

"I think that poor lady sitting beside her finally just passed out cold and she didn't have anyone to talk to," Piddie said. "I sure was proud to see that bag of wind hustlin' on away from our gate. I don't think I could've stood her all the way to Tallahassee!"

At 6:30, the Delta attendant called for our flight to board for the final leg of our trip. The early morning fog had cleared as we began our descent into Tallahassee. The flight pattern took us over the dry lakebed that had once been Lake Jackson as we approached the airport.

The pilot executed a smooth touchdown and we taxied by the tan and black airport terminal with *Welcome to Tallahassee* written in bold black letters across the front. Because of our early hour, the crowd awaiting our arrival was limited to a handful of homefolks. Stephanie and Bill rushed up to greet us. After collecting the luggage, Holston, Jake, and I piled into Betty with Stephanie at the wheel. Evelyn, Joe, and Piddie settled into the Towncar with Bill as the chauffeur.

"Hey! You gonna be okay to drive home?" I called out to Bobby.

He waved back. "I'm pretty rested. I slept the whole way home. We'll see y'all later!" He and Leigh rolled their luggage toward the long-term parking lot.

"I know y'all have a lot to talk about, but I'm sure you're awfully tired," Stephanie said. "Just lay the seats back, and Betty and I will drive all of you Miss Daisy's home."

"Did she give you any trouble?" I asked.

Stephanie grinned. "Nope. Oh, she cuts out a bit once you get her up over a hundred or so, but other than that, she's a great little ride."

I was too tired to rise to the bait. By the time we reached the entrance to Interstate 10, I was sound asleep.

POSITIVE RESULTS

Sinfully Decadent Chocolate Torte

Ingredients: ½ cup butter, 8 ounces semisweet chocolate, 5 eggs, ¾ cup white sugar, 1 cup ground almonds.

Melt margarine and chocolate over low heat. In mixing bowl, beat whites until stiff. In a separate bowl, beat together yolks and sugar. Blend in chocolate mixture and stir in almonds. Fold beaten whites into chocolate until no streaks of white remain. Scrape into 9 inch pan. Bake torte at 350°F for 45 to 50 minutes.

Smother in white chocolate torte icing and sprinkle with crushed nuts for the most sinful treat of a lifetime.

CHAPTER THIRTY

TWO DAYS FOLLOWING our exhausting, yet exhilarating, return from Alaska, Holston's ex-wife called from New York. His beloved ex-mother-in-law, Marilyn Beaumont, had fallen and shattered her right hip. Compounding the problem, she had developed pneumonia in both lungs, even with the best efforts of the health-care team.

Holston left from Tallahassee Regional Airport early the next day on Delta's first flight to Atlanta, with connections to New York's LaGuardia Airport. After I dropped him at the terminal, I continued to Dr. McCray's office for the appointment for my physical. The office churned with its usual beehive activity.

Kimberly Grant, ARNP, swept into the exam room where I huddled, chilled to the bone in my stylish paper ensemble. "Usual three thousand-mile check-up, Hattie?"

"Yep. Also, I've had some bleeding recently…rectal…cramping, too. I thought I'd mention it."

Her blonde brows knitted with concern. "How much? How often? What color?"

"It started about two months ago, I guess. Just a little at first—bright red with some rust color mixed in. My family and I just got home from a cruise. I had a couple of episodes on the boat where I bled quite a bit. The cramping's getting worse, even lasts after a bowel movement. I've been more tired than usual, and I've dropped some weight."

"Hmmm…" She scribbled on my chart. "Any family history of colon cancer?"

"Actually, yes. My father had some malignant polyps removed when he was around seventy. I recently found out that he'd also had a portion of his colon removed. He and Mom never told us. I found out from my aunt."

"We'll get you a referral in to the Digestive Disease Clinic. Hopefully, it's just internal hemorrhoids. It'd be a good idea to check it out, given your family history."

Other than being anemic, the physical went smoothly. Kimberly handed me a referral for my biannual mammogram (or slam-o-gram, as Stephanie and I called it) and a date and time for my initial visit to Dr. Lucas Thomas.

"Wow! That was quick! This appointment's this afternoon."

Kimberly grinned. "Hey, what can I say? I have pull. Actually, he had a cancellation. Otherwise, it would have been three weeks before you could get in to see him."

"I'll work my schedule around this. I'd rather get this taken care of. I have a wedding to plan."

Kimberly squealed. "Really?"

I showed her my engagement ring. She oohed and ahhed. Personally, I've never understood why women stuff their engagement rings in each other's faces as if they were honored awards. But, since I did love Holston, and was pretty excited about the prospect of sharing life's travails with him, I figured there was no harm in being a little proud.

After the midmorning clients, I left my Tallahassee clinic for the Digestive Disease Clinic at the end of Riggins Road. The spacious reception area on the first floor was filled with patients of varying ages. After I filled out the preliminary forms, a scrub-suited nurse escorted me into an exam room.

Dr. Lucas Thomas stepped into the room and introduced himself. My spirits sank to new depths. How could I possibly allow this gorgeous specimen of the male gender to see my bottom?

"You're a little young for me to suspect colon cancer, but I never take chances when someone has a positive family history. It's a good idea for you to have a baseline colonoscopy at your age," he said in a warm, gentle voice. "I believe in being proactive and preventative when it comes to colorectal cancer. It's curable, when found at an early stage."

He explained the colonoscopy procedure thoroughly, using a flip chart to illustrate the different parts of the rectum and large intestine he would be researching. His nurse, Connie, stepped in as he was leaving. She made an appointment the next week for the procedure, and reviewed the pre-op instructions.

As I left the clinic with a handful of papers, I marveled at the fact that I had just consented to have an incredibly handsome doctor stuff a long tube with a camera into a very private area. Suddenly, the absurdity of the situation struck me. Would I be able to order framed copies of the points of interest to pass around at parties?

"I need to stay for a few days," Holston said. "The old girl's pulling out of it, but she's still in intensive care. I really thought I'd be calling you with bad news. But, she's a fighter."

I toyed with the idea of telling him about the impending colonoscopy. No. He had enough on his mind at the present.

"Okay, sweetie. I miss you madly. Have you and your ex-wife scratched each other's eyes out yet?"

"She's been almost bearable. Dealing with her used to be pure hell. Now, it's just the fourth level of purgatory." He chuckled. "Claire has everything she's always wanted—money and social position. I told her about you."

"And..."

"She's thrilled. I keep waiting for the real viper to lash out. Since I don't stand in her way anymore, she treats me like some college boy she once had a mindless fling with before moving on to bigger and better things."

"Her loss, my gain."

"Yes, and you have my heart and soul. I'll call you in a couple of days. You can always reach me on my digital phone. Leave a message, and I'll get to you soon. I have to keep it turned off while I'm at the hospital."

❦ ❦ ❦

Jake and I cruised off the Thomasville Road exit of Interstate 10 in Tallahassee and turned on to Capital Circle. The blue jeep in the center lane suddenly had the automotive equivalent of a cat running-fit, swerving across two lanes of traffic before screeching on the brakes for a right-hand turn sans signal.

Jake grabbed the dashboard. "Gah! What bit him?"

I checked the rear view mirror. The pick-up truck behind me and the cars in his wake had almost become intimate on an insurance basis.

I glanced over at Jake. "Did you see his vanity plate? It said KILLER."

Jake snorted. "It should read IDIOT!" He jabbed at me with his index finger. "Don't think for a minute that I came along out of insane curiosity over your handsome doctor. I'm here because I get to drive Betty afterwards. You'll be way too loo-loo to operate heavy machinery. Leave that to us big girls." He batted his long eyelashes. "Besides, it's slow at the shop right now, so Jolene can handle it. Of course, I put in a tape to record Oprah."

I smirked as I pulled into the parking lot at the Digestive Disease Clinic. "Your concern is heartwarming."

"You sure get irritable when you don't have your morning caffeine fix, sister-girl."

I huffed. "You'd be irritable, too, if you had to drink damn near a gallon of cherry flavored Go-Lightly. Hah! There's a sick joke for you! I practically had to sleep in the bathroom. Then, I had to give myself an enema this morning to boot! Plus!" I stabbed the air dramatically. "I've had nothing to eat since 6:00 p.m. yesterday, and nothing to drink since midnight. I'm just a little edgy—okay?!"

Jake patted my hand. "There, there, sweet girl. They'll be giving you some sleepy juice pretty soon, and you won't care one way or the other."

Shortly after I registered at the desk, a smiling nurse called my name.

"You go, girl!" Jake gave me a thumbs-up. "I'll see you when it's behind you—no pun intended."

After removing my clothes and depositing them into a labeled plastic bag, I donned the mandatory air-vent-in-the-rear hospital gown, and settled on to a gurney. Several nurses stopped by my curtained cubicle, taking vital signs, double-checking the chart for allergies to medications, and confirming the planned procedure. One nurse started an IV, and the next gave the pre-op medications.

"You should start to feel this pretty quick," she said. "The whole procedure is fairly painless. We'll have you in the recovery area for a bit afterwards."

Soon, my eyes wouldn't focus, except for a few seconds at a time. A gentle warmth flowed through me as the drug took effect.

"Here we go," the attendant chirped as she wheeled the gurney through a set of double doors into the operatory.

"Good morning, Miss Davis," Dr. Thomas said.

"I really think this procedure should put us on a first-name basis, don't you?" My words slurred. "By the way—that Go-Lightly stuff was God-awful!"

"But, necessary, I'm afraid," he replied. "I've got to have you clean to be able to see clearly in there." Dr. Thomas and his nurse rolled me onto my side and raised one knee almost to my chest.

"You'll feel a little pressure, now," he said as he inserted the tube. "You want to watch on the monitor?"

My tongue was thick and dry. "Only if you give me a guided tour."

As he inched the scope through the rectum and descending colon, he stopped periodically to snap a freeze-frame picture.

He motioned to the video monitor. "You do have some internal hemorrhoids. See these little reddish bumps? That could possibly be the source of the bleeding."

A few centimeters up the colon, he stopped at a black spot with ragged margins. It reminded me of the appearance of a sunspot. I strained my eyes to focus.

"Hmm…here's something. Heather, let's biopsy this area." A small looped wire clipped a section of tissue.

Other than a few diverticuli, small out-pouch herniations of the colon, the remainder of the exam was uneventful.

"Okay, all through!" he announced. The attendant rolled the gurney to a private recovery area.

Jake peeked around the curtains. "How you doin', sister-girl?" He eased quietly onto a nearby chair. "I asked to come back with you as soon as they'd let me."

I moaned.

"You hurting?"

"Gas pains. They blow air up inside to open up the passageway."

"Well, just toot it out!"

I winced. "You know how much I hate to do that."

"It's either that, or leave here looking seven months pregnant. Do it!"

I never realized passing gas could feel so exquisite. Perhaps it could be a new hobby.

Jake dabbed at the corners of his eyes with an imaginary hankie. "I feel so close to you right now." He grabbed my hand.

The curtains parted and Dr. Thomas stepped into the cubicle. "How are you feeling?"

"Gaseous. Other than that—fine as frog's hair."

"Honey," Jake patted my hand, "don't say anything stupid under the influence of drugs that you'll kick yourself for later."

Dr. Thomas's wore a stern expression. Obviously, he wasn't here for a social call.

"Miss Davis, Hattie. We need to discuss your test." He glanced at Jake.

I shook my head, then waited for the dizziness to subside. "Jake's family. Go ahead."

He sat on the edge of the gurney. "Hattie, do you remember that one black spot where I took a biopsy?"

I nodded.

"It's a tumor. We're running a quick test that will, if it's positive, confirm my diagnosis. If the first test is negative, we'll have to wait on the biopsy results in a few days. I believe the tumor is malignant. Cancer."

Words tumbled around in my brain, but none came from my mouth. The mere mention of cancer had erased an entire vocabulary.

Jake grabbed my hand. "What will we do?"

Dr. Thomas stood. "I'll come back as soon as I know something."

I smiled weakly at Jake. "You always said I was a pain in the butt."

He got up and threw his arms around me. "I can't take it, sister-girl! You've got to be okay!"

Dr. Thomas returned shortly. His lips were drawn into a thin, serious line. "I'm sorry to say…it is cancer. When do you want to schedule surgery?"

"How 'bout now?"

"Are you sure? Do you have anything to be taken care of?"

"I want it out! And, I'm already prepared. I drank that stuff, and I haven't had anything to eat. I might as well go ahead with it."

"Do you have a surgeon in mind?"

I thumbed through my mental files for under: Medical, Surgery, Good Reference from Mary. "Dr. Crowley?"

Dr. Thomas nodded. "Excellent. I'll go call Tallahassee Memorial and see about coordinating a room for you. I'll have to call Dr. Crowley's office and check his surgical schedule. Connie can put it all together. Hopefully, we can get you worked into the schedule as soon as possible."

He rested his hand on my shoulder. "Hattie, the good part is that the cancer was located in the descending colon. Further up the pike, and you might have had fewer symptoms so early on. This gives us the best possible scenario: early detection with a good chance of a complete cure."

Connie appeared fifteen minutes later. I was slowly becoming more cognizant of the reality of my situation as the medication began to wane.

"You have a room on the third floor." She looked at Jake. "Can you drive her over to Tallahassee Memorial?"

"Of course," Jake replied.

"Good. Report to central registration in the atrium. They'll get you checked in to the hospital. We're coordinating with the hospital surgical unit and Dr. Crowley as to a time for your surgery. They'll be working you into an already full schedule."

I lowered the volume on Betty's stereo system. "You'll have to call Anna at the clinic here. She can route my clients to the other therapists, and Stephanie can reschedule the clients in Chattahoochee. Oh my God! Shammie and Spackle! Call Margie and John to help feed and water, and, umm...Evelyn, Joe, Piddie, Bobby, Leigh..." My head swam with the drugged effort at linear thought. "Holston!"

"Sister-girl, I know your schedule better than you do most of the time. I'll take of everything. As soon as we get you checked into a room, I can start making calls."

Jake entered the parking garage by the hospital and trolled for an open space. We curved around until we finally located a spot on the top level.

"Can you walk, or do I need to find a wheelchair?"

"I'm still a little wobbly...just need a little support."

Jake and I strolled arm in arm toward the elevators. "Someone will think we're in love," he said.

"Aren't we?" I slurred.

"You betcha."

THE HOSPITAL

White Chocolate Torte Frosting

Ingredient: 6 eggs, 1 cup white sugar, 3 ounces melted white chocolate, ¾ cup butter.

Combine eggs and sugar, and mix well. Cook in a double boiler, stirring constantly until thickened. Pour mixture into a medium size bowl, and add chocolate. Beat until cool. Beat in butter or margarine. Chill frosting until thick enough to spread. For an extra-tasty treat, embellish torte with fresh raspberries.

CHAPTER THIRTY-ONE

AFTER THE REQUISITE mound of paperwork, I was admitted to room 312. For the second time in one day, I shucked my clothes for the fancy hospital attire and crawled into bed.

Jake studied the tan-walled private room. "It could use a woman's touch."

I plopped my purse down on the bedside table. "Hey, I'm just glad to have a private room. This place is packed!"

"Well, we'll at least have to see about getting a few plants and flowers in here. This place needs some color."

"Maybe you can sign on as their interior designer."

He rolled his eyes.

We heard a soft rap on the door, and a lanky male nurse in dark blue scrubs whisked into my room. "Hello, I'm Jon Presley. I'll be your nurse this afternoon till about 11:00 p.m." He took my left hand and checked the identification band against the chart. "Your name?"

"Hattie Davis."

"Date of birth?"

"October 3rd, 1956. I'm a Libra."

The nurse smiled. "Who's your doctor?"

"My primary care physician is Dr. McCray, but now there's Dr. Thomas and Dr. Crowley."

"What procedure are you in for?"

"Colon surgery."

Satisfied that I was, indeed, Hattie Davis, he took my vital signs.

Jake cocked his head and smiled. "You any kin to the King?"

Jon rolled his eyes. "No. But, I have a Pomeranian named Elvis if that counts."

"Jake Witherspoon." Jake extended his hand to Jon.

"I thought you looked a little familiar," Jon said. "You were in ICU here, what, two or three years back?"

Jake's eyebrows flicked upward. "Memory like an elephant. Were you working in the intensive care unit then?"

"No, one of my dear friends has worked the unit for years. Of course, your face was splashed all over the *Tallahassee Democrat* for awhile."

Jon scribbled notations in my chart. "I'll check back in on you in a bit. If you need anything, just buzz. Have they told you what time your surgery is scheduled?"

"I'm a work-in. I guess Dr. Crowley will be by sometime soon."

Jon nodded. "Okay. We'll need to get an IV started on you with some fluids since you won't be able to eat."

I smiled weakly. "I lost my appetite about an hour ago."

After Nurse Jon left my room, Jake clutched his chest. "Is he a doll, or what!?"

"I guess my hospital stay just got a lot more interesting to you."

Jake huffed. "Now...Miss Evil Rita, you know I'm only here for you, dear love. If it was up to me, I'd steer as clear as possible from this place—not that they didn't take excellent care of me. I've just had enough for one lifetime!"

For the next half-hour, Jake busied himself on the telephone rounding up the troops. Soon, half of Tallahassee, and, I'm positive, all of Gadsden county knew of my impending surgery. Jillie stopped in with a small bag containing my toothbrush, toothpaste, hair brush, shampoo, deodorant, and several changes of underwear.

Jake tucked and smoothed the top sheet. "I'll go on home tonight and pack a big bag for you and me. I'll check on the kids. Then, I'll come over and stay with you after the surgery."

By five, Evelyn, Joe, Bobby, and Leigh were pacing my room, and several of my friends from Tallahassee Police Department and Leon County Sheriff's Office had stopped in to wish me Godspeed. Mary popped by for a few minutes on her break from the emergency room. Because Aunt Piddie was in the final stages of a head cold, she had opted to stay at Elvina Houston's house. Between the two of them, the old lady hotline would likely catch fire before the evening was out.

When Dr. Crowley hadn't shown up by eight, I sent the whole group packing. "I'm fine. You guys need to go on home and get some rest. It may be a long day tomorrow. All I'm going to do is sleep, anyway."

Jake leaned over and kissed me on the forehead. "I'll keep trying to reach Holston. I've left a couple of messages on his voice mail. I'm sure he'll call tonight."

I flipped the channel changer until I reached the Cartoon Network. After ten minutes of Bugs Bunny, I felt the weight of adulthood lift from my shoulders. Yosemite Sam was in his usual snit when Dr. Crowley knocked on my door.

"Miss Davis?" he asked as he walked into the room.

"Hi, Dr. Crowley. I'm sorry to see you again like this." I motioned to the hospital bed.

"Me, too." He held my hand for a moment. "The massage you gave me a while back—I can still recall how good I felt afterwards! I've been meaning to get back in to see you. I never seem to have any down time here lately."

"I guess Mary'll have to give you another gift certificate." The massage session had been Mary's way of thanking the doctor for his excellent care of her daughter, Carrie.

Dr. Crowley's easy cowboy-on-a-holiday manner was instantly soothing. His kind brown eyes and gentle nature immediately put me at ease. He slid a chair close to the bed.

"You and I need to talk about some things."

"Shoot."

"I don't believe in flowering things up, Hattie. Best case scenario: I go in, remove the tumor, suture the colon together, and you're good as new in a few weeks. Dr. Thomas assures me I have enough room to do just that." He paused, as if choosing his words carefully. "When cancer occurs in the descending colon, the patient will generally have recognizable symptoms early on, giving the best chance of successful treatment."

"Dr. Thomas said the same thing."

"Unfortunately, it presents a problem if the cancer excision doesn't leave me enough room to reconnect the bowel before the rectum. Dr. Thomas tells me that I have at least ten centimeters to work with, on the low end. Much less than that, and you will end up with a colostomy. That's the worst-case scenario."

A fist of fear clenched my heart. My throat closed around the words I wanted to speak. It had never crossed my mind that I might end up with any kind of permanent disfigurement.

Dr. Crowley held up his hands. "A colostomy is not the bug-a-boo it once was, now. We've come a long way. You just need to know all the possibilities going into this—not that you have a choice. Left to its own, that tumor would mean the end of your life. That is not acceptable. It has to go." He smiled warmly. "I will do everything in my power to take care of this for you, Hattie."

Dr. Crowley stayed a few more minutes, going over the sequence of events for the upcoming procedure. "I'll see you tomorrow. I don't know how the surgical schedule will pan out, exactly. It may be first thing in the morning. More than likely, it will be sometime after noon." He turned to leave. "I'll leave orders for a mild sedative to help you get some sleep."

After Dr. Crowley left, I freaked out. I'm usually calm under fire, taking control and getting things done. Later, I fall into a heap after it's all over and everyone else has calmed down. This was different. I was alone and scared witless.

Jon pushed his monitor unit into the room. "Hattie? You all right? I saw Dr. Crowley leaving."

"No. Not really." I burst into huge sucking sobs. Jon stood by the bed and held my hand until I calmed down a little. He handed me a cool washcloth for my face. "I'll be right back, Hattie. Let me get someone to cover my patients for a bit."

He returned shortly. "Do you want me to call your family?"

"No. They'll be here enough tomorrow. I can handle this. I just had a fear bubble."

Jon settled himself onto the hospital's version of a comfortable chair: a tan Naugahyde-covered high-back number with stiff rolled cushions. "I do understand your fear."

"I'm sure you've had a lot of patients in here facing surgery for cancer. It seems that it's all around us these days. Better detection...blah, blah, blah! I don't know if I buy that. Almost every week, someone I know—friend or client—tells me about someone in their family who's been diagnosed. I have two women friends who've had breast cancer, both barely over forty!"

Jon nodded. "It seems we've poisoned our poor bodies and planet so terribly. I often think it's Nature's way of shoving back." He paused, considering his next words. "Actually, my experience with cancer is more personal. To look at me now, you'd never guess I'd almost succumbed to leukemia when I was in my mid-teens. I've stared it in the face. So I do understand your fear, anger—the whole mish-mash of emotions."

"I guess I don't get the whole thing. I mean, I understand the genetic set-up in my case. But, I don't drink excessively. Heck, I'm singing under the table after one beer. I've never smoked. I eat a fairly good diet...well, some chocolate. Why did I develop cancer?"

"Why, why, why. Same questions I had, even at the age I faced it. Why would a healthy sixteen-year-old's blood suddenly turn against him?" Jon's soft brown eyes grew misty with the memory. "My mama was the sweetest woman who ever graced this planet. She wasn't educated formally past the tenth grade, but she had deep pools of wisdom and faith that lifted both of us, and my whole family, up and over crisis and heartbreak." He smiled. "There were seven of us stair-step kids. When someone flubbed up, she'd call the roll until she hit on the right kid's name. Of course, you knew you were the culprit, but you held your breath through the list of names, hoping she'd land on one of the others. I always knew when she meant to call me. She'd say sugar-monkey!"

I lifted an eyebrow. "Sugar-monkey?"

"Her nickname for me: mama's little sugar-monkey."

We chuckled together.

Jon wagged his index finger. "I don't tell that to many folks."

"Our secret."

He dipped his head. "Thank you for your discretion, miss. When my mom and dad heard my diagnosis, my dad just clamed up. He could-n't discuss it at all. But, my mama—she gathered information like a doc-toral student. 'Course, that was way before the internet. She wrote letters and talked to everyone she could. I'm sure I wouldn't be here without her dedication to my healing. That and the monetary support from several civic service groups. There's no way my family could've afforded the expensive treatment I had to undergo. I have a deep, abiding respect for service groups...like the Shriners, for example."

"I guess I've always associated them with the funny hats and motorcycle parades."

"Most people do. Not me, nor my family. They're one of the few organizations I regularly donate money to."

"How long's your mama been gone?"

His gaze fell to the floor and his shoulders slumped slightly. "Almost five years. My daddy passed about a year after she did—stroke."

I reached over and touched his hand. "I'm a mid-life orphan, as well. So's Jake—and Holston, my fiancée. A lot of us are, come to think of it. Your illness, just out of curiosity, was it the reason you went into nursing?"

"Partially, I suppose. My mama told me I was always nussin' some-thing. I'd find little hurt animals—wild or tame—and baby them back to health. She said she caught me a few times crying over the little grave of something I'd found dead in the yard." He paused. "The nurses are the people who got me through the treatments—the transfusions and chemotherapy. I have great love for the folks in my field."

"I think you have all the responsibility without enough compensa-tion."

"Money's not everything." He reached over and patted my hand. "As for you—my mama would say, get in touch with your God-side, Hattie. She was not what I would call religious—more, deeply spiritual.

Her faith was a cloak over me and my family. Just to believe in something—a higher power interested in your well-being. It certainly got me through then, and now."

"Jon! Location?" A voice sounded from the speaker above the bed.

"Three Twelve," he answered as he stood to leave. "Break's over. Back on my head! I'll make sure you get something to help you sleep. Dr. Crowley left the orders. My suggestion to you—between friends—get up early and have the nurse or one of your family members help you take a shower. It's amazing how therapeutic water can be. Brush your teeth, just don't swallow the water. I have friends in the O.R. and in recovery. Lots of eyes will be watching over you tomorrow."

"Jon?" I called as he reached the door. "Thank you, sugar-monkey."

He smiled, nodded, and scurried off.

The light sedative that Pat, the second nurse on the evening shift, administered through my IV began to soften the edges of my anxiety. I mused on my personal version of spirituality.

Raised Southern Baptist—the all-folks-are-miserable-sinners, hell-fire-and-damnation sort of religion. Though the church's party line had softened in the last decade, I was indoctrinated early with a healthy fear of an all-powerful God who kept a big ledger of transgressions.

When I reached my thirties, I began to question the validity, not of a higher power, but of the fear of recrimination that was used as a tool for control. I broke with the Baptist philosophy to search for my own truths, my own innate sense of value and goodness.

From the teachings of several Eastern religions, I gleaned a sense of oneness with all life (I still had issues with cockroaches, snakes, and mosquitoes), and the theory that you get back what you put in. Ultimately, I vowed daily to be the best person I could be, work diligently, and to overcome learned biases against people with different philosophies. As Piddie so often put it—live and let live. I failed miserably a great deal of the time. Being human, and flawed, was a tough habit to break.

Aunt Piddie served as my living example. She was technically a member of the Baptist church, but attended worship services with both black and white friends. The black services she found much more appealing.

They've just got more heart in what they do, she said. *When they sing, they throw back their heads and belt it out like their lives depended on God takin' notice! Not like the slow funeral dirges we white folks call singin'.*

Lucille Thurston stopped by on average of once a month to gather Piddie for church services. She would come back all filled with the spirit.

I called to that spirit now.

SURGERY

Excerpt from Max the Madhatter's notebook:

April 9, 1956: I have a deep scratch on my left hand. It has been there for three days now. At first, it was raw and sore, and I couldn't touch it. I am watching it heal. The edges have turned from bright red to light pink. Just the middle is still painful. Pretty soon, I will have to look hard to tell where it was.

CHAPTER THIRTY-TWO

THE FAMILY ARRIVED en masse at 6:15 a.m. After the eleven to seven nurse, Yolanda, took my vital signs, Evelyn helped me maneuver the rolling IV pole so that I could take a quick shower. Jon suggestion was on target. The warm water flowing across my skin felt wonderfully soothing. My caffeine-starved nervous system was sending bongo-drum throbs to my temples. At least the pre-op medication would squelch the dull, nagging headache.

"Has anyone heard from Holston?" I asked as Evelyn helped me towel dry.

"Jake finally talked to him this morning. He's trying to get a flight home."

When ten-thirty rolled around, we resigned ourselves to the fact that I wouldn't be included in the morning's surgery schedule. Leigh was feeling light-headed by eleven-thirty, so I insisted that she and Bobby grab lunch in the cafeteria. Evelyn and Joe went along, too, promising to hurry back.

Jake's foot tapped a staccato beat on the tile. "This waiting's making me want to ruin my manicure."

A loud rap sounded on the door, and a hospital attendant rolled a gurney into the room. "Time to go on down," he said. Holding my chart for reference, he went through the check-off sequence and compared the information against my wristband.

"Never begrudge that set of questions, sister-girl," Jake said as he accompanied the gurney down the hall, "even if everyone we meet needs to ask you who you are. You want them to operate on the right thing, you know."

When the elevator doors opened on the first floor, Jake kissed me gently on the cheek before the attendant wheeled the gurney through the double doors into the surgical holding area. Knowing Jake, he would hobble madly to the cafeteria to gather the troops and herd them back to the waiting room.

"Hi, Miss Davis, I'm Jaye Anderson. Jon Presley told me to keep an eye on you. I'll be with you until you are called back." Jaye checked my chart and wrist identification, and went through the question/answer routine. "I'll give you a little something to help you relax." She administered a sedative through the IV.

Gradually, the warming effects of the drug washed over me. I loved everybody and everything: the attendants rushing by, the warm blanket over my feet, the IV tubing, the mint-green mushroom hair cover on the woman in the cubicle across from me. The world was a wonderful place. Life was good.

"Nice hat," I mouthed to the woman.

She smiled back—a lopsided, drugged grin. She loved me, too. How beautiful.

Jaye appeared by the side of the gurney. "Here we go, Hattie." She wheeled me into the surgical operatory, where I was transferred to a steel table under glaring bright lights.

"Good afternoon, Miss Hattie." I dimly recognized Dr. Crowley's voice behind the mask. "Let's go get that bad boy out of you!" The flesh beside his eyes crinkled as he smiled.

The gas mask was fitted over my nose. "Breathe deeply now…"

❦❦❦

I heard dim, disembodied voices around me. *Where am I?* Conversations came in bits and pieces—beeping noises, something attached to my arm, pumping up, holding, then, releasing with a hiss. I began to shiver, deeply chilled. A warm blanket was spread over me. My chattering slowed...ceased. I drifted off to sleep.

❦❦❦

"Bag...bag..." I tried to whisper. My throat was sore and parched. Evelyn, Joe, Bobby, Leigh, Jake, and Holston huddled near the bed. "What's she saying?" Evelyn said. "Is she in pain?"

I tried to open my eyes. "Bag?"

Jake jumped as if he'd been stabbed with a hot poker. "Oh! Oh!" He bent over to whisper in my ear. "No colostomy bag, sister-girl. You're all in one piece. It's okay. The only bag you're gonna get is that cute little designer number we saw in Dillards. You know—the one you wouldn't buy for yourself right before you bought Betty on your Visa."

I managed a weak smile.

"She's back!" Jake said.

When I closed my eyes again, I dreamed of people in trench coats silhouetted by a bright light. They were here to take me. The shadowy crowd parted. My mother and father walked toward me, hand in hand. They smiled. Love. Support. I felt light and free—floating. My mother held a small bundle in her arms. A baby—newborn. The baby looked at me with beautiful blue eyes and smiled. Sarah...my sister...I never got to meet you. I wanted to go away with them.

I lifted away from my heavy body and hovered over the room, looking down at the woman on the bed. Poor thing! The people around her seemed worried. Other people rushed in and out of the room. Why were they so upset?

I turned back to my parents. From the shadows, an elfish little man stepped into the soft light. His clothes hung in limp folds around his small frame. A purple hat with a daisy in its brim dipped over his eyes. He looked oddly familiar. Max?

Max the Madhatter held up one hand. Though his lips didn't move,

I heard his voice. *You can not come here yet. You have many things to do before you can be with us. There will be a time.*

My spirit pulled down…down. I felt the heaviness of my physical body—the pain. I settled into its injured shell. I took a deep, shuddering breath, and opened my eyes.

Holston's eyes glistened with tears. "Hattie?"

The next two days were a drugged blur of familiar faces, flowers, cards, friends, and medical personnel. The family took shifts staying day and night. As the pain decreased, I weaned my body from the morphine pump. Three days post-op, Jon removed the catheter, and I began to slowly negotiate short trips to the bathroom and reclining chair. Eventually, I strolled the hall with the rolling IV pole Jake had fondly named Marvin.

On the fourth day after surgery, I had used little of the morphine, and the PCA unit (patient controlled analgesia) was removed from the room. The first meal was a lunch of beef broth (my father had fondly named it rusty nail soup), orange Jell-O, a lime Popsicle, and iced tea. A gourmet meal couldn't have tasted any better.

Twenty-nine and a half tiles lined the ceiling. Many times, I'd counted them as a mantra until the pain medication took effect. Four corner shelves were weighted with flowers and plants. Behind the recliner, a cheerful clump of helium balloons bobbed. A large round wall clock with black numbers ticked off the time at a maddeningly slow pace.

Aunt Piddie visited on the morning of the fourth day. "We've got ever' prayer circle in the county goin' for you, gal. Miz Lucille has all the black churches sendin' up pleas." She lowered her voice to a whisper. "They got a lot more ummph behind their prayers, I do believe. All that soul just boosts 'em straight up to Heaven."

I smiled at my aunt. She wore her new Cracker Jack sailor-inspired pantsuit. Miniature replicas of the Regal Queen sailed at various levels in her light blue curled hair. Designs by Evelyn had struck again!

I held her warm hand. "Have you enjoyed your extended visit with Elvina?"

Piddie huffed. "That old woman? I've got a headache from trying to talk to her! She's deaf as a stump. Couldn't hear a fart in a jug!"

I clutched a pillow over the nine-inch, stapled-and-dressed vertical abdominal incision. "Pid, please don't make me laugh right now."

Evelyn wagged her finger. "Mama! She's been cut up, now!"

"What'd I say? It's true. Elvina is near deaf! I have to yell at her to get her to understand. I get a permanent earache from her yellin' back at me!" Piddie reached up and stroked my hair. "You doin' all right, gal?"

"Better, now that I'm off the morphine. It was making me itch like mad all over—one of the side effects. I'm really not in a lot of pain. Just sore."

"Oh!" Piddie jumped. "I'd forget my head if it wasn't tied on! I wanted to tell you that I talked to Paul Wong late last night. It was mornin' over there, you know. He sends their love and best wishes. I gave him the number of that nice florist at Blossoms. I 'spect he'll be sending you some flowers."

Someone tapped lightly on the door. "Come in!" I called.

Patricia Hornsby ducked quietly into the room, holding Ruth by the hand. "We wanted to come by. We won't stay long." Patricia hugged me carefully. "Ruth has been begging to come see you since we found out you were here. I told her we had to wait a few days for you to feel up to company."

Ruth handed me a tall green vase full of daisies. "For you, Mama chuntian."

"How beautiful! How did you know that daisies were my favorite flower?"

She shrugged and smiled.

Jake settled on to the rollaway cot at the foot of my bed. "I kinda like these little slumber parties." He bounced a couple of times, and grinned at the sound of the squeaky springs.

"I'm really okay for me to stay alone, now. I'll probably be going home tomorrow. At least that's what Dr. Crowley said today."

He pursed his lips into a pout. "I don't want you to be by yourself.

Besides, it's my turn to stay with you."

"I don't remember a lot about the first night after surgery," I said.

Jake fluffed his pillows and settled back. "It was pretty scary for all of us. You almost stopped breathing! They said it was a reaction to the anesthesia. I think you were deciding if you were going to stay with us."

I shrugged. "Maybe."

"You know, all that week I roomed with Holston—all the times I've been around him, I've never seen his feathers ruffled at all. He's always so calm and controlled—so even. But, he broke down and cried like a baby after you started breathing okay. The man adores you, sister-girl."

I felt tears forming. "I thought he might not want me anymore."

Jake looked at me as if I'd grown a second head. "Why?"

"I don't know, damaged goods. The whole cancer thing."

"That you even thought that, is the only thing that is damaged!" He snorted dramatically.

"You know what really gets me?" Jake continued. "Holston does-n't realize how handsome and magnetic he is. I've known scads of men with half his looks and class, and they acted all stuck-up, preening in mirrors, not caring who they stepped on, or why."

"I think his ex-wife had a lot to do with his lack of self-esteem. From the little tidbits he's told me, Claire was a real ball-buster. She was okay with him as long as he earned the big bucks playing the high-roller's game, but dumped him like yesterday's dirty socks when he left Wall Street to follow his dreams of becoming a writer."

"Claire doesn't know what she lost."

I looked down. "I haven't shared this with anyone, but…"

Jake shifted to the edge of the bed and curled into a girl-talk position. "Like I'm just anyone? Really!"

"Holston was shy with me at first, you know, sexually. He had very little confidence."

Jake smoothed the pillow behind me. "I find that hard to believe. The man's an Adonis."

"Would I lie?"

"I'm certainly glad you turned him around, sister-girl. It'd been a cryin' shame for all that manliness to go to waste." Jake rubbed his stubby chin thoughtfully. "There's only one small thing I've found some-what…bizarre about Holston."

I grinned. "Three times every morning, right?"

I held the pillow over my stomach and tried not to laugh too hard, but Jake rolled around on the cot like a rabid skunk.

"Lordy, Jake. Don't you ever tell him that we discussed his morning gas ritual. He'd just die!"

"Some things are better just between us girls." Jake wiped the joy-tears from his eyes. "When will you find out about the biopsy results?"

"In a couple of days," I said.

His brows knit together. "I had the weirdest dream while I was napping here that first night. I won't say I was actually sleeping— about every two hours, the nurses came in and flung on the lights and threw a party. Anyway, in the dream, Little Ruth told me that everything would be alright, and that you were healed."

I paused. "Jake, I haven't told anyone about this. I don't even know if I have the words to describe it. Something happened to me, I suppose, when I almost stopped breathing that afternoon."

"Spill it…" After I relived the strange occurrence, Jake stared at me with his mouth hanging open.

"Close your trap. You'll catch flies."

"Gah! You had a near-death experience!"

I shrugged. "Yeah, suppose I did."

Jake shook his head. "I don't know how you can be so blasé about it! It's incredible!"

"Maybe. Now, Jake, don't fudge me. I know the real reason you want to stay here with me is roaming up and down the hall in blue scrubs."

He patted up and down his pants and shirt. "Do I have on my transparent clothes, today? Or…did your close brush with the Grim Reaper leave you physic…or would that be, psychotic?"

"You two would make a cute couple."

Jake studied his nails. "I know I grow enough cuticles to make a whole 'nother person."

"Jakey, changing the subject won't get it with me."

He huffed. "Okay! Jon said I could call him for dinner after you leave the hospital. He thinks it wouldn't be professional otherwise, even though I'm not his patient. He's really into this whole ethics thing."

I threw one hand into the air. "All right!"

Jake tilted his head and looked toward the heavens. "It really is so circular, when you think about it. My assault brought Holston into your life, and your surgery brought Jon into mine." He smiled and leaned forward, a rapt expression on his face. "Did you know that Elvis was the Georgia 2000 poster dog for December?"

"Amazing. I'll have to ask for his autograph when we meet."

Mid-afternoon, a pink-lady volunteer delivered an interesting oriental arrangement. The design was an asymmetrical yet perfectly balanced blend of live flowers, dried twigs, and moss. I admired the parity of light and dark hues, stillness and suggested movement—yin and yang. The small card read: *We are with you in spirit. For in spirit, there is no separation. Paul and Sushan Wong.*

Jake admired the arrangement. "The amazing thing about this— Piddie said he phoned this order in personally to Blossoms. He had to stay up late to call them during working hours!"

"Paul Wong's such a nice man. Hey, by the way, how's Jolene doing in the shop?" I asked.

Jake was studying the simple, yet intricate arrangement. Probably contemplating adding oriental designs to his repertoire. "Hmmm? She's doing great. She still gets a little wigged-out under fire. I haven't had any big events in the last two weeks, so she's handling the workload just fine. And, she's really very clever. She makes these lady-hat arrangements that are nothing short of genius. She finds old pillbox felt hats at flea markets and yard sales, then uses them, lined of course, as containers for floral designs. They've become the rage of Gadsden County! She's even had women bring their own old hats in for her to work with."

"I know having her help takes a big load off of you." I sighed. "This cancer thing has forced me to make some decisions; I told Garrett I'd sell the townhouse to him."

Jake flipped through a stack of get-well cards. "Really? You want to make the Hill your full-time home?"

"Yeah, I think so. Heck, I've already moved most of my belongings to the Hill. I have to dump some stress from my life, Jake. I'll probably close my massage practice over here. I can delegate my clients to Anna or one of the other therapists at the clinic."

"Biggie decisions, sister-girl." He pushed a stray sprig of hair from my eyes. "The pace in Chattahoochee is a lot slower than over here. Besides, you'll be an old married woman soon. Oh! Did I tell you about the idea for the Witherspoon mansion?"

I winced as I rearranged myself on the bed to alleviate a muscle cramp in my back.

"Mandy, Stephanie, and I want to turn the house into a day spa. We haven't been to the town council yet to get the clearance. It's zoned residential right now. But, I think we can prove that the type of business we'd attract wouldn't have a harmful impact on the neighborhood. I still plan to live there after you and Holston are married, of course."

"That's a great idea! I just knew you'd come up with a way to make things happen."

"Hasn't happened yet. That pompous butt-hole attorney, Hank Henderson, sits on the council. If it doesn't grease his palm, he won't support it. And, he doesn't like queers." Jake chuckled. "Piddie's put in to help us push it through. She says she knows a lot about ole Hankie-boy. We'll just have to see how things pan out."

Jake flipped channels on the television. The more stations we had, the less there was to watch. "You and Holston set a date yet?"

"I hoped for mid-to-late October."

He twirled around. "That's only four months away!"

"I know, I know. We'll have to see. I don't want a big fancy free-for-all. Neither does Holston. I hate lace and frou-frou, and I refuse to waste gobs of money on a big show for its own sake. If it was up to me, I would get married in blue jeans!"

"It's your wedding. You can wear plastic wrap and a ribbon if you want."

"There's a thought."

Jake grinned. "Now, you're scaring me."

A knock on the door announced the arrival of the family, with the exception of Holston, who was at the townhouse resting.

"I'm glad you're here. Jon said I can take a shower if we can figure out a way to keep my incision dry."

"Just a minute," Evelyn said. She left the room, returning shortly with a trash can liner and a roll of cloth tape she'd borrowed from Jon. "Necessity is the mother of invention. I'll just make a quick patch, and cover up that cut like nobody's business!"

Since I was wobbly and weak from the aftereffects of pain medications and inactivity, Evelyn and Leigh supported me as I shuffled to the small bathroom's shower stall. All three of us giggled like kids in a summer rainstorm as they washed my hair and body. Clean hair, after five days, was a near-orgasmic luxury. They towel-dried my skin, removed the protective plastic over my dressed incision, then used a blow-dryer to style my hair.

As anyone who's ever experienced abdominal surgery can attest, to leave the hospital, you must perform the three P's: pee, pass gas, and poop. Everyone who wandered into my room looking the least bit medically inclined wanted to know about my bodily functions. I became so accustomed to reporting the latest update, I even told Mevlyn, the pink-lady volunteer who delivered a dish garden from Reverend and Lucille Jackson.

Dr. Crowley bustled into the room around 11:00 a.m. on the fifth day of my incarceration. "Well?"

"I've done everything—except the poop part. I wish I had great things to report. I only started eating solid food yesterday. If it counts, I did have the very teeniest bowel movement." I held up my fingers as a measure.

Evelyn said, "We'll take good care of her, Doctor. We have my daughter's old room set up and ready, just waiting on her to come home."

Piddie chuckled. "And everyone'll start bringing food over as soon as I say the word—so Evelyn won't send her back here with her cookin'."

"Now, Mama…" Evelyn said.

Dr. Crowley checked the notations in my chart. "I don't see any reason why you can't go on home. Call my office in the next couple of days to set up a four-week post-op appointment, and I'll want to see you in my office in a week to remove the staples."

The nine-inch vertical stainless steel-clamped incision on my belly resembled a huge zipper. "Great! I'll be happy to give them back to you."

Dr. Crowley scribbled release orders. "Hattie, we should have the biopsy results on the lymph nodes in a couple of days. I'll call you as soon as I have the papers in my hands." He smiled. "I just have a good feeling about it."

THE WEDDING

Excerpt from Max the Madhatter's notebook:

March 2, 1957: Good comes out of bad. All the time. Like when I have one of my spells, and I'm shocked by the simple beauty of what my hand has drawn on a blank page. Beauty and goodness can paint over hate and meanness, given half a chance.

CHAPTER THIRTY-THREE

IN THE SNIPPETS of time Evelyn and Jake had taken from watching over me during my—as the family now referred to it—cancer scare, Karen's old bedroom had been transformed into a light, airy guest room. The dark mausoleum that had served as a memorial for her lost daughter now sported pale buttercup-yellow walls, pressed flower prints, and windows shaded with white plantation blinds framed with wispy folds of unbleached muslin. Heavy oak furniture that had anchored all four corners of the room had been replaced with natural wicker nightstands and a white crackled-paint iron headboard. Unlike the outdated avocado-green shag monstrosities, two sisal rugs complemented the pale hardwood floors.

The remainder of the house was slowly being transformed within the parameters of Evelyn's new decorating scheme. Brass porthole mirrors, miniature lighthouses that lit from within, and ocean-scene watercolor prints infiltrated the living room. Joe carried his honey-do list around as he gathered materials to strip the Jamaican-print wallpaper from the kitchen.

My homecoming to Joe's and Evelyn's house was followed by a

parade of casserole-bearing well-wishers. Aunt Piddie kept a careful inventory of the incoming food, and sent thank you cards in the following day's mail. Dr. Crowley called two days after I came home to relate the wonderful news that all of the twelve lymph nodes he'd stripped during surgery were clear of cancer cells. Thank heaven, no chemotherapy would be necessary.

Two weeks following my release from the hospital, Evelyn and Joe hosted a small celebration in the newly redecorated kitchen-family room. The navy blue and gold paper ware complemented the crisp white and gold tablecloth. A carved watermelon filled with chilled cantaloupe, honeydew, and watermelon balls provided the centerpiece for the buffet. Joe dashed in and out of the screened porch carrying platters of chicken, beef, and pork to the barbecue pit. For the occasion, Evelyn had designed a white chef's hat for Joe and a coordinating navy-trimmed white apron with an anchor emblem in the center.

As we were finishing the meal, I grabbed Holston's hand. "We have something to discuss with all of you...since we're all here together."

Piddie nearly dropped the sauce-slathered pork rib she'd been nibbling. "Lordy mercy! This family's beginnin' to get a reputation for suspense and surprise announcements. It's a good thing I don't have a heart condition!"

"Holston and I have set a date for our wedding. It will be held on Saturday, October 26th. The weekend after The Madhatter's Festival."

Evelyn put her hand over her heart. "Mercy! That's only three months away! How can I possibly make your dress in time, Hattie?"

"Here's the other part. The dress code will be casual—like a big picnic. We're going to wear blue jeans and white shirts for the ceremony. Jake wants to decorate. We don't want to waste lots of money on this. It will be very simple—just friends and family."

Evelyn wrung her hands "Have you called Reverend Ghent? What about the reception? We'll have to reserve the Women's Club."

"Actually, I've asked Reverend Julie Crews from Tallahassee Unity Church to perform the service."

"May I?" Jake interrupted. "I've asked Hattie and Holston to allow me to decorate for the wedding—like she said. They have agreed to have an outdoor service. At Turkey Point."

Silence cloaked the room.

Jake stood and paced around the table. "I know it seems kinda odd, with what happened to me there, but I need desperately to paint good over bad. We all do." He stopped and rested his gaze on us, one-by-one. "By having a joyous union by the lake, I just know that the love and commitment within you all—my family—will wash the evil away." Jake paused. "Turkey Point is a beautiful spot with a perfect overlook of Lake Seminole. I will transform it into a magical place for a commitment ceremony."

"This is a fine fare-thee-well," Piddie said.

I stepped up to the plate. "Holston and I think it's a wonderful idea, and we're looking forward to having our wedding there. The covered picnic pavilion is available. We've already reserved it for the combination reception," I glanced toward Leigh and Bobby, "for both Holston and I, and Bobby and Leigh."

"Are you sure you want to do that?" Leigh asked.

"Absolutely. You two never had a party to celebrate your marriage. We can pool our resources and spend the money on a big catered cookout. I know the owner of Sonny's Barbecue in Tallahassee. They will do it up right! That way, we can all enjoy ourselves with as little stress as possible."

Piddie clapped her hands together. "You know what this means? We're all headin' into a good cluster!"

"Amen, honey!" Jake said.

Evelyn sat straight up. "Can I at least make the white his and hers weddin' shirts?"

"Sure, as long as you keep it simple. No frou-frou on mine..."

"A few seed pearls?"

"Very few."

October 25th:

Without the flash of police crime scene tape whipping in the lake breeze, Turkey Point was tranquil—a shady hill with a postcard-perfect view of Lake Seminole framed by towering pine and live oak trees. I paused on the same spot where Jake had suffered, searching the area for hidden signs of menace—a black stain left by Marshall Thurgood's release of white-hot violence. The balmy late October breeze rustled the pine needles, unleashing a whispering call.

"Sister-girl, don't just stand there drawing gnats, help me with these boxes of lights. They're light, so you won't hurt yourself lifting them. Jolene, Stephanie, and Evelyn will be here in a few minutes ready to get started."

"You really think it's okay to put these up today? I mean, people steal lights, even at Christmas. It is pretty deserted up here."

"Not to worry. I have friends in high places." He grinned. "Rich's going to swing by several times tonight and keep an eye on the area. He also said he'd set some roadblocks up to keep vehicles out until tomorrow."

Roadblocks had been in place on this road before. It didn't stop Marshall Thurgood. I shivered.

"What'sa matter? Rabbit run over your grave?" he asked as he pushed by me with a box of lights.

"Something like that, yeah." I returned to Pearl's truck bed, grabbed an armload of white trellises, and followed Jake to the crest of the hill.

It took most of the day to decorate Turkey Point to Jake's specifications. Two white trellises intertwined with ivy and white lights formed the pulpit at the crest of the hill. On either side of the archway, the tree trunks were wrapped with strands of white lights to six feet above the ground. Several linked extension cords snaked through the trees to the pavilion to provide electrical power.

Four stands of candles stood near the pulpit, positioned to a throw soft, glistening glow on the area where the wedding party would stand. Stephanie and Jolene had carved gallon plastic milk jugs into stenciled luminaries. They were filled with sand and a single candle to illuminate the path leading to the picnic pavilion reception area.

Jake's plan was timed to work with Nature's days-end light show. As the sun set over the lake, we would take our vows. The miniature white lights and candles would glow as the fall evening darkness settled over the woods.

❧❧❧

The morning of October 26th dawned with the slight hint of upcoming winter. By noon, the temperature was a balmy seventy-five degrees with clear, crystal blue skies dotted by a few wispy clouds. Since Jake and Evelyn were handling the arrangements, and Holston and I were observing the age-old tradition of separation before the ceremony, I took a leisurely walk to the fishpond.

While Spackle chased small frogs at the edge of the water, my mind to drifted to memory.

Daddy and I, hand in hand. Bobby blazing a trail far ahead of us. Walking through the woods to check the fence lines around the property. The first frost had driven the snakes underground, and we shuffled through the leaves with little fear of startling a rattlesnake. Daddy pointed out trees and called them by name—loblolly pine, hickory, water oak, sweetgum. Our footfall sent startled rabbits and lizards scrambling for cover. Up ahead, Bobby pretended to take aim and fire at an unsuspecting fox squirrel. The musty aroma of rich, dark loam filtered through the air, laced with a hint of distant wood smoke.

The heavenly scent of homemade beef and vegetable soup welcomed us as we stepped onto the back porch, clumping our shoes on the flooring to remove the trail dirt. Mama was humming in the spacious country kitchen, calling for me and Bobby to set the table for dinner and pour the sweet iced tea. The growing darkness outside was held at bay by the glow of kitchen lights as my family settled into the worn wooden chairs for soup and day's end conversation.

I snapped back to the present with a start when Spackle plopped into my lap and slapped me with his wet tongue. "I could take you back, you know." I ruffled his mottled fur. "But, no one else would love you like I do."

The rumble of the ATV announced Jake's arrival. He negotiated the steep earthen steps carefully, using one of his many everyday canes.

"Whew!" He plopped down beside me. Spackle lunged over to share kisses. "Sister-girl, you gonna sit down here all day by yourself?"

"No, I just needed some space. Why does something we tried to keep so simple seem so complicated all of a sudden?"

"Because everything worth doing always turns into a big pile of poop before it comes out right. You'll see. A few hours from now, you'll be married to lover-boy, and up to your armpits—in a white shirt, no less—in Sonny's barbecue sauce, having the time of your life."

"I'll have to trust you on that. Evelyn has worked herself up to a high rollin' boil over my shirt. She can't seem to get the collar to iron down flat."

Jake laughed. "Evelyn just lives to be in a fizz. Haven't you figured that out yet?"

He put his hand over mine. "You okay, sister-girl? You seem a little...misty. You having the pre-marriage blues?"

I sighed. "No. I was just thinking about Mama and Daddy. Even though I know they're just on the other side of here, wherever heaven is. I can't help wishing they could be here."

Jake put his arm around my shoulders. "I was lucky enough to know Mr. and Mrs. D. You are the very best blend of both of them. So, in a way, they are going to be there today."

I smiled at my soul-deep friend. I didn't trust words to tell him how much he'd enriched my life by simply being himself.

Jake used his cane to help him stand, and wiped the dried grass from his jeans. "C'mon, I'll give you and the mutt a ride to the Hill. We've got to have time to do something with that hair of yours!"

A small crowd of wedding guests were seated around the Turkey Point clearing in folding chairs when Evelyn, Joe, Piddie, and I arrived in the Towncar. Betty was parked next to Bobby's beat-up pick-up truck by the curb, as Holston, Jake, Leigh, and Bobby had arrived earlier.

"Let me check your shirt one last time." Evelyn frowned as she straightened the collar. "There." She patted my shoulder. Tears threatened at the corners of her eyes.

"Don't fail me now, Matron of Honor. If you lose it, so will I!"

Evelyn and Joe looked stiff and out-of-character in their blue jeans and white shirts. Piddie had opted for a long denim shift with a soft pink sweater.

"Joe, go tell Jake we're here. Then, come on back to take your place," Evelyn said. We helped Aunt Piddie into her wheelchair, and Rich Burns escorted her to the front row close to the arbor. From the trunk, I grabbed the cluster of silk daisies and dried ferns that Jake had fashioned to look as if I'd been just strolling along in a wildflower field idly picking flowers.

As the October sun began to fall toward the horizon, the soft strains of *Jesu, Joy of Man's Desiring* quieted the crowd. Reverend Julie stood with her back to the water at the crest of the hill. Jake, resplendent in dark blue jeans and white tuxedo shirt, stood beside Holston. The music continued as Evelyn walked dramatically up the aisle and took her position on the opposite side of the groom and the best man.

Joe offered his arm. "Shall we?" The opening strains of the wedding march sounded as Joe and I walked together. Joe placed my hand in Holston's, then stepped back to the edge of the crowd next to Aunt Piddie.

The service was brief. Reverend Julie spoke of love, commitment, and the universal God-spirit that flows through all life. We exchanged plain gold bands. Holston drew me close to his warmth, and kissed me softly on the lips, lingering for a moment before pulling back and smiling. His dark eyes told me all. I love you. I will honor you. I am your home. We were silhouetted by the soft peach and yellow skies of the sun set over Lake Seminole.

Reverend Julie announced, "I present to you—for your love and support—Mr. and Mrs. Holston Lewis."

The crowd erupted with applause. Bobby wolf-whistled. Leigh slapped him playfully on the arm. The familiar faces I loved looked at Holston and me: Bobby, Leigh, Joe, Evelyn, Piddie, Jake, Jon Presley, Stephanie, Mandy, Julie, Mr. Bill, Rich and Carol, Chris and Kathy from TPD, Kelly from LCSO, Mary Mathues, Reverend and Lucille Jackson, Garrett, Jillie, Patricia and Rainey with Ruth, Elvina Houston, and a host of my clients and acquaintances from Tallahassee and Chattahoochee. Jon Presley, holding Elvis, who was dressed in a smart sequined white-satin doggie tux, dabbed his eyes with a tissue.

I strained to see the edge of the crowd in the dusk darkness. One face seemed to glow—a slow, knowing smile, a nod, an understanding beyond words. I turned quickly to Jake. He was frozen in place, staring at the same spot in the sea of faces. I jerked my head around to locate the glowing face. It had disappeared.

Jake looked at me, his eyes intense. *Yes, I saw him, too. Marshall Thurgood.*

"Hattie?" Holston's voice made me start. "You okay?"

I nodded.

"Let's go celebrate then, Mrs. Lewis."

Holston and I walked arm in arm through the luminary-lighted path toward the picnic pavilion. The crowd trickled behind us. The caterers from Sonny's had prepared two long tables of cooked chicken, beef, and pork ribs, baked beans, coleslaw, and toasted Texas toast garlic bread. A separate table held iced tea, water, lemonade, and urns of fresh coffee. A towering six-layered cake, baked using Piddie's Best Damn Chocolate Cake recipe, waited on a decorated table. All four of us planned to cut the cake together in celebration of our unions.

After the meal had been consumed, and everyone lounged around looking like an advertisement for stain remover products, the disc jockey Jake had hired cranked up the music by the makeshift dance floor in the parking lot. Deep into the Fall evening, with the music man spinning old disco, Motown standards, and big-band tunes, the fine folks that Holston and I called family and friends shook a leg, cut a rug, and busted a move. Other than exchanging knowing nods to each other, Jake and I never discussed our mysterious experience.

Some things you just don't question.

ADOPTION

Excerpt from Max the Madhatter's notebook:

April 1, 1960: Nurse Marion talks with me about all kinds of things: the beauty of the dogwood trees and azalea bushes blooming across the hospital grounds, the laughter of her children, and just everyday life.

Once, when I asked her about happiness, she said, "Max, running after happiness is like a dog chasing his tail— going 'round and 'round and always coming up short. But, when happiness finds you by itself, that's the true magic. You'll be busy living and it'll sneak up and sit down beside you. Just like that! Reminds me of little Dorothy in the Wizard of Oz. She thought her happiness was somewhere far off, a ways over the rainbow. Only, she found out it was with her at home, all along."

CHAPTER THIRTY-FOUR

HOLSTON AND I spent our first night of wedded bliss in the private, newly redecorated master suite on the Hill—a present from Joe and Evelyn. The next day, we packed Betty with an assortment of clothing, camping gear, and coolers, and headed north toward the Blue Ridge Mountains of North Carolina. It ruffled my sphinctered feathers not to have any set plans or advance reservations, but Holston convinced me to tempt the travel gods and just get in the SUV and drive. In the two days it took to reach the Great Smokey Mountain National Park, we stopped at least ten times a day to explore anything that tickled our imaginations—a pottery kiln opening in south Georgia, three roadside flea markets, an old black man weaving split oak laundry baskets on his front porch, five fresh produce stands, and nearly every Dairy Queen franchise between Chattahoochee and Asheville, North Carolina.

When we were hungry, we ferreted out a local eatery. When we got tired, we pulled Betty over to a rest area, and napped in her reclining seats. We pitched the five-person dome tent in mom-and-pop campgrounds, state parks, and rustic national forest tent sites close to babbling mountain streams. Personal hygiene fell to an all-time low, depending on the available running water.

Two weeks after we had left for our adventure, we blew into the 'Hooch, disheveled, odiferous, and relaxed. Upon our return, we initiated the lengthy process toward the adoption of a Chinese national orphan. Patricia outlined the procedure for us—the mounds of authenticated paperwork necessary before we could travel abroad to receive our adopted daughter.

Patricia patiently calmed my overwhelming frustration as we waded through the necessary documentation: medical exam reports, a home study, bank-account summaries, financial sheets, FBI clearance, child-abuse clearance, police reports, and a certified copy of our marriage license. The results of my follow-up colonoscopy, six months following the surgery, were tagged on to the medical report. Because Holston had been married previously in New York State, a certified copy of his and Claire's divorce decree had to be authenticated by the secretary of state for New York.

Once all the state-certified, original documents were compiled, the package was sent to the Chinese Embassy in Houston, Texas, for authentication by the Chinese officials. The package was forwarded to our adoption agency in China, where the papers were translated into the Chinese language and turned in to the government for approval.

We breathed a huge sigh of exhausted relief when the documentation finally reached China. At that point, it was out of our hands and into the clutches of foreign bureaucracy. Dr. Paul Wong, alerted by Aunt Piddie, became actively involved. The time span usually took most couples nine months to a year. We received an announcement the first week of April, six months from the time we initiated the adoption. The package contained a medical evaluation and a color picture of the little girl who had been chosen for us.

A brief note, penned by Paul Wong read: "I must tell you what I know of this little child. She is most alert and intelligent for one so young. A fierce spirit resides in this baby.

"She was found in a small, white hand-woven basket, surrounded by wild daises, wrapped in soft clothing. She had a piece of parchment paper attached to her blanket with one Chinese character drawn in black ink. The sign for the word Spring in your language, the word chuntian in our language. She has hence been called Baby Chuntian since she was left in the care of the orphanage three months ago."

The formal color photograph of Chuntian showed a beautiful infant with a thick head of shiny black hair, and a small dimple on one side of her slight smile. Holston purchased a carved frame for our daughter—Sarah Chuntian Lewis.

Couples across the States collectively held their breaths as the United States and China engaged in a superpower pissing contest following the tragic midair collision involving one of our reconnaissance aircraft en route over international waters off the Chinese mainland, and one of two Chinese jets sent out to sniff around the spy plane. For several weeks, we prayed with each newscast that our government would say and do the right things to salvage our chances for adoption. If relations between the two countries ground to a halt, so would our hopes of seeing Sarah Chuntian Lewis. As quickly as it had flared, the tension subsided. Both superpower tomcats stalked to different parts of the alley without losing any fur.

By mid-April, the back bedroom where I'd spent my childhood had been transformed into a cheerful nursery painted pale yellow with a daisy wallpaper border. To allow us to hear any cries from the baby's room, Holston installed an intercom system similar to the one my parents had owned many years prior. A small crib stood ready in the master suite. Initially, Sarah would sleep close to us.

My nephew, Joshua Mason Davis, 8 lbs., 7 oz., debuted two weeks late on February 14, 2001. Josh was a stoic, mellow baby with Leigh's black hair and striking blue eyes. His features hinted of the Native American heritage from his mother's side of the family.

Bobby and Leigh told the story of the late-night truck ride down Bump Nose Lane, an unpaved stretch of washboard country forestry road whose teeth-clattering potholes had finally jarred Leigh into labor. In the two months he'd been part of the family, Josh had acquired a room filled with toys and clothes. An average of one new outfit per week didn't faze him. He spit up on the designer rags as easily as the inexpensive diaper shirts from the thrift store.

In anticipation of Sarah's arrival, Evelyn was frantically designing ensembles with an oriental flare. For Sarah's homecoming, she'd found a buttery-soft daisy print flannel material for a receiving blanket. Josh's birth, and the impending arrival of Sarah, shook Evelyn from her extended gloom over Karen. Joe reported that her attempts to contact her daughter had almost ceased with the flurry of baby-clothing design.

The official call from our adoption agency came the final week of April. We had one week to pack, make travel arrangements, and prepare mentally and emotionally for the long, exhausting trip. Dr. Paul and Sushan Wong had arranged to meet us at the airport in Beijing. They would be our Chinese guardian angels in a foreign land where we didn't speak the language or know the customs.

While Holston and I waded through the maze of bureaucracy leading toward the adoption, Jake, Stephanie, and Mandy fought city hall to rezone the Witherspoon mansion and grounds as a mixed residential-business. All of the councilmen and women were in favor of the move, except for one holdout—Daniel "Hank" Henderson, attorney-at-law. The reasons for his opposition were unclear.

Along with the proposed sale of the golf course to a group of south Florida investors, and the opening of a second bed and breakfast inn, the day spa and salon would provide a draw to weary vacationers looking for a small-town respite from south Florida's urban sprawl. Chattahoochee was emerging as a warm, friendly Mecca for antique-seeking northerners escaping the harsh winter weather.

After two months of haggling, the zoning change came abruptly, surprising the council and the three prospective spa owners. Behind the scenes, with one brief phone conversation to Hank Henderson, Aunt

Piddie had, as she put it, snatched the overblown mule's patootie by the short hairs. No one knew what markers she had called in. She was tight-lipped, vowing to keep her methods to herself until the Good Lord called her Home.

The double doors to the Witherspoon mansion stood open. A Superior Interiors delivery van blocked the circular drive, so I pulled Betty around to the side entrance.

"Jakey!" I called as I entered the front parlor. I stopped short to admire the transition of the once-formal room into a spacious waiting area, complete with upholstered high-backed chairs, teak occasional tables, oriental area-rugs, and a bubbling rock fountain. The tall windows were shaded with almond-colored plantation blinds. In one corner, an antique armoire housed a small television and stereo system. Two bold modern paintings dominated one wall. The spa's logo, three gilded C's connected to form a triangle, was centered on another wall so that it was the first thing a visitor would see upon entrance.

"What'cha think?" Jake asked from behind me.

"It's like...this place was made to be a resort spa!"

"C'mon, I'll give you the three-dollar tour. We're still working on some parts. The old mud room is being tiled so that Steph can set up a wet massage table for full body sea-salt scrubs and body wraps. If all goes according to plan, we're aiming to open by the first part of June."

He shuffled into the dining room. "This will be the reception-reservations desk area. Stephanie found an old mahogany desk and armoire at an estate sale that will go right here." He pointed to the center of the room. "She also located an antique glass and wood display case for her line of skin care products. And..." He led me toward the rear of the house. "Of course, the kitchen will stay as it is now, and Holston's private office will remain back there, but the other four downstairs bedrooms will be used as treatment rooms.

"The next two rooms—here—will be combined into one large room. This is not a supporting wall, so we're putting two large, arched doorways in so that it will create the illusion of one room, but with a little privacy for the hairstylists and patrons. Wendel Dixon up at the Antique Mini Mall found the mahogany archways in Cairo, Georgia. They came from an old home that was being demolished. That's one of Mandy's wheel and deals. Old Wendel's probably going to get free haircuts for a year."

I shook my head. "Mandy got the better end of that pact. Wendel has one of the worst comb-overs in Gadsden County. He has less hair than my new little nephew."

"Wendel insists that he has a really high forehead."

I smiled. "Has Mandy found another hairdresser for the shop?"

"She's interviewing now. Gah! You should've seen the strange little woman who came by this morning. She looked like she could've been Hannibal Lechter's mama!"

I laughed. "Maybe she could handle the more extreme styles."

"I don't think so! Actually, we all liked this one woman from Naples, Florida, who wants to move up to this part of the state. She's a hoot! Wanda Jean Orenstein. Great New Jersey accent—wonderful sense of humor. All of us think she'd fit right in."

"Sounds like everything's falling into place."

He nodded. "Yeah, 'bout time things work out like they should. Now, Stephanie will have the room farthest from the others for massage therapy. She said you could share the room with her if you want to." Jake raised an eyebrow.

"I like my spot at the Madhatter, unless you get to the point you need the extra room for the flower shop. Besides, who knows what my schedule will be after Sarah's with us."

"Speaking of the luckiest, most soon-to-be-spoiled-rotten child in the world, have you heard any news?"

"Yep…that's one of the reasons I stopped by." I filled him in on the travel plans. "I hope you can take us to the airport. Leigh and Bobby have Joshua now, and I hate to ask them to get out and about that early with a new baby. Evelyn and Joe have done so much already, and it's getting more difficult for Piddie to travel."

"Not a prob-lemo, sister-girl. If you don't mind letting me borrow Betty after I drop you and Holston off at the airport, I'll plan to stay at Jon's over the weekend, and get some things done while I'm over there.

Otherwise, I'll haul you over in the back of the delivery van. Wouldn't that be a class act?"

"Class positively oozes out of our every pore." I breathed a tired sigh. "We'll be ready around 4:30 a.m. Friday's going to be a long day. By the way, the two original art pieces in the front parlor. Are they—"

"Ruth's? Absolutely. When I saw the daisy and rainbow spring painting she did for your wedding present—the focal point of the nursery—I asked her and Patricia if I could commission two paintings for the spa." He shook his head. "That child is going to be famous! And, you and I have some of her first pieces."

Jake flipped a business card from his pocket. "Jon designed our business cards. What'cha think?"

The three C's spa logo was tastefully engraved in gold script on a gray flannel background.

"What do the three C's stand for?"

Jake grinned. "Cut, curl, and coddle."

I laughed. "Catchy"

"We thought so."

The Dragonfly Florist van pulled into the carport on the Hill at 4:00 a.m. Friday morning.

"Mornin' glory!" Jake called as he let himself in the back door. "China Express, all aboard!"

I emerged from the kitchen.

"Ewww! Sister-girl! You already look tired. Didn't you sleep?"

"Too excited. I think I saw every hour on the clock."

"Maybe you'll just pass out on the plane. I bet this will be the charmed trip where you'll finally learn to sleep sitting up on an airline seat."

"One can hope."

Jake picked up the small wheeled duffle. "I've seen you pack more bags to go out of town for a weekend."

"Patricia and Rainey warned us to be prepared for any mode of travel. The less we have to keep up with, the better."

"Hattie and I are both a bit nervous about carrying so much money on us," Holston said. "We have to pay the orphanage a cash fee to take Sarah with us. Then, we start the two-week process of getting her visa and papers to bring her back to the States."

"Lucky that Paul Wong will be over there to help out. Where's all the dough? Surely not in your carry-on."

Holston lifted the edge of his shirt to reveal a thick money belt. "Hattie and I are wearing these."

Jake patted Holston's middle. "And, here I thought you were both so blissfully happy that you were putting on a spare tire."

❧❧❧

At the airport, Jake walked us to the gate. "Atlanta first, of course."

I rolled my eyes. "Naturally. Then, the cross-country route to L.A., then the nightmarish trans-Pacific trip to Beijing."

"They haven't invented the beam-me-up thing yet, sister-girl." He cut his eyes toward Holston. "I hope you brought loads of sedatives."

Holston patted his breast pocket. "Benadryl—it knocks her out cold."

"Give her one before you leave the ground in Atlanta. Then, drug her again—maybe twice—for the last leg of the trip."

"Oh, come on! I'm not that bad. I can fly without being a whiney puss."

Jake stared at me like I'd announced I was going to run for political office. "Sure. And I can wax my behind and ski to China."

Jake grabbed his camera. "Almost forgot! Mary at the *Twin City News* wants a picture of you two at the gate. Just wave or something. She's putting a blurb in the paper about your trip."

Holston and I hammed it up as Jake flashed several angles.

"There. Now, don't worry about Shammie and Spackle. I'll take extra time with them. They probably won't even realize you're gone." He paused. "Except for Shammie. The princess puss is going to sling major cat-itude when you come home after two weeks, and with a baby, no less!"

"Tuna packed in spring water seems to calm her down," Holston said.

"I see she has you trained, too," Jake said. "Kisses, loves, Godspeed—and all that." He squeezed his eyes shut. "I won't cry."

The Delta attendant called for general boarding.

My stomach was a butterfly hatchery. "Well, here we go."

"Oh! Wait!" Jake fumbled in his pocket and handed me a sheet of copy paper. "I was flipping through the *Madhatter's Guide to Chocolate* yesterday looking for Piddie's best damn chocolate icing recipe, and I noticed the drawing on the very last page. It never meant anything much to me before."

Many times in the past, I had contemplated the series of coincidences that had led me to this juncture: Mama's death, Jake's assault, meeting Holston, and my brush with cancer. Standing at the gate with my husband and my best friend, I looked down at the scratchy line drawing of a little girl kneeling by a spring surrounded by daisies. I understood that there was no such thing as mere chance. Divine order prevailed.

A small orphan girl and a madman had foretold the happy ending.

Rabid Press
Trade Paperback Books

The Madhatter's Guide to Chocolate at $14.95 each: _____

Sales Tax (if applicable): _____

Shipping: _____

Total: _____

Please include $3.95 for shipping and handling for first book and $1.25 for each additional. Texas residents must include applicable sales tax. Payment must accompany orders.

Allow 3 to 4 weeks for delivery.

Name: _____

Date: _____

Shipping Address
Street: _____

City: _____ State: _____ Zip Code: _____

Phone: _____ Fax: _____

Email: _____

Card Type:　o Visa　　o MasterCard

Name on Card: _____

Card #: _____

Exp. Date: _____ Signature: _____

Make your check payable and return to:

Rabid Press
P.O. Box 4227
Cedar Park, TX 78630

www.rabidpress.com

Rhett DeVane is a true southerner, born and raised in the piney woods of the north Florida panhandle. Originally from Chattahoochee, Florida, she now lives in Tallahassee where she is completing a series of southern fiction novels. Rhett is owned by two cats, Sisko and Saki, and a rescued Florida Cracker Retriever named Shelly.